RICKSHAW

RICKSHAW

the novel *Lo-t'o Hsiang Tzu*

by Lao She

TRANSLATED BY JEAN M. JAMES

The University Press of Hawaii
Honolulu

Published originally in serial form in
the periodical *Yü-chou-feng*, September 1936 to May 1937.

This edition copyright © 1979 by
The University Press of Hawaii

Manufactured in the United States of
America

Maps by William C. Stanley

Library of Congress Cataloging in Publication Data

Shu, Ch'ing-ch'un, 1898–1966.
    Rickshaw = the novel Lo-to Hsiang Tzu.

    I. Title. II. Title: Lo-to Hsiang Tzu.
PZ3.S5619Rh   895.1'3'5   79–10658
ISBN 0–8248–0616–6
ISBN 0–8248–0655–7 pbk.

CONTENTS

MAPS

A NOTE ON THE TEXT
AND THE TRANSLATION

The edition used for this translation is a recent Hong Kong reprint. I have compared it with a 1949 Shanghai edition lent to me by the Hoover Institute at Stanford University. The two editions are, to the best of my knowledge, identical.

Those who have read Evan King's translation published in 1945 as *Rickshaw Boy* will wonder if *Rickshaw* is the same novel. It is. King cut, rearranged, rewrote, invented characters, and changed the ending. The girl student and One Pock Li are King's, not Lao She's. King also added considerable embellishment to the two seduction scenes.

This new translation omits nothing and alters nothing. Some small additions to the text have been made whenever necessary to clarify terms and allusions which the non-Chinese reader will not understand. This method is the least obstructive to the flow of the narrative and does supply the supplementary material necessary for clarity of meaning.

Lao She wrote eloquently rather than elegantly. He used the dialect of Peking, which was famous for its liveliness and colorful idioms. I am, of course, solely responsible for errors but I have done what I can to convey his style and his strength.

TRANSLATOR'S INTRODUCTION

Shu Ch'ing-ch'un, whose pen name was Lao She, was born of Manchu parents in Peking in 1899. After graduating from normal school at the age of sixteen, he went to work to support his widowed mother. He was able to spend some time studying at Yenching University and became an instructor in Chinese at Nankai Middle School in 1923. In 1924 he went to London to teach Chinese at the School of Oriental Studies in the University of London. After his return to China in 1930 he taught at Cheeloo University, Tsinan, Shantung province, until 1934 and at other universities elsewhere until the outbreak of the Sino-Japanese war in 1937. He then went to Hankow. He spent the rest of his life writing patriotic and exhortative novels and plays. He left China in 1946 for the United States, where he remained until his return in 1949. He was an active and respected writer under the People's Republic of China up until the Great Cultural Revolution when, no one is sure why, he committed suicide in 1966. Ranbir Vohra has written a full-length study of Lao She's life and works, *Lao She and the Chinese Revolution* (Cambridge, 1974).

Like Charles Dickens, whom he greatly admired, Lao She was a social novelist, a chronicler of life in Peking as Dickens was the chronicler of London. The terrible life of the poor depicted in *Rickshaw* is hard to believe, but sociological studies conducted in Peking in the twenties describe the same conditions and worse. Everything we read in *Rickshaw* about the housing, sickness, ignorance, poverty, and almost hopeless struggle to survive agrees with the information gathered by Sidney Gamble and published in two books. The first, *Peking, a Social Survey* (New York, 1921), looks at all aspects of life in Peking including its history, size, topography, and climate. The second, *How Chinese Families Live in Peking* (New York, 1933), deals with living costs and budgets. Lao She's calculations of how much a rickshaw man needs to live are confirmed by the figures in this book.

Other sources on Peking in the early thirties are Robert W. Swallow's *Sidelights on Peking Life*, published in China in 1927, and Osvald Siren's *The Imperial Palaces of Peking* (1976 reprint) and *Walls and Gates of Peking* (1924).

Recent photographs of the enormous square in front of the T'ien An Men do not show the city the rickshaw puller Hsiang Tzu knew. Old Peking, unchanged for hundreds of years, is gone now and can be found only in old photographs and novels.

Lo-t'o Hsiang Tzu, published in 1937, is set in Peking (known then as Peip'ing). The name of the city was changed from Peking to Peip'ing in 1928 when the government of the Republic of China shifted the national capital to Nanking. Peking, the former capital, kept itself alive more out of habit than out of necessity. It had no industry and had lost its only business, governing the country. It was a city in limbo. The name was changed back to Peking in 1948 when the People's Republic of China was established. Peking will be used here even though Lao She used Peip'ing.

The novel probably begins in 1934 when the area around Peking was menaced by both Japanese and warlord troops and leftish political views were best kept to oneself although political demonstrations by students and other groups did take place. It ends shortly before the attack on the Marco Polo Bridge southwest of Peking which led to open war between Japan and China.

Rickshaw is Lao She's eighth novel but the first to have a leading character who is not of the educated class. His earlier works made fun of scholar-officials, professional students, and useless bureaucrats. He concentrated on a single theme with many variations: what was wrong with China and the Chinese. Here he chooses not an educated man but an illiterate laborer, a rickshaw puller. *Rickshaw* is the first important study of a laborer in modern Chinese fiction. Hsiang Tzu is not mocked, not blamed, not praised, but analyzed and despaired of.

Lao She waits until the last chapter to state his message. Whereas previously he had seen the conservatism of the traditionally educated with their blindness to the necessity to modernize China and the Chinese as the obstacle to progress, he now goes deeper. It is the self-centeredness of the Chinese, which he calls Individualism, that is their crucial failing.

In his early novels Lao She's target was the traditional ideal of success; a man's primary goal was to become an official and get rich, which would redound to the greater glory of his family and his ancestors. By his seventh novel, *Niu T'ien Tz'u chuan* (The biography of Niu T'ien Tz'u), published in 1936, he had worn the subject out. He had also given up. Lao She was convinced that the Chinese lacked a spirit of national solidarity, a larger vision, and a sense of commitment to a greater cause. They had no sense of mission larger than self and self-aggrandizement. He says of Hsiang Tzu: "He who works for himself knows how to destroy himself. These are the two starting points of Individualism."

Lao She's "Individualism" is selfishness; Hsiang Tzu is the personification of this great flaw. He is not a victim of a sick society but one of its representatives, a specimen of a malady that must be cured. A sick society produces sick individuals.

Lao She shows real compassion for the actual victims: the poor, young and old. But he has no hope for them; they are a part of life in Peking. It is in the passages describing life in Peking that the influence of Dickens is obvious. Dickens' dry wit, his irony, his tongue-in-cheek gibes, are also emulated by Lao She, whose lavish use of the exclamation point informs us that the statement preceding it is meant to be ironic.

Peking and the life of Peking are woven into the novel's fabric. Hsiang Tzu is not depicted in a vacuum. He is a part of this city which can feed and shelter him much better than his country village ever could. Yet this great city is neutral toward him. It neither helps nor hinders. All it gives him is a slightly better chance to survive.

Hsiang Tzu is not a sympathetic character. He is a bit pigheaded. "Hsiang Tzu" means good omened but everything he touches turns out badly. "Hsiao Fu Tzu," the name of the girl he loves, means Little Lucky One but she dies of poverty and despair. He has more than one chance to save himself from poverty but he fails to put his opportunities to good use. His rejection of Hsiao Fu Tzu for fear of having to support her two brothers as well dooms both her and himself. When he resolves to try one more time, but only if she helps him, it is too late. Her death kills his spirit. Without any reason to go on living he does not go back to work for Professor Ts'ao. He gives up. He is trapped in a blind alley of his own making. There is no hope for him and there is no hope for the society that spawned him. Hsiang Tzu is the offspring of the womb of a diseased society: its product, not its victim. Hsiang Tzu is victimized only once, by the detective who shakes him down. In other instances he always has a choice and always, whether out of fear for his own selfish interests or out of pride or greed, he chooses badly.

Hsiao Fu Tzu, on the other hand, like the other dwellers in their crumbling courtyard, is a victim. There is no escape for her. She is trapped in a snare not of her own making.

The cry of indignation that rises in the last chapter is not Hsiang Tzu's, it is Lao She's. Here is this city, its inhabitants living, working, playing, as if nothing else mattered and nothing else were happening. The people simply do not care.

Lao She uses the story of Yuan Ming and Professor Ts'ao to present a secondary theme—the ever-present menace of the political police and the stupidity of the masses who are blind to it. Professor Ts'ao is an amiable armchair Socialist. Yuan Ming is a student who will do anything, except study, to get a good grade. He toadies to Professor Ts'ao and when that doesn't get him a passing grade he accuses Ts'ao of Communism. Hsiang Tzu loses both his job and his savings as a consequence while Professor Ts'ao escapes unharmed. Later, Yuan Ming worms his way into the government and becomes a functionary in the Nationalist Party and also takes bribes from the opposition. He then sets out to unionize the rickshaw pullers. Finally, Hsiang Tzu, needing money, informs on Yuan Ming.

The reaction of the people to Yuan Ming's execution is, in fact, a condemnation not simply of their callousness but also of their blindness. Yuan Ming is, after all, a political prisoner, not a felon. The populace does not care. People do not see any difference or any threat to themselves in his execution.

Is there a hero in this novel? Hsiang Tzu is but a pawn. Is there a villain? When people are struggling to survive they do so by climbing higher on the bodies of others. When nobody cares about his fellow man, executions become amusements for the public.

Lao She's indictment of China is similar to the one made by Lu Hsün twenty years before in *Diary of a Madman*. Lao She is also convinced that there is no hope for the Chinese; they all "Eat people." But Lao She does not cry out "Save the children!" as the madman does. He sees China lost in a blind alley. There is not a glimmer of optimism in *Rickshaw* only sarcasm and despair, the result of his frustration and deep rage at this seemingly unchangeable impervious society. Lao She has lost all the hope for a better future he spoke of in 1929 in *Erh Ma*

(The two Mas). On the other hand, he never looks back to the past bemoaning a lost Golden Age.

If there is an explicit political message anywhere in this novel, it is voiced by the old rickshaw man in his parable of the grasshopper which, alone, can do nothing to preserve itself. But when one of a horde this same grasshopper becomes invincible. The poor must unite; collective action can save them.

One more point remains to be made here. During the twenties and early thirties the Chinese literary world expended a lot of time and ink on the question of proletarian literature. All the left-wing writers were convinced that such literature was needed and must be written. In fact, they believed it was the only kind of fiction worth writing. Others on the center and right insisted that literature must be separate from politics. With so much energy going into polemics over the need for proletarian literature, the left-wing writers did not actually do much creative work.

In *Rickshaw* we have what is, in fact, a proletarian novel of the most realistic reportorial sort, written in the language of the people. Lao She was not affiliated with any literary society or literary school. He did, however, write the novel the left wing so conspicuously failed to produce, a novel concerned with a worker and his life and the society in which he lived, worked, suffered, failed, and, finally, died.

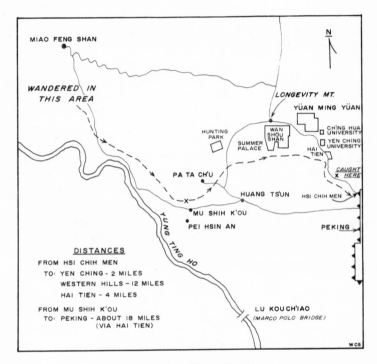

HSIANG TZU'S JOURNEY

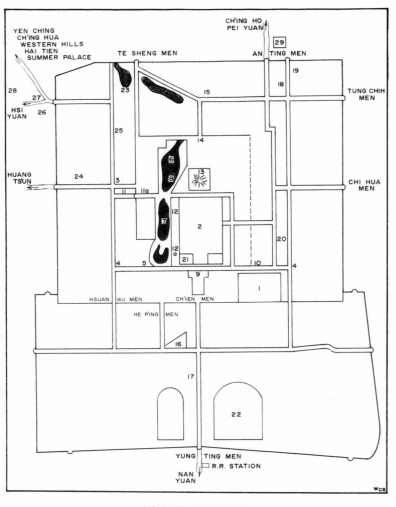

HSIANG TZU'S PEKING

1. THE LEGATION
   QUARTER
2. THE IMPERIAL PALACE
3. DOUBLE EAST & WEST
   P'AI LOU
4. SINGLE EAST & WEST
   P'AI LOU
5. HSIN HUA MEN
6. NORTH LAKE
7. MIDDLE & SOUTH LAKES
8. THE WHITE DAGOBA
9. T'IEN AN MEN

10. CH'ANG AN STREET
11. HSI AN STREET
11a. HSI AN MEN
12. PEI CH'ANG STREET
12a. NAN CH'ANG STREET
13. COAL HILL
14. HOU MEN
15. DRUM TOWER
16. PA TA HU TUNG
17. T'IEN CH'IAO
18. TEMPLE OF CON-
    FUCIUS

19. LAMA TEMPLE
20. TUNG AN MARKET
21. SUN YAT SEN PARK
22. TEMPLE OF HEAVEN
23. CHI SHUI T'AN
24. WHITE PAGODA
25. HSIN STREET
26. THE WHITE HOUSES
27. KAO LIANG BRIDGE
28. ZOOLOGICAL & BO-
    TANICAL GARDENS
29. ALTAR OF EARTH

CHAPTER ONE

T HE PERSON we want to introduce is Hsiang Tzu, not Camel Hsiang Tzu, because "Camel" is only a nickname. We'll just say Hsiang Tzu for now, having indicated that there is a connection between Camel and Hsiang Tzu.

The rickshaw men in Peking form several groups. Those who are young and strong and springy of leg rent good-looking rickshaws and work all day. They take their rickshaws out when they feel like it and quit when they feel like it. They begin their day by going to wait at rickshaw stands or the residences of the wealthy. They specialize in waiting for a customer who wants a fast trip. They might get a dollar or two just like that if it's a good job. Having struck it rich they might take the rest of the day off. It doesn't matter to them—if they haven't made a deal on how much rent they'll have to pay to the rickshaw agency. The members of this band of brothers generally have two hopes: either to be hired full time, or to buy a rickshaw. In the latter case it doesn't make much difference if they work for a family full time or get their fares in the streets; the rickshaw is their own.

Compare the first group to all those who are older, or to all those who, due to their physical condition, are lacking in vigor when they run, or to all those who, because of their families, do not dare waste one day. Most of these men pull almost new rickshaws. Man and rickshaw look equally good so these men can maintain the proper dignity when the time comes to ask for the fare. The men in this group work either all day or on the late afternoon and evening shift. Those who work late, from four P.M. to dawn, do so because they have the stamina for it. They don't care if it is winter or summer. Of course it takes a lot more attentiveness and skill to work at night than in the daytime; naturally you earn somewhat more money.

It is not easy for those who are over forty and under twenty to find a place in these two groups. Their rickshaws are rickety and they dare not work the late shift. All they can do is start out very early, hoping they can earn the rickshaw rental and their expenses for one day between dawn and three or four in the afternoon. Their rickshaws are rickety and they run very slowly. They work long hours on the road and come out short on fares. They are the ones who haul goods at the melon market, fruit market, and vegetable market. They don't make much but there's no need to run fast either.

Very few of those under twenty—and some start work at eleven or twelve—become handsome rickshaw men when older. It is very difficult for them to grow up healthy and strong because of the deprivations they suffer as children. They may pull a rickshaw all their lives but pulling a rickshaw never gets them anywhere. Some of those over forty have been pulling rickshaws for only eight or ten years. They begin to slow down as their muscles deteriorate. Eventually they realize that they'll take a tumble and die in the street sooner or later. Their methods, charging all that the traffic will bear and making short trips look like long ones, are quite enough to bring their past glory to mind and make them snort with contempt at the younger generation. But past glory can scarcely diminish the gloom of the future and for that reason they often sigh a little when they mop their brows. When compared to others among their contemporaries, however, they don't seem to have suffered much. They never expected to have anything to do with pulling rickshaws. But when faced with a choice between living and dying, they'd had to grab the shafts of a rickshaw. They were fired clerks or dismissed policemen, small-time merchants who had lost their capital, or workmen who had lost their jobs. When the time came when they had nothing left to sell or pawn, they gritted their teeth, held back their tears, and set out on this death-bound road. Their best years are already gone and now the poor food they eat becomes the blood and sweat that drips on the pavement. They have no strength, no experience, and no friends. Even among their coworkers they are alone. They pull the most broken-down rickshaws. There's no telling how many flats they get in a day. They'll get a fare and then beg for "understanding and pardon." Fifteen cents is a large fee but they want a tip, too.

Besides these groups, there is yet another one composed of those distinguished by background or knowledge. Those born in Hsi Yuan and Hai Tien, west of the city, naturally find it advantageous to work the

Western Hills or the Ch'ing Hua and Yen Ching University routes. Similarly, those born north of the An Ting Gate make trips to Pei Yuan and Ching Ho. Those born south of the Yung Ting Gate go to Nan Yuan. They are the long-haul men. They refuse to take short-run customers because wearing yourself out on little three or five cent trips isn't worth it. But they yield to the prowess of the pullers in the Legation Quarter. These specialists in foreign trade run from the quarter to the Jade Foundation Mountain, the Summer Palace, or the Western Hills in one trip. But stamina is not what matters. The reason all the other rickshaw men cannot compete for the foreign trade is because these "eaters of foreign food" have a smattering of exotic knowledge. They have picked up some foreign words. These fellows understand when British or French soldiers say "Longevity Mountain" or "Summer Palace" or mispronounce *pa ta hu t'ung* (the red light district). They know a few foreign words and do not pass what they know along to others. Their running style is also peculiar to them. They run at a moderate pace with their heads down and eyes fixed straight ahead while keeping to one side of the road. They have an air of superiority, of not being at odds with the world, about them. Because they work for foreigners, they can do without vests with numbers on them so passengers can hail them. Regulation dress for them is a long-sleeved white jacket and white or black trousers with full legs tied tightly with white cords around the ankles. They wear very thick-soled black cloth shoes and have a smooth clean appearance. Other rickshaw men don't argue over resting places or challenge them to races when they see these clothes. These fellows seem to be engaged in another occupation.

And with this simple analysis we can, we hope, be just as precise when talking about Hsiang Tzu and his position as we are when describing the location of a certain bolt in a machine. Hsiang Tzu, before the events which produced the nickname "Camel," was a comparatively independent rickshaw man. That is to say, he belonged to that group made up of the young and strong who also owned their own rickshaws. His rickshaw, his life, everything was in his own hands. He was a top-ranking rickshaw man.

Becoming independent was not a simple matter at all. It took one year, two years, at least three or four years, and one drop of sweat, two drops of sweat, who knows how many millions of drops of sweat, until the struggle produced a rickshaw. By gritting his teeth through wind and rain, depriving himself of good food and good tea, he finally saved enough for that rickshaw. That rickshaw was the total result, the entire reward, of all his struggle and suffering. It was the equivalent of the campaign medals worn by a soldier who has gone through a hundred battles.

When Hsiang Tzu rented someone else's rickshaw he ran from dawn till dark, from east to west, from south to north. He had no say in the matter. He was like a top someone else was spinning. But in the midst of all this twirling his eyes certainly had no spots before them nor was his mind confused. His thoughts were fixed on that distant rickshaw, the rickshaw that would make him free and independent, the rickshaw that would be like his own hands and feet. He would no longer have to put up with the bad temper of rickshaw agency owners or be hypocritically polite to others when he had his own rickshaw. With his own strength and his own rickshaw, he would have something to eat when he opened his eyes in the morning.

He did not fear hardship and had none of the bad habits of the other rickshaw men, habits which all of them could understand and pardon but were certainly not to be taken as examples of proper behavior. His intelligence and exertions were enough to realize his ambitions. Had his environment been a little better, had he had a little education, he certainly would not have ended up in the "rubber tire corps." Furthermore, no matter what he worked at, he certainly would never have failed to make the most of his opportunities. Unfortunately, he was compelled to pull a rickshaw. All right, he could prove his ability and intelligence in this occupation, too. He seemed to be just the sort of person who would even be a good demon in hell if he had to.

Born and reared in a village, he lost both his parents and the few pieces of family land as well. He came to the city when he was eighteen. Bringing with him a country boy's muscles and forthrightness, he earned his keep by selling his strength in one day labor job after another. But he realized before long that pulling a rickshaw was the easiest way of all to earn money. There are limits to the income from other laboring jobs. There was more variety and opportunity in pulling a rickshaw; you never knew when you might gain a reward greater than you had ever hoped for. Naturally he was aware that such an encounter did not come about entirely by chance. It was essential that both man and rickshaw have a handsome air. You can do business with a man who recognizes quality when you have the goods to sell.

After thinking it over, he believed that he did have the qualifications. He was strong and the right age. The trouble was he had never done the running. He didn't dare just grab hold and take off with a fine-looking rickshaw. But this was no insurmountable difficulty. With his physique and strength as a foundation, he would need only ten or fifteen days of practice to be able to run with style. Then he would rent a new rickshaw. Perhaps he'd get hired on a private basis very quickly and then, after eating sparingly and spending very little for one year, or two years, or even three or four years, he would certainly be able to get his own rickshaw, and one of the best! Looking at his youthful muscles, it seemed to him it was only a question of time until he achieved his ambition and reached his goal. It was no dream at all.

His height and strength had both developed beyond his years; by twenty he was already very large and tall. Although his physique had yet to be molded into a definite form by the passage of time, he already looked like a mature man, a grown man whose face and form still had something naive and mischievous about them. While watching the top-notch rickshaw men he thought about how he would pull in his waist to really show off his "iron fan" chest and hard straight back. He'd turn his head to look at his shoulders; how very broad they were and how very impressive! Once he had his waist bound tightly, he'd put on wide white pants and fasten them down at the cuffs with rubber bands to show off that pair of great big feet! Yes, there was no doubt he could become a most outstanding rickshaw man. He grinned at himself like a simpleton.

There was nothing remarkable about his face. It was his enthusiastic expression that made him likable. His head was not very large; it had two round eyes, a thick nose, very short and very bushy eyebrows, and a scalp that was always shaved and shiny. There was no fat on his cheeks and even so his neck was almost as thick as his head. His face was always red. A large scar between his left ear and cheekbone was particularly lurid. He had been bitten by a mule while asleep under a tree when a boy. He took very little notice of his face. His love for it was the same as his love for his body: both had the same tough strength. He regarded his face as if it were one of his limbs; it needed only to be strong and that was fine. Yes indeed, he could do a headstand for quite a long time after he came to the city. In this position it seemed to him he was very like a tree: up or down, there was no place that wasn't straight and strong.

He was almost like a tree; sturdy, silent, and yet alive. He had his own plans and some insight, but he did not enjoy conversation. Each man's grievances and difficulties were topics of public discussion among the rickshaw pullers. They all reported, or described, or yelled about, their affairs at the rickshaw stands, in the small teahouses, and in front of mixed courtyards, the horizontal tenements of Peking. Afterwards these tales became everyone's property and like a folk song were passed along from one place to another. Hsiang Tzu was a peasant; his speech was not as glib as the city fellows'. Assuming that cleverness of speech comes from innate ability, what was innate with him was an unwillingness to talk. He was also, therefore, not inclined to copy the spiteful lips and wicked tongues of the city folk. He minded his own business and did not enjoy discussing it with others. Because his mouth was often idle, he had plenty of time to think; his eyes seemed always to be peering at his mind. He needed only to decide; then he would follow the road his mind had opened. If it happened that his path was blocked, he would remain silent for several days, grinding his teeth, just as if he were chewing up his heart.

He decided to pull a rickshaw, so he set out to get one to pull. First he rented a battered one and practiced. He did not make any money the first day. He didn't do too badly the second day but then he had to spend the next two days lying down; his ankles had swelled up like gourds and he couldn't lift his feet. He endured it. He didn't care how much it hurt. He knew it was unavoidable, a stage of rickshaw pulling he must experience. He would be unable to run fearlessly unless he had been through it.

He dared to run after his ankles healed. This made him extraordinarily happy because now there was nothing more to fear. He was well acquainted with place names. It wouldn't matter much if he made a mistake once in a while and had to go the long way round, he had plenty of stamina. His experiences while pulling, hauling, and carrying things on poles guided him in the technique of rickshaw pulling, so he didn't think it was very difficult. Furthermore he had his own notions; concentrate a lot and don't be pushy and you probably won't do anything wrong! His way of stammering and then blurting out his words hindered him when shouting out his price and competing for passengers with the other pullers. He couldn't get the better of all those fast talkers. He was aware that he had this shortcoming so he hardly ever went to a rickshaw stand. He waited for customers where there were no other rickshaws. In these out-of-the-way places he could discuss fees calmly. Sometimes he didn't set a price; he simply said, "Get in. Pay me what you want." His manner was so honest, his face so open and likable, that it seemed all people could do was trust him. It didn't occur to anyone that this great simpleton could be an extortionist. If people did wonder about him, it was only to suspect that he was a fellow from the country and new in town. He probably didn't know the streets so he didn't know how much to charge. When someone asked him "Do you know how to get there?" he just smiled in a way that looked as if he were trying to be clever by pretending to be stupid, which left the passenger at a loss what to think.

He got his stride right after three weeks of work. He knew his way of running really looked good. The way a rickshaw man ran was proof of his ability and qualifications. That splayfooted fellow, flapping his feet down onto the ground like a pair of rush leaf fans, is undoubtedly a beginner fresh from the village. That man with his head sunk way down and his feet scraping the ground, who puts on a show of running but isn't moving much faster than he walks, is one of the fellows over fifty. The ones who have all the experience they need but not much strength have another method. They push their chests way out and hold their stomachs way in. They raise their knees high. They stretch their necks and heads forward when they move. They look like they are running with all their might, but in fact they aren't a bit faster than anyone else. They rely on exaggerated gestures to maintain their dignity.

Hsiang Tzu certainly never chose to conduct himself in any of these ways. His legs were long, his stride was long, his torso was firm. There was scarcely a sound when he set out. His stride seemed to expand and contract. The rickshaw shafts did not wobble, which made the passenger feel secure and comfortable. Tell him to stop and no matter how fast he was going at the time, he'd be standing still in two more light steps. His strength seemed to permeate every part of the rickshaw. He ran with his back bent forward, his hands gripping the shafts lightly; he was energetic, smooth in his motions, precise. He didn't appear to be in any hurry and yet he ran very fast, but without jeopardizing anyone. Indeed, even among rickshaw men hired by families such a technique was regarded as very valuable.

He changed to a new rickshaw, asked a few questions, and learned that one like it, with soft springs, bright brass work, a rain cover, two lamps, and a brass horn, was worth something over one hundred dollars. A similar rickshaw could be easily got for one hundred if the lacquer and brass work were slightly defective. So in all probability he only needed a hundred dollars to buy a rickshaw. Suddenly he thought, if I could save ten cents a day I'd have one hundred dollars in just one thousand days! He couldn't figure out how many years were in one thousand days but, he decided then and there, one thousand days were all right. Even ten thousand days were all right. He just had to buy a rickshaw! The first thing he had to do, he knew, was to get hired by a family. If he were hired by someone who had many social engagements and went out to ten or so dinners a month, he could collect two or three dollars in tips from the hosts. Add that to the dollar eighty he could save each month and maybe he could save as much as five dollars, and have maybe fifty or sixty dollars in one year! His hope came much closer that way. He did not smoke, did not drink, did not gamble, wasn't addicted to anything, and had no family burdens. All he needed to do was grit his teeth and he wouldn't fail. He swore an oath to himself: in one year and a half he would have his own rickshaw or else! It would be a new one, too. He wanted no old rebuilt rickshaw that passed for new.

He actually did get hired by a family, but it didn't do much to advance his hopes. He gritted his teeth all right, but after a year and a half he was nowhere near fulfilling his vow. He'd get private jobs and take great pains to be careful in everything he did. Unfortunately, affairs in this world have more than one face. He would perform his duties punctiliously but he'd be fired anyway. It might take two or three months or only eight or ten days and out he'd go. He'd have to look for another job. Naturally he'd have to look for private work and look for fares at the same time—he was "riding a horse while looking for a horse" and had no time off at all. He made mistakes frequently during this period. He drove himself. He paid no attention to how much food he needed every day. After all, he had to save his money to but a rickshaw. But forcing your strength is never a sound practice. He always seemed to be thinking of something else and couldn't keep his mind on his work when running. The more he thought, the more frightened and anxious he became. If things kept on like this, when would he ever be able to buy a rickshaw? Why was it like this? Could anyone say he had no goal in life? In the midst of these confused thoughts he would forget his customary caution; the tire would run over bits of brass or broken pottery and blow out, and all he could do then was quit for the day. Sometimes he ran into pedestrians, which was even worse. The limit was reached when the rickshaw had its top ripped off because he was in a hurry to get through a crowd. Certainly none of these mistakes would have occurred if he had been working for a family. His mind was not very quick and after losing a job he was muddled. It is understood that if you smash up a rickshaw you must pay for the repairs. This vexed him even more; it was like throwing oil on a fire. Sometimes, because he was afraid of bringing on some greater catastrophe, he just slept all day in a kind of stupor. A whole workday had been wasted when he finally opened his eyes and he felt even worse and hated himself. At such times he was even harder on himself as his anxiety increased and his meals became irregular. He thought he was made of iron but even he could get sick.

He was very stubborn and would not let go of his money for medicine when he fell ill. The illness would get worse and worse. He not only had to buy more medicine, he also had to force himself to rest for quite a few days. All these problems made him grit his teeth and work even harder, but the money for a rickshaw didn't pile up any faster.

It took three whole years but he saved one hundred dollars!

He couldn't wait another minute. He had originally planned to buy the latest model, the one that was most completely outfitted and pleased him the most. Now the best he could do was see what he could get for his money. He couldn't wait any longer. Perhaps something else would come up that would lose his money for him! As it happened there was a new rickshaw, one that had been ordered but never paid for, which was not much different than the sort he had hoped to get. Its original price was over a hundred dollars but the maker was willing to cut the price a little because the deposit had been forfeited.

Hsiang Tzu's whole face was red. He took out ninety-six dollars, his hand shaking. "I want this rickshaw!"

The maker decided to press for a round hundred. He talked and talked, he pulled the rickshaw back and forth through the gateway, raised the top and lowered it, and squeezed the horn, accompanying each action with a stream of superlatives. The finale to his performance was to kick the steel spokes twice.

"Listen to the sound! Like a bell! Take it. You can bring it back and throw it in my face if one spoke is weak or even if you pull it to pieces. One hundred dollars. Any less and it's no deal!"

Hsiang Tzu counted his money again. "I want this rickshaw. Ninety-six dollars!"

The maker knew he had run into a clever man. He looked at Hsiang

Tzu and sighed. "For friendship's sake, the rickshaw is yours. Guaranteed for six months. I'll repair everything free unless you smash up the frame. Here's the warranty, take it!"

Hsiang Tzu's hands shook even harder. Almost weeping, he took the warranty and the rickshaw. He pulled it to a quiet spot and carefully examined his own rickshaw. He tried to see a reflection of his face in the lacquered panels! The longer he looked, the more he loved it; even those features which weren't exactly what he had wanted could be overlooked because it was his rickshaw now. Looking over the rickshaw led him to feel he ought to take a little time off. He sat on the perforated footrest and stared at the gleaming brass horn on the front end of one shaft. Suddenly he realized he was twenty-two years old this year. His parents had died too soon for him to know what day his birthday was and he had never celebrated a single birthday since coming to the city. All right, today he had bought a new rickshaw. Let today be his birthday, his and the rickshaw's. It would be easy to remember. Besides, the rickshaw was his heart's blood. There was simply no reason to separate man from rickshaw.

How did they spend this double birthday?

Hsiang Tzu decided that his first customer must be a well-dressed man. It absolutely must not be a woman. Best of all would be a man who wanted to go to the Ch'ien Gate; the Tung An market was next best. What he ought to do when he got there was go to the best food stall and have a meal—hot pancakes stuffed with fried mutton or something similar. Then, after he'd eaten, he'd take one or maybe two fares if they were profitable. If there weren't any he'd put up his rickshaw; this was his birthday!

His experiences in life became much more interesting after he got his own rickshaw. Working for a family was fine, and so was working by the day. He never had to worry about a rental fee—whatever he earned was all his. He felt very much at ease and was more polite to others than before; consequently his business was very satisfactory. Why if things went on like this, by working two more years, two years at the most, he could buy another rickshaw. One, two, why he could even open a rental agency!

But hopes for the most part come to nothing and Hsiang Tzu's were no exception.

CHAPTER TWO

Hsiang tzu ran much faster after buying his rickshaw. His courage grew because he was happy. Of course, with his own rickshaw, he had to be especially careful. But when he looked at himself and looked at this rickshaw, he realized it just wouldn't be right if he didn't run hard.

He had grown an inch since coming to the city and it seemed to him he ought to get even taller. It was true his skin and face were both firmer and more set, and his upper lip had a smallish mustache too, but in his opinion he still ought to grow some more. Although he never said anything, he was secretly delighted whenever he went through a doorway or gate and had to duck his head—which told him he was very tall and still growing. He seemed to be both an adult and a little boy; it was a lot of fun.

How could a man so tall, pulling such a gorgeous rickshaw, his own rickshaw too, with such gently rebounding springs and shafts that barely wavered, such a gleaming body, such a white cushion, such a sonorous horn, face himself if he did not run hard? How could he face his rickshaw? This was not false pride. It seemed to be a kind of duty. He couldn't show off his strength and exhibit the excellence of his rickshaw to full capacity if he didn't fly. That rickshaw was really endearing. It seemed to understand everything and have feelings after he had pulled it for six months. It responded promptly when he turned or squatted or straightened up and gave him the most compatible kind of assistance. There was not the slightest separation or disharmony between them. When he came to a flat stretch with little traffic, Hsiang Tzu might hold the shafts with only one hand and fly along safely with the whisper of the rubber tires urging him on like a damp cool breeze. You could wring the sweat out of his clothes when he got to his destination. It was just as if they had come out of the washtub.

He felt exhausted, but it was a happy, honorable exhaustion, like that following a long ride on a famous horse.

If you are bold, it does not follow that you are careless. When Hsiang Tzu ran boldly, he was certainly not careless. Not to run hard would make him feel he had failed his passenger. To run hard and wreck the rickshaw would make him feel he had failed himself. The rickshaw was his life; he knew how to be careful with it. With caution and boldness combined he gained more self-confidence as he went along. He was convinced that both he and the rickshaw were made of iron.

Accordingly, he not only dared to run boldly, he didn't worry much about what time he took the rickshaw out. He knew that earning your living by pulling a rickshaw was the occupation with the most moral integrity in the whole world. No one could prevent him from working when he wanted to. He paid no heed to rumors of events outside the city. He paid little heed to reports of soldiers being billeted in the military camp at Hsi Yuan again, about fighting south of Chang Hsin Tien, about press gangs active outside the Hsi Chih Gate again, or about the Chi Hua Gate having been shut for half a day. Of course he did not go out deliberately looking for trouble when all the shops shut their doors and the streets were full of armed police and the local militia. He scurried to put away his rickshaw like everyone else. He knew how to be cautious, especially since it was his rickshaw. But after all, he was a country boy and not like the city folks who hear the wind and immediately expect the rain. In addition, his physique led him to believe that he was bound to have some way out if by ill fortune he was put on the spot. He wouldn't suffer much loss. He wasn't an easy person to browbeat; he was so big and had such broad shoulders.

Every year rumors and news of battles seemed to flourish along with the spring wheat. Ears of wheat and bayonets might be regarded as the symbols of the hopes and fears of the northerner. It was just at the time when the young wheat needed the spring rain that Hsiang Tzu's rickshaw was six months old. Spring rain does not invariably fall in accord with the wishes of men, but battles always come no matter whether anyone wishes for them or not. Rumors, truths—Hsiang Tzu seemed to have forgotten the farmer's life he once led. He didn't much care if the fighting ruined the crops and didn't pay much attention to the presence or absence of spring rain. All he was concerned about was his rickshaw; his rickshaw could produce wheat cakes and everything else he ate. It was an all-powerful field which followed obediently after him, a piece of animated, precious earth.

The price of food went up due to drought and news of warfare; this much Hsiang Tzu knew. But like the city folk, he could only grumble about the high cost of food. There was nothing he could do about it at all. So food was expensive; did anyone know how to make it cheaper? This kind of attitude made him concerned only about himself; he put all other disasters and calamities out of his head.

If there was nothing else the city folk could do, they could still make up rumors. Sometimes they fabricated them from nothing. Sometimes they added nine parts talk to one part truth to prove they were definitely not stupid and incompetent. They were like little fish who, when they have nothing to do, poke their mouths up to the surface of the water and blow utterly useless bubbles to their own great satisfaction. The most interesting of rumors are those that have to do with war. Other kinds of rumors are nothing but verbiage from beginning to end, like ghost stories and fairy tales, which never produce a spirit no matter how many times they are told. Rumors about fighting arise because there is no accurate news. Rumors, on the other hand, do produce an immediate effect. Perhaps there are discrepancies between rumor and fact in the details, but eighty or ninety percent of the rumor is accurate as to the existence or nonexistence of the fighting itself. "There'll be fighting!" Once these words have been uttered there'll be a skirmish sooner or later. Everyone has his own explanation as to who is fighting whom and for what. And yet, while laborers, and rickshaw men are among them, do not welcome war, they do not invariably take all the hard knocks when wars break out. The ones who get the most upset every time a battle takes place are the rich. They decide to flee as soon as they feel an ill wind. Money enables them to come and go quickly. But they cannot run by themselves because money makes their feet sink down deep. They must hire others to serve as their legs. Trunks must have porters; grandparents and children must have their rickshaws pulled. At such times the price of the arms and legs of the brothers who have theirs for sale goes way up.

"Ch'iengate, Eaststation!"

"Where?"

"East . . . Railway . . . Station!"

"Oh. That'll be just a dollar forty. No use haggling. The armies are on a rampage!"

It was in precisely this sort of situation that Hsiang Tzu took his rickshaw outside the city. There had been rumors around for ten days. The price of everything had gone up, but it looked like the battles were far away and not likely to hit Peking soon. Hsiang Tzu worked as usual; he certainly didn't snatch a little time off because of rumors. One day he took a fare to the west side and noticed something was up. Not one of the rickshaw men at the stands at the major west side intersections was calling "Anyone for Ch'ing Hua?" "Anyone for Hsi Yuan?"

He walked in circles for a while. He heard that no traffic dared leave the city. Carts were being confiscated by warlord soldiers outside the Hsi Chih Gate; big ones, little ones, mule carts, rickshaws, all were grabbed. The silence around the rickshaw stands meant real danger. He decided to have a cup of tea and then head south. He was brave enough to face danger but there was no point to deliberately risking his neck. Just at this moment two rickshaws came up from the south; the passengers looked like students. The pullers shouted as they ran, "Anyone going to Ch'ing Hua? Hey! Ch'ing Hua?"

Not one of the rickshaw pullers at the stand said a word. Some of them looked at the two rickshaws with faint smiles. Some sat with their pipes in their mouths and didn't even lift their heads. The two men kept bawling. "Are you all deaf? Ch'ing Hua!"

"Give me two dollars and I'll go!" Noticing that no one was saying anything, a very short young fellow with a shiny shaved head answered jokingly.

"Go ahead! We still need one more!" The two rickshaws halted. The shiny-headed fellow stared a while, as though he didn't know what to do. No one else moved. Hsiang Tzu was well aware that it was dangerous to leave the city. Otherwise why wasn't anyone grabbing a two dollar fee to go to Ch'ing Hua University when the usual fare was thirty cents or so? He didn't consider going either, but that shiny-headed colleague seemed to have decided to take his chances and go if he could get someone else to go along. He stared at Hsiang Tzu.

"Hey Big Boy, how about you?"

The phrase made Hsiang Tzu laugh; it was a compliment. He changed his mind. It looked like he'd better lend a hand to this short-of-body, long-on-courage bald-head to justify the compliment. Furthermore, two dollars is two dollars and not something you pick up every day. Danger? With a stroke of luck like this? Besides, two days ago there were people who said the Temple of Heaven was overrun with soldiers and he'd seen with his own eyes that there wasn't even one hair of a soldier's head there. With this thought in mind, he picked up his rickshaw.

There was not a single person in the tunnel through the Hsi Chih Gate. Hsiang Tzu's heart grew chilly. The bald-head realized things didn't look too promising but said, still smiling, "Pay attention, partner! We can't avoid either good fortune or disaster now. What happens next is what happens!"

Hsiang Tzu knew the situation might turn out badly but he'd spent so many years on the streets he couldn't claim he'd never thought of that! He couldn't act like a nervous old woman.

There wasn't a single cart to be seen outside the Hsi Chih Gate. Hsiang Tzu ran with his head down, not daring to look around. His heart seemed to be in his throat. He looked around in all directions from the Kao Liang bridge; there wasn't even one soldier. He relaxed a little. Two dollars, after all, is two dollars. In his opinion, how could you get such a good deal without a little boldness? Ordinarily he didn't like talking at all but now he spoke a few sentences to this shaven-headed shrimp quite willingly; the silence on this road was unnerving.

"Take the dirt path? The road. . . ."

"Why mention it?" The short man guessed his meaning. "If we take the side road we can figure we'll make it."

But before they reached the side road Hsiang Tzu, the shaven-headed shrimp, and the two passengers as well were seized by ten soldiers!

Although it was already late June, and time to open the doors and take incense into the Miao Feng temple, the coldness of the night could not be kept out by an unlined jacket. There was no burden of any kind on Hsiang Tzu's frame except a gray army jacket and blue uniform trousers, both reeking with sweat even before they got to him. These bits of tattered army uniform made him think of the clean white shirt and blue jacket and trousers he had been wearing before; how clean and handsome they were! True enough, there are other things in the world more handsome than his blue outfit, but Hsiang Tzu knew how difficult it had been for him to achieve that clean and tidy appearance. Smelling his present stinking sweaty stench made all his earlier struggles and successes seem exceptionally glorious, ten times more glorious than they had in fact been. The more he thought of the past, the more he hated those soldiers. They had taken away his clothes, hat, shoes, rickshaw, and even his long sash. All they left him was a bunch of purple and black bruises and blisters all over his feet! But clothes don't count for much, and the sore spots on his body would heal soon. His rickshaw, that rickshaw earned with years of blood and sweat, was gone! He hadn't seen it since he pulled it into the bivouac! All the misfortunes and suffering and difficulties of the past could be forgotten in the wink of an eye, but he would never forget his rickshaw!

He was not afraid of hardships. But to get another rickshaw would take several years! It was not a matter of say it and it's as good as done. All his accomplishments were futile; he was right back where he'd started from! Hsiang Tzu wept! He not only hated those soldiers, he hated everything in the world. What made them think they could cheat and insult someone like that? What for?

"What for?" He cried out.

His outcry, although very brief, reminded him of the danger he was in. He just had to escape; nothing else mattered.

Where was he? He could not say for certain. He had been following the troops for days with sweat running down to his heels. He was forced to carry or pull or push their stuff when they marched. He had to carry water, light fires, and feed the pack animals when they halted. All he was conscious of all day long was the need to keep himself moving; his mind was blank. He fell asleep at night when his head touched the ground. It was just as if he had died; never opening his eyes again was not all that terrible.

He seemed to recall that at first the soldiers had been retreating into the Miao Feng Mountains. Once they were in the mountains he concentrated entirely on climbing. He kept thinking that there was no telling when he might slip and fall into a ravine and then his flesh and bones would be eaten up by wild eagles and so he ignored everything else. They had wandered around in the mountains for many days and then suddenly there were fewer and fewer hilly paths. He could see level ground off to the east when the sun was at his back. That night, when the evening mess call sounded, bringing in the outpost sentries, some who had rifles were leading camels.

Camels! Hsiang Tzu's heart heaved. All at once he could think again. Like a man who has lost his way and then suddenly comes to a landmark he knows, he put everything together in his mind very quickly. Camels cannot cross mountains so he must be near the plain. In the Ching Hsi district west of Peking, there were, as far as he knew, villages like Pa Li Chuang, Huang Ts'un, Mu Shih K'ou, and others where camels were raised. Could it be they had wandered back and forth and come to the Mu Shih pass? What kind of strategy was that? If this gang of soldiers who only ran here and there stealing and plundering had a strategy, he couldn't figure out what it was. But he knew for sure that if this place was indeed near the Mu Shih pass, then the soldiers had not gone across the mountains and were heading back to the plain to find another escape route. Mu Shih K'ou was a nice place. You could get to the Western Hills from there by going north-east. You got to Chang Hsin or Fu T'ai by going southeast, and due west there was a road through the mountains. That, in his opinion, was how the soldiers had it figured so he'd better plan an escape route for himself, too. The time for him to flee had come. Perhaps the soldiers would have to retreat into the confusing mountains again; if he waited until then to run away he'd still be in danger of starving. He'd better take advantage of this opportunity if he wanted to escape. He thought that by running away in this area he'd get back to Hai Tien in one trip! He knew just how to go, even though there were quite a few villages in between to be avoided. He shut his eyes and promptly had a mental map; here is Mu Shih K'ou—please let it be Mu Shih K'ou—he'd head northeast, passing several villages, and then he'd be near the famous Buddhist temples. But the road there was exposed so he'd have to stick close to the foothills. Continuing to head northeast-ward, he'd pass more villages until he came to the Ching I Yuan, the old Summer Palace. Then he could find his way to Hai Tien with his eyes shut. His heart leaped joyfully. These last four days it seemed to him that all his blood had run down into his arms and legs; now it seemed to have rushed back to his heart. His heart was hot and his arms and legs began to get cold. Hot hope made his whole body trem-ble!

It was already midnight and he still had not closed his eyes. Hope made him happy, apprehension made him fearful. He wanted to sleep but could not do it; he lay there, his arms and legs looking like they'd been scattered on the dry grass. There was no sound of movement anywhere; only the stars above kept his leaping heart company. The camels suddenly groaned; they were not far from him. He enjoyed this music, it was like suddenly hearing a cock crow in the middle of the night, a sound that made you feel both sad and comforted as well.

There was cannon fire in the distance. The sound was faint but it was unquestionably cannon fire. He didn't dare move but the camp broke out in disorder immediately. He held his breath; his chance had come! He knew the soldiers would have to retreat again and they'd make for the mountains for sure. His experiences lately had taught him that these soldiers fought like a bee trapped inside a house; all they could do was strike out wildly. They would certainly run away if there was cannon fire. In that case, he ought to keep alert. Very slowly, holding his breath, he crawled along the ground; his goal was those camels. He knew quite well that the camels couldn't help him but they were prisoners of war together so they ought to feel some sympathy for each other. Things were getting more disorganized in the camp. He found the camels crouched down in the darkness like mounds of earth. There wasn't a sound except their hoarse breathing; it was as if the world were at peace everywhere. Feeling bolder, he lay down alongside the camels, like a soldier hiding behind sandbags, and thought fast.

The sound of the shelling is coming from the south. If it doesn't mean a real battle, at least it must be a warning that the road is cut. Well, then, these soldiers will have to retreat back into the mountains and if they really do climb the mountains they can't take the camels along. Accordingly, the fate of the camels was his fate as well; he would be done for too if they didn't leave the camels behind. If they forgot the camels, then he could escape. He pressed his ear to the ground and listened for footsteps; his heart beat rapidly.

He had no idea how long he waited, but no one ever came to get the camels. He felt braver and sat up. He looked across the camel humps and couldn't see anything. It was black in all directions.

Escape now! Never mind whether for good or ill, flee!

CHAPTER THREE

Hsiang tzu stopped after about thirty steps; he couldn't leave those camels behind. At this moment, of all the wealth he had in the world, only his life remained. If there had been a bit of rope on the ground, he would have picked it up with pleasure; it could still comfort him a little even though it was useless. At least he would have a length of rope in his hand and it wouldn't be completely empty. He had to escape, but what good was a stark naked life? He could take those camels along even though he hadn't any idea what they might be good for. They were objects and quite large objects at that.

He pulled at the lead rope. He didn't know much about handling camels but he had no fear of them; he wasn't afraid of animals because he was from a village. The camels stood up very, very slowly. He didn't stop to find out whether they were all hitched together or not. He lengthened his stride once he knew he could get them moving; he didn't care if he was leading one of them or the whole train.

He set out and then regretted his decision. Camels, those used to carry heavy loads, that is, are slow walkers. Not only did he have to go slowly but he had to go with great caution. Camels are afraid of slipping; a puddle, a patch of mud, either one could make them break a leg or twist a knee. The value of a camel lay in its four legs; if one leg was done for, everything was done for! And Hsiang Tzu had been thinking of escaping!

But he was unwilling to let go of them. Let it all be up to Heaven; camels got for nothing are not to be discarded. Hsiang Tzu had a good sense of direction because he was a rickshaw man but even so, right now he was confused. When he went to find the camels, he concentrated on them alone. After he got them on their feet, he didn't know which direction was which. The sky was so black and he was so nervous that although he could see the stars and get his bearings from them, he was simply too upset to do it. The stars seemed to be more nervous than he was; they were shifting around and bumping into each other all over the black sky. Hsiang Tzu didn't dare look up at the sky any more. He lowered his head and, frantic to hurry but not daring to walk fast, moved forward. He thought: I am leading camels so I must follow the road. I can't go along the edge of the foothills. There's a direct road from Mu Shih K'ou, if I am near Mu Shih K'ou, to Huang Ts'un. It's a road that camel trains take and it doesn't twist and turn at all. A direct road is worth quite a lot to a rickshaw puller but there's no place to hide on that road! Wasn't he certain to meet soldiers again? And even if he didn't, how could the tattered uniform he was wearing, the dirt on his face, and his unshaved head convince anyone that he was a camel driver? He was nothing like, absolutely nothing like, a camel driver, but he was just like a deserter! A deserter! It wouldn't amount to much if he were caught and taken to the magistrate, but if villagers nabbed him the least they'd do was bury him alive! He began to tremble when he thought of that. The soft thud of camel pads behind him made him jumpy. He had to get rid of this excess baggage if he wanted to save his neck. But he couldn't let go of the lead rope after all. Keep going, keep going to wherever it is and do and say what you have to. You're a couple of pack animals to the good if you live and if you die, that's fate!

He took off his uniform jacket, however, ripped the collar off, and threw it away. The two brass buttons that still remained to carry out their duty were also thrown into the darkness without the slightest sound. He then flung this collarless, buttonless, garment over his shoulders and tied the sleeves in front, as if it were a cape. In this way he believed he could reduce any suspicion that he was a defeated soldier on the run. He rolled up his trousers too. He didn't actually look like a camel driver but he didn't look much like a deserter, either. The dirt on his face and the sweat on his body were probably enough to make him look like a coal hauler with his camels.

His thought processes were very slow but he considered all the details and acted upon his ideas promptly once they were formed. No one could see him in the darkness. He really did not have to prepare himself immediately, but he could not bear to wait. He did not know what time it was; it could be dawn at any minute. He couldn't keep to the foot of the mountains so he'd have no chance to hide in the daytime. He must make people think he was a coal hauler if he planned to show himself on the road in broad daylight. He felt much better as soon as he had acted upon his idea, as if the danger were now past and Peking lay before his eyes. He had to get to the city safe and sound quickly. He had no money and not a scrap of dried food so he couldn't waste time. When he realized that, he considered riding on a camel; saving his strength would enable him to endure hunger longer. But he didn't dare ride. Riding was safe, but he still had to get the camel to kneel so he could get on and he didn't dare take the time. Besides, it would be very difficult to see the footing if he were up that high. If the camel stumbled and fell, he would fall too. No, just go along as you are.

He was pretty sure he was following a main road, but uncertain where it was or where it went. It was very late. The fatigue from days of work plus the terrors of flight made him utterly miserable in mind and body. His footsteps became so plodding and slow when he had been on the road for a while that he seemed to be running down. The night was still dark; there was a little damp chilly mist in the air and he felt even more bewildered. He stared at the ground as hard as he could; it looked like little mounds, one after another, until he put a foot on them, and then he realized that it was only level ground. To be so attentive and still be fooled made him very upset, almost furious. Never mind the ground, look ahead, walk with your feet striking the earth. He couldn't see anything in any direction. It seemed as if all the darkness in the whole world had been waiting for him. He came out of darkness and he went into darkness; behind him came those silent camels.

Gradually the darkness became habitual to him. His heart seemed to have stopped beating; his eyes closed by themselves. He didn't know if he was still moving forward or had already stopped. All he was conscious of was wave after wave of motion like a stretch of rolling black ocean. Darkness and his mind met, joining to make one feeling of vagueness, of rising and falling, of uncertainty in everything. Suddenly there was a heave in his heart, as though he'd thought of something, and yet it also seemed as if he'd heard a slight sound but couldn't tell what it was. He opened his eyes wide again. He was still going straight ahead. He forgot what he'd just been thinking of. There was no noise anywhere. His heart pounded and then slowly calmed down. He ordered himself not to close his eyes again, not to think nonsense again. Getting to the city quickly was the first order of business. But his eyes closed so very easily when he wasn't thinking. He must think about something in particular. He must stay awake. He knew he could sleep for three days if he fell down. Think of what? His head got dizzy, his sweating was unbearable. His hair began to itch, his feet got sore, and the inside of his mouth was dry and rough. He couldn't think of anything except feeling sorry for himself. But he couldn't even think carefully about himself, either. His head was so empty and befuddled it seemed that no sooner had he thought about himself than he forgot what he was thinking. His mind was like a candle about to burn out that can't even illuminate itself. The thick darkness surrounded him and made him feel afloat in a sea of blackness, even though he knew he still existed and was still walking onward. With no other object around to show him where he actually was, he might as well be floating all alone on an empty ocean, not daring to believe even in himself. He had never experienced the agony of this sort of bewilderment and utter desolation before. He didn't enjoy making friends ordinarily, for he would never be afraid standing alone with the sun beaming down on him and everything revealed right before his eyes. He was not afraid now, only it frustrated him not to feel certain of anything. If those camels had been as unruly as donkeys and horses, they might have made him wake up and pay attention to them, but they were so amenable their very tameness upset him. In a fit of fear, he suddenly doubted that they were really still behind him and he jumped in alarm. He seemed to be convinced that those big creatures could have light-footedly insinuated themselves down a side path and into the darkness without his knowing a thing about it, the way a cake of ice slowly turns into nothing while you drag it along.

He sat down at one point, he had no idea when. If he were just going to go die, well, he'd know after he'd died. But he wouldn't be able to remember how or why he sat down. He sat for five minutes, perhaps an hour, he couldn't tell. And he didn't know if he sat first and then slept, or slept first and then sat. Probably he had gone to sleep first and then sat down, since he was exhausted enough to go to sleep on his feet.

He awoke. It was no normal awakening but a startled falling from one world into another in the blink of an eye. Darkness was what he saw but he heard a cock crow very distinctly. The sound was so clear it was just like something drawing a line through his brain. He woke up completely. The camels? He couldn't think of anything else. The rope was still in his hand and the camels were still there next to him. He calmed down. He was too worn out to stand. He felt sore and listless. He didn't want to stand up but didn't dare go back to sleep again. He had to think, think very carefully and make the correct decision. It was just at this moment that he thought of his rickshaw and cried out again, "What for?"

"What for?" But meaningless yelling is utterly useless. He went to feel the camels; he still didn't know how many he was leading. Now he knew: he had three all together. He didn't know if that was too many or too few; he collected his thoughts and concentrated on these three bodies. He still wasn't settled in his mind about how it was to be done, but his vague mullings did lead him to conclude that his future depended entirely upon these three beasts.

"Why not sell them and buy another rickshaw?" He almost jumped in the air! But he did not move, probably because he felt ashamed of himself for not having thought of such an obvious and troublesaving plan already. Joy overcame his mortification; he had made up his mind. Wasn't that a cock crowing just now? It's true that cocks do crow in the middle of the night sometimes, but dawn could not be far off anyway, and where cocks crow there must be a village. Could it be Pei Hsin An? There were camel breeders there. He'd better get a move on quickly. If he could get there by dawn and get the camels off his hands then he could buy a rickshaw as soon as he got to the city. In times when soldiers were out on a rampage surely rickshaws must be a little cheaper. Buying a rickshaw was all that concerned him. He seemed to think selling camels was easy.

His spirits improved and his body didn't seem to be sore anywhere once he began thinking about the connection between the camels and a rickshaw. Not even thinking of selling the camels for one hundred *mou* of land or perhaps exchanging them for several pearls would have made him this happy. He didn't know what the going rate for camels was now, but he had heard that in the old days, before there was a railroad, the price of one camel was a fifty dollar silver piece because camels are very strong and eat less than horses and donkeys. He did not expect to get three fifty-dollar silver pieces, but he did expect to get eighty or one hundred dollars for them, enough to buy a rickshaw.

The sky became brighter and brighter the longer he walked. Yes, the lighter spot was directly ahead. He was walking east all right. He couldn't mistake the direction even if he took the wrong path. The mountains were in the west, the city was in the east—he knew that much. Gradually, the blackness coating everything began to thin out; fields and distant trees all took shape in the general grayness. Colors could not be distinguished yet. The stars faded and the sky was obscured by a layer of gray, like cloud and like mist, but much higher up than before. Hsiang Tzu felt he could lift his head. He also began to smell the fragrance from the grasses along the roadside and hear birdcalls. His eyes, ears, mouth, and nose all seemed to be recovering their proper functions. He could see all of himself too, and ragged and embarrassing as his condition was, he could now believe he had returned to life. It was just like awakening from a nightmare and realizing how precious life is. After looking himself over, he turned his head to regard the camels. They were just as hard on the eyes as he was, and just as precious. It was the season for animals to shed their coats. The camels were already showing patches of reddish gray hide, while hanks of loose long hair hung here and there, waiting to be pulled off. They looked like the largest beggars of all the animals. Most pitiable of all were their long hairless necks; they were so long, bald, curved, and stretched out so far, they looked like skinny disappointed dragons. But Hsiang Tzu did not reject them no matter how ugly they were; after all, they were living things. He realized he was the luckiest man on earth. Heaven had sent him three living treasures which could be turned into a rickshaw. This kind of thing didn't happen every day. He couldn't help laughing.

A trace of red came through the gray in the sky. The ground and the distant trees looked much darker. Gradually the red and gray began to mingle; in some places the sky became a gray purple, in others it was noticeably red. The color of the greater part of the sky was a grape-purple gray. After a short period a gleam of gold shone through the red and each color grew brighter. Suddenly everything stood out quite distinctly. At the same time, the morning clouds in the east became deep red and the sky above them turned blue. The red clouds scattered and golden beams shot out. The streaky clouds made a warp, the rays of light made the woof; together they wove a marvelous gleaming spiderweb in the east. The green of the fields, trees, and wild grasses was transformed from a dark green to a shimmering emerald hue. The trunks of the old pines were dyed orange, the wings of the flying birds shone with glints of gold, and all things wore a smile.

Facing this red glow, Hsiang Tzu wanted to shout out loud. It

seemed to him he had not seen the sun since the soldiers captured him.
With his mind full of curses and his head always down he had forgotten that there was still a sun and a moon; he had forgotten the sky.
Now he walked freely along the road, the brightness increasing while he walked. The sun lent a touch of gold to the dew on the grass and leaves, shone on Hsiang Tzu's brow, and warmed his heart. He forgot all his trials, all the danger, all the pain. Never mind how ragged and filthy he was. He would never be cast out of the sun's bright light and heat. He lived in a universe with light and heat in it. He was elated and could have shouted for joy.

Looking again at his torn clothes and then back at the three shedding camels behind him, he smiled. That four such unlikely creatures could have actually escaped from danger and could now walk on a road in the sunshine was a miracle indeed! Why worry any more about the rights and wrongs of things? Everything, in his opinion, was as Heaven had decreed. He stopped worrying and walked on slowly. He had nothing to fear as long as Heaven protected him. Where was he going? He didn't think to ask any of the men and women who were already coming out to the fields. Keep going. It didn't seem to matter much if he didn't sell the camels right away. Get to the city first and then take care of it. He longed to see the city again. He had no parents or relatives there, nor property of any kind. Still, in the end, it was his home; the entire city was his home. He'd find a way after he got there.

There was a village in the distance, and not a small one. The willow trees outside it were like a row of tall green sentries. He could see the low buildings; a little smoke was floating above them. Even from this distance he could hear the dogs barking, a wonderful sound. He headed straight for the village. He didn't think he'd done anything illegal by taking the camels. It seemed to him that all he had to do was show he was not afraid of anything. He was a good man so why should he have anything to fear from the law-abiding people in the village? Everyone these days lived beneath the bright and peaceful sun.

He thought he'd like some water to drink. But it wouldn't matter much if he couldn't get any. He hadn't died in the mountains, so what did being thirsty for a little longer matter?

The village dogs barked at him. He ignored them. But the stares of the women and children made him uneasy. He certainly was a very peculiar camel driver. If that wasn't it, why else would they be looking at him like that? He thought it was too much to bear. The soldiers hadn't treated him like a man and now everyone in this village thought he was a monster too! He didn't know what to do. His strength and courage had, until recently, given him a measure of pride and self-respect, but lately he had been subjected to nothing but mistreatment and hardship for no reason at all. He looked up above the ridgepole of a house and saw that brilliant sun again, but it wasn't as precious as it had been a short time ago!

Pig piss, horse piss, and filthy water made reeking puddles along the only wide street in the town. Hsiang Tzu was afraid the camels would slip and fall and wanted to rest awhile too. There was a house on the north side of the street that looked impressive; there were tiled-roof buildings in the back and the main entry was closed by a latticed gate. There was no solid wooden gate and no gatehouse. Hsiang Tzu's heart leaped; a tiled roof means a wealthy owner and a lattice gate and no gatehouse mean a camel dealer! Very well, he'd just rest right here and it was a safe bet he'd have a good chance to get rid of the camels.

"Sze! Sze! Sze!" The only camel talk Hsiang Tzu knew was that "sze" meant kneel, so he ordered them to kneel. He used the word very smugly, deliberately making it clear to the villagers that he was no outsider to the camel trade. The camels really did kneel. Hsiang Tzu then sat himself down underneath a small willow tree with dignity. Everybody looked at him and he looked right back; he knew it was the only way to lessen the villagers' suspicions.

An old man came out of the impressive house after Hsiang Tzu had been sitting for a while. He wore a blue gown and a short jacket. His shiny face looked friendly. One look and Hsiang Tzu knew this was the village rich man. Hsiang Tzu made up his mind.

"Sir, is there any water? I'd like some."

"Ah!" The old man's hand brushed at a spot of mud on his jacket. He inspected Hsiang Tzu and then took a close look at the camels. "We have water. Where have you come from?"

"The west." Hsiang Tzu didn't dare mention a place because he didn't know where he was.

"Aren't there soldiers in the west?" The old man's eyes stared at Hsiang Tzu's uniform trousers.

"I was forced to work for some soldiers. I just got away from them."

"Ah. Wasn't there some danger this side of the pass with those camels?"

"The soldiers all went into the mountains. The roads were quiet."

"Um." The old man nodded his head slowly. "You wait, I'll get you some water."

Hsiang Tzu followed him. When he got to the middle of the courtyard he saw four camels.

"Sir, could you make up a camel train if you kept my three?"

"Humph! A camel train? I had more than three camel trains thirty years ago. Times have changed. Who can afford to keep camels?" The old man stood still, gazing at his beasts. After a pause he said, "A few days ago I was actually planning to go in with a neighbor and send them all west of the pass to graze. But there are soldiers fighting everywhere, so who dares go anywhere? If you keep them around all summer it makes you miserable just to look at them. Miserable! Look at all those flies! Soon it will be hot and we'll have mosquitoes too and then have to watch these fine animals suffer so. It's too much!" The old man shook his head continually, as if there were no end to his regret.

"Sir, take my three so you can make up a train and send them out to graze. A summer here would make such healthy animals half dead from flies and mosquitoes." Hsiang Tzu was almost imploring him!

"But who has cash to buy? These are no times to raise camels!"

"Keep them. Pay what you want. I want to get them off my hands so I can go the city and decide how to make a living."

The old man looked Hsiang Tzu over carefully for a while; he realized Hsiang Tzu was certainly not one of the bandit kind. Then he turned to look at the animals outside. He really seemed to like those three camels. He was well aware it would do him no good to buy them but, like a bibliophile who sees a book and promptly wants to buy it and a horse breeder who sees a horse and can't do without it, this former owner of more than three camel trains could not let these camels go. Besides, Hsiang Tzu said he could buy low. It is easy for men who understand business to forget that when they get a bargain they are stuck with the items once they have been paid for.

"Young colleague, if I had the money I'd really consider keeping them!" He spoke the truth.

"Just keep them anyway. Whatever you decide is fine!" Hsiang Tzu was so earnest it made the old man a little embarrassed.

"To tell the truth, they would have been worth three fifty-dollar silver pieces thirty years ago. In these times, what with the soldiers pillaging on top of everything else, I . . . you'd better try somewhere else."

"I'll take what you give me!" Hsiang Tzu couldn't think of anything else to say. He realized the old man's words were honest, but he didn't want to trudge all over the world selling camels. If he didn't sell them now perhaps some other kind of trouble would turn up.

"See here, see here. Twenty or thirty dollars isn't really what I'd like to offer, but it really is difficult to take them any farther, isn't it? In these times it can't be done!"

Hsiang Tzu's eagerness cooled off somewhat. Twenty or thirty dollars? That's a long way from enough to buy a rickshaw! But he wanted to settle the deal right away; besides, he did not believe he would be lucky enough to find another buyer. "Sir, I'll take what you give."

"What do you do, young fellow? It's quite obvious you are not in this trade."

Hsiang Tzu told him the truth.

"Oh, so you risked your life to get them."

The old man sympathized with Hsiang Tzu and felt greatly relieved as well. The camels were not stolen goods, although not far from it. But after all, a wall of soldiers came in between; nothing in the wake of a military rampage could be said to follow ordinary rules.

"Well then, young fellow, I'll give you thirty-five dollars. If I claim that isn't cheap then I am a small dog. If I could add another dollar I'd be a small dog too. I am over sixty . . . humph, what else can I say?"

Hsiang Tzu was without a plan. He had been very grasping about money in the past but now to suddenly hear this old man's honest and sympathetic words after days with those soldiers made him too embarrassed to bargain. Furthermore, thirty-five dollars cash in hand seemed much more reliable than ten thousand dollars in hopes, even though getting only thirty-five dollars in exchange for risking his life seemed all wrong! Indeed, it was impossible, really impossible, to claim three live camels were only worth thirty-five dollars! But what could he do? "The camels are all yours, sir. I ask only one thing. Please find me a jacket and something to eat."

"That I can do!"

Hsiang Tzu had a drink of cold boiled water and put on a poorly fitting white jacket. He took thirty-five dollars in bright silver and two hunks of biscuit and set out. He wanted to get to the city in one trip!

CHAPTER FOUR

Hsiang tzu lay for three days in a small inn in Hai Tien, his body shaking with chills and fever. He was delirious at times and had great purple blisters on his gums. Water was all he wanted, not food. Three days of fasting brought his temperature down and left his body flaccid as soft taffy. It was probably during these three days that, either by talking in his sleep or babbling deliriously, he let others find out about the camels. He was Camel Hsiang Tzu even before he recovered.

He had been simply Hsiang Tzu, as if he had no family name, ever since he came to the city. Now that Camel was put before Hsiang Tzu, no one would care what his family name was. Having or not having a family name didn't bother him, but to have sold three animals for only thirty-five dollars and then been stuck with a nickname to boot was nothing to brag about.

He decided to take a look around once he struggled to his feet, but he never expected his legs to be so weak. He collapsed feebly onto the ground when he got to the front door of the inn. He sat there, dizzily, for a long time, his forehead covered with cold sweat. He put up with it and then opened his eyes. His stomach rumbled; he felt a little hungry. He stood up very slowly and went over to a won ton peddler. Then, with a bowl of won ton soup, he sat down on the ground again. He took a mouthful and felt nauseated, but held the soup in his mouth awhile and forced it down. He didn't want any more. After a short wait it finally went straight down to his belly and he belched loudly twice. He knew he still had life in him.

He looked himself over after getting a little food in his stomach. He had lost a lot of weight and his ragged trousers couldn't have been dirtier. He was too tired to move but he had to get himself cleaned up immediately; he refused to enter the city looking like a wreck. Only he'd have to spend money to make himself clean and neat. It would take money to get his head shaved and buy a change of clothes and shoes and socks. He ought not to disturb the thirty-five dollars he had in hand. But after all, even if he didn't, wasn't it still a long way from enough to buy a rickshaw? He took pity on himself.

Although it wasn't so long ago that he had been captured by the soldiers, it was all like a nightmare when he thought about it now. This nightmare had aged him considerably; it was as if he'd taken on many years in a single breath. When he looked at his big hands and feet it was obvious they were his, but they looked like they might have been picked up any old place. He didn't dare think of all the hardship and danger he'd just gone through, but it was still there even though he didn't think about it. It was like knowing the sky is overcast during a succession of dark days, even though you do not go out to look at it. He knew his body was especially precious; he should not make himself suffer. He stood up, aware that he was still very weak, intending to go get properly dressed without another minute's delay—as if all he needed was to get his head shaved and his clothes changed to be strong again instantly.

It took a total of two dollars and twenty cents to get properly turned out. A jacket and trousers of fine-looking unbleached rough cloth cost one dollar, black cloth shoes were eighty cents, cotton socks were fifteen cents, and a straw hat cost twenty-five cents. He gave the tattered things he took off to a ragpicker in exchange for the usual two boxes of matches.

He headed down the highway with his two boxes of matches, his goal the Hsi Chih Gate. He had not gone very far before he felt unsteady and exhausted. But he gritted his teeth; he could not ride in a rickshaw. No matter how he looked at it he could not take a rickshaw. Couldn't any peasant make the trip? And besides, he was a rickshaw puller! What a joke to let his energy be drained by such a piddling sickness. He absolutely would not give in to weakness. Why even if he had an accident and couldn't crawl, then he'd roll and roll all the way to the city. If he did not reach the city today it was all up with him; his body was the only thing he had confidence in, never mind being sick!

Wobbly and shaky, he lengthened his stride but gold stars appeared before his eyes not far from Hai Tien. He leaned against a willow tree and pulled himself together. The turning earth and reeling sky made him dizzy for a while, but still he refused to sit down. The whirling earth and sky eventually slowed down and his heart seemed to come rolling back to its place again from somewhere far away. He wiped the sweat off his head and set out once more. He'd had his head shaved and got his clothes changed. Surely, he reasoned, this was enough to compensate for his weakness. Well, then, his legs had better do their duty and walk! He got almost to the northwest gate in one stretch.

When he saw the bustle of people and horses, heard the ear-piercing racket, smelled the dry stink of the road, and trod on the powdery, churned-up gray dirt, Hsiang Tzu wanted to kiss it, kiss that gray stinking dirt, adorable dirt, dirt that grew silver dollars! He had no father or mother, brother or sister, and no relatives. The only friend he had was this ancient city. This city gave him everything. Even starving here was better than starving in the country. There were things to look at, sounds to listen to, color and voices everywhere. All you needed was to be willing to sell your strength. There was so much money here it couldn't be counted. There were ten thousand kinds of grand things here that would never be eaten up or worn out. Here, if you begged for food, you could even get things like meat and vegetable soup. All they had in the village was cornmeal cakes. When he reached the west side of the Kao Liang bridge he sat down next to the canal and dropped quite a few hot tears!

The sun was setting; the old willow branches bending above the canal had tiny glints of gold on their tips. There wasn't much water in the canal but there was a lot of trailing waterweed like an oily belt, narrow, long, and deep green, which gave off a slight rank smell of damp. The wheat on the north bank had already spit out its shoots. They were stunted and dry, with a layer of dust on their leaves. The pads of the water lilies along the southern embankment of the canal floated limply on the surface. Little bubbles were released around them at intervals. People were coming and going on the east side of the bridge. They all looked hurried in the light of the setting sun, as if they felt a kind of uneasiness as evening approached. It was all very enjoyable and precious to Hsiang Tzu. Only a little canal like this one could be considered a canal. These trees, the wheat, the water lily pads, the bridge, were the only real trees, wheat, water lilies, and bridge, because they were all part of Peking.

He was in no hurry sitting there. Everything he saw was familiar and dear. If he were to die while sitting there, he'd be content. He rested for some time and then crossed the bridge and bought a bowl of bean curd from a street vendor. Warmed by the scalding hot snow-white bean curd, the vinegar, soy sauce, chili pepper oil, and scallion tips gave off an absolutely wonderful smell that made Hsiang Tzu want to hold his breath. His hands couldn't stop trembling while he held the bowl and gazed at the dark green scallion tips. He took a mouthful. The bean curd opened a path in his body. He added two more spoonfuls of chili pepper oil. When he'd finished, sweat soaked his wasteband. With his eyes half shut he held out the bowl. "Give me another bowlful!"

He felt like a man again when he stood up. The sun had sunk to its lowest point in the west. The evening clouds reflected in the canal made the water slightly red. His elation made him want to shout. He forgot all about being sick, forgot everything, as he rubbed the slick scar on his face, rubbed the coins in his pocket, and looked at the sunlight on the watchtower. Then, as if he had a conviction to act upon, he went determinedly into the city.

The gateway tunnel was jammed with every kind of cart and all sorts of people. Everyone wanted to get through it quickly but no one dared hurry. The cracking of whips, shouts, curses, honking of horns, ringing of bells, and laughter were blended into a continuous roaring by the megaphonelike tunnel, making a "weng weng." Hsiang Tzu's big feet cut forwards and jumped backwards while his hands fended off people to left and right. He pushed his way into the city like a great skinny fish which follows the waves and jumps for joy. He caught sight of Hsin street; it was so broad and straight it made his eyes sparkle when they saw it just as brightly as the sunlight reflected off the roofs above him. He nodded his head.

His bedroll was still at the Jen Ho rickshaw agency; naturally he intended to hurry there. Although he did not always rent one of their rickshaws, he stayed at this agency because he had no home of his own. Liu, the owner, was a man who would soon be sixty-nine. He was old but not dignified. In his younger days he had served as a guard in the Imperial Treasury, operated a gambling house, trafficked in women, and practiced loan sharking. Liu had all the qualifications and abilities needed to carry on these enterprises: audacity, tact, skill, social contacts, reputation, and so forth. During the last days of the Ch'ing dynasty he had fought in mob wars, abducted women of good family, and "knelt on iron chains." Kneeling before the magistrate on iron chains, Liu never wrinkled his brow, never confessed, never once said "spare my life." The magistrate admired his unflinching fortitude under torture. This is called making a name for yourself.

As it happened, Liu came out into the new republic when he got out of jail. Liu could see that the police were becoming more and more powerful and the role of local bravo had already become a thing of the past. Even if those great old heroes Li K'uei and Wu Sung had still been alive, they wouldn't have been able to carry on either.

Liu opened a rickshaw agency. He had started out as a local bravo, or neighborhood bully, so he knew how to treat poor people: when to squeeze them and when to let up a little. He excelled in his genius for fast footwork. None of the rickshaw pullers dared try to outsmart him. One stare or guffaw from Liu would leave them completely stymied, as if they had one foot in heaven and one foot in hell. All they could do was let him persecute them.

Liu now had over sixty rickshaws. He did not rent out worn rickshaws—the very worst of his was almost new. He charged a somewhat higher rental fee but allowed two more rent-free days during the three yearly festivals than the other rickshaw agencies did. The Jen Ho agency also had sleeping rooms, so unmarried men who pulled its rickshaws could stay there free, but they had to pay promptly for using the rickshaws. Anyone who couldn't pay up and tried to beg off would be thrown out the door like a broken teapot and have his bedroll confiscated. But if any of them had a serious problem or was ill, all he had to do was tell Liu about it. Liu would not sit idly by. He'd even go through fire and flood to help. This is called making a name for yourself.

Liu had the physiognomy of a tiger. He was nearly seventy but his back was still straight and he could still walk ten or twenty li. He had big round eyes, a big nose, a square chin, and a pair of tigerish canine teeth. His open mouth looked just like a tiger's. He was almost as tall as Hsiang Tzu. His head was shaved so it glistened and he had not grown a beard. He claimed to be a tiger, but alas he had no son, only a thirty-seven or so year old tiger daughter. Anyone who knew about old Liu also knew about Hu Niu, Tiger Girl. She, too, had grown up with the head and brains of a tiger and so she frightened men off. She was skillful at helping her father manage the business but no one dared ask for her as his wife. She was the same as a man in everything; she had a man's bluntness when swearing at someone and even added a few embellishments all her own. Under the rule of the Lius, the Jen Ho agency was like a length of steel tubing: nothing out of place. This agency had a great deal of prestige and influence in the world of rickshaws. The methods of the Lius were often on the lips of rickshaw owners and pullers, the way scholars quote from the Confucian classics.

Until he bought his own rickshaw, Hsiang Tzu had pulled one of theirs. He had deposited his profits with Liu at interest, and when he finally had saved enough, he withdrew it all and bought his rickshaw. "Mister Liu," he'd said, "look at my new rickshaw!" He had taken his new rickshaw back to the Jen Ho agency.

The old man had looked at it and nodded. "Not bad!"

"I'll still have to stay here. But whenever I work for a family, I'll go live there," added Hsiang Tzu rather proudly.

"Very well." Liu had nodded again.

And so, when Hsiang Tzu had a private job, he lived there. He lived at the agency when he was out of a private job and had to work the streets.

In the opinion of the other rickshaw men, it was unheard of to have someone who no longer pulled a Jen Ho rickshaw go on living there. They wondered about it. The most farfetched guess was that Hsiang Tzu was related to old Liu. Many others said old Liu probably had a high opinion of Hsiang Tzu and planned to fix Hu Niu up with a husband who would live there. Speculations like these were colored by a little envy, but perhaps things really would turn out like that. The Jen Ho agency would certainly be left to Hsiang Tzu when old Liu died, that was what mattered. All they did was make foolish guesses about the situation. Naturally none of them dared be so rude as to say anything to Hsiang Tzu himself.

In fact, old Liu's good treatment of Hsiang Tzu was on quite another account. Hsiang Tzu was the sort of man who held fast to his old habits in a new environment. Suppose he joined the army; he certainly would not start right in pretending to be ignorant of what he was doing and cheat and swindle people the way most soldiers did as soon as he had put on his uniform. At the agency he started looking for something to do as soon as he came back each day and had wiped the sweat off his brow. He was never idle. He dusted off rickshaws, pumped up tires, spread the rain covers out to dry in the sun, and greased wheels. No one had to tell him to do these things; he did them voluntarily.

Working made him very happy, as if it were the best of all amusements.

Ordinarily, there were about twenty men living at the agency. They either sat around talking or were dead asleep after putting away their rickshaws. Only Hsiang Tzu's hands were never idle. When he first came there everyone thought he was putting on a show for old Liu, trying to get himself in good like a stray dog. After a while they realized he was not putting up a false front in any way. He really was that forthright and natural, so there was simply nothing more to be said. Old Liu never praised him, never gave a sign he had noticed Hsiang Tzu; he simply made a mental note. He knew Hsiang Tzu was a good worker, so he was glad to have him around even if he wasn't pulling a Liu rickshaw. The courtyard and doorway, not to mention anything else, were always kept clean when Hsiang Tzu was there.

Hu Niu liked the big oaf even more. Hsiang Tzu always listened attentively when she spoke and never argued with her. The other rickshaw pullers were contrary because of all their miseries. She wasn't afraid of them in the least but preferred not to have much to do with them, so she saved all her comments for Hsiang Tzu. It was as if the Lius had lost a friend when Hsiang Tzu had a private job and was living out. And when he was there, even the old man's swearing seemed more to the point and a little kinder.

Hsiang Tzu entered the Jen Ho agency carrying his two boxes of matches. It wasn't dark yet and the Lius were still eating dinner. Hu Niu put down her chopsticks when she saw him come in.

"Hsiang Tzu! Did you let a wolf catch you or did you go to Africa to dig in the gold mines?"

Hsiang Tzu said nothing; he grunted.

Liu's big round eyes gave Hsiang Tzu the once-over. He didn't say anything either.

Hsiang Tzu sat down facing them, his new straw hat still on his head.

"In case you haven't eaten, here's some." Hu Niu behaved as if she were taking care of a good friend.

Hsiang Tzu didn't move. His heart was suddenly full of a feeling of warm friendship he couldn't put into words. He had always regarded the Jen Ho agency as his home. On private jobs his masters changed frequently, and when working the streets his passengers changed with every trip. This was the only place he was allowed to stay and there was always someone to chat with. He had just escaped with his life and come back to his friends and here they were, inviting him to have something to eat. While he wondered if they could be mocking him, he almost wept, too.

"Just had two bowls of bean curd." He showed a little courtesy.

"What did you go away for? Where's your rickshaw?" Old Liu's eyes were still fastened on him.

"Rickshaw?" Hsiang Tzu spat.

"Come have a bowl of rice first. It won't kill you. What are two bowls of bean curd?" Hu Niu pulled at his sleeve like a wife fussing over a younger brother-in-law.

Hsiang Tzu did not take the rice bowl. He took out his money instead. "Sir, keep this for me. It's thirty dollars." He put the change back in his pocket.

Liu inquired with his eyebrows. Where did it come from?

Hsiang Tzu ate and told how he had been captured by the soldiers.

"Humph! You idiot!" Liu shook his head. "If you'd brought them to the city and sold them for the soup pot, they'd have been worth more than ten dollars a head. If it had been winter and they'd had their heavy coats, three head would have brought sixty dollars!"

Hsiang Tzu already regretted it; hearing this made him feel even worse. But, he went on to think, it was hardly virtuous to let three living animals have their throats cut for the soup pot. They had all escaped together so they should all live. That was all there was to say about it and he felt at peace in his mind.

Hu Niu cleared the table. Liu looked up as though he'd thought of something. Suddenly a laugh showed two teeth that looked more and more like tiger teeth the older he got. "Dolt! Did you say you were sick at Hai Tien? Why didn't you come straight back on the Huang Ts'un road?"

"I had to go the long way round by the Western Hills. I was afraid that if I took the main road someone would catch me. I was pretty sure the villagers would grab me as a deserter if they thought things over."

Liu smiled and his eyes rolled back and forth. He had been afraid Hsiang Tzu was lying about the money. Maybe it was stolen. He wasn't going to hide anyone's loot for him. He had done every lawless thing there was to do when young, but he had to be careful now that he had taken up the role of reformed character. He knew what to watch out for, all right. There was only one flaw in Hsiang Tzu's story, but he had explained it away without mumbling. The old man relaxed. "Now what?" he said, pointing to the money.

"Whatever you say."

"Buy another rickshaw?" The old man stuck out his tiger teeth again as if to say, "You buy another rickshaw and still think you're going to stay at my place free again?"

"There isn't enough. I've got to buy a new one!" Hsiang Tzu did not look at Liu's teeth. He was concentrating on his own thoughts.

"Lend you the money? One percent interest. Anyone else gets charged two and a half."

Hsiang Tzu shook his head.

"Buying on installments from a dealer is not as good as giving me one percent."

"I won't buy one on installments either," Hsiang Tzu said intensely. "I'll save up until I get enough. Ready cash buys ready goods."

Old Liu stared at Hsiang Tzu as if he were trying to read a strange word he couldn't figure out and detested, but could hardly get angry at. He waited awhile and then picked up the money. "Thirty dollars? You're sure about the amount?"

"That's right." Hsiang Tzu stood up. "I'm going to bed. I've brought you a box of matches, sir." He put the box on the table and stood blankly for a moment. "There's no need to tell people about the camels."

CHAPTER FIVE

OLD LIU did not spread tales about Hsiang Tzu, but the story of the camels came from Hai Tien anyway. While people hadn't found any faults in Hsiang Tzu, most of them thought he was eccentric and contrary because of his absolute stubbornness. But they looked at him with different eyes after the story of the camels got around, even though he was still working just as glumly and unsociably as ever. Some said he'd got hold of a gold watch; some said he'd got three hundred dollars for nothing. Those who were convinced that they had the most accurate information would nod their heads and say he'd brought thirty camels back from the Western Hills! The stories were all different but they amounted to the same thing: Hsiang Tzu had struck it rich!

As a rule, when it comes to those who have struck it rich, most people respect them no matter how unpopular they are. It isn't all that easy to make a living when you sell your strength, so everyone hopes for a little easy money. Easy money is so rarely got hold of that anyone who does have a bit of luck must be exceptional. Good luck means a great destiny in store for you. And for this reason, Hsiang Tzu's silence and eccentricity were gradually converted into the "sparse speech of a great man." Well, if he was a great and generous man then they ought to run after him and get him on their side.

"Good job, Hsiang Tzu! So tell me, how did you get rich?"

Hsiang Tzu heard talk like that every day. He never made a sound. Finally, when he was infuriated, his scar would get red and he'd say, "Get rich! So where'd my fucking rickshaw go?"

Oh yes, that's true. Where *had* his rickshaw gone? They began to think things over again. Feeling happy for someone is not like being worried about him, and they had forgotten about his rickshaw, thinking about his good luck instead. And in a few days they saw him out pulling a rickshaw again. He hadn't changed his trade and hadn't bought a house or some land, so they cooled towards him. From then on, whenever Camel Hsiang Tzu was mentioned, no one went to ask him why he was called Camel. Camel seemed to have been his name from the start.

Hsiang Tzu himself could not forget the whole thing so nonchalantly. He couldn't stand not being able to buy another new rickshaw right away! The more upset he got, the more he thought of his original rickshaw. He worked hard all day, but not without hatred, thinking of his disaster over and over again. When he thought of it he began to realize there was something in his way and he couldn't help wondering what good it did to have a goal anyway. This world was certainly not the least bit fair to him just because he was ambitious. But why the hell did anyone have the right to take away his rickshaw? And if he got another one soon, how could he be sure the same thing wouldn't happen all over again? What had happened to him was like a nightmare. It almost made him afraid to have hope for the future ever again. Sometimes he almost felt envious when he watched the other men drinking, smoking opium, and running off to brothels. Ambition was useless. Why not enjoy what you had? They were right. Even if he didn't run off to a brothel, he ought to be able to have a few drinks when he felt like it. Cigarettes and liquor appealed to him right now. He knew you didn't have to spend too much on them and they were sure to comfort him. They would help him move ahead on his bitter road and let him forget the pain of the past at the same time.

Still, he did not try them. He had to save all he could; otherwise he couldn't get his own rickshaw soon. Even if he bought one today and lost it tomorrow, he still had to buy one. This was his ambition, his hope, even his religion. It would simply be a waste of his life if he didn't buy a rickshaw. Thoughts of becoming an official, getting rich, buying property, these were all beyond him. Pulling a rickshaw was all he was good for. To be able to buy a rickshaw was the only reliable hope he could have. He could not face himself if he didn't buy a rickshaw. This hope filled his mind all day long as he counted and recounted his money. Should a day come when he forgot it then he would have forgotten himself and would know he was only a beast of burden, running along the streets without any promise and without any manhood. No matter how fine the rickshaw, if it was rented his pulling never had vigor. It was as unnatural as if he were bearing a burden on his back. Of course he wasn't careless with a rented rickshaw. He always kept it clean and never ran into things, but merely as a precaution, not because he was really interested or enjoyed what he was doing. But taking care of his own rickshaw was the same as counting his money, always a real pleasure.

So he went on not smoking or drinking. He didn't even drink good quality tea. Rickshaw men as imposing as he was would always go to a teahouse after a flying trip and drink the better tea with two lumps of white sugar in it to restore their spirits and cool off. When he had run so hard the sweat dripped from his earlobes and his chest felt on fire, Hsiang Tzu wanted to do the same. And not because it was the thing to do. Gulping down two cups of good tea like that was really necessary. But all he did was think about it and go right on drinking cheap tea made from dust and stems. Sometimes he really wanted to scold himself for making himself suffer. But how else could a rickshaw puller who wanted to save money do it? He hardened his heart. Buy a rickshaw first! Buy a rickshaw first! Get that rickshaw and you'll have enough to pay for everything else.

With such a deathlike grip when it came to spending money, Hsiang Tzu never let up a minute when it came to earning money. He just worked the whole day when he didn't have a private job. He went out early and came back late; he didn't quit until he had earned a certain amount. Never mind how long it took, never mind how his legs felt. Sometimes he worked stubbornly right through a day and a night. In the past, he had never tried to steal someone else's customer, particularly when the rickshaw man was either old or very young. How could they get their share if a man with a body like his and a rickshaw like his fought for their customers? He didn't care about that now. All he saw was money. More was more. Never mind how hard or easy the job, never mind who you have to fight with; getting the job was all he cared about. He was a hunger-crazed beast. All he knew was that the only way to buy a rickshaw was to never stand still; he felt much better when running with a fare.

Bit by bit, Camel Hsiang Tzu's reputation departed from plain Hsiang Tzu's. Often a string of curses would follow him when he swiped a fare and ran. He never swore back. He lowered his head and ran instead, telling himself, "If I didn't have to buy a rickshaw I wouldn't do such dishonorable things!" He seemed to be begging everyone's pardon with these words, but he was unwilling to say them out loud. When he saw everyone staring at him at the rickshaw stands or in the teahouses he wanted to explain things then and there until he noticed how aloof they were. Besides, as a rule he never drank with them, or gambled, or played checkers, or even gossiped, and so his words merely churned around inside him and never came out. Gradually his discomfiture turned into shame and rage and he'd almost lose his temper. They'd stare at him and he'd stare right back. He recalled how respectful everyone had been when he had returned after escaping from the soldiers. Now he was regarded with such contempt that he felt he couldn't stand it. It took all his strength to hold in his fury while he sat alone with his pot of tea in a teahouse or counted his just-won pennies at a rickshaw stand. Although he wasn't afraid of a fight, he didn't want to start one. The others weren't afraid of a fight either, but lifting a hand against Hsiang Tzu was worth thinking about twice. Not one of them was his match yet it wasn't exactly honorable for all of them to fight him at the same time.

He repressed his anger and decided not to go work in a different part of town. He'd just have to put up with it until he bought his rickshaw. Then he could work things out. He wouldn't have to worry about the rental fee once he had his own rickshaw so he could be generous and never offend others by stealing their passengers again. He stared at them with this thought in mind as if to say, you'll see!

He should not have taken such chances, considering his health. He didn't even wait until he was fully recovered to start work after he got back. He was often worn out even though he didn't actually feel bad, but he dared not rest even when he was exhausted. He had always believed that the way to wash away aches and pains was to go for a long run until his body ran with sweat. He didn't dare deprive himself of food, but he didn't dare spend the money for good food either. He knew he had lost a lot of weight but he was still tall and his bones and muscles were still hard and firm, so he stopped worrying about himself. He had always held that he could stand more hardship than anyone else because he was bigger and taller. It never occurred to him that a large body working so hard might need a lot more food. Miss Liu had said to him time and time again, "You fathead, if you go on like this you'll be spitting blood and it will be your own fault!"

He knew she was right but he couldn't help flying off the handle at her because his life had become so frustrating and he was always a little hungry as well. He'd say, with a cross glance, "Yeah, and if I don't work all the time, how can I buy a rickshaw?"

If anyone else had looked at her that way, Hu Niu would at least have cursed him up one side of the street and down the other. She was exceedingly polite and solicitous towards Hsiang Tzu; she merely turned down the corners of her mouth.

"You'd better control yourself if you want to buy a rickshaw, but of course you are made of iron! You ought to take a few days off." When she saw that he wasn't paying any attention to her, she'd add, "All right, so stick to your same old plan. Don't blame me when you drop dead!"

Old Liu also thought rather less of Hsiang Tzu; his recklessness and long working hours were certainly not doing Liu's rickshaw any good! Even though he put no time limits on rickshaws rented by the day and the men could take them out and bring them back when they wished, still, if everyone worked himself to death like Hsiang Tzu, a rickshaw wouldn't last six months. You don't take solid and useful things and go nail them up in a privy hole! Besides, all Hsiang Tzu cared about was work. He never took time to polish the rickshaws and such anymore, and that was another loss. The old man began to brood. He couldn't say anything because not having a time limit was a general rule and helping out with the rickshaws was a matter of friendship, not a duty. A man with a reputation like his wasn't going to invite ridicule by revealing any of this to the likes of Hsiang Tzu. All he could do was glance at Hsiang Tzu out of the corner of his eye and compress his lips tightly to show his displeasure. Sometimes he considered throwing Hsiang Tzu out and then looked at his daughter and didn't dare do it. She certainly liked the clod, so why make trouble? He hadn't the least intention of bringing Hsiang Tzu in as his son-in-law, but she was his only child and he couldn't see any possibility of marrying her off, so he couldn't drive away her friend. To tell the truth, Hu Niu had her uses; he really didn't want her to leave home. He realized this selfishness of his was unfair to her and was a little afraid of her for that reason. The old fellow who had never feared anything in heaven or on earth in all his life now began to fear his own daughter when he was old. But he had a consoling thought in his discomfiture; he only needed to be afraid of one person and that would constitute the proof that he was not a lawless man. The establishment of this fact might perhaps save him from meeting an awful retribution when he died. All right, he admitted he was afraid of his daughter so he didn't chase Hsiang Tzu away. This was not to say that he would offhandedly allow her to do anything she liked, of course, such as getting married to Hsiang Tzu. No indeed. It was obvious to him that she might well have such a notion but he was fairly certain Hsiang Tzu would never look so high.

Well, then, he'd be wary and that was good enough; being the first to make her unhappy just wasn't worth it.

Hsiang Tzu paid no attention to the old man's mood; he hadn't the time for such trivial matters. If he had any intention of leaving the Jen Ho agency, it would be because he'd got a private job, not because of quarrels over trifles. He was already fed up with working the streets; swiping passengers made everyone despise him and he did not take in the same amount every day. He'd make a lot today and a little tomorrow. There was no way he could tell how long it would take to save enough to buy a rickshaw. He wanted to have a definite time in mind. Even though there was less profit in private work, what he wanted was the assurance that he would save a certain amount each month. Then he would feel there was hope and he could stop worrying. It was all right with him if he never spoke to anyone again.

He did get a job. Humph! It was just as disagreeable as day work. He worked for the Yang family. Mr. Yang was from Shanghai, the senior Mrs. Yang was from Tientsin, the junior Mrs. Yang was from Soochow. The combination of one husband and two wives, of southern singsong and northern tune, produced who knows how many children.

Hsiang Tzu almost fainted after his first day at work. The senior wife had to be taken to the markets to shop for food first thing in the morning. The young masters and mistresses had to be taken to school as soon as Hsiang Tzu and Mrs. Yang returned. Their schools were all different; some went to elementary school, some to primary school, some to kindergarten. They came in all ages and didn't look alike but they were equally obnoxious, particularly when riding in the rickshaw; even the most well behaved had two more hands than a monkey. Mr. Yang had to be taken to his office after the children had been delivered. Then Hsiang Tzu had to rush back to take the junior wife to the Tung An market and to visit friends and relations. And when he'd brought her back, he had to collect the children, bring them home for lunch, and take them back to school again. Hsiang Tzu thought he could get his own lunch after delivering the scholars but the senior wife sang her Tientsin tune, ordering him to haul water. Although their drinking water was delivered, water for washing was hauled in by the rickshaw man. This job was not one of the regular duties of a rickshaw man, but Hsiang Tzu thought he'd better go along with it. He said nothing and filled the stone cistern. Then the junior wife ordered him to go out and buy some things as soon as he put down the water buckets and was about to get his lunch.

The two wives never agreed on anything. When it came to household management, however, they saw eye to eye. The central item in their policy was never to let a servant rest for a minute. Another item was their reluctance to let a servant eat. Hsiang Tzu did not realize this; he thought it was only coincidence that he had come on a day when the household was unusually busy. He said nothing and went out and bought his lunch with his own money. He loved money as his life but he had to be brutal to himself in order to survive in this situation.

The senior wife told him to sweep out the courtyard when he came back from doing the shopping. The master and the two mistresses of the Yang household were all quite well dressed when they went out, but their house was like a garbage dump. Hsiang Tzu felt sick to his stomach when he looked at the courtyard. He had to forget that a rickshaw man didn't double as a houseboy so he concentrated on sweeping the place out. The junior wife called him a willing worker after he'd swept and tidied the courtyard and told him to sweep out the other rooms. Hsiang Tzu didn't argue then either. What astounded him was how two such pretty ladies could so litter their rooms that there was no place even to put down a foot! Once he had the rooms straightened up and tidy, the junior wife handed him a muddy little one-year-old imp. He didn't know what to do. He could manage any job that took strength but he had never held a child and there he was with the young master in his hands. If he didn't hold him tightly, he feared the baby would slip out; and if he held him too tightly, he feared the baby would be injured. He was sweating. He thought he'd better hand this treasure over to Chang Ma, a big-footed woman from the north. He was scolded roundly to his face when he found her.

Servants in the Yang household changed every three or four days; they were just household slaves to the master and mistresses. The

Yangs felt that these poor people wouldn't have earned their wages if they weren't worked to within an inch of their lives. This Chang Ma was an exception; she had been with them for five years already and the only reason for it was that she had the nerve to open her mouth and give everyone hell. It didn't matter if it was the master or one of the mistresses. Annoy her and there'd be a string of oaths. Take Mr. Yang and his venomous nautical blasphemies, the senior Mrs. Yang and her vigorous Tientsin accent, the junior Mrs. Yang and the flowing bites of her Soochow dialect and you have persons who had never met their match anywhere before. But when they encountered Chang Ma's barbaric fierceness they began to feel they were engaged in a kind of exchange of courtesies. It had some of the flavor of an encounter between one hero and another. They were, therefore, able to appreciate her and made her their bodyguard.

Hsiang Tzu had been born in a northern village where such casual use of gutter language was completely taboo, but he didn't dare strike Chang Ma because a gentleman does not quarrel with females nor did he care to give her as good as he got. He merely glared at her. Chang Ma said nothing more, as if she sensed the approach of danger.

Just at this moment the senior wife yelled at him to go fetch the scholars. He carefully gave the grubby infant back to the junior wife. The junior wife thought this meant he felt contempt for her. She let loose and called him names until his faced looked like a multicolored melon. It had been the senior wife's feeling that she didn't much care for having Hsiang Tzu hold the junior wife's baby for her, so she had yelled at him. But when she heard the junior wife swearing at him, she opened her oleaginous throat and joined in; he was her target, too, and had to bear it all. Frantically, he grabbed the rickshaw and left. He even forgot to get angry. He simply had never seen anything like it before and was stunned when it hit him head on so suddenly.

He brought the children home bunch by bunch. The courtyard was noisier than a marketplace. The billingsgate of the women and the howls of a herd of kids made the place as chaotic as the theater district when the plays were over, and it was a futile chaos besides. Fortunately, he still had to go fetch Mr. Yang so he rushed out again. The noises and shouts and traffic in the streets seemed much easier to bear than the misrule in that household.

Hsiang Tzu kept right on running in circles until midnight when he finally found a moment to breathe. He was aware not only of his exhaustion but also of a constantly buzzing noise in his head. Everyone in the Yang family was asleep but the master and the mistresses still seemed to be screaming in his ears like voices from three different victrola records all spinning wildly in his brain at once. It drove him wild. He couldn't be bothered with thinking about anything any more; he wanted to sleep.

A chill hit his heart when he entered his tiny room; he wouldn't be able to sleep either. The room was part of a larger one next to the front gate which had been divided by a partition and furnished with two doors. Chang Ma was on one side, he was on the other. There was no lamp in the room but there was a two-foot-wide window on the street side, which fortunately, was under a streetlamp that gave the room a little light. The place was damp and smelly and dust was thick on the floor. There was a plank bed next to the wall and nothing else. He felt the bed planks and realized that if he lay with his head down, his feet would climb up the wall. If he had his legs flat, he'd end up half sitting. He'd never get any decent sleep at all. He thought it over for a while then pulled the plank bed out crossways, putting the ends in the corners. This way he could lie down, though his feet would still stick out a little.

He brought his bedroll in from the gateway, spread it out, and lay down with his feet dangling in the air. He wasn't used to that and couldn't sleep. He shut his eyes hard and consoled himself. You've put up with all kinds of mistreatment. Why must this be the one kind you can't stand? Go to sleep. You still have to be up early tomorrow. Never mind that they don't feed you well and the work is so wearing. Maybe they'll play mahjong a lot, have company, go out to dinner parties. Why are you here, Hsiang Tzu? Isn't it for the money? You can put up with anything if you get a lot of money coming in.

Thoughts like these made him feel much better. He sniffed a few times; the room didn't smell as bad as before. Slowly he slid into a dream. Sort of confusedly he thought there might be a bedbug but he didn't care enough to catch it.

After two days Hsiang Tzu was as downhearted as he could be. But on the fourth day guests were coming. Chang Ma officiously set up a mahjong table. Hsiang Tzu's heart was like a little frozen pond when suddenly a breath of spring wind blows across it. The children were all handed over to the servants when the ladies began to play. Chang Ma had to tend to the tea, napkins, and cigarettes, so naturally the entire horde of monkeys was turned over to Hsiang Tzu to mind. He despised them all but had stolen a peek into the house and noticed that the senior wife was in charge of the money. She looked like she was taking it very seriously. He said to himself, don't assume this woman is so awful. Maybe she really isn't stupid. She must know enough to take advantage of these parties to give the servants a few extra coins. He was careful to use very patient methods with the monkeys; there was a tip in the offing so he treated the little monsters like little ladies and gentlemen.

The mahjong game broke up and the senior wife ordered him to take the ladies home. The two guests were very anxious to leave at the same time so another rickshaw had to be hired. Hsiang Tzu went and hailed one. The senior wife fumbled around in her sash vaguely for some money, as if preparing to pay for the second rickshaw. The lady demurred twice. The senior wife said in tones of feigned courtesy, "Don't be silly, sister! Here you've come to my house and I am not to pay for the rickshaw? Sister, please get in!" And not until then did she extract ten cents.

The bitter truth was obvious to Hsiang Tzu; her hand shook when she handed over that coin.

After taking the guest home and helping Chang Ma put away the table and pick up, Hsiang Tzu stood and looked at the senior wife. She ordered Chang Ma to get some boiled water, waited until Chang Ma had left the room, then took out a coin.

"Take it. None of this saucy staring at me!"

Hsiang Tzu's face suddenly turned purple. He stood up so straight it almost looked like his head would hit the roof beam. He grabbed the ten cents and threw it in her face.

"Give me my four days' wages!"

"What's biting you?" She looked at him and then gave him his pay without another word.

He had just reached the street with his bedroll in the rickshaw when he heard furious curses erupting in the courtyard.

CHAPTER SIX

AMONG THE SHADOWS of leaves cast by the starlight Hsiang Tzu raised his head in the slight breeze. Looking at the far-off Milky Way on this August night, he sighed. His chest seemed just as broad as this cool sky but he felt as if there weren't enough air; his chest was very tight. He wanted to sit down and cry for a while. He had a strong body, a patient disposition, ambition, yet he allowed people to treat him like a pig or a dog and he couldn't keep a job. It wasn't only that he hated people like the Yangs. He wanted to cry because he had begun to wonder if it wasn't all hopeless. He was afraid he'd never amount to anything again in his whole life. He dragged the rickshaw slower and slower, as though he was no longer the Hsiang Tzu who just lifted his foot and ran ten li.

Pedestrians were already scarce when he got to the main street; the streetlights were very bright. He felt even more confused and at a loss. Where could he go? Back to the Jen Ho agency, of course. He felt even worse. Merchants and peddlers weren't afraid of failure. On the other hand they were afraid of missing a sale; having a customer come into a restaurant or a barber shop, look around, and walk out, for instance. Hsiang Tzu knew perfectly well that getting a job and losing it was an everyday affair, after all. "When one place isn't fit for a gentleman like me there's always another place that will do." But he had kept his voice low and held his temper to keep that job. He had lost face so he could buy a rickshaw and all he got was another three and a half day job. He was not better than those good-for-nothings who were hired and fired all the time. It made him feel sad. It even seemed to him he would be disgraced if he went back to the Jen Ho agency again and gave them all a chance to crack jokes. "Hey, look! I'll bet Camel Hsiang Tzu has been bounced in three days again! Ha!"

But where else could he go if he didn't go to the Jen Ho agency? To avoid having to think about this question any more, he went directly to the street the agency was on.

The Jen Ho agency had three rooms facing the street that led from the Hsi An Gate. The room in the middle was used as an office. It was there the rickshaw pullers went to make their arrangements and pay their fees. They were not allowed anywhere else because the other two rooms were the Liu's bedrooms. The rickshaw entry on the west end had a big double gate lacquered green. There was a bent iron rod over the gate with a bare light bulb hanging from it. Just above the gate was a slab of iron with the name Jen Ho Rickshaw Agency in gold characters. All the rickshaw pullers used this gate when coming or going with their rickshaws or when off work. The deep green of the gate complemented the gold characters above it, which cast back gleaming reflections in the bright light from the naked bulb.

All the agency rickshaws were handsome and lacquered either black or yellow. They all had the same smooth sheen to them which matched the snow white covers on the cushions. The rickshaw pullers were a bit proud, as if they considered themselves the aristocracy of rickshaw men.

After going through the gate you went by the side wall of the west room and came to a big square courtyard with a locust tree in the middle. The rickshaw stalls were along the east and west walls. There was another smaller courtyard on the south side with rooms both around it and between it and the main courtyard; these rooms were the dormitories for the men.

It was probably a little after eleven when Hsiang Tzu caught sight of that very bright but strangely solitary light bulb. There were no lights in the office or in the east room but the west room was still lit up. He knew Miss Liu was not asleep yet. He thought he'd tiptoe in very quietly and not let her see him. He didn't want her to be the first person to witness his defeat because ordinarily she respected him greatly. He had just pulled the rickshaw past her window when she came out the gate. "Ah, Hsiang Tzu? What. . . ." She was about to continue when she noticed his dejected manner and his bedroll in the rickshaw. She swallowed her words.

If you are afraid of something happening, then it's bound to happen. The shame and despair in his heart froze together in a lump; he stopped and stood there, wordless. Unable to speak he just stared at her idiotically. She looked different tonight. He didn't know whether it was the light or the face powder, but her face looked much paler than usual. This added pallor veiled most of the fierceness in her looks. Her lips actually had a little rouge on them, which made her rather attractive. Hsiang Tzu felt very peculiar when he saw all this and his heart fluttered. He never thought of her as a woman ordinarily and to see those red lips so unexpectedly made him uneasy all of a sudden.

Hu Niu was wearing a pale green silk jacket and full black silk trousers. The silk jacket gleamed with a soft and melancholy sheen in the lamplight. A bit of white sash, revealed by the shortness of her jacket, emphasized the purity of the green color. A light breeze made her wide black trousers flutter like dark spirits which wanted to flee the glaring bright light and reunite in the darkness.

Hsiang Tzu didn't dare look anymore and lowered his head in confusion, a shiny little green jacket still in his mind. He knew she usually didn't dress up like that. What with the Liu wealth she could easily wear silk and satin every day, but dealing as she did with rickshaw pullers all day she always wore cotton which, while rather colorful, was nothing to catch your eye. Hsiang Tzu felt he was looking at some extraordinary new thing. It was both familiar and novel so he was a little confused.

He'd been feeling miserable to start with and now with this strange new creature he'd met under the glaring light added in he hadn't a notion in his head. He didn't want to move. He wished she would go inside quickly instead, or else order him to do something. He simply couldn't stand the suspense of being in a situation where nothing is as it appears and everything is perplexing.

"Well!" She took a step forward and said softly, "Don't just stand there! Go in and put the rickshaw away and hurry right back. I've got something to tell you. See you in my room."

Accustomed as he was to working for her, all he could do was obey. But she was not the same tonight and he wanted time to think about it. He didn't move. There he stood, like a post, getting more confused, until he gave up, for he hadn't an idea in his head, and took the rickshaw in. He glanced at the south rooms. No lights were on. Probably they were all asleep or else no one had come back with a rickshaw yet. He went to her room after putting the rickshaw away. All of a sudden his heart began to pound.

"Come in. I've got something to tell you." She peeked out at him and spoke in a half laughing, half annoyed manner.

He came in very slowly.

On the table were some pears, their skins still green, a wine jug, three white porcelain cups, a large platter with half a chicken braised in soy sauce, smoked liver, braised tripe, and such.

"You see." Hu Niu waved him to a chair, watched him sit down, and continued. "You see, I gave a feast to reward myself today. You have some too." With that she poured him a cup of baigan, a strong liquor. The fumes of the potent spirits mingled with the aromas of smoked and braised meats making them thick and rich. "Drink up! Have some chicken. I've already had mine, don't wait for me. I was just telling my fortune with dominoes. I knew you were coming back. Isn't that amazing?"

"I don't drink." Hsiang Tzu stared fixedly at the cup.

"If you don't drink then bugger off! 'A good heart has good intentions,' so what's this refusal to accept a gift all about? You silly camel! It won't kill you! Even I can drink more than two cups. If you don't believe it, just watch!" She picked up the cup and drank most of it, shut her eyes, and exhaled. She raised her cup. "Drink up. Or else I'll grab you by the ears and pour it down your throat!"

The fury that filled Hsiang Tzu's belly was bottled up with no way out. He did think of staring her down when she teased him like that but he knew she usually didn't treat him badly and she was always blunt with everyone, so he ought not to offend her. On second thought, since he didn't want to offend her, he could just tell her frankly about all of his grievances instead. He usually hadn't much use for talk but now a thousand words, ten thousand phrases, seemed to be burdening his mind and he'd be miserable if he didn't speak up. Looked at that way, she wasn't teasing him, she was obviously concerned about him. He took the wine cup and drained it. A burning taste relentlessly, forcefully, descended. He stretched out his neck and let out two not entirely helpful belches.

Hu Niu began to laugh. It hadn't been all that easy for him to get the mouthful down and he quickly looked towards the room on the east when he heard her giggles.

"There's no one there." She held back her giggles but a smile still lingered on her face. "The old man has gone off to wish Auntie a happy birthday. He'll be there two or three days. Auntie lives in Nan Yuan.'' She poured him another cup as she spoke.

His mind turned a corner when he heard this; he realized something was not quite right here. At the same time he didn't want to leave. Her face was so close to his, her clothes were so clean and shiny, her lips so red, it all made him aware of a new urge. She was just as old and ugly but had more life to her than before. It was as if she had suddenly become a different person; yet she was still herself, only with something added. He didn't want to think too carefully about this new whatever it was. He hadn't the nerve to accept it casually but he couldn't bear to reject it, either. His face reddened. He had another drink to bolster his courage and forgot all about his woes just at the very moment he was going to tell her about them. He got even redder in the face. He couldn't help staring at her some more. The more he looked the more excited he got. She was revealing more and more of that whatever it was that he didn't understand and it was sending more and more of some sort of hot fierce force towards him and she became an abstraction of something bit by bit. He warned himself to look out but he needed more courage, too. He downed three cups in a row and forgot what looking out meant. Befuddled, he did not know why he felt so extraordinarily happy and brave when looking at her. Full of courage, he wanted to seize this new experience and feel this new joy immediately. Ordinarily he was afraid of her but now there was nothing the least bit frightening at all. He, on the other hand, had been transformed into a man of awesome strength. It seemed to him he could treat her like a kitten and hold her in his hands.

The light was turned off inside. The sky outside was deep black. Once in a while stars stabbed into the Milky Way or streaked across the blackness with gleaming reddish or whitish tails trailing behind. They hovered lightly or fell swiftly; they fell straight down or swept across the sky. Sometimes they moved just a little, trembling and lending bright excitement to the sky above, lending brilliant flashes to the darkness. Sometimes only one star, sometimes many, flew down causing commotion in the silent sky and confusing all the stars. Sometimes one great star stabbed into a corner of the sky, its gleaming tail long and shooting out star flowers of red and pale yellow. At the last entrance of all, one made an entire corner of the sky white with a sudden outburst of joy as if it had cut the impenetrable darkness open, piercing it and leaving a milk-white glow behind. The remaining light dispersed and the darkness moved down and enclosed everything like a curtain, while silently and slowly the clustered stars resumed their original positions and smiled gently above the breeze. Some lovelorn fireflies fluttered above the ground making their own meteor shower.

Hsiang Tzu got up very early the next day, took a rickshaw, and went out. His head and throat were both rather sore but that was because it was the first time he had had a drink, so he didn't pay any attention to it. He sat at the head of a small side street letting the light morning breeze blow on his head. He knew this slight headache would be gone before long. But there was something else on his mind which made him extremely depressed and there was no quick way to get rid of it. The events of the night before filled him with doubt; he was ashamed, puzzled, and also conscious that there was some danger now.

He didn't understand what Miss Liu was up to. She hadn't been a virgin for a long time; he'd found that out a few hours ago. He had really respected her up to now and had never heard anything scandalous about her. She was free and easy with everyone, but no one had ever talked about her behind her back that way. The rickshaw pullers said nasty things about her among themselves, but that was only because she was too hard on them. There wasn't anything behind it. Well, then, what about that business last night?

This question only showed how stupid he was, but Hsiang Tzu did have his doubts about the goings on of the night before. She knew he wasn't staying at the agency so why was she waiting up for him so devotedly? If it was a matter of pleasing anyone who happened to come along. . . . Hsiang Tzu hung his head. He came from a village; while he hadn't thought of getting married yet, it certainly wasn't because he had no such plan in mind. If he had his own rickshaw and life was a little easier, and if he were also willing to take a wife, he would definitely go to the country and get a strong young girl who was used to hardship and who knew how to wash clothes and keep house.

Other fellows his age had parents over them, so who didn't sneak out to the white houses? But Hsiang Tzu would never go along. First of all he regarded himself as a man with a goal; he couldn't waste money on girls. Second, he had seen those foolish wastrels with his own eyes in the public privies—some of them were only eighteen or nineteen—beating their heads on the wall and still they couldn't manage to piss. And last, he must stick to the rules because when the day came for him to marry, the girl must be clean and pure and so must he. But now, now. . . . He thought of Hu Niu. She wasn't so bad if he thought of her as a friend. But as a woman? She was ugly, old, nagging, and shameless. It seemed to him that those soldiers who had stolen his rickshaw and had almost done him in were nowhere near as detestable and disgusting as she was! She had done away with all the pure vigor he had brought from the country and made him a woman-izer!

Worse, if this affair got around and old Liu heard about it, what then? Does he know his daughter is shopworn goods? If Liu doesn't know, how could he, Hsiang Tzu, get out of taking the blame all by himself? And if Liu has known about it right along and won't control her, well what kind of father and daughter are they anyway? And if he got mixed up with people like that, what would that make him? He couldn't possibly want her even if father and daughter were agreed to it. Never mind if old Liu has sixty rickshaws, or six hundred or six thousand! He must get out of there right away, just cut them off with one stroke. He had his ability. He'd rely on it to buy a rickshaw and take a wife. That was the right way to do it!

Hsiang Tzu looked up. He knew he was a good man. There was nothing to fear, nothing to worry about. He was bound to make it as long as he worked hard.

He tried to get passengers twice. No one hired him. That glum feeling came back. He didn't want to think about it but his mind was so congested and confused he just had to get things cleared up. This affair seemed to be totally unlike other problems. It wouldn't be easy to forget even if there were a way to get around it. Not only was it as if something had been glued onto his body. His heart also seemed to have been soiled by black smudges and they could never be washed away. No matter how much he hated her, how much he despised her, she seemed to have got hold of his mind. The more unwilling he was to think about it again, the more she kept popping up in his thoughts naked and offering everything ugly and fine to him all at the same time. It was like buying junk; in the midst of all the rusty iron and bits of copper are some gleaming and colorful little things you cannot resist. He had never been this close to anyone before. It was the kind of relationship you just can't forget as you please even though it had happened so suddenly and it was she who had seduced him. There you are, thinking you've shoved it away to one side and yet it can go and curl up in your mind as if it had grown roots. It was not only a new experience for him, it was also a kind of vexation he couldn't describe and it left him not knowing what to do. There was nothing he could do about her, about himself, about the present or the future. It was as if he were a little insect caught in a spider's web trying to break free and never succeeding.

He absentmindedly hauled several fares. He still couldn't get it out of his head even when he was running hard. He couldn't seem to get it clear or find a beginning or end to it. But an idea that there was something pleasing, maybe just an emotion of some kind or other, kept occurring to him. It was very vague and very persistent. He wanted very much to go off by himself and get drunk. Drink wipes out a man's troubles. Perhaps it might make him a little happier, because he couldn't stand much more of this torment.

But he didn't dare get a drink. He refused to ruin himself because of this business. He tried thinking about buying a rickshaw but couldn't keep his mind on it; there was always something getting in the way. This little thing had already sneaked out and occupied his mind even before he thought about a rickshaw. It was like a black cloud that covers the sky and cuts off the light. He felt even more at wits end when evening came and it was time to return the rickshaw. He had to go back but was really afraid to go back. What if he ran into her? What could he do? He pulled the empty rickshaw around and around the streets. He wasn't far from the agency two or three times but he turned away and went somewhere else. He was just like a schoolboy who has played hooky for the first time and dare not go home.

Strangest of all, the more he worried about avoiding her, the more he thought about meeting her. These thoughts became more urgent as it grew darker. An apprehensive boldness that knew it mustn't but was determined to try anyway clutched his heart. He felt just the way he had when, as a boy, he would take a stick and go poke at a hornets' nest. Frightened and with his heart pounding, he had to try it out, as if some evil impulse were urging him on. He became vaguely conscious of an urge much more powerful than himself that was squeezing him into a ball and throwing him into a fire. There was nothing he could do to stop his forward motion.

He came to the Hsi An Gate again. He wouldn't put it off again; he'd just go right to the office and look for her. She wasn't anyone, merely a female. His whole body got hot.

A man of about forty was walking past just under the light when

Hsiang Tzu arrived at the gate. He thought he recognized the man's face and manner but was too timid to call out. It was almost reflexively that he said, "Rickshaw?"

The man stared at him, startled. "Hsiang Tzu?"

"Yes, sir." Hsiang Tzu grinned. "Mr. Ts'ao?"

Mr. Ts'ao smiled and nodded. "Well, now, if you aren't working for anyone now, how about working for me? The man I have is too lazy. He never pays any attention to cleaning the rickshaw although he does run with the strength of a horse. Will you come or not?"

"How could I not come, sir!" Hsiang Tzu seemed to have forgotten the right way to smile and mopped his face with a small towel repeatedly. "Sir, when should I start?"

"Well," Mr. Ts'ao thought about it. "Day after tomorrow."

"Yes sir!" Hsiang Tzu thought about it too. "Sir, shall I take you home?"

"There's no need to. I've been in Shanghai for a while and haven't been living in the old place since I came back. I live in Pei Ch'ang street now and go out for a walk in the evening. See you day after tomorrow." Mr. Ts'ao gave Hsiang Tzu his new address and added, "And you'll use my rickshaw."

Hsiang Tzu was so happy he wanted to fly. He felt like a white stone road that had been pelted by heavy rain; the troubles of the last few days had all been washed away like the dirt on the stones. Mr. Ts'ao was an old employer of his. They hadn't been together for long but the feeling between them was good. Mr. Ts'ao was an extraordinarily agreeable man and there weren't many people in his family, only a wife and a small son.

He pulled the rickshaw right into the Jen Ho agency. Was Miss Liu's light still on? One look at the lamp light and Hsiang Tzu turned into a doltish tree.

He stood there for a long time until he decided to go in and see her. He'd tell her he'd found a job. He'd hand over two days' rental fee and then say he wanted to take out his savings. And with that he'd have cut the rope in two with one blow. Of course it wouldn't do to tell her that was what he was doing but she would catch on anyway.

He put the rickshaw away and then went back and very bravely called her name.

"Come in!"

He opened the door. She was lying across her bed wearing her everyday clothes and barefoot. She lay there and said, "What's up? Had a bit of the sweet stuff and now you're back for more, is that it?"

Hsiang Tzu got as red in the face as the red-dyed egg you send a new mother. After standing there tongue-tied he finally said haltingly, "I've got another job set up. Start work the day after tomorrow. They have their own rickshaw."

She took in his words. "You punk. You don't know what's good for you." She sat up and pointed a finger at him, half smiling and half annoyed. "There's food for you here, clothes for you too. But if you don't go out and get in a stinking sweat you're not content, is that it? The old man doesn't run me and I won't stay a spinster all my life! And I have my own resources if the old man gets bullheaded. We two can rent out two or three rickshaws and bring in a dollar eighty or so in a day. Isn't that better than running all over town on your own stinking feet? So what's so wrong with me? I'm only a little older than you, but not much. I can take care of you, love you!"

"I want to pull a rickshaw." Hsiang Tzu couldn't think of any other argument.

"What a head full of dough you have! You sit down. I won't bite!" Then she grinned and showed her tigerish teeth.

Hsiang Tzu sat down very warily. "What about my money?"

"The old man has it. It won't be lost. There's nothing to be afraid of. But you'd better not ask him for it. You know how he is, don't you? Ask for it when you have enough money to buy a rickshaw. Not one cent will be missing. But if you ask for it now it will be a miracle if he doesn't curse the soul right out of your body. He doesn't think badly of you. It won't be lost. I'll make it up to you double if it's short. You and your village smarts! Don't make me do something I'll be sorry for!"

Hsiang Tzu had nothing to say. He hung his head and fumbled in a pocket. Taking out two days' rental, he put it on the table.

"Two days' worth." He was about to leave when he remembered something. "I'm turning in the rickshaw now and taking tomorrow off, so that's what the money is for." He hadn't actually intended to take a day off but this was the way to show his honesty. He'd turn in the rickshaw and not stay at the agency afterwards.

Miss Liu came over, picked up the money, and stuffed it back in his pocket. "No charge for me or the rickshaw. You're in luck, you sap! Don't 'forget favors and turn your back on kindness,' that's all!" With that she turned around, shoved him out, and locked the door.

CHAPTER SEVEN

Hsiang tzu went to the Ts'ao house.

He felt a little chagrined about Miss Liu, but she was the one who started up the affair with her seductive ways and besides, he wasn't after her money. There wasn't anything he had to apologize to anyone for, in his opinion, now that he had made a clean break with her. What he did worry about, however, was the money he had left with old Liu. He was afraid the old fellow would get suspicious if he went and asked for it back right away. But Miss Liu would probably get angry if he never went to see them again and tell her father bad things about him and that would be the end of his money. It would be difficult to be polite to her if he left the money on deposit with old Liu and then ran into her every time he went to the agency. He couldn't think of any workable plan and being without a plan made him even more worried.

He'd rather ask Mr. Ts'ao for advice, but how could he explain it? The part about Miss Liu was something he couldn't tell anyone. And then he really felt bad; he began to realize that a clean break just wasn't possible. Incidents like that can never be washed away; they are like black moles on the skin. His rickshaw had been lost for no reason at all and now, again for no reason at all, this complication had turned up. He realized he would never amount to anything. Never mind how ambitious he was, it was all futile. He thought and thought. He did see this much: in the end he would probably have to forget about his dignity and go ask for Miss Liu in marriage. Wasn't not wanting her the same as not wanting Liu's rickshaws? A latecomer has to eat warmed-up leftovers! He couldn't stand the thought, but when the time came there'd probably be nothing else he could do. The best thing for now was to keep working; working for the best and waiting for the worst. He no longer had the nerve to be as self-

confident as he was in the past. His height, strength, and will didn't
amount to a thing. His life might be his own, but it was controlled by
someone else. It was controlled by a first-class bed-hopper!

Rationally speaking he ought to be delighted now because the Ts'ao
household was the most agreeable of all he had worked for, and not
because the pay was any higher. Except for the standard bonuses at
the three annual festivals, there wasn't much spare change around for
tips. But Mr. and Mrs. Ts'ao were unusually amiable and treated
everyone like a human being. Hsiang Tzu wanted to earn a lot of
money fast and would kill himself to get it, but he also wanted a room
that was fit to live in and enough food to fill him up. The Ts'ao house
was spotless; even the servants' rooms were clean. The Ts'ao food was
not bad and they never fed the servants garbage. He had a large room
to himself and could eat his three meals in peace. When you added
polite employers not even Hsiang Tzu could put money ahead of
everything else. When food and living quarters are agreeable and the
work is not exhausting, you don't lose anything by getting yourself
well taken care of. He certainly would not have eaten that well if he
had spent his own money on food. Well, then, since the food was provided and it wasn't the sort that gagged you, why not eat your fill for
free? Food cost money; now there was an account he knew how to add
up. To eat well, sleep soundly, and be able to keep himself clean like a
human being were advantages not easy to come by.

Furthermore, although the Ts'aos did not play mahjong and didn't
entertain often and had no spare change, he always got a coin or two
when some extra job had to be done. If Madam told him to go get pills
for the little boy, for instance, she gave him an extra coin and told him
to take a rickshaw although she knew quite well he could run faster
than anybody else. These bits of money didn't add up to much but
they made him aware of the sort of human relationships and consideration that made a person pleased at heart. Hsiang Tzu had had
quite a few employers, and nine out of ten of them would pay him late
if they could to emphasize to him that working him for nothing was
best. After all, servants were really dogs and cats, perhaps not even as
good as dogs and cats. The Ts'ao family was an exception so he was
delighted to be there.

He went out to pick up in the courtyard and water the flowers without waiting to be told. And they always complimented him every time
they saw him doing these things. Sometimes they would use such occa-

sions to fetch some worn clothes and tell him to trade them for matches even though they were still usable, just so he could keep them for himself. He felt a little like a human being there.

In Hsiang Tzu's eyes, old Liu was like Huang T'ien Pa, the leader of the Yellow Turban rebels ages ago. He was a harsh stern person but you could still say that he was honorable and had made a name for himself. He wasn't entirely bad. The other admirable man he knew besides Huang T'ien Pa was Confucius. He was altogether vague about what sort of person Confucius really was, but according to what was said about him, he could read a lot of words and was very reasonable. There had been both military men and literary men in all the households he had worked for. There wasn't a single one of the military types who was better than old Liu, nor had he ever met a single literary gentleman who was reasonable, even though they were professors at the university or had good government jobs and of course could read lots of words. Even if the Master was reasonable, Madam and the young Mistresses were still hard to work for. Only Mr. Ts'ao could read and was also reasonable, and Mrs. Ts'ao was so polite you felt grateful to her. Well, then, Mr. Ts'ao must be like Confucius. Even though Hsiang Tzu couldn't imagine what Confucius was like, he ought to be like Mr. Ts'ao, never mind what Confucius thought about it.

In fact, Mr. Ts'ao wasn't all that brilliant. He was only an ordinary man who sometimes taught school by the hour and sometimes did other things. He thought of himself as both a Socialist and an aesthetician, having been somewhat influenced by the writings of William Morris. He had no deep opinions about government and art but he did have one good point: what he believed in could actually be acted upon in the small affairs of everyday life. He seemed to have realized that he had no talent that would astonish mankind and enable him to perform some earthshaking deed, and so he arranged his work and household according to his own ideals. Even though his ideals added nothing to society, at least he spoke and acted toward the same end and didn't go around passing off bravado as ability. He paid close attention to small matters as if to say that he needed only to regulate this little household; society could do as it liked. Still, sometimes he was ashamed of himself and sometimes he was pleased. He apparently saw his household as a small oasis of green in a desert. It could offer a little water and a little food only to those who came there; it had no greater significance.

By a lucky chance Hsiang Tzu had come to this oasis after days of wandering in a desert. He thought it was a miracle. He had never known anyone like Mr. Ts'ao and looked on him as a true sage and worthy. This might have been because his experience was limited or simply because you don't see many men like Mr. Ts'ao in the world. When he took Mr. Ts'ao out his clothes were so simple and elegant and the man himself was so gracious and dignified and he, Hsiang Tzu, was so clean and neat, stalwart and handsome, that he just had to run with delight as if he were the only man to pull Mr. Ts'ao. It was always so quiet in the house and so clean everywhere it made him feel comfortable and secure.

When he was a boy in the country he had often watched the old men on winter days or under the autumn moon sitting silently with their bamboo pipes. Although he was very young and couldn't imitate them, still he loved to look at them and the way they sat so silently. It must, he worked it out, have some satisfaction in it. Now, although he was in the city, the silence in the Ts'ao household reminded him of the village. He longed to smoke a pipe and taste a little of that satisfaction.

Alas, that woman and that money wouldn't let him relax. His mind was like a green leaf being rolled up by a caterpillar preparing to make its cocoon. He couldn't stop worrying about his problems. He was often inattentive to others, even to Mr. Ts'ao, and the answers he gave did not correspond to the questions people asked. This situation made him very uncomfortable.

The Ts'ao household retired very early; by nine in the evening there was nothing left to do. Hsiang Tzu sat in his room by himself or in the courtyard, working over his thoughts, thoughts about those two problems. He even considered getting married right away. That would put an end to Hu Niu's plans. But how could he take care of a family when he depended on pulling a rickshaw for his living? He knew about his long-suffering brothers in the mixed courtyards. The men pulled rickshaws, the women sewed, the children scavenged for bits of coal. In the summer they gnawed on watermelon rinds dug out of garbage heaps and in the winter they all went to get handouts of rice gruel at the soup kitchens for the poor. Hsiang Tzu couldn't stand that. Besides, he'd never get his money back from old Liu if he got married and it wasn't likely that Hu Niu would let him off lightly either. But how could he let that money go? He'd risked his life for it!

His own rickshaw he had purchased last autumn. More than a year had passed since then and now he had nothing except thirty-odd dollars he couldn't get at and all these entanglements. He became gloomier and gloomier the longer he thought about them.

In early October, some ten days after the mid-autumn festival, the weather began to get colder. He figured he'd have to get some more clothes. Money again! You can't buy clothes and have something left over at the same time. He simply dared not hope to buy a rickshaw again. Even if he always worked for somebody, what did a life like that amount to anyway?

One evening Mr. Ts'ao came back from the east side a little late. Being cautious, Hsiang Tzu used the east-west thoroughfare passing in front of the T'ien An Gate. He ran with vigor in the light cool breeze along the broad empty road lit by the silent streetlights. The depressing thoughts that had filled his mind for a long time were forgotten. Listening to his own footfalls and the slight noise from the seat springs in the rickshaw, he forgot everything. He unbuttoned his jacket and the light wind whistled across his chest. He felt happy, as if to run just like this straight to some unknown destination and then simply drop dead was all there was. He ran faster and faster. There was a rickshaw ahead of him; he yelled to make way and passed it. In a minute more they had passed the T'ien An Gate. His legs were like two springs that almost touched the ground and then bounced up again. The wheels were turning so fast you couldn't see the spokes; the rubber tires seemed to have left the ground. Both man and rickshaw seemed to be blown along by a fierce wind.

Mr. Ts'ao was lulled by the cool breeze. Probably he was half asleep; otherwise he would surely have put a stop to Hsiang Tzu's flying pace. Hsiang Tzu lengthened his stride; he had a vague notion that if he got up a good sweat he'd sleep soundly that night instead of lying there worrying.

The north side of the avenue just east of Pei Ch'ang street was obscured by the locust trees outside the red wall of the park. Hsiang Tzu had just decided to slow down when his foot hit something piled up high. Where the foot went the wheel went too. Hsiang Tzu fell and the rickshaw crashed.

"What happened?" Mr. Ts'ao tumbled out after his words. Hsiang Tzu said nothing and scrambled to his feet. Mr. Ts'ao sat up quickly. "What happened?"

A pile of cobblestones recently unloaded for repairing the road was there, but no red lantern had been left on the heap.

"Are you hurt, sir?" asked Hsiang Tzu.

"No. I'll walk. You bring the rickshaw." Mr. Ts'ao was still composed. He felt around on the pile of stones for anything that might have been dropped.

Hsiang Tzu felt the broken shaft. "There's not much broken, sir. You can still ride. I can pull it!" He pulled the rickshaw away from the heap of stones. "Get in, sir."

Mr. Ts'ao had no intention of riding any more, but when he heard the tears in Hsiang Tzu's voice all he could do was get in.

When they came to the streetlights at the intersection with Pei Ch'ang street Mr. Ts'ao saw that a patch of skin had been rubbed off his left hand. "Hsiang Tzu! Stop!"

Hsiang Tzu turned his head; there was blood all over his face. Mr. Ts'ao was shocked. He didn't know what to say. "Quickly, you. . . ."

Hsiang Tzu was confused. Thinking he was being told to hurry, he pulled himself together and ran all the way home. He saw the blood on Mr. Ts'ao's hand when he put down the shafts and ran frantically into the courtyard, intending to get some antiseptic for it from Mrs. Ts'ao.

"Never mind me. Take care of yourself first." Mr. Ts'ao hurried in.

Hsiang Tzu looked himself over and finally realized he was hurt. Both knees and his right elbow were scraped and what he thought was sweat running down his cheeks was actually blood. Too upset to do anything, or even think, he sat down on the stone step inside the gateway and stared stupidly at the broken shafts on the rickshaw. A brand new black lacquered rickshaw looks ugly and awful when it gets its first cracks and bare wood shows through. It is like a paper doll for funerals with the feet not glued on yet so that the ends of the millet stalk legs still show. Hsiang Tzu stared blankly at the two broken shafts.

"Hsiang Tzu!" The woman servant, Kao Ma, called him. "Hsiang Tzu, where are you?"

He sat motionless, his eyes nailed to those broken shafts. Those two white ends seemed to be piercing his heart.

"What kind of a jerk are you? Not saying anything, hiding here. Look here, what a fright you gave me! Master is calling you!"

Kao Ma always mixed the facts and her reactions to them together when she talked; the effect was confusing and touching. She was a widow of about thirty-two or thirty-three. Clean and energetic, she did her work quickly and carefully. People in the other families she had worked for suspected her of being too boastful, of having too many notions of her own, and even of being a little two-faced about things. The Ts'ao family enjoyed having a clean and sprightly person around and paid little attention when she shaved the rules and so she had been with them for three years already. Even when they went away somewhere the Ts'aos took her along.

"The Master is calling you!" she repeated.

When Hsiang Tzu stood up and she saw blood on his face clearly, she added, "You'll be the death of me. What is all this? You haven't even changed your clothes! When you catch cold, that'll fix you. Hurry up! Master has the stuff for it inside."

Hsiang Tzu went in with Kao Ma clucking along behind him. They entered the study together. Mrs. Ts'ao was there too. She had just medicated Mr. Ts'ao's hand and was now bandaging it. She gasped when she saw Hsiang Tzu.

"Madam, he's really gone and messed himself up proper!" Kao Ma was afraid only that Mrs. Ts'ao couldn't see everything, so she quickly poured some water into a basin and said even faster, "Didn't I know it all along? He never takes care when he runs so he was bound to crash sooner or later and isn't that just what happened? Here. Haven't you washed yet? Clean up, put a little antiseptic on, that's the right way!"

Hsiang Tzu covered his right elbow with his left hand and didn't move. The study was so clean and elegant it was all wrong to have a big bloody-faced fellow like him standing there. Everyone seemed to be aware that something was out of place. Even Kao Ma was silent.

"Master." Hsiang Tzu hung his head, his voice very low but forceful. "Master, get someone else. Keep this month's wages to repair the rickshaw. The shafts are broken and the lantern on the left side has some glass broken out, but everything else is all right."

"Get washed up first and get the antiseptic on. Then we'll talk about it." Mr. Ts'ao looked at his hand while he spoke. His wife was still slowly winding a bandage around it.

"Get washed first!" Kao Ma decided to speak up again. "Master hasn't said anything about the rickshaw so don't you be so hasty!"

Hsiang Tzu still did not move. "There's no need to get washed. It'll be all right soon. When a private rickshaw man dumps someone, bangs up the rickshaw, he's shamed. . . ."

Hsiang Tzu's vocabulary was not large enough to enable him to express his thoughts clearly, but all of the emotion he felt had poured out already; only the sobs were lacking. Quitting and forfeiting wages was almost in the same class as suicide to Hsiang Tzu. But this time his duty and his reputation seemed much more important than his life. The person he had dumped was not just anyone, it was Mr. Ts'ao. Suppose he had dumped that Mrs. Yang? So dumped is dumped and she deserved it. He could behave like a rowdy in the streets toward Mrs. Yang. She did not treat him like a man so he didn't have to be polite to her either. Money was everything to people like the Yangs. What did they care about "face" or whatever it is that's called "propriety"? Mr. Ts'ao was not that sort of man at all.

Hsiang Tzu had to sacrifice money to protect his own reputation. He wasn't interested in hating anybody; he only hated his fate. He was on the brink of deciding that after he left the Ts'ao house he would never pull a rickshaw again. He could still risk his own life, since it wasn't worth anything, but someone else's life? If he actually got someone killed what could he do? He had never thought of that before but now, because he had got Mr. Ts'ao injured, he became aware of the possibility. All right, he could do without his wages, he would do something else from now on and never dare work at a trade where you carried someone else's life on your back again. Pulling a rickshaw was the ideal profession to him; to give it up was the same as casting away his hopes. He realized his life would be spent muddling through and there was no need to give another thought to becoming a good rickshaw man. He'd grown so big for nothing!

He had been stealing business from others and having them curse him for it when he was working by the day, but that sort of dishonorable behavior was due to his ambition. He could excuse himself because he wanted to buy a rickshaw. But what was there to say now that he was working privately and had caused a disaster? Others would find out about it. Hsiang Tzu had dumped his employer and cracked up the rickshaw. What a joke this business of working privately was! Hsiang Tzu was trapped! He couldn't wait until Mr. Ts'ao fired him; he'd better leave first.

"Hsiang Tzu." Mr. Ts'ao's hand was nicely bandaged now. "You go get washed up. There's no need to talk about leaving your job. It wasn't your fault. The men who left the stones ought to have left a red lantern there. It's all over now. Go wash and have the antiseptic put on."

"Yes indeed, Master." Kao Ma had thought of something more to say. "Hsiang Tzu is hard to get through to. Where did it all begin? He dumped the Master and got himself in this mess. But Master said it wasn't your fault so you needn't go on being contrary. Look at him, so tall and no weakling and still he's like a little boy! It's really exasperating! Madam, say something. Tell him to stop worrying." Kao Ma's speech was like a phonograph record; it went around and around in circles, mentioning everything, no trace of a beginning or end to it.

"Get washed quickly. The blood frightens me!" was all Mrs. Ts'ao said.

Hsiang Tzu was completely mixed up. Finally, when he heard Madam say she was frightened by the blood, he seemed to have found something helpful to do that would calm her. He took the basin out and washed off outside. Kao Ma waited for him in the doorway with the bottle of antiseptic.

"What about your arm and legs?" Kao Ma dabbed at his face. Hsiang Tzu shook his head. "No need."

Mr. and Mrs. Ts'ao went to bed. Kao Ma took the bottle and went with Hsiang Tzu. When they got to his room she put the bottle down and stood in the doorway. "You can put it on yourself later. I say, you needn't eat your heart out over such a trifling affair. I quit lots of jobs too when I was young and my husband was alive. In the first place, there I was out slaving and he had no ambition and it made me furious. In the second place, I was young and rough tempered. One sentence that was uncalled for and off I'd go! I sell my strength to earn a living but I'm no slave. 'You bosses have your stinking money and we mud people have an earthy nature, but waiting on old women is not for me!' I'm better off now with my husband dead. I have nothing to be anxious about and my temper is a little milder too. And this place, well, I've been here three years. Yes indeed, I started work the ninth of September at the Chung Yang festival. There isn't enough in tips but still they don't treat you too badly. We sell strength and do it for money. Struggling for compliments doesn't mean a thing. But I can say this. There are some advantages to taking the long view of things. If you quit every few days you will have had six months off out of a year and no profit. That's nothing like as good as meeting up with a good-natured boss. So don't make a fuss about working more. You can count on a steady job to let you save a few dollars even if the tips are rare. About that business right now, Master hasn't said anything, so what's done is done and what else matters? Now I'm not getting above myself but you are a little brother and easily ashamed and angered. There's no need to be that way. A hot temper isn't something you can eat. Someone as simple and hasty as you are will find staying here and quietly getting through the day much more profitable than pointlessly wandering around all over the place. I'm not speaking for them. I think you and I get along very well together." She took a breath. "Good enough. See you tomorrow. It's no use being bullheaded. There's nothing tricky about me. I say what I have to say."

Hsiang Tzu's right elbow was very painful and he didn't sleep well most of the night. He recalculated everything. He knew Kao Ma's words were reasonable. Everything was false. Only money was real. Save your money and buy a rickshaw. You can't count on anger to serve as food. And with that idea in mind the calmness that brings sleep came too.

CHAPTER EIGHT

MR. TS'AO had the rickshaw repaired and didn't dock Hsiang Tzu's pay at all. Mrs. Ts'ao gave him two cure-all pills but he didn't take them nor did he bring up the subject of quitting again. Although he felt very embarrassed, Kao Ma's words won out in the end and life was back in its rut after a few days. Gradually, he forgot about the incident and all his hopes put out new sprouts again.

Hsiang Tzu's eyes sparkled when he sat alone in his room figuring out ways to economize and buy a rickshaw. His lips wouldn't stop muttering; it was as if he had some mental illness. He didn't know much about arithmetic and his mind and mouth kept on repeating "six times six is thirty-six." The calculation had little relation to how much money he actually had, but the repetition filled his mind. It was just as if he had a bill due him.

He had great respect for Kao Ma for he knew she had more ability and wit than most men and her words came from a grasp of the root of a problem. He didn't dare go looking for a chance to chat with her but he was quite willing to listen, if she had time for a few words, when he ran into her in the courtyard or gateway. She'd only make a brief comment but it was always enough to give him something to think about for a long time so he'd grin like a dolt every time he met her to make her understand he respected what she said. Kao Ma felt rather proud of herself and would always pull out a few sentences even if she didn't have the time.

But when it came to ways to manage money he didn't dare follow her judgment rashly. Her judgment, in his opinion, while not actually bad, was more or less risky. He listened to her willingly, for if he could learn better maneuvers from her, his heart would be more at ease. But he held onto his same old notion in practice: don't scatter your money recklessly.

Yet it was true that Kao Ma did indeed have a way to make money. Ever since she was widowed she had taken whatever surplus cash she had each month and loaned it out at interest. One or two dollars was enough. She loaned the money to servants, low-ranking policemen, street vendors, and the like for at least three percent. People like these were often red-eyed and desperate over one dollar, so even if someone wanted two dollars back when lending one, they would still have to reach out their hands for it. They'd never know what cash looked like any other way. Poison was on the money they did see; accept it and it would drain them dry, but they still had to take it. Generally they had the nerve to take just enough to give them a breathing space. Life was one reprieve after another and they'd take care of tomorrow tomorrow.

Kao Ma herself had taken this poison while her husband was living. He would get drunk and come looking for her and she couldn't get rid of him without a dollar. If she didn't have it he'd just stand outside the gate where she was working and rant drunkenly. Then she would have to go out and borrow the money no matter how high the interest; there was no other way. She learned her method from that kind of experience. She was not thinking of getting some of her own back. She thought this method was quite reasonable and almost a benevolence toward those seeking help. There were those who needed the money and those who were willing to lend it. It was mutual aid! She didn't see anything wrong with the theory and so she was a little sharp in practice. She wasn't about to toss her money into a stream so she could watch it float. If she could undertake something she'd say so. To do this required sharp eyes, skill, and caution. No one was going to put something over on her. She certainly did not take fewer pains than a bank manager. In fact she had to be a great deal more careful and circumspect.

No matter how much the capital, the theory is the same. Ours is a capitalistic society and for that reason it sifts coins bit by bit like an enormous fine sieve. As the money shifts from top to bottom, only the smallest coins pass through. The theory is also sifted at the same time but there is just as much of it below as above because a theory, unlike coins, doesn't care how small the holes are. It is something disembodied and can flow through the tiniest of holes if it pleases.

Everyone said Kao Ma was tough and she admitted it herself, but the origin of her harshness lay in the bitter discipline of the poverty she had suffered. Recalling the hardships of the past, when even her husband was heartless and unreasonable, she would grind her teeth. She could be very friendly and very nasty for she knew that you can't go on living in this world otherwise.

She advised Hsiang Tzu to lend his money, too, and, if he was willing, she'd help him entirely out of the goodness of her heart.

"I'm telling you, Hsiang Tzu, keep it in your pocket and a penny will always be a penny. Lend it out and money breeds money! After all, what are our eyes good for anyway? Let go of the money when you see the right prospect but don't lend it to any deadbeat. Lend it to a policeman, say, and if he can't pay the interest when the time's up or can't return the principal, go to his superior! One word and he's out of a job. You can do it! Find out for certain when his payday is, blockade the nest, and grab the money. Not get your money back? That would be a wonder!"

"Now, for example, take a group of ten. Whoever we lend to must have some collateral. Just to lend it without checking up is like groping for a pot in the ocean and will that work? You listen to what I tell you. I guarantee I'm right!"

Hsiang Tzu didn't need to say anything. His expression was enough to show how deeply he respected what Kao Ma had said. Until he went and added it all up by himself, that is. Then he felt sure that it was a lot safer to keep his money in his own hands. It was true there wouldn't be any action and his money wouldn't make more money but it was also true that it wouldn't be lost. He took out the few dollars he'd saved during the last few months; all his money was in silver and he turned the coins over quietly one by one, afraid they'd clink. The silver was so white and gleaming, so thick and real and eye-catching, that he felt even more he could not let go of it except to buy a rickshaw. Every man has his own methods and it was of no advantage to him to follow Kao Ma in everything.

He had once worked for a family named Fang. All of them, parents, children, even servants, had postal savings accounts. Mrs. Fang urged Hsiang Tzu to open one too. "You can open an account with one dollar so why don't you start one? The proverb is right when it says 'When the sun is shining always think of the day when it won't be; don't end up wishing for time when time has gone.' You are still young. If you don't use your youth and strength to advantage and save something now, what will you do later? It is impossible that all three hundred and sixty-five days of the year will be sunny. This method doesn't take any trouble. It is reliable and pays interest too. Whenever you are in a pinch you can take some out and use it. Could anything be handier? Go get an application blank and I will fill it in for you as a favor if you can't write."

Hsiang Tzu knew she meant well and he knew that the cook and the nurse had passbooks. He even considered giving it a try but then one day Miss Fang asked him to deposit ten dollars for her. He peered at the passbook. Huh! It was just as weighty as a handful of paper. When he deposited the money they put more marks in the passbook and stamped it with a seal. He knew this was no swindler's place and yet it must be. You put in beautiful silver and all they give you for proof is some marks in a book and that ends the whole business. Hsiang Tzu was not falling into that trap. Besides, he suspected the Fangs were in business with the Post Office. He had always believed that the Post Office was a business with branch offices all over and it probably had quite an old trademark. At least it wasn't much different from other long-established shops in Peking. That was why the Fangs were so eager to bring in more business. Even if it wasn't really like that, cash in hand, after all, is much better than cash in a passbook, a whole lot better! The money in a passbook is only a few marks!

All he knew about banks was that they were good places to pick up fares. He'd be sure to get a passenger if the policeman didn't prevent him from waiting there, but he couldn't guess what kind of business went on inside. True, there must be lots of money inside but he could not understand how people could go in there and shake it out. In any case it wouldn't be easy for him to start up a connection with a bank so it wasn't worth distressing himself thinking about it. There were many things in the city which he did not understand, and listening to friends discussing them in teahouses made him even more confused because everyone had his own point of view and none of them ever got to the point. He didn't want to hear any more or think any more. He knew that if you wanted to steal, it would be best to rob a bank and since he had no intention of becoming a bandit it was pointless to bother about such things. He might as well hang onto his money. In his opinion this was the most dependable method of all.

Kao Ma knew he was determined to buy a rickshaw so she suggested a plan. "Hsiang Tzu, I know you don't want to lend your money but here's another way to get your own rickshaw in a hurry. If I were a man and I pulled a rickshaw, I would certainly pull my own. I'd pull for myself and shout for myself and not beg anyone for anything! If I could do that, you could offer me the mayor's job and I still wouldn't trade. Rickshaw pulling is hard work but if I were a man, and strong, I'd stick to a rickshaw and never join the police. It's always the same with them, always standing in the street winter and summer for just a few dollars a month and no tips and no freedom. Let him grow a mustache and poof! He's fired. There's simply no profit in it.

"As I was saying, if you want to buy a rickshaw right away here's a good way to do it. Start up a money-lending club and get ten members, twenty at most. Each member puts in two dollars a month but you arrange to get first crack at the pot and you'll have forty dollars right off. You have some savings, too, so add some more and you'll have a rickshaw to pull. The general arrangement is quite simple. Then, when you get your rickshaw, you can change the club into a lottery association and you won't have to pay any interest. Besides, its quite respectable and really fits your needs. So if you want to start a club I'll be the first to join. No kidding! So how about it?"

This plan made Hsiang Tzu's heart jump for joy. Really, if he collected thirty or forty dollars and added them to the thirty in old Liu's hands plus the money he had on hand could it fail to add up to eighty dollars? It wasn't enough to buy a new rickshaw but one about eighty percent new would do very well! Besides, if he did things this way he could go to old Liu and get his money back and save it from just lying there like nothing at all. Eighty percent new is eighty percent but he'd pull it anyway and wait until he'd made a pile and then trade it in.

But where could he find those twenty people? Even if he did get them together, this was a matter involving your reputation. When people like me need money we get up a club but then don't the others expect me to do my part the next time around? Starting a club in these hard times is often a waste of time. A hero never asks for help. Obviously, if it's in my destiny to buy a rickshaw, I'll buy one. I won't beg from others.

Kao Ma noticed that he was not reacting and actually considered prodding him but then she remembered that direct and honest nature of his and knew there wouldn't be any great satisfaction in teasing him. "You do it your way! Chasing a pig down an alley, doing things in a straightforward way, is a good idea too!"

Hsiang Tzu said nothing. He waited until she went away and then nodded his head to himself as if agreeing that his deathlike grip on his money was worthy of respect. He felt very happy.

It was early winter already. The low lugubrious call of the chamber pot sellers was added to the cries of the vendors who sold peanuts and sugar-roasted chestnuts in the side streets in the evenings. One of these sellers had some chamber pots with lids in the shape of a bottle gourd on his pole. Hsiang Tzu bought a big one. Since it was his first sale the seller couldn't make change but Hsiang Tzu felt accommodating. He saw a small chamber pot with a nice deep green glaze and a raised rim.

"Don't bother to look for change. I'll take this."

He put the large pot away and took the little green one into the main house. "Young Master, are you still up? I brought you a nice toy!"

Everyone was watching Hsiao Wen, the son of the house, take his bath. One look at this toy and they couldn't help laughing. The Ts'aos didn't say anything. They must have realized this was a rather stupid kind of toy but Hsiang Tzu's kind intentions ought to be honored so they smiled at him to show their thanks. Kao Ma, however, could not keep still.

"Well, really now, Hsiang Tzu! Such a big fellow and you come up with such a brilliant idea. It's too disgusting!"

Hsiao Wen was delighted with the toy. He splashed water from the tub into the pot and said, "This little teapot has a big mouth!"

Everyone laughed harder. Hsiang Tzu straightened up and went out because he didn't know how to react when he was pleased. He was very happy; never before had everyone looked at him with smiling faces as if he were some important personage. He smiled a little while he got out the rest of his money and gently tossed it, coin by coin, into the pottery gourd, saying to himself, this is safer than anywhere else! When there's enough, then I'll smash it against the wall, wham! and there'll be more coins than pieces!"

He certainly would not beg from anyone again. Yet he was always a little uneasy about his thirty dollars. Old Liu was very reliable and the money wouldn't be lost in his hands; but still, there were times when Hsiang Tzu became depressed about it. This thing money was like a ring: it is always best to have it on your hand.

Deciding to hang onto his money made him very happy, and he felt just the way he did when he tied his sash tightly and made his torso much straighter.

The days got colder and colder but Hsiang Tzu seemed not to notice. He had a definite plan in mind and everything he saw looked bright. He couldn't feel the chill in the brightness.

Ice was seen on the ground for the first time. Even the surface of the unpaved side streets was getting hard; it looked dry and parched everywhere and the color of the black earth began to look slightly yellow, as if all the moisture were completely gone. It was on these cold mornings, when the ridges made by big wheels were inlaid with lines of frost, when little breezes cut through and scattered the morning clouds revealing the lightest, bluest, gayest of skies, that Hsiang Tzu went out eagerly for an early morning run. The cold wind whistled up his sleeves, making his whole body shudder the way it did in a cold bath. Sometimes a wild wind rose, making it hard for him to breathe, but he lowered his head, gritted his teeth, and charged onward like a big fish swimming against the current. The greater the wind the stronger his resistance to it; it was as if he and the wild wind were in a battle to the death. When a blast made it utterly impossible for him to get his breath he'd shut his mouth, wait a while, then belch, as if diving into water. After the belch he continued to push forward; on he'd struggle, for nothing could stop this big man who hadn't a single relaxed muscle in his body. His entire frame fought back like a green insect surrounded by ants. And what sweat! When he put down the rickshaw, let out a long breath, and wiped the yellowish sand out of the corners of his mouth he knew that he was a man no one could match! Watching the gray dust-filled wind sweeping across in front of him, he nodded.

The wind blew around the trees along the roadside, shredded the cloth signs hung outside the shops, stripped the posters off the walls, and obscured the sun; it was singing, calling, bellowing, whirling. Suddenly it charged straight ahead like a great demented spirit in a wild rush that lashed out at heaven and earth. Suddenly it went into a frenzy, punching furiously in all directions like a frustrated evil spirit that has decided to strike out wildly at everything. Suddenly it swept crossways, using a surprise attack which no one had anticipated, to assault everything on earth and snap off branches, blow off roof tiles, and break down power lines. But Hsiang Tzu was there watching. He had just come through that wind—that wind wasn't anything to him!

The victory was his! And when he had a following wind, all he had to do was hold the shafts firmly. There was no need for him to pull; the wind could turn the wheels for him like a good friend.

Of course he wasn't blind and must have noticed the old and weak rickshaw pullers. The slightest wind would go right through the worn-out clothes they wore; a strong wind would just rip them; and who knows what they had wrapped around their feet? They shivered at the rickshaw stands, eyes lingering over everything like a thief's. They'd all shout "Rickshaw!" at anyone. When they got a passenger and got warmed up, the sweat would soak through those thin and tattered clothes. Their sweat would turn to ice on their backs when they stopped. When they met a head wind and could hardly take a step, they still had to keep on grimly dragging the rickshaw. When the wind struck down at them from above they had to go on with their chins on their chests. When the wind came from below, their feet simply couldn't find the ground. When the wind came from in front it blew their hands upward the way it blows a kite. When the wind came from behind there was no way they could keep control of the rickshaw or themselves. But they used every trick there was and all the strength they had because dead or alive they had to get to their destinations! They'd kill themselves for a few pennies. After a tour with the rickshaw the gray dust was turned into mud by the sweat on their faces and stayed there, leaving only three red ovals of eyes and mouth showing.

The days were so short and so cold that there were not many people on the streets and working so hard all day did not always earn enough for a single full meal. But the old rickshaw men had wives and children at home and the young ones had fathers, mothers, brothers, and sisters! In winter each of them was in hell. They had more life in them than ghosts but hadn't a ghost's comfort and leisure. And ghosts didn't have to wear themselves out to eat. To die like a dog in the street would be their greatest peace and comfort. It is said that the ghosts of those who have frozen to death have little smiles on their faces!

How could Hsiang Tzu not have seen them? But he had no time to worry about them. Although he shared their lot he was young and strong, could take suffering, and didn't fear the cold. He had a place to stay at night and proper clothes during the day so he felt he could not be put in the same category with them at all. While they all suffered, the degree of suffering was not entirely the same. He bore fewer hardships now and would be able to escape them in the future. He thought that if he reached old age he certainly would not be pulling a broken-down rickshaw and suffering from hunger and cold. He believed his present superiority would guarantee the triumph to come. He was just like the chauffeurs he met outside restaurants and big houses; they had no interest in passing the time of day, for chauffeurs felt it would diminish their prestige if they were to have anything to do with rickshaw pullers. The attitude of chauffeurs toward rickshaw men surely bore some resemblance to the way Hsiang Tzu behaved toward those poor old defeated soldiers. They were all in hell but not in the same circle.

Since it never occurred to them to stand together, each went his own way; each man's hopes and exertions obscured his vision. Each man thought he could found a family and maintain his livelihood with his bare and empty hands. Each of them went groping for his own path in darkness. Hsiang Tzu did not think of others or pay attention to them. He thought only about his money and future success.

Slowly signs and portents of the three-week New Year holidays appeared in the streets. Even though it was very cold, lots of color lined both sides of the streets when it was bright out and not windy. New Year's paintings, gauze lanterns, red and white candles, silk flowers to wear in the hair, and honey-covered dough cakes all came out in rows. The sight made people look happy and a little worried, too. While everyone thought about the days of happiness at New Year's, everyone also had to pay their debts.

Hsiang Tzu's eyes got brighter. It occurred to him, while looking at all the sights along the streets, that the Ts'aos certainly ought to be sending out presents and each present sent should get him a few coins in tips. The New Year's bonus must be two dollars at least. That wasn't much, but when the New Year callers came he'd take each one of them home and every trip would bring in twenty or thirty cents too. It would all add up to something; he had no fear it would be too little. His pottery gourd would not do him wrong as long as the spare change got into his hand. When he had nothing to do at night he would stare fixedly at his clay friend who only ate money and never spit it out. Softly he urged it, "Eat a lot, eat a lot, pal! When you're full up I'll be all set!"

New Year's was coming closer and closer; in a twinkling it was January 8. Joy or apprehension impelled people to make plans and put things in order. There were still twenty-four hours in a day but these were not ordinary days. They would not let anyone follow his own predilections. Everyone had to do something in preparation for the coming holidays. It was as if time suddenly had consciousness and emotions which made people obey it in their thoughts and their rush of activity.

Hsiang Tzu was one of the happy ones. The commotion in the streets, the shouts of the vendors, his hopes for the New Year bonus and tips, time off for the holiday, and visions of good food, all made him as delighted and full of hope as a child. Aha, he thought to himself. Get out a dollar and take eighty cents of it to buy a little gift for old Liu. A gift is a trifle but a man of mark is important so he'd better take a little something to apologize. He'd say he hadn't been to call on the old man all this time because he had been so busy. And he could get that thirty dollars back then, too. It was smart business to waste one dollar and get that large an amount back. Once he had his idea worked out he shook the pot gently, imagining how much deeper and enjoyable the sound would be once thirty more dollars were added. Yes indeed, all he had to do was get that money back and he'd have nothing to worry about!

One evening Kao Ma called to him just as he was about to give his treasury a shake. "Hsiang Tzu! There's a young lady at the door looking for you. I just came home and she wanted me to tell her all about you." Hsiang Tzu came out and she added in a low voice, "She's like a big black pagoda. What a fright!"

Hsiang Tzu's face suddenly reddened as if he were surrounded by flames. He knew something must have gone very wrong.

CHAPTER NINE

HSIANG TZU almost hadn't the strength to go out in the street. In confusion he had already peeked out at Miss Liu by the glow of the streetlight with his feet still inside the gateway. She had probably rubbed some powder onto her face again; the reflection from the streetlight made it look slightly ashy green, like a layer of frost on a blackened and dried up leaf. Hsiang Tzu simply hadn't the nerve to look at her directly.

The expression on Hu Niu's face was mixed. In her eyes there was a glimmer of earnest longing to see him, but her lips were stretched in a bit of a cold smile. There were lines across her nose, which was wrinkled up to show her disdain and anxiety. Her eyebrows were arched; in the peculiar way she had powdered her face they looked both seductive and tyrannical. When she saw Hsiang Tzu emerge her lips pouted and the expressions on her face failed to unite in a suitably nasty response. She gulped, as if suppressing various emotions. Mustering a little of the savoir-faire she got from old Liu, she chuckled in a half angry and half laughing way, pretending to be nonchalant about it all.

"You can still come back even though you're like a dog who's been beat with a package of meat and not looking back beats a retreat!" Her voice was very high, just the way it was when she was scolding the rickshaw pullers and there wasn't a trace of a smile left on her face once she'd said her piece. Suddenly, as if she felt ashamed and cheap, she gnawed her lip.

"Don't make a fuss!" Hsiang Tzu seemed to have put all his strength into his mouth as he blurted these words. His tone was soft but very forceful.

"Humph! What do I care!" She grinned evilly but lowered her voice in spite of herself. "I don't blame you for avoiding me. It's no

wonder, not with a seductive vixen like her here. I knew you were no
fool a long time age so don't stand there looking like a clod. 'A
Mongol may throw away a tobacco pouch but he's no fool even
though he pretends to be.' " Her voice rose again.

"Don't fuss!" Hsiang Tzu was only afraid that Kao Ma might be
eavesdropping in the doorway. "Don't fuss! Come over here!" He
went toward the avenue as he spoke.

"I don't care where we go. I'm not afraid. I have a loud voice." Her
mouth rebelled but she went with him.

Once across the avenue they went along a side street and then stood
by the red-painted brick wall surrounding the public parks. Hsiang
Tzu still hadn't forgotten his rural habits and squatted. "What have
you come for?"

"Me? Lots of reasons!" She thrust her left hand into her waistband
and a curved belly stuck out a little. She looked down at him thought-
fully, as if to express benevolence and show some mercy on him.
"Hsiang Tzu, there was a reason for me to look for you. A very important reason."

The low gentle sound of "Hsiang Tzu" did away with a lot of his
anger. He raised his head and looked at her. There still was nothing
lovable about her but the sound of "Hsiang Tzu" echoed softly in his
heart, bringing a gentle feeling of intimacy. It was as if he had heard
such a sound somewhere before and it evoked a feeling he couldn't fail
to recognize, a feeling he wanted to break off but couldn't. His voice
was still low but a little kinder. "What's up?"

"Hsiang Tzu!" She came closer. "I have something!"

"What do you have?" He was startled.

"This!" She pointed at her belly. "So decide what to do."

Stunned, he groaned. Suddenly everything was clear. Ten thousand
things he'd never thought of came rushing into his mind. They were so
numerous, so upsetting, so turbulent, that his mind retreated in a
panic and became an empty white space, like a movie screen when the
film breaks.

The street was unusually quiet. A few gray clouds covered the
moon. There was a slight breeze now and then which rustled the life-
less branches and dried leaves. The piercing yowling of cats came
from far off.

Hsiang Tzu's mind went from panic to emptiness. He didn't even
hear these noises. Hands under his chin, he stared at the ground and

stared at it so hard it seemed about to move. He couldn't think of anything and didn't want to think of anything. All he knew was that he was getting smaller and smaller but couldn't shrink away into the ground entirely. His whole life seemed to be standing here at this unbearable moment and there was absolutely nothing else in the world. Then he realized he was cold; even his lips were trembling slightly.

"Don't sit there hugging yourself! Can't you talk? Get up!" She seemed to be getting cold, too, and wanted to move around.

Hsiang Tzu stood up stiffly and walked north with her. He still couldn't find anything to say. His whole body seemed wooden; it was like just being waked up by the cold.

"You haven't decided?" She glanced at Hsiang Tzu, an expression of love for him in her eyes.

There was nothing he could say.

"You'd better come to call on the twenty-seventh. It's the old man's birthday."

"Too busy. End of the year!" In the midst of his great mental confusion Hsiang Tzu still did not forget about his own affairs.

"I know a rascal like you reacts to the hard but not to the soft. Talking nicely to you is a total waste!" Her voice rose again and the chill silence in the street made it especially clear. "You think that I'm afraid of anyone? What do you intend to do? If you don't want to listen to me, I haven't the time to play around wasting spit on you! If you abandon me I'll stand at your boss's doorway and curse three days and three nights in a row! I'll find you anywhere you go. I'm not interested in who's to blame!"

"Don't yell, all right?" Hsiang Tzu took a step away from her.

"If you are afraid of a fight you shouldn't have come panting after a free ride in the first place. You had a taste and now you make me take the blame all by myself. Why don't you pull back the skin on your dead prick and take a look at who I am!"

"Talk slower. I'm listening." Hsiang Tzu was very cold but all this abuse suddenly made him feel hot; the heat wanted to break out of this frozen-stiff skin of his. His whole body began to itch all over and his scalp was burning unbearably.

"This doesn't settle anything. I'm not looking for ways to upset you." She curled her lips revealing two tiger teeth. "I'm not trying to hurt you, I really love you and you don't know what's good for you! Getting bullheaded with me won't do you any good, I'm telling you."

"No. . . ." Hsiang Tzu wanted to say "No need to sock me once and bat me thrice" but couldn't remember the whole phrase. He knew quite a lot of sarcastic Peking slang but couldn't speak it freely. He could understand it when others used it but couldn't manage it himself.

"No what?"

"Have your say!"

"I've got a good plan." Miss Liu stood still and spoke to him face to face. "You look here. If you get a go-between to do the talking it's a sure thing the old man won't agree. He's the one who owns the rickshaw and you're the one who pulls it. He isn't about to go beneath himself for a son-in-law but I don't care. I like you and I get what I like and that's that. So why should I care about any other motherfucking business? Anyone who sends a go-between for me will get nowhere. Mention marriage to the old man and he just regards it as a plot to get hold of all those rickshaws of his. Even someone better off than you wouldn't do. This business will never get anywhere unless I do something about it myself, so I picked you. We'll just assume we have the right to 'behead first and report later.' And besides, I've already been knocked up so neither of us can get out of it. But for us to just march right in and ask his permission wouldn't do either. The old man is getting stupider the older he gets so if a rumor about us gets around he might just go get himself a concubine and shove me right out. He still has what it takes all right, never mind that he's almost seventy. He really might want to take a young wife. While I wouldn't go so far as to say he'd have lots of children, he could still father two or three kids at least. Believe it or not, as you prefer!"

"Let's walk a while and talk about it." Hsiang Tzu saw a policeman who had come by twice already and he decided it wasn't a good idea to stay there.

"We can talk right here. It's nobody else's business!" She followed his glance and saw the policeman. "You aren't pulling a rickshaw, so what are you afraid he'll do? Why would he go bite off someone's cock for no good reason? What's so suspicious about us? We're talking about our own affairs. Look, here's my idea. When the old man's birthday comes on the twenty-seventh, you go make three kowtows to him. Then wait until New Year's Day and come again to wish him a happy New Year and make him feel good. I'll see to it that he's cheerful. I'll get him some baigan or something and let him drink too much. When he's pretty far gone you strike while the iron is hot and simply offer yourself as his foster son. After that, I'll gradually let him know that all is not quite right with me. But I'll make like Hsu Shu in Ts'ao Ts'ao's camp and won't talk, so he'll have to ask me questions and then I'll put him off. When he's really frantic I'll give the man a name. I'll say it was Chiao Erh who died a little while ago. He was assistant manager of the funeral paraphernalia rental agency just east of us. He had no relatives and no friends. He's already buried in the potter's field outside the Tung Chih Gate, so where could the old man go to find out the truth? He won't know what to do but we can help him along by hinting that the best thing to do is give me to you. After all, you are the foster son and serving as a son-in-law isn't much different anyway. We'll 'pole a boat with the current' and save us from disgracing ourselves in public. So tell me, have I got it figured right or not?''

Hsiang Tzu was speechless.

Feeling that she had finished her story, Hu Niu walked on northwards with her head down as though she were relishing her own tale while seeming to give Hsiang Tzu a chance to think it over. At this moment the wind blew the clouds apart revealing the moon; the two of them had come to the head of the street.

The water in the Imperial Canal, the moat surrounding the Forbidden City, was already frozen. Silently, grayly glittering, smoothly, firmly, it reflected the reddish-purple wall of the Forbidden City. Inside the Forbidden City there was not a single sound; the splendid watchtowers, the gold and green honorific inscriptions, the vermilion gates, and the pavilion on Coal Hill were all peaceful and silent, as if waiting for a sound most unlikely ever to be heard again. A slight breeze blew by like a melancholy sigh, winding around through the towers, pavilions, and palaces, as if it wanted to tell a little tale of the past.

Hu Niu went westwards and Hsiang Tzu followed her to the bridge over the narrow stretch of water between the North and Middle Lakes just west of the Forbidden City. There was no one on the bridge. Thin moonlight coldly, silently, shone on the great flat fields of ice above and below the bridge. The gray shadow of a distant pavilion seemed to be frozen in the lake but its yellow roof tiles reflected a little light. The trees scarcely moved and the moonlight was nebulous. The White Dagoba on its hill on an island in the North Lake reached loftily to the clouds and its simple whiteness shed cold solitude and lonely desolation to its surroundings. The three lakes made the cold barrenness of the northland manifest among all the man-made stonework.

When they reached the highest point on the nine-arched bridge the chilly exhalations from the ice made Hsiang Tzu shudder all of a sudden. He wanted to go no farther. Ordinarily when he pulled a rickshaw across this bridge he put all his vigor into his legs and dared not even glance to the left or right because he was afraid of tripping. Now he could look around freely but he felt in his heart that this scenery was a little horrifying. All this cold gray ice, barely moving shadows of trees, and dreary Dagoba seemed on the verge of shrieking and running madly away! This great white marble bridge beneath his feet had become unusually desolate, especially white and chilly; even the streetlights were miserable.

He wasn't interested in walking any farther or looking around again. Even less was he interested in accompanying her. He actually thought about jumping off the bridge all of a sudden. His head would hit and crack the ice and he'd sink down and freeze there like a dead fish.

"See you later!" He turned around abruptly to go back.

"Hsiang Tzu! Do it my way! See you on the twenty-seventh!" She spoke to his broad back. Then she glanced at the White Dagoba, sighed, and went on homeward.

Hsiang Tzu didn't even turn his head. He ran wildly, as if pursued by a ghost, and almost ran into a wall. He leaned against the wall, supporting himself with one hand, and couldn't help wanting to cry. He was momentarily dazed. Then a shout came from the bridge. 'Hsiang Tzu! Hsiang Tzu, come here!" It was Hu Niu's voice.

He dragged his steps back towards the bridge. Hu Niu came to meet him, leaning foward a little with her lips slightly stretched.

"I said, Hsiang Tzu, you come here. I've got something for you." She met him before he had come back very far. "Here's the thirty dollars you left plus some interest. I added enough to make it a round dollar. Here it is. It's just to show you how I feel and not for any other reason. I think about you all the time. I love you. I'll take care of you. There's no need to say any more. Just don't 'forget favors or be ungrateful for kindness' and that'll be fine. Here, take good care of it. If it's lost you can't blame me!"

Hsiang Tzu took the money, a handful of bills, and blankly

watched her until her head disappeared as she went down the other side of the bridge.

The gray clouds covered the moon again. The lights were brighter and the bridgeway exceptionally white, vacant, and cold. He turned around and began to walk. He hurried back as if he'd gone crazy. The image of that desolate and melancholy bridge was still lodged in his mind when he arrived at the front door as if only the time it took to blink an eye separated him from it.

The first thing he did when he got to his room was count and re-count the money. When he'd counted the bills three times the sweat on his palms made them sticky and of course he couldn't be sure he'd counted them correctly. When he finally finished he stuffed them into the gourd-shaped pot and then sat on his bed, staring stupidly at the ceramic object. He didn't want to make any plans because with money you have an out. He really believed this piggy bank could solve everything for him and he needn't worry again. The Imperial Canal, Coal Hill, the White Dagoba, the bridge, Hu Niu and her belly . . . were all a dream. Now you wake up from that dream and there are more than thirty dollars in the pot. Really!

He hid the pot carefully after he'd looked long enough. He figured that the big troubles of the day would all be slept away after a good night's sleep. Why not talk about them tomorrow!

He lay down and couldn't close his eyes! All those problems were like a nest of hornets—you come out, I go in—and there was a sting on the end of every one of them.

He did not want to think; and, in fact, there was nothing he could think about. Hu Niu had already blocked all the roads and there was no way for him to escape.

The best thing would be to get out of town. Hsiang Tzu could not go. He'd still be happy even if he were forced to stand guard over the White Dagoba but he simply could not go back to the village. Go to another city? He couldn't think of any place better than Peking. He could not leave. He'd rather die here.

Since leaving was impossible there was no point wasting his energy worrying about other problems. With Hu Niu, action followed words. She was quite capable of keeping after him constantly if he didn't give in and she'd find him as long as he was in Peking. To tell the truth, there was no point trying to be sly with her. Get her mad enough and she'd go get old Liu; and if he hired a couple of thugs, not to mention a gang of them, they could do him in in any secluded spot in town.

After thinking over what Hu Niu had said from beginning to end, he felt he had tumbled into a pitfall. His hands and feet were caught in the snares and there was absolutely no way to escape. He wasn't smart enough to criticize her plan point by point and so he could find no loopholes in it. All he knew was that she had cast a net that would entrap him and put an end to his family line and respectability. Not even a fish an inch long could have escaped it! He couldn't think systematically so he simply lumped everything together; the whole mess was as heavy as a half-ton sluice gate and the whole thing was weighing down on his head. Crushed by this pressure, he couldn't resist. He realized that the entire course of a rickshaw puller's life was described in two words: tough luck! A rickshaw puller, and only a rickshaw puller, had better never put a foot wrong or get involved with a woman. Get stuck like that and you've made a mistake as big as the sky. Old Liu relied on all his rickshaws, Hu Niu relied on her stinking cunt—to humiliate him! It was useless for him to think about anything anymore. If he were to give in to his fate, good. Then he'd go kowtow and acknowledge a foster father, and after that wait to marry that stinking vixen. Not to give in to your fate is suicidal!

He put Hu Niu and her story off to one side when he got to that point. The problem wasn't that she was cruel, it was that a rickshaw puller's fate had to be cruel. It was the same as the fate of a dog who has to put up with thrashings and bad temper and even the smallest child could beat it with a stick for no reason at all. What's a life like that good for anyway? You want a fight? Okay, fight.

He couldn't sleep. He kicked off his quilt and sat up. He decided to go out and get some baigan and get really drunk. So what's it all about? Who makes the rules anyway? Go fuck your grandmother! Get drunk and go to sleep. The twenty-seventh? I won't go kowtow on the twenty-eighth either. We'll just see who can do what to Hsiang Tzu! Throwing his padded coat over his shoulder, he grabbed the rice bowl he used for a teacup and ran out.

The wind had risen, the gray clouds had already scattered, and a small moon spread its cold light. Hsiang Tzu had just got out of a warm bed and couldn't help gasping in the cold. There were no pedestrians in the street and only two rickshaws waiting. The pullers covered their ears with their hands while they stamped their feet to keep warm.

Hsiang Tzu ran straight to a small shop. The door was shut to keep the warmth inside and you had to open a sliding panel in a small window to buy what you wanted. Hsiang Tzu wanted four ounces of baigan and three cents' worth of peanuts. He had to keep the bowl level so he didn't dare run back to his room. He slid his feet quickly along the road like a sedan chair bearer instead. Frantically he dived under his quilt with his teeth chattering when he got back and didn't want to sit up again. The baigan on the table gave off its sharp pungent aroma; he didn't like it at all. He wasn't interested in touching the peanuts now. The wave of cold air had waked him up like a basin of cold water sloshed in his face but now he was reluctant to reach out a hand and his head wasn't all that hot anymore either.

He lay there for a long time staring at the bowl on the table from over the edge of his quilt. No, he wasn't going to ruin himself on account of that entanglement or break his resolution not to drink. While there was really no good way to handle the situation, still there must be some crack he could escape through. But even if there was absolutely no way out he shouldn't roll himself into a mud hole ahead of time either. He'd better open his eyes wide and take a hard look at how, in the end, he had allowed himself to be shoved down by others.

He put out the lamp and covered his head with the quilt completely, intending to go right to sleep. But he couldn't sleep. He pulled off the quilt and looked around.

The paper window shone greenly in the light from the setting moon like the sky brightening at dawn. The tip of his nose felt the chill in the room and the cold air brought the smell of baigan with it. He sat up abruptly, grabbed the bowl, and swallowed it all in one big mouthful!

CHAPTER TEN

HSIANG TZU wasn't smart enough to devise any other solution nor had he the force of character to cope with the whole situation. There wasn't a thing he could do. Each day was just another bellyful of grievance. His life was no different from the life of anyone else who, after being injured and not at all sure what to do about it, thinks only of how to recoup the loss. The cricket who loses his hind legs in a fight still expects to crawl with the two legs he has left. Hsiang Tzu had made no decision; he thought only of getting through each incident as it came, day by day, and then worry about where he was after he'd crawled there. He never thought of jumping.

The twenty-seventh was still more than ten days away. All his thoughts were focused on that day; the twenty-seventh was all his mind pondered, all his mouth mumbled about, all his dreams dreamed of. It was as if there must be some way to solve everything once the twenty-seventh was past although he was clearly aware he was only hoodwinking himself by thinking that way.

Sometimes he thought of going somewhere far away—taking all his money and going to Tientsin, for instance. When he got there, if he was lucky, he might change his trade and not pull a rickshaw again. Could Hu Niu follow him to Tientsin? All the places you took a train to were very far away to him. She'd never be able to catch up with him there, no matter what. It was a good idea, but in his heart he knew it would be his last resort. If there were the least chance of staying in Peking, he'd stay there! So his thoughts returned to the twenty-seventh. Suppose he just did the things the easy way and slid through this tight spot. Maybe he could get out of the whole mess and not have to change his entire life. Even if he couldn't get rid of it once and for all, just getting past one crisis was enough.

But how could he slip past this one crisis? He had two plans. One was to pay no attention to her at all and simply not go to the birthday party. The other was to do as she demanded. These two plans were opposites, but they amounted to the same thing. If he didn't go, she certainly wouldn't smile sweetly and release him. If he did go, she still wouldn't let him off.

He remembered something that had happened when he was new at the game and copied the way other rickshaw men took shortcuts. He'd seen a side street and went down it to shave the distance a little, but it turned out to go in a circle and he came out where he'd begun. Now he'd got himself into another street like that one. He was ending up in the same place no matter which way he went.

There was nothing he could do so he tried thinking about the good side. If he simply wanted her, was there any reason why he shouldn't go through with it? But no matter which way he thought about it, he always felt depressed. He could only shake his head when he thought of her looks. Never mind her looks, think of her way of life . . . faugh! He was an ambitious and proper man. He could never face anyone again if he went and married a shopworn item like her. He wouldn't even have the nerve to face his parents after he died. Who knew for certain if that baby in her belly was his or not? Oh sure, she could bring some rickshaws along but was there any guarantee? Old Liu was not a man to annoy! And suppose everything was to his interest? He still couldn't stand it because how could he ever get the better of Hu Niu? She had only to extend a finger and she could send him on errands until his head was spinning, his eyes had spots in front of them, and he couldn't tell which way he was going. He knew all too well how awful she was! If he wanted to start a family he absolutely would not do it with her. There was nothing else to be said. If he wanted her that would be the end of him and he was definitely not a man who despised himself. There was no solution at all!

There was no way to put her in her place, so he turned to hating himself and thought a lot about slapping himself across the mouth sharply. But, to tell the truth, he really hadn't made any mistakes. She was the one who had arranged everything so nicely and then simply waited for him to come fall in the trap. The trouble with him was that he was too honest. Be honest and it's a sure thing you'll suffer for it. And there's no "reasonableness" you can appeal to.

What made him even more upset was that there was no place he could go to complain of his wrongs. He had no parents, no brothers, no sisters, no friends. Ordinarily he thought of himself as a fine fellow without ties or hindrances. His head reached the sky and his feet pressed the earth. He was involved in nothing and entrapped in nothing. Now he realized how wrong he was; men cannot exist by themselves.

This was especially true when he thought of his relationship with his fellows; they all seemed to have something likable about them now. He began to think that if he had made friends with a few like himself along the way he wouldn't be afraid of any number of Hu Nius now. They would have lent a hand and done everything they could to help him get rid of his problem. But the truth was he was one lone person and it wasn't all that easy to scrape up a friend on short notice. He felt a kind of terror he had never known before. He was afraid that anyone could cheat and trample on him if he went on in the same old way. Keeping to yourself was no way to have your head reach the sky!

This terror began to make him have doubts about himself. In winter when his master went out to dinner or to a play he customarily put the water can for the carbide lamp inside his coat because it would just freeze up if left on the rickshaw. The combination of hot sweat after a run and the ice-cold water can close to his chest made him shudder instantly. He wasn't sure how long that can took to warm up. Ordinarily he hadn't thought there was anything demeaning about doing this. Sometimes he felt a sense of superiority when he held it. After all, those pullers of broken-down rickshaws don't always have carbide lamps.

But now it seemed to him that he earned such a little bit of money each month and had to bear so many hardships to get it, and even his own chest, that chest the little water can had to be held against so it wouldn't freeze, his own broad chest, wasn't even worth as much as that water can. There was a time when he believed that being a rickshaw man was the ideal job for him. He could get his living and start a family by pulling a rickshaw. Now he shook his head to himself. No wonder Hu Niu browbeat him. After all, he was only a man who wasn't even as good as a water can!

On the third day after Hu Niu found him, Mr. Ts'ao and some friends went to an evening movie. Hsiang Tzu waited for him in a small teahouse with that lump of ice of a water can inside his coat.

The weather was very cold so the door and windows of the teahouse were shut fast. The place reeked of coal fumes, sweat, and the dry smoke of cheap stinking cigarettes. Even so, the windows still had a covering of frost flowers on them. Almost all the tea drinkers were rickshaw men with private jobs. Some of them tilted their chairs back against the wall and, taking advantage of the warmth, took naps. Some had cups of baigan which they drank slowly after "offering" a drink to everyone else. When they'd swallowed a large mouthful they'd lick their lips and the chill inside them was liberated noisily below. One of them had hold of a huge pancake which he ate by biting off half at a time and his neck was thick and red with the effort of chewing. Another was grim-faced and telling everyone all about his woes; he'd been running from early morning until now without stopping and getting soaked with sweat and drying off and getting soaked again he didn't know how many times. Most of the others had been chatting about nothing at all until they heard his speech. They were all silent for a moment while they recalled their own troubles that day and then began to tell everyone else about them. Suddenly the place sounded like it was full of birds with their nests on fire. Even the fellow eating the huge pancake made enough room in his mouth so he could shift his useless grudges off the tip of his tongue. Trying to swallow and talk at the same time made the muscles on his face jump.

"So you think this motherfucking private work doesn't grind you down? I got up at a motherfucking two A.M. and no water or food has hit my teeth till now! Speaking only of going from the Ch'ien Gate to the P'ing Tzu Gate, I made three motherfucking round trips. Today I got my motherfucking asshole so cold it cracked and what farting!" He looked around at them all, nodded, and went back to chewing his pancake.

This outburst got them all talking about the weather; they all regarded it as the center of their difficulties.

Hsiang Tzu said nothing the whole time but was very interested in what they had to say. Their stories were full of curses and disgruntlement even though their tones of voice and the stories themselves were all different. These tales fell upon the grievances in his own heart and were totally absorbed, like a few raindrops falling on dried up earth. He had no way, and didn't know how, to tell his story from beginning to end. He was able only to take in some of the bitterness of life from the stories told by others. They were all suffering and he was no exception; he recognized that he was one of them and began to feel sympathetic toward them. He frowned when they spoke of the sad bitter parts and smiled when they spoke of the comic parts. And so he thought he had become one of them for they were all fellow sufferers. Not saying a word himself didn't make any difference. He used to think they were all disgusting foulmouths. You'd never get rich if you spent the day grumbling the way they did. Today he realized for the first time that they did have something to say. They were talking about him, talking about his hardships and those of all other rickshaw pullers.

The door suddenly opened right in the middle of their noisy heated chatter, letting in a blast of cold air. Almost everyone looked up angrily to see who was so lacking in consideration as to open the door wide. They all got angrier as the person outside moved more slowly; he seemed to be doing it on purpose to annoy them. A waiter called half in anger and half pleasantly, "Hurry up, uncle! Don't let all the warm air out!"

The man came in before the waiter had finished speaking. He was a rickshaw man too. He was over fifty from the look of him. He was wearing a sort of middle-length threadbare padded coat with the cotton wadding coming out at the lapels and elbows. His face apparently hadn't been washed for days. You couldn't see the color of his skin except for the redness of his two cold ears which were red as an apple about to fall. Gray hair stuck out in all directions from under a small cap. Beads of ice hung from his eyebrows and short beard. He fumbled at a plank bench as soon as he came in, sat down, and just managed to gasp "Fix a pot of tea."

The teahouse was a gathering place for privately employed rickshaw men and a rickshaw puller like this old fellow would certainly never have come in on an ordinary day. They looked at him as if their recent remarks had gained a deeper and sharper meaning and no one had more to say. Ordinarily there would have been a few naive and silly young men there making fun of customers of his sort with sarcastic cracks, but not one of them made a sound this time.

Before the tea was ready the old man's head sank slowly down and down and down until he slid onto the floor.

They all jumped up at once saying "What happened! What happened!" and began pushing forward.

"Don't move!" The manager of the place knew what had happened

to the old man and held them all back. He loosened the old man's collar, lifted him up, and propped him up with a chair against his back
while supporting his shoulders. "Sugar water, quick!" Then he listened to the old man's throat and said to himself "He isn't choking on
phlegm."

No one moved but no one in that smoke-filled room sat down,
either. They all blinked and looked toward the old man near the door.
All seemed to have the same thought in mind: "There's our future!
When our hair is gray each one of us will make that one last deal—the
one where we'll fall and break our necks!"

The old man groaned twice just as the sugar water was put to his
lips. He raised his right hand, so black it glistened as if it had been lacquered, and wiped his mouth with the back of it without opening his
eyes.

"Have a little sugar water," the manager said in his ear.

"Ah?" The old man opened his eyes. When he saw that he was on
the floor he moved his legs, intending to stand up.

"Drink some water first. There's no hurry." The manager let go of
the old man's shoulder.

Almost everyone pressed forward to help.

The old man sighed and looked around. Holding the cup in both
hands, he drank the sugar water sip by sip. He drank it down and
looked at them again. "Ah, thank you all very much, gentlemen." He
spoke so softly and gently that it really did not seem possible the
words could have come from that mouth with its ragged mustache.
He tried to stand up once more when he had finished and three or four
men hurried over to help him. There was a trace of a smile on his face
and again he said very gently, "No, no, I can manage. There's no
problem! I was very cold, and hungry too, and I fainted. I'll be all
right." That trace of a smile told them they were looking at a face that
was clean and benevolent even though covered with dirt.

They all seemed to have been touched by the scene. The middle-
aged fellow with the cup of baigan had already finished it. His eyes
were bloodshot and a little teary. "Hey, bring two more ounces here!"

The old man had already sat down on a chair against the wall
when the baigan arrived. The man was a little drunk but he held the
cup before the old man's face with great ceremony.

"Be my guest, have a drink. I am forty and more and I won't de-
ceive you. This private work is only a way of making the best of a bad

ob. You may get by one year at a time but the legs know. I'll be the
ame as you in two or three years. Are you almost sixty?"

"Not quite. Fifty-five." The old man drank. "It's so cold and there
ren't any passengers. My belly was empty and when I got a few pen-
ies they all went for baigan to get a little warmer. I got this far and
ouldn't hold out so I thought I'd come in and warm up but the room
vas too hot inside and I hadn't had anything to eat so I fainted. It
loesn't amount to anything. Gentlemen, my brothers, thank you so
ery much!"

This time the old man's gray grasslike hair, the dirt on his face, his
harcoal-colored hands, and that torn cap and padded coat all
eemed to emit beams of pure light like the image of a god in a ruined
emple which, although damaged, was still dignified.

They all looked at him as if they were afraid he'd leave. Hsiang Tzu
ust stood there saying nothing the whole time. He suddenly ran out
vhen he heard the old man say his belly was empty and came flying
ack with his hands full of ten mutton-stuffed steamed buns wrapped
p in a huge cabbage leaf. He put them directly in front of the old
nan saying "Eat!" and then sat down again in his original place and
ut his head down as if utterly exhausted.

"Oh!" Looking both delighted and on the verge of tears, the old
nan nodded to them. "We are brothers, after all. When we haul a pas-
enger we sell him all our strength and then at the end of a trip when
ve want an extra penny for it he thinks it's outrageous!" He stood up
nd was about to go out.

"Eat!" Everyone spoke in almost the same breath.

"I'm going to call Hsiao Ma, my grandson. He's watching the rick-
haw outside."

"I'll go. You stay there," said the middle-aged man. "You won't
ose your rickshaw here. You don't have to worry about it. There's a
olice box just across the street." He opened the door a crack. "Hsiao
Ma! Hsiao Ma! Your grandfather wants you! Bring the rickshaw over
ere."

The old man patted the buns several times but didn't take one. As
oon as Hsiao Ma came in he picked one up. "Hsiao Ma, good boy, for
ou!"

Hsiao Ma was only about twelve or thirteen. His face was very thin
nd he was all bundled up. His nose was red with cold and two drib-
les of snot hung from it. His ears were covered by worn-out earmuffs.

He stood beside his grandfather; his right hand took a bun, his left hand took a bun, and without being told he bit into them alternately.

"Hey! Slow down!" The old man had one hand protectingly on his grandson's head and took a bun with the other. Slowly he took a bite. "Grandfather will eat two. That's plenty. The rest are for you. When we've eaten them all we'll quit work and take the rickshaw back home. Maybe it won't be so cold tomorrow and we can go out a little earlier. Right, Hsiao Ma?"

Hsiao Ma nodded to a bun and snuffled. "Grandfather must eat three. What's left is mine. I'll pull grandfather home in a few minutes."

"You don't have to!" The old man smiled with satisfaction at everyone. "In a moment we'll both walk back. Riding in a rickshaw is too cold."

The old man finished his share, drained the cup of baigan, and then waited for Hsiao Ma to finish eating. He pulled out a rag and wiped his mouth and nodded to them all again. "Son went for a soldier. He's gone and hasn't come back. His wife. . . ."

"Don't talk about it!" Hsiao Ma's cheeks were stuffed and looked like two peaches. He kept on eating while interrupting his grandfather.

"A little talk doesn't matter. We are all friends here." Then he said in a low voice, "Grandson is serious-minded, not to mention that he's very ambitious. The wife went off too. The two of us depend on our rickshaw. It's worn out but it's ours, so we keep what we get every day and don't worry about a rental fee. But the two of us are still very hard up no matter how much we earn. What else can we do?"

"Grandfather," Hsiao Ma had almost finished the buns, "we must get one more fare. We don't have any money for coal tomorrow morning because of you. If it had been up to me I would have made that trip to the Hou Gate just now but you wouldn't go! So there'll be no coal tomorrow morning and we'll see what you do about that!"

"There's a way. Grandfather can get five pounds of coal balls on credit."

"Will they let us have some kindling too?"

"Sure! Good boy, eat, eat up. We ought to get moving." With that, the old man stood up and nodded to each of them in turn. "Gentlemen, thank you all so very much!" He reached out for Hsiao Ma

Hsiao Ma stuffed the remains of the last bun into his mouth all at once.

Some of the men stayed in their seats and some went out with them. Hsiang Tzu was the first out the door. He wanted a look at that rickshaw.

It was a very dilapidated rickshaw. The lacquer was cracked and the shafts were so worn the grain of the wood showed. There was a battered carbide lamp and the ribs supporting the hood were tied together with rope.

Hsiao Ma pulled a match out from under his earmuff and struck it on the sole of his shoe. Cupping it in his small black hands he lit the lamp. The old man spit in the palms of his hands, sighed, and picked up the shafts. "See you tomorrow, brothers!"

Hsiang Tzu stood outside the doorway in a daze, staring at the old man, the young boy, and that worn-out rickshaw. The old man went right on talking while he pulled. His voice was sometimes high and sometimes low, just as the street was sometimes bright from the streetlights and sometimes in shadow. Hsiang Tzu watched and listened while feeling a new and unbearable emotion in his heart. It seemed to him that he saw his own past in the figure of Hsiao Ma and his future in the figure of the old man. He had never spent a single cent frivolously before and now he felt very happy because he'd bought ten steamed buns for them. He waited until he could no longer see them and then went back inside. They had all begun to talk and laugh again but he felt confused so he paid for his tea, went out again, and took the rickshaw to the movie theater to wait for Mr. Ts'ao.

It was really cold. A little gray sand floated in the air. The wind seemed to be rushing along up above and the stars couldn't be seen very clearly except for the big ones, which shivered in the sky. There was no wind at all there below, but cold air was coming up from the ground. The ruts already had long cracks in them made by the cold and the ground was grayish white, as shiny as ice and as hard.

Hsiang Tzu stood outside the movie theater awhile. He was cold already but didn't want to go back to the teahouse. He wanted to think quietly by himself. These two seemed to have shattered his fondest hope: the old man owned his own rickshaw! He had been determined to buy his own rickshaw from the first day he pulled one and he was still willing to run fast all day long on account of that ambition. As he saw it, he'd have everything once he had his own rickshaw. Phooey! Look at that old fellow!

And wasn't this reluctance of his to take Hu Niu due to his old hope of buying a rickshaw? Of buying a rickshaw and saving money and then getting himself a proper wife? Phooey! Look at Hsiao Ma! If he had a son, wouldn't he be like that? There didn't seem to be any real need to resist Hu Niu's demands once he thought about things that way. He couldn't escape, no matter what, and what kind of wife was undesirable anyway? Besides, she might bring a few rickshaws along, so why not enjoy a period of ready-made prosperity? There was no reason to look down on anyone now that he had seen through himself. Hu Niu was Hu Niu, so why bother to say anything more!

The movie ended. He got out the water can and quickly lit the lamp. He took off his padded coat which left him wearing a short jacket. He wanted to get home in one flying trip, to run and forget everything and it wouldn't matter if he fell and broke his neck, either!

CHAPTER ELEVEN

THINKING ABOUT Hsiao Ma and the old man made Hsiang Tzu want to throw away his hopes and enjoy each day for itself, period. What good did it do to grind his teeth at things he couldn't do anything about? It seemed obvious to him that the fate of the poor was like a date pit: pointed at both ends. If you avoid dying of starvation when young, good for you. But it was almost impossible to avoid dying of starvation when old. You can be a real man only during the period in between—when you are young and strong and not afraid of the hard grind to feed your hunger. You are an absolute idiot if you are afraid of enjoying yourself then when you should be happy. There won't be another inn once you've passed through this village! Such thoughts made him think even the business with Hu Niu wasn't all that depressing.

But then he'd look at his pot and change his mind. No, I can't do as I please. Forty dollars more and then I can buy a rickshaw. I can't waste my effort. I can't blindly waste the money piled up in that pot. It wasn't that easy to save! I just have to stay on the right path, there's no doubt about that. But what about Hu Niu? There still wasn't any answer. And he was still upset because of that detestable twenty-seventh.

When his distress got so bad he felt helpless, he'd hug the pot and mumble to it: have it however you like, this money is mine no matter what! No one can take it away! I have my money and I'm not afraid of anything. Make me desperate and I can run away. With money you can really move!

The bustle in the streets was increasing. Vendors of candied melon pieces, candy offerings for the Kitchen God and such, filled the streets and you could hear voices shouting "Rock candy here! Candy!" wherever you went.

Hsiang Tzu used to look forward to New Year's but now he wasn't interested. He was getting tenser and tenser as the confusion in the streets increased; that horrible twenty-seventh was right in front of him! His eyes were sunken and even the scar on his face was dark. The streets were so busy and the ground was so slippery that he had to be extremely careful when he pulled the rickshaw. His worries and the need to be constantly on the lookout attacked him doubly. He realized that he just didn't have the energy to cope with both; he'd think of this one and forget about that one. Often a sudden scare would make him itch all over like an infant in the summer with prickly heat.

The east wind brought along some little black clouds on the afternoon of the day of the offerings to the Kitchen God and the weather suddenly warmed up a little. By the time to hang lanterns the wind had dropped considerably and scattered snowflakes were falling. The sellers of candied melon were already worried about the warm air and now there was snow in addition. They promptly sprinkled chalk on the sugar, afraid that otherwise the pieces would stick together in a lump. The snowflakes changed to tiny ones before many large ones had fallen and they whitened the ground with a swishing sound.

The ceremonies for the Kitchen God began in the shops and houses after seven o'clock. The snowflakes were squeezed closely together in the midst of the gleam of incense and the flash of firecrackers and lent something dark and mysterious to all the furor. The people still on the streets looked alarmed and worried; pedestrians and rickshaw passengers were anxious to get home in time for the offerings but the ground was slick and wet and no one dared walk fast. The hawkers who sold the candy were anxious to get rid of their seasonal goods and shouted in unremitting frenzy and hearing it was strangely upsetting.

It was around nine o'clock and Hsiang Tzu was bringing Mr. Ts'ao home from the west side. They passed the busy market at the west single *p'ai lou* and turned east onto Ch'ang An street where the traffic gradually began to thin out. The smooth flat asphalted thoroughfare was covered with a layer of pure white and the glitter reflected from the streetlights dazzled the eyes. Now and then an automobile would come along, its headlights shooting out far ahead. The tiny snowflakes became golden glints in the beams from the headlights like the scattering of a million bits of golden sand. Soon they would reach the Hsin Hua Gate. The road here was broad to begin with and the addition of light snow made you feel broad of vision and exalted in spirit; and besides, everything seemed to be very solemn. The Ch'ang An Memorial Arch, the building on top of the Hsin Hua Gate, and the red wall of the southern end of the park, all wore peaked white mourning caps which went well with their vermilion columns and red walls. Beneath the lamplight they solemnly displayed the honor and dignity of the old capital. This time and this place made you feel as if no one lived in Peking and there was nothing there but jasper palaces and jade mansions with only a few old pine trees to receive the snow in silence.

Hsiang Tzu had no time to gaze at these beautiful vistas. He stared at the "jade road" directly ahead and thought only about getting home in a few more steps. That straight white cold and silent thoroughfare seemed to let his mind's eye see directly to the door of the house. But he couldn't speed up because even though the snow on the ground was not thick, it grabbed your feet and soon there was a thick layer stuck to the bottoms of your shoes which you'd kick off but another layer would stick itself on right away. The particles of snow were small but very heavy and they accumulated rapidly. He couldn't really run because they grabbed his feet and got in his eyes. The snow piled on him didn't melt easily either; a thin layer already covered the shoulders of his coat and while it didn't amount to much, the dampness of it disgruntled him. There were no shops along this route but the sound of firecrackers in the distance never stopped. Now and then a twice-exploding rocket would shoot into the dark sky. The sparks would scatter and fall and the darkness would look even darker; it was almost frightening. He heard the bang and saw the sparks and the darker dark in the sky and wanted to get home right away, but he did not dare speed up. It was annoying!

What made him even more unhappy was that beginning on the west side he had become aware of a bicycle following them. When he got to Ch'ang An street there was less noise and he was even more conscious of being followed. The bicycle wheels crunched on the snow and although the sound was not loud he was still aware of it.

Hsiang Tzu, and other rickshaw pullers were the same, found bicycles extremely obnoxious. Cars were hateful but they made a lot of noise and you could avoid them well ahead of time. Bicyclists would squeeze through every opening they saw, wandering eastwards and wobbling westwards, and watching out for them made you dizzy. Furthermore, never tangle with them. If anything goes wrong the rickshaw puller is always to blame. No matter what, the police figure the rickshaw pullers are easier to handle than the riders of bicycles, so they always go after the rickshaw man first.

Hsiang Tzu thought more than once of skidding to a stop to make that fool behind him crash, but he didn't dare because rickshaw pullers have to hold their tempers at all times. He had to shout "Stopping!" every time he knocked the snow off his shoes.

They had come to the gate at the south end of the park; the road was very wide there and that bicycle was still close behind. Hsiang Tzu got even angrier. He deliberately stopped and shook the snow off his shoulders. He stood still and the bicycle went on past. The man on the bicycle even turned around to look. Hsiang Tzu deliberately waited, delaying until the bicycle was far off, then picked up the shafts, cursing.

Mr. Ts'ao's humanitarianism made him unwilling to have the windbreak put up to keep the wind off. He didn't even allow the top to be put up unless it was pouring with rain, in order to make the rickshaw man's work easier. He didn't think this trifling snowfall made it necessary to put the top up and besides, he loved to look at the winter scenery at night. He, too, had noticed this bicycle. He waited until Hsiang Tzu had finished swearing and said softly, "If he continues to follow, don't stop when we get to the house. Go right on to Mr. Tso's house. Now don't get flustered."

Hsiang Tzu was already a little flustered. He knew about the obnoxiousness of bicyclists but not that there was something about them to fear. This bicyclist must have a lot of history behind him since Mr. Ts'ao didn't even dare go home. Hsiang Tzu went a short distance and caught up with the bicyclist again; he had waited for them intentionally. He let them pass and then Hsiang Tzu got a good look at him. He understood in a glance; the man was a police spy. He had often seen these men in teahouses and while he had never spoken to them, he knew their manner and how they dressed. This one wore the usual long black gown and a felt hat pulled down low.

Hsiang Tzu seized the opportunity to look back when he turned the corner into Nan Ch'ang street; the man was still following them. He seemed to forget about the snow on the ground and put more effort into his stride. They were in a long straight bright white street with its cold lights and with a detective pursuing them! Hsiang Tzu had never had such an experience and he broke out in a sweat. He looked back again when they passed the back gate of Sun Yat-sen Park; the man was still there. He didn't dare stop when they got to the house but he really didn't want to keep going. Mr. Ts'ao made not a sound so all he could do was keep heading north. He ran straight to the north end of the street; the bicycle was still following. He went down a little side street; still there! He came out of the side street; still following. He was heading for Mr. Tso's house and shouldn't have gone down that street. He woke up when he was almost at the northern end of it and realized he was mixed up which made him angrier.

He ran to the back of Coal Hill and the bicycle kept going on north to the Hou Gate. Hsiang Tzu wiped off his sweat. There was less snow falling now but large flakes were coming down among the small ones. Hsiang Tzu almost loved the way those snowflakes flew and danced in the air everywhere. They didn't make people uncomfortable the way the tiny flakes did. He turned around and asked, "Where to, sir?"

"Still to the Tso's house. If anyone asks you about me, say you don't know who I am."

"Yes sir." Hsiang Tzu's heart began to thump but it wouldn't do to ask questions.

When they arrived at the house, Mr. Ts'ao told Hsiang Tzu to bring the rickshaw inside and shut the gate tightly. Mr. Ts'ao was still very composed but his face was pale. He went inside after giving Hsiang Tzu his orders. Hsiang Tzu had just got the rickshaw parked inside the gateway when Mr. Ts'ao came back with Mr. Tso. Hsiang Tzu recognized him and knew he was a good friend of Mr. Ts'ao's.

"Hsiang Tzu," Mr. Ts'ao spoke rapidly, "you take a taxi back. Tell Madam I am here. Tell them to come here too. Come in a cab, but call another one. Don't ask the one you take to wait. Understand? Good. Tell Madam to bring what we'll need and the two scroll paintings hanging in the library. Did you get that? I am about to telephone Madam. I'm telling you, too, because I'm afraid she might be upset and forget what I tell her, so you remind her."

"Shall I go?" asked Mr. Tso.

"There's no need. That man might not have been a detective but that other business is on my mind and I must take precautions. You go call a cab, all right?"

Mr. Tso went to the telephone to call a cab. Mr. Ts'ao gave Hsiang Tzu another order. "When the cab comes I'll pay him. Tell Madam to pack quickly, never mind anything else. Just be sure to bring the boy's things and those hanging scrolls in the library, those hanging scrolls.

Wait until Madam is all packed and then tell Kao Ma to call a cab. Do you understand all that? Lock the front gate after they've gone and sleep in the library. The telephone is in there. Do you know how to telephone?"

"I can't call but I can answer it." In fact, Hsiang Tzu didn't even like answering the telephone but he didn't want to make Mr. Ts'ao worried so that was the best answer to give.

"That's good enough," answered Mr. Ts'ao and then he continued, still speaking very fast. "Perhaps there'll be a disturbance but don't you open the gate! They certainly won't let you go with all of us gone and you there alone. If it looks like trouble you put out the light, go to the rear courtyard, and jump over the wall into the Wang's courtyard. Do you know their servants? Right. Hide out there for a while and then leave. Never mind watching out for our things or your things. Just get out and over the wall and avoid getting caught. I'll make it up to you if you lose anything. Here's five dollars for now. All right, I'll go call Madam. You tell her all of it again when you get there. And don't say anything about arresting anyone. Maybe that bicyclist just now was a detective and maybe he wasn't. And don't you get panicky either!"

Hsiang Tzu was completely bewildered. He had lots of questions he wanted to ask but he was so worried about remembering Mr. Ts'ao's orders that he didn't ask any of them.

The cab came. Hsiang Tzu sat inside it with a numb brain. The snow was still falling and things outside couldn't be seen very well. He stiffened his spine and sat bolt upright. His head almost hit the roof. He had to think things over but all he could do was stare at the red arrow on the radiator cap up front; the red made it so delightful. Those little brushlike things hanging down in front of the driver outside that moved back and forth by themselves to clean the glass were rather interesting too. He was getting tired of watching them when they arrived at the house. He got out without any enthusiasm.

He was just about to press the doorbell when someone who seemed to have come right out of the wall grabbed his wrist. Hsiang Tzu's instinctive reaction was to yank his hand away but he had already recognized the fellow and did not move. It was that bicyclist, the detective.

"Hsiang Tzu, don't you recognize me?" Grinning, the detective let go of his wrist.

Hsiang Tzu gulped and didn't know what to say.

"You remember the time we took you to the Western Hills? I am Lieutenant Sun. Remember?"

"Ah. Lieutenant Sun." Hsiang Tzu couldn't think. He had paid no attention to who was Lieutenant and who was Captain when those soldiers had dragged him off to the Western Hills.

"If you don't remember me, I still remember you. That scar on your face is a fine identification mark. I've been following you around for some time. I couldn't be sure it was you at first but I couldn't be mistaken about that scar after a good look!"

"You want something?" Hsiang Tzu wanted to press the doorbell.

"Of course there's something, and it's important besides! We'll go inside to discuss it, all right?" Lieutenant Sun, a detective now, pressed the doorbell.

"I'm busy!" Hsiang Tzu's forehead suddenly broke out in a sweat and he said to himself fiercely, I can't slip away from him but how can I ask him in!

"You needn't get so upset. I've come to do you a favor!" The detective wore a little smile of cunning. When Kao Ma opened the door he stepped right up and said, "Thank you very much, thank you very much!" He pulled Hsiang Tzu in behind him before he could speak to Kao Ma and pointed to the gatekeeper's room. "You stay here?" He entered and looked around. "This little room is remarkably clean. Your job mustn't be so bad!"

"You want something? I'm busy!" Hsiang Tzu couldn't bear any more chit-chat.

"Didn't I tell you? My business is important." Detective Sun was still smiling but his tone was stern. "So I'll tell you right out. The man Ts'ao is a revolutionary. He'll be shot as soon as he's caught. He can't get away! I figure we already have an acquaintanceship. After all, you served me in the camp and we are both street people besides. I took a big risk in coming here to warn you. But if you wait to leave, you'll find the nest here has been blocked up for cleaning out and no one will get away! We have to sell our strength to eat so why should we get mixed up in their troubles with the law? Right?"

"How could I face them?" Hsiang Tzu was still thinking of the orders Mr. Ts'ao had given him.

"Who do you have to apologize to?" The corners of Detective Sun's lips turned up in a smile and his eyes squinted. "They brought this calamity on themselves. So what do you have to apologize to them for? Since they were bold enough to do it let them take responsibility for the consequences. It's just not right for us to take the rap along with them. Not to mention anything else, say you are cooped up for three months in a dark cell. Could you stand it with those wild bird habits of yours? And what's more, if they go to jail, they've got the money for bribes. They won't suffer. And you, little brother, haven't a thing. They'll tie you to the piss bucket for sure. Of course, this whole business doesn't really amount to much and they'll only have to put up with a few years in jail once they spend the money to put influence to work. But you haven't got the dough to fix the judge. It'll be a miracle if you aren't the fall guy. Simple guys like you and me who never do anything wrong always end up in front of a firing squad at T'ien Ch'iao. Is there anything fair about that? You are a man who knows what's what and a man like that doesn't lose out because he doesn't see what's right in front of his nose. What's all this talk about giving anyone respect? Ha! Let me tell you something, brother. There's no one on earth that has any respect for poor saps like us!"

Hsiang Tzu was frightened. He remembered the awful time when he'd been captured by the soldiers. He could imagine what it would be like to be in jail. "So I have to get out and forget about them?"

"If you take care of them, who'll take care of you?"

There was nothing Hsiang Tzu could say in reply. He was silent for a while until even his conscience nodded his head. "All right. I'll scram."

"You think you can leave just like that?" Detective Sun laughed coldly.

Hsiang Tzu was even more confused.

"Hsiang Tzu, my good fellow, you are so thickheaded! I'm a detective. How could I let you go?"

"What. . . ."Hsiang Tzu was so upset he didn't know what to do.

"Don't pretend to be so dumb!" Detective Sun's eyes pinned Hsiang Tzu down. "I'll bet you have a nest egg, so get it out and buy your life. I don't earn as much as you do every month. I have to eat, buy clothes, and support a family. I depend on getting a little on the side. That's why I'm speaking to you privately. Think about it. Can I just let you go with a wave of my hand? Friendship is friendship and would I have come to tell you all this if we weren't friends? But business is business and I have to get something out of this affair. Otherwise my family would have to eat air, wouldn't it? Men of the world don't need to waste words. You'd better come clean."

"How much?" Hsiang Tzu sat on his bed.

"As much as you have. There's no standard price."

"I'll go wait it out in jail, that's all."

"Can this be you I hear? Mightn't you regret it?" Detective Sun's hand went inside his coat. "Take a look, Hsiang Tzu. I could haul you in right now. If you resist arrest I get out my gun. So if you don't want to talk money and I take you in right now, even your clothes will be stripped off you when you get to jail. You know what's what, don't you? You can figure it out for yourself."

"You have the time to put the bite on me. How come you don't squeeze Mr. Ts'ao?" Hsiang Tzu was choked with rage and it took him a long time to say anything.

"Now he's a real crook. There's a nice little reward when I catch him but I'd have to take the blame if I let him get away. But as for you, my idiotic little brother, letting you go is like farting and killing you is like squashing a bedbug. Hand over the money and you go on your way. Don't hand it over, okay, it's T'ien Ch'iao for you! Don't go making a big thing out of it. After all, you're such a big man! And besides, I can't keep all the money for myself. My colleagues get a little. I don't know how much will be left for me after it's divvied up. But there's nothing I can do for you if you can't manage to buy your life so cheaply. How much money do you have?"

Hsiang Tzu stood up. His brains were bursting and his fists were raised.

"Move a hand and that's the end of you. I'm warning you. I have friends outside who'll help. Hurry up, get the money. Here I respect face and you don't even know what's good for you!" Detective Sun's eyes were extremely ugly.

"What did I ever do to anyone?" Hsiang Tzu sobbed and sat down on the bed again.

"You never did anything to anyone but you are right on the spot. People are lucky only in the womb and we are the ones who were born at the bottom. There's nothing more to say." Detective Sun shook his head as if he were infinitely sad. "All right. So you think I'm doing you wrong, so what. Just quit dragging things out."

Hsiang Tzu tried thinking again but there was nothing he could do. He took the pot out from under his quilt with shaking hands.

"I'll look!" Detective Sun smiled, took the pot, and smashed it against the wall. Hsiang Tzu watched the money scatter on the floor and his heart was torn apart. "Is that all there is?"

Hsiang Tzu was silent. He could only shudder.

"Good enough. I don't drive people to their deaths. A friend is a friend. But you'd better realize that buying your life with so little is a real bargain!"

Hsiang Tzu was still silent. Shuddering, he wanted to wrap up in the quilt.

"Don't touch that!"

"It's so cold." Hsiang Tzu's eyes glared.

"If I tell you don't touch it, don't touch it! Beat it!"

Hsiang Tzu swallowed his anger, chewed his lip, pushed open the door, and went out.

The snow was already over an inch thick. Hsiang Tzu walked with his head down. A pure whiteness was everywhere except where he left his black footprints behind.

CHAPTER TWELVE

HSIANG TZU decided to look for a place to sit down and straighten things out in his head. Why should he be afraid if he cried afterwards? At least he'd know what his crying meant. His situation had changed so fast his wits couldn't catch up. Only there was snow every place he went and nowhere he could sit. It was after ten o'clock and all the teahouses were shut, but he wouldn't have wanted to go to one even if they had still been open. He wanted a quiet place for he knew that the tears waiting in his eyes could fall there.

There was no place to sit. All he could do was walk slowly, but where? This silver-white world had no place for him to sit down, no place for him to go. In all this white world only hungry birds and cast-out wanderers knew what a sad sigh was.

Where could he go? That made a problem all right. There was no need to think of anything else. Go to a cheap inn? No good. He could count on "losing" something during the night because of the good clothes he was wearing, not to mention the horrible fleas in those inns. Go to a better inn? He couldn't do that either. He only had five dollars and besides, that was his entire capital. Go to a bathhouse? They closed at midnight and you couldn't spend the night there. There was no place to go.

Not having any place to go made him realize just how badly off he was. He'd worked in the city for all these years and all he had now was his clothes and five dollars. Even his bedroll was gone! Then he thought of tomorrow. What would he do tomorrow? Go pull a rickshaw, keep on pulling a rickshaw. Nuts to that! All he'd got out of pulling a rickshaw was that someone had stolen his money and he couldn't find a place to stay.

Be a street vendor? All he had for capital was five dollars. And besides, the carrying pole had to be bought beforehand. And what kind of goods brought in enough to live on anyway? Pull a rickshaw and you could make thirty or forty cents easy but you needed capital to be a street vendor and there was no guarantee you'd be able to clear enough to pay for three meals. Wait until he'd eaten up his capital and then go pull a rickshaw? But wasn't that the same as pulling down your pants to fart and a waste of five dollars? He couldn't piddle this five dollars away in pennies and dimes—it was his very last hope!

Go work as a house servant? Not his line of work at all. He didn't know how to be a servant. Wash clothes, cook, he didn't know how! Nothing was any good; he couldn't do anything. He was only a big dumb black thick hunk of junk.

He had gone as far as the Middle Lake without realizing it. When he got to the top of the bridge and looked around, snow was all he could see everywhere he looked. It now occurred to him that it was still snowing. He rubbed his head. His woolen knit cap was already quite damp. There was no one on the bridge; even the policeman had gone off somewhere. The snow beating at the streetlights made them look like they were constantly blinking. Hsiang Tzu looked at the snow surrounding him and felt lost.

He stood on the bridge for some time. It was as if the world had already died; there was not a sound and nothing to disturb the silence. Apparently the gray-white snowflakes had seized their opportunity and were falling vigorously, as they chaotically, silently, and quickly tried to bury the world before anyone, man or ghost, realized it. In his silent isolation Hsiang Tzu heard the tiny voice of his own conscience. He must not think of himself first. He must find out what had happened. Mrs. Ts'ao and Kao Ma had been left there without a man! Was there any question that the five dollars had been given him by Mr. Ts'ao? He dared not speculate any longer. He lifted his feet and walked back very quickly.

There were footprints in front of the doorway and new tire tracks on the street. Could Mrs. Ts'ao possibly have left already? Why hadn't that fellow Sun arrested her?

He didn't dare push at the door; he was afraid someone would grab him again. He looked around and saw no one. His heart began to thump. Try taking a look. There's no other house to go to. Anyway, if someone arrests me, then I'm arrested. He pushed gently at the front door and it opened. He took two steps in, staying close to the wall, and saw the light on in his room. In his own room! He felt like crying. He crept up to the window to listen and heard a cough. It was Kao Ma's voice. He opened the door.

"Who? Oh, you! Scared me to death!" Kao Ma patted her heart to calm herself and sat on the bed. "Hsiang Tzu, what's going on here?"

Hsiang Tzu couldn't answer. He felt like he hadn't seen her for years and years and his mind was blocked up by a wall of heat.

"What's it all about?" Kao Ma asked. She felt like crying too. "Here you two weren't back home yet and then the Master telephones and tells us to go to Tso's and says you are coming right away. You come and wasn't I the one who opened the door for you? I look and you have a strange man with you. So I don't say a word and hurry off to help Madam get the things together. So there we are with no lights on which makes Madam and me snatch blindly. Young Master is already sleeping sweetly so we have to get him out of his warm bed first. We get him all wrapped up and then go get the hanging scrolls in the library and there's never a glimpse of you so what were you doing anyway? I'm asking you! So we got the things together any old way and I go look for you. Well, there's not even your shadow! Madam is very angry, partly it was from worry, and trembling. So all I can do is call a cab but we don't dare trick anyone by trying the 'Empty City ruse' and all of us leave and hope no one realizes that the house is empty. All right, I promise Madam. I say, 'Madam, you go and I'll watch the house. I'll hurry straight to the Tso's right away as soon as Hsiang Tzu comes back. And if he doesn't come back, I'll just accept what comes.' So what's it all about? What have you been up to? Tell me!"

Hsiang Tzu had nothing to say.

"Speak up! Do you think silence will do any good? What's going on?"

"You go!" Hsiang Tzu managed two words. "Go!"

"You'll watch the house?" Kao Ma calmed down a little.

"You just tell the Master when you see him that a detective arrested me except, except, he didn't arrest me."

"What sort of a story is that?" Kao Ma almost laughed, she was so exasperated.

"Now you listen!" Hsiang Tzu got angry. "Tell Master to get away quick. The detective said he really was going to arrest Master. The

Tso house isn't a safe place for them either. They have to get away quick! I'll jump over the back wall into the Wang's yard when you leave and spend the night there. I'll lock the door. Tomorrow I'll go look for a job. I apologize to Mr. Ts'ao.''

"The more you talk the more mixed up I get." Kao Ma sighed. "All right, I'll go. Young Master may be getting cold and I'd better hurry up and tend to him. When I see Master I'll just say Hsiang Tzu said to tell Master to get away quickly. Hsiang Tzu will lock the gate tonight, go over the wall, and sleep at the Wang's. Tomorrow he'll go look for a job. Is that right?''

Utterly mortified, Hsiang Tzu nodded.

Hsiang Tzu locked the door and went back to his room after Kao Ma left. The broken pot still lay in pieces on the floor. He picked up a piece, looked at it, and threw it down again. His bedroll hadn't been touched at all. It was very strange. Just what did it all mean? Could it be that Sun was not a real detective? Impossible! If Mr. Ts'ao hadn't seen danger, why else would he have decided to drop everything and run? "I don't understand! I don't understand!''

He sat on the edge of the bed without realizing it. As soon as he sat down he jumped up again, as if startled. "I can't hang around here! What if Sun comes back again?" His mind spun around. "I haven't done right by Mr. Ts'ao but Kao Ma is taking a message back telling him to get away quick so I can face myself, at least." When it came to his conscience, he had never intended to cheat anyone at all. And besides, he was the one who had been wronged. His own money was the first to go and there was no way he could take care of Mr. Ts'ao's things now.

He mumbled along to himself while he made up his bedroll. Then he hoisted it onto his shoulder, put out the lamp, and hurried to the rear courtyard. Putting the bedroll down, he held onto the top of the wall and called softly, "Old Ch'eng! Old Ch'eng!" Old Ch'eng was the Wang's rickshaw puller.

No one answered. Hsiang Tzu made up his mind. He'd jump over first, then discuss it. He threw the bedroll over and it fell onto the snow without a sound. His heart jumped. Carefully, he climbed over the wall and jumped down. He got his bedroll out of the snow and quietly went to look for Old Ch'eng. He knew where his room was.

Everyone seemed to be asleep for there wasn't a single sound in the whole place. Hsiang Tzu suddenly felt that it wasn't very difficult to

be a thief at all. He got a little bolder and walked with his feet really
striking the ground. The snow was very firm and made only a little
noise. When he found Old Ch'eng's room, he coughed.

Apparently Old Ch'eng had just gone to bed. "Who is it?"

"Me! Hsiang Tzu! Open the door!" Hsiang Tzu spoke very naturally and warmly, as though hearing Old Ch'eng's voice was like hearing
the comforting words of a loved one.

Old Ch'eng turned on the light, put an old fur-lined coat over his
shoulders, and opened the door. "What is it? Hsiang Tzu, it's after
midnight!"

Hsiang Tzu went in, put his bedroll on the floor, and sat down on it
firmly, still without a word.

Old Ch'eng was more than thirty years old and had pimples all
over him that were so hard they had corners. He and Hsiang Tzu
didn't have much to do with one another ordinarily but they always
nodded and spoke when they met. Sometimes Mrs. Wang and Mrs.
Ts'ao would go out shopping together and the two of them would
have a chance to rest and have some tea together. Hsiang Tzu did not
have a high regard for Old Ch'eng. He ran very fast but in a nervous
hurry and his hands never seemed to have a good firm grip on the
hafts. Even though Old Ch'eng was just fine as a person, he still had
this one failing and Hsiang Tzu certainly could not give him his entire
respect.

Now Hsiang Tzu found Old Ch'eng entirely likable. He sat there
not saying anything and feeling grateful and friendly at heart. A short
while ago he was standing on a bridge at Middle Lake and now he
was sitting with a friend inside a room. The rapidity of the change
emptied his heart and yet it pulsed with warmth at the same time.

Old Ch'eng burrowed under his covers. Pointing to the old coat, he
said, "Hsiang Tzu, have a smoke. There're some in the pocket."

Hsiang Tzu was not a smoker but this time he couldn't refuse. He
took a cigarette, stuck it between his lips, and let it hang there.

"What is it?" asked Old Ch'eng. "Quit?"

"No." Hsiang Tzu sat on the bedroll as before. "Trouble! All the
Ts'aos ran away and I don't dare stay to watch the house."

"What trouble?" Old Ch'eng sat up again.

"Can't say for sure. Anyway, it's big trouble. Even Kao Ma left."

"And all the doors are open and no one is in charge?"

"I locked up properly."

"Hmm." Old Ch'eng pondered for a while. "I'll go tell Mr. Wang, all right?" He put his coat over his shoulders.

"Let's talk about it tomorrow. I simply can't explain it clearly." Hsiang Tzu was afraid Mr. Wang would question him.

This is the trouble Hsiang Tzu couldn't explain clearly.

Mr. Ts'ao was paid to teach by the hour at the university. There was a student there named Yuan Ming who, hitherto, had had nothing against Mr. Ts'ao and had often come to chat with him. Since Mr. Ts'ao was a Socialist and Yuan Ming's ideas were even more radical, the two of them had a lot to talk about. Differences in age and social position, however, caused them to have several little differences of opinion.

Mr. Ts'ao thought that a teacher ought to put his heart into teaching and the students ought to put their hearts into attending to their lessons. A teacher must not be lax about grades because of his personal feelings.

As Yuan Ming saw it, an ambitious youth in this shattered and chaotic world ought to do something to aid the revolution. It was irrelevant for the time being whether lessons were well or poorly prepared. He continued to see Mr. Ts'ao. First, because they still had this and that to discuss; second, he hoped this personal relationship would get him high enough grades to pass no matter how low his examination scores were. After all, haven't the heroes in times of anarchy and disorder frequently been scoundrels? There are quite a few excusable examples of this type in history.

When examination time came Mr. Ts'ao did not give Yuan Ming a passing grade. Yuan Ming's other final grades were quite low enough to flunk him out even if Mr. Ts'ao had passed him, but he hated Mr. Ts'ao in particular. In his opinion, Mr. Ts'ao did not understand face at all; and in China, face and revolution are of equal value. Yuan Ming viewed learning with contempt because he was anxious to accomplish something, and he gradually became accustomed to sloth because he viewed learning with contempt. He saw no need for gaining the respect and loving protection of others—no matter what was said about him, his thoughts were progressive! Since Mr. Ts'ao had not given him a passing grade, obviously he did not understand a youth with ambition. Well, then, they hadn't been that intimate after all! Since they had been on good terms ordinarily, making things in-

olerable for a fellow at exam time convinced him that Mr. Ts'ao was
ly and crafty.

Since grades are unalterable and there was no way to avoid flunk-
ng out, he decided to take his anger out on Mr. Ts'ao. Now that he'd
ost his place in school he'd just drag a teacher along with him for
ompany. And so, he not only had something to do, he could show off
iis fierceness too. Yuan Ming was not a good man to provoke! More-
over, if he could beat his way into a new group by means of this affair,
hat would certainly be a lot better than having nothing to do.

He took what Mr. Ts'ao had said in lectures and private discussions
about government and society, rearranged it a little, and went to lay
an accusation against him at Kuo Min Tang headquarters. He
laimed that Mr. Ts'ao was spreading seditious thoughts among
outh.

Mr. Ts'ao had ears, of course, but he thought it was all very com-
cal. He knew how shallow his socialism was. He also knew how his
ove for traditional culture and art prevented him from doing any-
hing excessive. It was absurd to find himself called a leader of the
Communist revolution; it was so contrary to what anyone might have
xpected. It was ridiculous, and so he didn't give it much thought,
ven though his students and colleagues told him to be careful. Your
peaceful ways cannot protect you in times of chaos.

Winter vacation was a good time to tranquilize the schools. Detec-
ives got very busy investigating and arresting. Mr. Ts'ao had been
aware of somebody following him on quite a number of occasions.
The shadow of someone behind him made him exchange his amused
miles for a more sober expression. He thought he'd better reconsider
iis position. Here was a good opportunity to make a reputation and it
vas a lot less troublesome to go to jail for a few days than throw a
pomb. It was just as reliable and had the same publicity value. In-
leed, going to jail was one qualification for being an important man.
3ut that wasn't for him. He could not resort to fakery to make a false
eputation for himself. He would, if he listened to his conscience, hate
aimself for not being a real warrior, for if he followed his conscience
ie would not want to be an imitation soldier. He went to find Mr. Tso.

Mr. Tso had a plan. "When the moment strikes move to my house.
They won't go so far as to check up on me!" Mr. Tso knew the right
people and the right people are much stronger than the law. "You

come and hide out here for a while. Let them assume we are afraid of them. Then you can get things cleared up later, and you'll probably have to spend some money too. Spend enough for everyone's face and once you get the money into the right hands, you can go home again and there'll be no more trouble."

Detective Sun knew that Mr. Ts'ao went to the Tso house often. He also knew that when the pursuit got hot he'd certainly run there for cover. "They" didn't dare offend Mr. Tso, but if they could intimidate Mr. Ts'ao they'd do it. They'd have some hopes of cashing in and getting lots of prestige too, once they had forced him to run to Tso's house. Obviously, picking on Hsiang Tzu had not been part of their plan but once Sun had spotted him as a sitting duck, why not pluck a few more dollars at the same time?

Right. Hsiang Tzu was caught on the spot and it served him right! Everyone else had a way. Everyone else had an out somewhere. Hsiang Tzu was the only one who couldn't get away because he was a rickshaw puller. Bran is what a rickshaw puller gets to eat and blood is what bursts out of him. He puts forth the greatest effort and gets the least reward. He has to take the lowest place among men and wait for the blows from every person, every law, and every hardship.

He'd smoked his cigarette and still hadn't figured out any reason for it all. He was like a chicken in the hands of a cook. If he breathed slowly everything would be all right. He had no other plan. He wanted desperately to talk to Old Ch'eng but there was nothing he could say. He didn't know enough words to express his innermost thoughts. He had experienced every hardship yet his mouth did not open. He was like a deaf mute. He'd bought a rickshaw and lost a rickshaw. Saved his money and the money was gone. He had worked as hard as he could only to benefit others who came along and took it all away. He'd never had the nerve to provoke anyone. He even avoided the dogs that ran loose. And in the end others still robbed him and he couldn't even spit out his rage!

But it was pointless now to think about the events of the past. What about tomorrow? He couldn't go back to the Ts'ao house so where could he go? "Is it all right if I sleep here tonight?" he asked. He was like a feral dog who'd found a corner out of the wind to hide in and had to make the best of it for the time being. But he'd better make sure even in such a simple matter. He'd better find out whether he was inconveniencing anyone or not.

"Well, you're here. It's cold out and there's snow on the ground so where else could you go? Is the floor okay? You can squeeze in up here, too."

Hsiang Tzu didn't want to squeeze in. The floor was fine by him.

Old Ch'eng went to sleep. Hsiang Tzu kept turning over and over and couldn't get to sleep. The cold air on the floor soon made the quilts as icy as a slab of iron so he tried curling up and then his legs got cramped. The cold wind coming in around the door stabbed at his head like a bunch of little needles. He shut his eyes hard, covered up his head, and still couldn't sleep. Listening to Old Ch'eng breathing irritated him and he longed to get up and hit him; he'd feel happier then. It got colder and colder. The cold made his throat feel itchy and he was afraid he'd wake up Old Ch'eng if he coughed.

Since he couldn't sleep, he thought about going back to the Ts'ao place for a look around. Why not go get a few things if the crisis had blown over and no one was there? Someone had stolen the money he'd had such a hard time saving and all because of a Ts'ao family problem, so why shouldn't he go steal something? He'd lost his money because of them. Wasn't it fair to get it back from them? When he thought of that his eyes lit up and in a moment he had forgotten all about the cold. Go to it! The money hadn't been all that easy to get and now it was gone but it was a snap to get it back. Go get it!

He was already sitting up. Then frantically he lay down again, as if Old Ch'eng were looking at him. His heart jumped. No. No, it was impossible to be a thief. Impossible! He was already humiliated because he had not carried out Mr. Ts'ao's orders while trying to avoid being arrested. So how could he turn around and rob him? He just could not do it! He'd die of poverty before he'd steal!

But how would anyone know that others hadn't gotten in and robbed the place? If that fellow Sun took some things who would know the difference? He sat up again. A dog howled somewhere in the distance. He lay down again. He still couldn't go. If someone else wanted to steal, let him. His own conscience was clear. He was so poor now he just couldn't afford the least misstep!

Besides, Kao Ma knew he'd gone to the Wang's. If something went missing during the night, it was him. It must be him. If it wasn't him it still was him! He not only hadn't the nerve to go steal something, now he was afraid someone else would get in. If something did disappear tonight, even jumping into the Yellow River wouldn't make him clean! He wasn't cold. On the contrary, he felt sweat on the palm of his hand. What to do? Go back over the wall and look around? He hadn't the nerve. He had given money in exchange for his life; he couldn't throw himself into the net again. If he didn't go, what if something disappeared?

He couldn't decide. He sat up again cross-legged with his head bent down and almost touching his knees. His head was heavy, his eyes wanted to close, yet he dared not sleep. The night was long, but it wasn't the time for Hsiang Tzu to shut his eyes.

Sitting for he didn't know how long, he changed his mind countless times; and then an idea came to him. He reached out and poked Old Ch'eng. "Old Ch'eng, Old Ch'eng, wake up!"

"What?" Old Ch'eng didn't want to open his eyes. "Piss? There's a chamber pot under the bed."

"Wake up. Turn on the light."

"Is there a thief or what?" Befuddled, Old Ch'eng sat up.

"Wake up. Are you wide awake?"

"Um!"

"Old Ch'eng, look here! This is my bedroll, these are my clothes, this is the five dollar bill Mr. Ts'ao gave me. There's nothing else, is there?"

"Nothing. So what?" Old Ch'eng sneezed.

"Are you awake? All I have is just these things. I haven't taken one leaf of grass from the Ts'ao family, right?"

"Nothing. We brothers have earned our living from households for a long time. Can we let anything stick to our hands? What we can do, we do. What we can't do, we don't do. We can't take things from others. Is that what this is all about?"

"Did you see everything?"

Old Ch'eng smiled. "Of course! Say, aren't you cold?"

"I'm all right."

CHAPTER THIRTEEN

THE SKY seemed to brighten a little earlier due to the reflection from the snow. The end of the year was at hand and since many households had bought poultry to fatten up, the racket made by chickens was ten times greater than usual. Cocks were crowing everywhere. The prospect was one of an abundant harvest thanks to the seasonable snow. But Hsiang Tzu hadn't slept well that night. He had endured several naps during the latter part of the night in a sort of daze that was like being asleep but not sleeping, or like floating on water and suddenly rising and falling. There was no peace in his heart. The more he slept the colder he got. By the time he heard chickens cackling and crowing outside, he really couldn't stand it any longer. He didn't want to alarm Old Ch'eng so he pulled in his legs and used a corner of the quilt to muffle his coughs but he still didn't dare get up. Enduring it and waiting made him very nervous. It wasn't easy to wait for daylight. He sat up when he heard the sound of cart wheels and the shouts of drivers in the street. It was cold sitting, too. He got up, buttoned up, and opened the door a crack to peek out. The snow wasn't really very deep. It had probably stopped falling around midnight. The sky seemed to have cleared but he couldn't see very well in the gray dampness; even the snow seemed to have a layer of thin gray on it. He saw in a glance the big footprints he'd left behind him the night before. Although they had been covered by snow, the hollows were still clearly visible.

In order to have something to do and also to get rid of those tracks, he got a broom out of a corner of the room and went to sweep the snow. The snow was heavy and hard to sweep but he couldn't find a larger bamboo broom at the time. He bent way over and pushed strongly. When the top layer was swept away some snow was still left sticking to the ground. It looked like the earth's skin had been snatched away. He had the whole courtyard swept up and all the snow piled under two small willow trees after he'd straightened his back twice. He was a little sweaty, warmer, and more relaxed. He stamped his feet and blew out a long breath, very long and very white.

He went back in and put the broom where he'd found it. He thought he'd roll up his bedroll. Old Ch'eng woke up, yawned, and before he shut his mouth asked, "Is it late?" His words were slurred. He rubbed his eyes and groped in the pocket of his old fur-lined coat for a cigarette. After two puffs he was awake and alert. "Hsiang Tzu, don't go right away. Wait until I get a little boiling water and we'll have a pot of tea. You had a lot to put up with last night."

"Should I go get it?" Hsiang Tzu offered a courtesy too. But as soon as he spoke he thought of the horrors of the night before and suddenly a formless lump blocked his thoughts.

"No, I'll go. I invited you, after all." Old Ch'eng pulled on his clothes and didn't bother to button them. He threw his old coat on over his shoulders and ran out, cigarette dangling. "Hey! The court-yard is all swept! You're a good one! I'll treat you!"

Hsiang Tzu felt a little better.

Old Ch'eng came back after a while carrying two bowls of sweet congee and lots of fried cakes and oil cakes. "I haven't made the tea yet. Have some congee first. Here, eat up. If it isn't enough I'll go buy more. We'll get credit if I don't have the money. We work hard and well, so we can't shortchange our mouths, can we? Here."

It was completely light out now and bright and cold inside. The two men began to drink from their bowls; the noise was loud and pleasing to the ear. Neither said anything. They ate up all the oil cakes and fried cakes.

"What now?" Old Ch'eng picked a sesame seed out of his teeth.

"I've got to go." Hsiang Tzu stared at his bedroll on the floor.

"Tell me about it. I still don't understand what it's all about." Old Ch'eng gave Hsiang Tzu a cigarette. Hsiang Tzu shook his head.

Hsiang Tzu thought it over and was embarrassed not to tell Old Ch'eng about it. Event by event he told the story of the night before and although it took a lot of effort, it can't be said that he didn't tell it completely.

Old Ch'eng pursed his lips for some time, as if ruminating. "The way I see it, you'd still better go find Mr. Ts'ao. You can't simply lay the whole business aside! Your money can't be lost just like that

Didn't you say that Mr. Ts'ao ordered you to run away if you saw that things didn't look good? Well, then, you were stopped by that detective as soon as you got out of the cab, so who's to blame? It wasn't that you weren't loyal. The situation was ugly and there was nothing you could do but put your own life first! The way I see it, there's nothing you have to apologize for. You go and find Mr. Ts'ao and tell him truthfully about everything that happened to you from beginning to end. I don't see how he can blame you and with any luck he might even replace your money. Leave your bedroll here and go find him right away. The days are short and it's already eight o'clock by the time the sun comes up, so get going!"

Hsiang Tzu perked up. While he still felt he had to apologize to Mr. Ts'ao, what Old Ch'eng said did come close to the heart of the matter. A detective had taken a gun and stopped him. How could he have done anything about the Ts'ao family's business?

"Get going!" Old Ch'eng added another sentence. "I noticed last night that you were a little stymied. When you meet up with trouble who can help being baffled? I absolutely guarantee that I am heading you in the right direction. I'm a bit older than you are so of course I've been through a lot more. Get going. Isn't the sun up?"

The thin light from the morning sun had brightened the entire city by borrowing the reflection from the snow. The blue sky, the white snow, the brilliance of the sky, the brilliance of the snow, and the golden flower shining between the blue and the white made people so cheerful they couldn't open their eyes!

Hsiang Tzu was about to leave when someone knocked on the front door. Old Ch'eng went to see and called from the door. "Hsiang Tzu! Someone looking for you!"

The Tso manservant, Wang Erh, stood in the doorway, his nose dripping with cold. He was stamping the snow off his feet. Old Ch'eng saw Hsiang Tzu come out and then said, "Let's all go sit inside." The three of them went back inside Ch'eng's room.

"Well, ah. . . ." Wang Erh rubbed his hands while he spoke. "I came to watch the house but I don't know how to get in. The door is locked. Well, ah, the cold after a snow is real cold. Well, ah, Mr. Ts'ao, Mrs. Ts'ao, they all went off bright and early. Went to Tientsin, or maybe it was Shanghai, I'm not sure. Mr. Tso told me to come watch the house. Well, ah, it's real cold."

Hsiang Tzu suddenly felt like crying! Here he was, all set to follow

Old Ch'eng's advice and look for Mr. Ts'ao, and Mr. Ts'ao had gone! He was stunned for a while and then asked, "Didn't Mr. Ts'ao say anything about me?"

"Well, ah, no. It still wasn't light out but they all got up. They simply didn't have time to say anything. The train was well, ah, leaving at seven forty or something. Well, ah, how can I get in there?" Wang Erh was in a hurry.

"Jump over the wall!" Hsiang Tzu glanced at Old Ch'eng as if he were handing Wang Erh over to him. He lifted up his bedroll.

"Where are you going?" asked Old Ch'eng.

"The Jen Ho agency. There's no other place I can go."

This one sentence expressed all the grievance, mortification, and helplessness in Hsiang Tzu's heart. All he could do was go and surrender because there wasn't any other solution. Every other path was blocked and so, on this snow-white earth, he could only go to that black pagoda of a Hu Niu. The respectability, the ambition, the loyalty, and the integrity he had put so much store in would never do him any good because his was a dog's fate!

Old Ch'eng came with him to the front door. "You take care of yourself. This isn't for Wang Erh to hear. You never touched a blade of grass in the Ts'ao house. Get going. Drop in for a while when you're back this way. I can recommend you if I hear about a good job. I'll take Wang Erh over after you go. Is there any coal?"

"There's coal and kindling in the storeroom in the back court." Hsiang Tzu picked up his bedroll.

The snow on the street wasn't so white anymore. It was all pressed down by wheels and looked a little like ice on the paved road. Horses' hooves had made it into black and white patches on the dirt streets. It looked very sad. Hsiang Tzu didn't think about anything but carrying his bedroll and walking forward. He went to the Jen Ho agency without a pause. He didn't dare halt because he knew once he stopped he just wouldn't have the courage to go on. He went right in, his face burning hot.

He had his line ready. He would say to Hu Niu, "I'm here. Let's look over the plan. It's all right with me, whatever it is. I haven't any ideas." But when he saw her, the words turned over and over in his mind and he never managed to say them out loud. His lips just wouldn't do the job.

Hu Niu had just got up. Her hair was tangled and her eyelids somewhat swollen. Her darkish face had little bumps on it like the skin on a freshly plucked chicken.

"Oh, you're back!" She was very friendly indeed and her eyes lit up in a smile.

"Rent me a rickshaw." Hsiang Tzu hung his head and stared at the unmelted snow on the toes of his shoes.

"Go talk to the old man," she said in a low voice and made a face at the east room.

Liu was drinking tea in his room just then. There was a big white brazier in front of him and the flames were over six inches high. When he saw Hsiang Tzu come in he said, half annoyed and half smiling, "So, you're still alive, you clod! You forgot all about me! Let's see, how long has it been since you were here last? So what's going on? Bought a new rickshaw yet?"

Hsiang Tzu shook his head with something like a stab wound in his heart. "Let me have another rickshaw to pull again, sir."

"Humph! You've been fired again! All right, go pick one out yourself." Old Liu poured a bowl of tea. "Here, have some tea first."

Hsiang Tzu took the bowl. Standing in front of the brazier he drank in great gulps. The tea was scalding and the fire extremely hot; he felt a little drowsy. He had put the bowl down and was about to leave when Liu told him to stop.

"Wait a minute. Are you in a hurry? I'll tell you something. You came at the right time. The twenty-seventh is my birthday. I'm having a mat shed put up and inviting guests. If you can help me out for a few days, good. You don't have to pull a rickshaw right away. They," he pointed at the courtyard, "are none of them reliable. I don't want to have those rapscallions banging and clanging around and starting a rumpus. You are good help. If something has to be done you do it and don't wait for me to tell you. Go sweep away the snow first. Come here at noon for a fire pot lunch."

"Very good sir!" Hsiang Tzu figured he'd just hand everything over to the Lius now that he was back there again. It was all right with him if they wanted him to work at something different. He recognized his fate when he saw it!

"Didn't I say so?" Miss Liu figured this was the right moment to come in. "Hsiang Tzu's always the one. The others just haven't quite got it."

Old Liu smiled. Hsiang Tzu hung his head even lower.

"Come on, Hsiang Tzu!" Hu Niu went out. "I'll give you the money. Go buy a broom. Get a bamboo one good for sweeping snow. The place must be swept clean because the mat shed builders are coming today." When they got to her room she gave him the money and said softly, "Try to be a little more energetic! Make the old guy happy! There's some hope for us."

Hsiang Tzu had nothing to say and didn't get angry. It was as if his heart had died. There wasn't anything to think about any more so he'd just get through one day at a time. He'd eat what there was to eat, drink what there was to drink, do what there was to do. He'd keep his hands and feet moving and in a few turns the day would be over. He'd better copy the donkey who turns the millstone; it knows nothing about anything and all it does is keep going in circles turning the stone.

He might just as well admit that he wouldn't be very happy no matter what. He didn't want to think, didn't want to talk, didn't want to lose his temper, and there was always something clogging his heart anyway. He'd forget about it for a time when he was working but he'd become aware of the thing immediately when he took a few moments off. It was soft and weak but always large. It hadn't any definite taste to it and it choked him; it was like a sponge.

With his heart blockaded by this thing, he drove himself to work so hard he'd be too tired to move and could just fall dead asleep that night. He would hand the affairs of the night over to his dreams. He gave the affairs of this day to his hands and feet. He seemed to be a dead man doing the work of the living. He swept up the snow, he did the shopping, he went to light gas lamps, he brushed off the rickshaws, he moved tables and chairs, and he ate old Liu's "Reward for the Workers Banquet." By the time he went to sleep that night he hadn't a thought in his head or a word in his mouth. He didn't know anything except for an inward awareness of that hunk of spongelike something.

The snow on the ground had been swept away and the snow on the roof had gradually melted entirely. The mat shed men had climbed onto Liu's roof and started to attach the roof and the walls of the shed to the agency building. Liu had contracted for an enclosed and heated structure that would fill the entire courtyard. It would have felt walls hung on its three sides with railings and glass windows. There would be decorative room dividers and painted screens inside. Any wood that showed would be covered with red cloth and the center door and side doors would have festoons of cloth. The kitchen would be set up in the back courtyard.

Old Liu wanted a big noisy party because it was his sixty-ninth birthday. Therefore it was most important to have a proper mat shed. The days were short and the mat shed men wouldn't be able to do more than put up the frame and get the roof and walls on. The interior decorations and festoons for the doors would have to wait until early next morning. Old Liu raged at the mat shed men about it and his face was all red.

Worried about this situation, Liu had sent Hsiang Tzu to hurry up the delivery of the carbide lanterns and remind the cook he was not to neglect his duties. Actually, these two arrangements couldn't go wrong but the old man was worried nonetheless. Then old Liu sent Hsiang Tzu out again as soon as he returned to borrow three or four mahjong sets; Liu simply had to do his gambling that day with style. When Hsiang Tzu came back with the mahjong sets he was sent right out again to borrow a victrola. You must have music at a birthday party. Hsiang Tzu's feet didn't stop for a moment; he kept on going right up until eleven that night. He was accustomed to pulling a rickshaw and found running around practically emptyhanded much more exhausting than working. When he returned from his last trip he, even he, could scarcely lift a foot.

"Good boy! You'll do! If I had a son like you I wouldn't have minded living a few years less. Go to bed. There are things to do tomorrow, too."

Hu Niu, standing to one side, winked at Hsiang Tzu.

The mat shed men came to finish up early the next morning and the painted screens were erected. The paintings showed famous battles from the period of the Three Kingdoms with all the warriors, great and small, riding their horses and brandishing their swords. Old Liu peered at them closely and felt content.

The furniture men came to unload the rented furnishings. There were eight tables inside the mat shed. The cushions on the chairs and stools all had large red flowers embroidered on them. An altar was set up in the central section. The incense burners and candleholders were all cloisonné enamelware. Four felt rugs were laid in front of the altar. Old Liu promptly sent Hsiang Tzu off to buy apples. Hu Niu gave Hsiang Tzu two more dollars behind Liu's back to pay for an order of noodles and the "longevity" peaches made of dough which have pictures of the Eight Taoist Immortals on them and symbolize long life.

Hsiang Tzu bought the apples and they were set out nicely. After a short wait the noodles and peaches arrived and were placed behind the apples on the altar. Painted on the peaches were open red mouths with a picture of an immortal stuck inside. They were very grand. Hu Niu fixed it so it would look like Hsiang Tzu had sent them by saying, "Hsiang Tzu sent these. Look how very thoughtful he is!" Hu Niu stuffed old Liu's ears with kind words and old Liu smiled at Hsiang Tzu.

The altar still lacked its large scroll with the character for "Long Life" written on it. According to custom, it ought to be presented by your friends so you need not prepare one yourself. But no one had sent one yet. Old Liu had an impatient nature and he got very angry again.

"I've gone to every wedding, birthday, and funeral at everyone else's house and got there first, too. Now when it's my turn they give me a bare stage so screw their mothers!"

"Tomorrow is only the twenty-sixth and the tables won't be ready until then, so what's the hurry?" Hu Niu said consolingly.

"I want it all arranged right now. This bits and pieces business makes me nervous. I told Hsiang Tzu to tell those guys the carbide lanterns had better be set up properly today and I'll slice them up into little pieces if they don't get here by four o'clock!"

"Hsiang Tzu, go back and hurry them up!" Hu Niu deliberately gave him all sorts of little tasks and always managed to tell him to do them when her father could hear. Hsiang Tzu said not a word, got her instructions straight, and left.

"Though I'm not the one to say so, Papa," she said with slightly pursed lips, "if you had a son, if he wasn't like me he'd be like Hsiang Tzu. But alas, an unkind fate put me in my mother's womb and there's nothing we can do about it. But making him your foster son wouldn't be so bad. Look at him. He works all day without even stopping to fart and he gets everything done just the same!"

Old Liu didn't answer. He was thinking. "What about the victrola? Let's hear it!"

It was an old wind-up victrola borrowed from who knows where and every sound it made was as mind-curdling as a cat's yowl when ts tail is stepped on. But old Liu didn't care; as long as it made some kind of noise it was marvelous.

Everything was in order by afternoon and all they were waiting for was the cook who would come to set up his kitchen tomorrow. Old Liu made a tour of inspection; the red of flowers and the green of willows was everywhere and he nodded his head in approval.

That evening he went to invite the owner of the T'ien Hsün Coal Company to come keep the account book. His name was Feng, he came from Shansi, and he kept accounts with great care. Mr. Feng came right over to look at things. He sent Hsiang Tzu out to buy an account book bound in red and a length of fancy red paper. He cut the paper into sections, wrote "Long Life" on them, and stuck them up here and there. Old Liu realized that Mr. Feng really knew what he was doing and he wanted to get two more people to play a few hands of mahjong with Mr. Feng then and there. Mr. Feng knew what a cardsharp old Liu was and didn't dare risk it.

Being deprived of his game annoyed old Liu, so he tried to get some of the rickshaw pullers to play another game of chance. "Any of you have the nerve to play?"

They were all willing but not if they had to play with him. Who didn't know he used to run a gambling house?

"You bunch of pantywaists, what are you good for?" Old Liu lost his temper. "When I was as young as you fellows I'd play even if I didn't have a cent in my pockets. If I lost I'd worry then. Come on!"

"Play for pennies?" asked one man tentatively.

"Keep your pennies. Liu doesn't play with children!" The old man gulped down a cup of tea and rubbed his bald head. "Enough. I wouldn't play if you asked me! Listen, you go tell the others they can only work part time tomorrow. My relatives and friends will be calling in the late afternoon so all the rickshaws must be put away by four. You are not to confuse things by dragging rickshaws all over the place. I don't want any rental fees tomorrow but you must bring the rickshaws in by four. I'll let you have one day free, so all of you wish me good fortune in your hearts a few times. And you'd better mean it! My birthday is day after tomorrow and no one will be allowed to take out a rickshaw. I'll have six main dishes, four side dishes, and one soup, all for you, at eight thirty that morning. Everyone must wear a long gown and whoever comes with his rump showing gets kicked out! After you've eaten, do me a favor and beat it so I can entertain my friends and relations. They'll be fed three seafood courses, six cold meats, six stir-fried dishes, four main courses, and one soup. I'm telling you all this ahead of time so you needn't stand around watching greedily. Relatives and friends are relatives and friends, after all, and I'm not asking you for anything. Of course, those who are generous will give me ten cents and I won't grumble that it's too little. If you don't bring even a penny, just kowtow three times. I'll accept that. But it must be done properly, understand? In the evening I'll let you come back for more. You can come back after six and everything that's left over, no matter how much or how little it is, is all yours. But it won't do you any good to come back early! Do you understand?"

"But the night-shift men tomorrow, sir," said a middle-aged puller. "How can they turn in their rickshaws at four when that's when they start work?"

"The night shift can start after eleven! In any case, they must not come milling in when guests are in the mat shed! You pull the rickshaws and Liu certainly is not one of you. Is that clear?"

There wasn't anything more to be said and they didn't know how to get out of there, so they stood there paralyzed. Old Liu's speech had angered and upset them. While it was an advantage to have one day's rental canceled, who wanted to eat this "free" meal? It would cost them an offering of twenty cents in cash at least. Furthermore, old Liu's words were so rude it looked like they would have to hide away like mice when he celebrated his birthday. And besides, while forbidding them to take the rickshaws out on the birthday itself meant that old Liu would sacrifice that day's income too, it also meant they'd all have to lose a whole day's take on one of the best days for business in the New Year holidays! They stood there, bold enough to be angry but not brave enough to speak up. There were no kind wishes for old Liu in their hearts.

Hu Niu pulled at Hsiang Tzu and he left with her.

Their anger seemed to have suddenly found an exit and they glared at Hsiang Tzu's shadow. They'd all felt during the last two days that Hsiang Tzu had become a mere lackey of the Liu house, desperately currying favor, slaving without complaint, and swallowing his grievances just to be their errand boy.

Hsiang Tzu didn't know about any of this. He helped the Lius in order to get rid of the vexation in his heart. He had nothing to say to the other men in the evening. There was nothing to talk about. They

didn't know about his grievances; they thought he couldn't be bothered to chat with them because he was so busy making up to old Liu.
All the attention Hu Niu paid to him left a particularly sour taste in
their mouths. They thought about the approaching party. Old Liu
wouldn't let them wander around in the mat shed but of course
Hsiang Tzu could stay and eat better food all day long. He was a rickshaw puller just like they were, wasn't he? So why was he any different from them? Look! Hu Niu is calling Hsiang Tzu away again!

Their eyes followed Hsiang Tzu. Their legs felt like moving, too,
and they all went out listlessly. Hu Niu was talking to Hsiang Tzu
under the gas lamp just then; they all nodded to each other.

CHAPTER FOURTEEN

OLD LIU's birthday party was very merry and he was quite pleased to have so many guests come to kowtow and wish him well. A great many old friends had also come to offer their felicitations, which was even more gratifying. He could tell from the presence of these old friends that he had not only staged a successful affair but had managed a "change for the better" as well. Their clothes were shabby now while his gown and short jacket were recently made. From the standpoint of business, quite a few of them had been wealthier than he in the past but now, after the changes of the last twenty-five years or so, they had sunk lower and lower and some even found it difficult to get enough to eat. Looking at them and then at his festive mat shed, the altar, the painted screens, and the great banquet, he realized that he certainly topped them by a head. He had "changed for the better." Even the gambling was a step up, for he had provided tables for mahjong, which was more elegant than shell games.

But in the midst of all this merrymaking, he also began to feel a little lonely and glum. Habituated to a solitary life, he had assumed that the guests at his birthday party would all be shopkeepers and shop managers as well as some of his bachelor friends from the old days. He had never expected that any womenfolk would come along. Hu Niu could take care of them but suddenly he became aware of his solitude in a household with only a grown daughter who was like a man.

If Hu Niu had been a son, of course, she would have set up a household already and would have had children. Even though he was an old widower, perhaps he wouldn't have been so lonesome. True enough, there was nothing he lacked except a son. The older he got the slighter his hopes for a son became. By rights, a birthday ought to be a joyful affair but tears seemed to be appropriate, too. No matter how great his change for the better, there was no one to carry on his business. Hadn't it all been done for nothing?

He was extraordinarily elated during the first part of the day. Here they all were, congratulating him on his birthday, and he received them imperially. He seemed to think he was a hero seizing glory but by the latter part of the day his spirits were sinking. Watching female guests leading their children by the hand made him envious but he didn't dare make friends with the children, and not being friendly made him feel even more out of sorts. He longed to lose his temper but not just at that moment. He knew he was a man of the world and he couldn't expose himself to ridicule in front of his relatives and friends. He wanted the day to end quickly so he wouldn't have to endure any more of this mental agony.

There was another flaw in the midst of his joy. Hsiang Tzu almost got into a fight at the feast he gave for the rickshaw pullers that morning.

The meal had been ready a little after eight but the rickshaw men were a little reluctant to come. They'd had a rent-free day the day before, but no one could come to eat with empty hands. Ten cents would do; forty cents would do, too. Any amount, large or small, contributed to the gift money. Ordinarily, each of them was a hardworking fellow and Liu was the boss. Today, as they saw it, they were guests. They shouldn't be treated like this. Besides, they had to leave as soon as they finished eating and they weren't allowed to take out a rickshaw either—and right at New Year's too!

Hsiang Tzu knew perfectly well that he wasn't in the "eat and beat it" class but he wanted to eat with them anyway. In the first place, he could eat early and get right to work; in the second place, he could show his friendliness. He sat with them and they dumped all their dissatisfaction with Liu on him. He'd just sat down when someone said, "Hey, you are an honored guest so how come you're sitting with us?"

Hsiang Tzu smiled foolishly; he hadn't caught the implication of the words. He hadn't been chatting with anyone lately and his wits didn't seem to be tending to business much.

They hadn't the nerve to start anything with Liu but at least they could gobble up all they could hold. There wouldn't be any seconds on food but there couldn't be limits on the drinks because it was a party! And so, by an unspoken agreement, they all used liquor to smother their rage. Some drank glumly and some played guessing games. Old Liu couldn't prevent them from doing that.

Hsiang Tzu watched them drink. It wouldn't do for him to stay completely out of things so he drank a few cups with them. They drank and drank until their eyes were bloodshot and their lips wouldn't behave.

Someone said, "Hsiang Tzu! Hey Camel! What a sweet job you've got! Plenty to eat every day when you are waiting on the old man and young lady! Pretty soon you won't have to pull a rickshaw. You'll be their number one boy!"

Hsiang Tzu sort of knew what he meant but didn't really take it in. After returning to the Jen Ho agency he had decided not to try to be any hero or stout fellow again. He'd just do as Heaven willed in all things. If someone wanted to say something, let him say it. Hsiang Tzu held his temper.

Someone else said, "This guy Hsiang Tzu ain't in our world. We make our dough by using our muscles but this guy has an inside job!"

They all began to laugh. Hsiang Tzu realized they were teasing him but he'd suffered too many wrongs to care about wisecracks. He still said nothing.

Those at the next table took advantage of the moment. One of them stretched out his neck and yelled, "Hsiang Tzu! Don't forget your brothers when you are the boss!"

Hsiang Tzu still said not a word. Then a man at his table added, "So say something, Camel!"

Hsiang Tzu's face got red and he said in a low voice, "So how could I be boss?"

"Hoo! Why couldn't you? Watch out, there'll be thumping and strumming soon!"

Hsiang Tzu couldn't figure out what "thumping and strumming" meant. He imagined the words were aimed at the relationship be- tween him and Hu Niu. His face slowly went from red to white. He thought of all the wrongs he'd suffered all heaped on top of his heart. He couldn't go on enduring everything in silence. Like dammed-up water, his resentment was ready to burst out as soon as it found an exit.

Another rickshaw man picked this moment to point at his face and say, "Hsiang Tzu, I'm talking to you! There you sit stuffing yourself in silence but you really get the idea, don't you? Tell us yourself, Hsiang Tzu! Hsiang Tzu?"

Hsiang Tzu jumped to his feet, his face a dead white. He said to the man, "We'll talk outside if you have the nerve."

They were all silent. Actually they were only teasing him to pass the time and certainly weren't looking for a fight. Now the silence was like that of twittering birds when they see a hawk. Hsiang Tzu stood there alone. He was taller than other men and aware of his isolation. But his heart was full of fury and apparently he was really convinced they were no match for him even if they all ganged up. He rapped out one sentence. "Do you have the nerve or not?"

Old Liu saw the whole thing. "Hsiang Tzu! Sit down!" Then he said to the rest of them, "We'll have none of this insulting a man just because he's honest and well behaved. Make me angry and I'll kick you all out! Hurry up and eat."

Hsiang Tzu left the table. The rickshaw pullers peeked at Liu out of the corners of their eyes and began eating. It wasn't long before they were all chattering again like the forest birds that chirp lightly once more when danger has passed them by.

Hsiang Tzu squatted in the gateway for some time, waiting for them. If there was any one among them who dared talk more scandal, he'd sock him! He didn't have anything left to lose so he'd just let them have it regardless of the consequences.

But they came out in groups of three or five and no one so much as glanced at him. Even though there wasn't a fight, he did get rid of some of his anger, more or less, after all. Something more occurred to him: this show he'd put on might have offended a lot of people. As a matter of fact he really didn't have any close friends and no one to tell his sorrows to when he had them, so how could he possibly afford to offend anyone? He felt a little sorry. The things he had just eaten lodged crossways in his stomach and became painful. He stood up. What about it? Don't those fellows who get into fights two out of every three days to keep from starving live happily and enjoy it too?

Does being honest and law-abiding really have any good points?

Thoughts like these led him to consider another road for himself. The Hsiang Tzu on this road was quite unlike the Hsiang Tzu of his former hopes. This new one was a guy who made friends with everyone he saw, took advantage every chance he got, drank someone else's tea, smoked someone else's cigarettes, borrowed money and never returned it, didn't get out of the way when he saw a car, pissed wherever he happened to be, and played tricks on the cops all day long, thinking it didn't matter much if he was hauled off to the police station and jugged for a few days. Yes indeed, rickshaw pullers like that did live and were happy. At least they were happier than he was. All right, since honesty, good manners, and ambition were all useless, turning into someone as wild as that wouldn't be so bad. It would even have some of the air of the hero, the stout fellow, about it as well. The kind of guy who was not afraid of Heaven or anything on earth and absolutely never suffered in silence! Right! That's the way he ought to act!

Blackguards are carved out of good men.

Now he began to feel sorry for the opposite reason: he hadn't fought it out! Fortunately there was no hurry; he wouldn't hang his head in front of anyone from now on.

Old Liu didn't have to rub any sand out of his eyes. He'd put together what he'd seen and heard, and understood almost everything already. "Well now, my daughter has been especially obedient lately. Humph! Because Hsiang Tzu has come back! Look at her eyes, always following him." The old man deposited each incident in his heart and found his loneliness even more intolerable. "Think about it. There's no son to begin with so it's impossible to get a larger and larger family. As for a daughter, she goes off to her husband's family and that's the end of her!" He'd expended all his care and thought all his life for nothing! Of course, Hsiang Tzu wasn't bad, but to consider taking him as a combination son and son-in-law, that double blessing, well, that was different! A stinking rickshaw puller! Old Liu had toiled all his life, fought in the mobs, knelt on chains, and now, approaching his end, was he the man who'd let a country bumpkin make off with his daughter and his estate? "Well, you don't get anything that cheaply! And if you could, you needn't expect to get it from old Liu! Not from a man who all his life had caved in a privy every time he farted!"

Still more guests came to congratulate him between three and four in the afternoon. The old man already felt bored by it all. The more they praised him for his good luck and for being so vigorous, the more he felt it was meaningless.

The guests departed one by one after the lanterns were hung up. Only about ten or so, those who lived nearby and those who were close friends, were still there; they gathered to play mahjong.

Looking at the empty mat shed in the greenish light from the carbide lamps, and at the empty tables, made the old man feel empty and depressed, as if he were seeing the time after his own death. It would look just like this; all you'd have to do was change the hangings from red to white, but no son and grandson dressed in white would be kneeling in front of the coffin. There'd only be a few people who didn't care, playing mahjong to get through the night watch! He actually considered driving away the guests who were still there; he ought to inspire awe as long as he had a breath of life left in him! But after all, it would be embarrassing to use his friends to release his anger.

Then his rage turned a corner. The more he looked at his daughter, the less she pleased his eye. And there was that Hsiang Tzu sitting inside the mat shed: a man in shape but a dog by nature. The greenish light made the scar on his face resemble a bit of jade. The more the old man looked at the two of them the more revolting they were!

Miss Liu was accustomed to doing without decorum but today she was dressed up from top to toe, making a great show of entertaining the guests because she desired their approval and wanted to show off in front of Hsiang Tzu. She had thought the party very interesting during the first part of the day but by afternoon she was a little tired. She found everything obnoxious and rather thought she'd like to find someone to swear at. By evening she hadn't a speck of patience left and it took an enormous effort to force her eyebrows to stay in a straight line in spite of themselves.

Old Liu was a little sleepy by seven o'clock but refused to give in to old age and go to bed. They asked him to join them in a few hands of mahjong. He didn't want to say he didn't feel like it, so he said mahjong was dull and other games were more to his taste. No one wanted to change games in the middle so all he could do was watch. Then he had to have a few more drinks to renew his energy. Then he grumbled that he hadn't had enough to eat and complained that the cook had made too much money on the deal. After all, the food certainly had not been abundant! Using the food as a starting point, he then took the features of the day that he had previously believed to be satisfactory and reviewed them one by one. The mat shed, the furnishings, utensils, food, cook, and everything else—nothing was worth what he had paid for it and everyone was taking advantage of him and it was all unfair!

By this time, Mr. Feng, the accountant, had got the books totaled. They had taken in twenty-five scrolls with appropriate poems, three batches each of longevity noodles and peaches, one jug of baigan, two pair of candles, and about twenty dollars in cash. The number of contributions was by no means small, but most of them were gifts of forty cents or less.

Old Liu was infuriated when he heard this report. If he had known it was going to be like that, he'd have ordered fried vegetables with noodles! Come and eat a huge banquet and give ten cents? Why that was simply taking an old man like him for a fool and making a sucker out of him! He'd never put on another party like this one again! He'd never get back the money he'd thrown down the rathole! But what good did it do to talk about it? Why they had even brought their own relatives and friends and all of them expected to get free eats off him, a man sixty-nine years old! Though he'd been clever all his life, he'd been stupid just this once and now he'd been eaten up by a lot of whoreson bastard monkeys!

The old man got angrier and angrier the longer he thought about it. He even regarded the satisfaction he'd felt during the day as befitting his stupidity. With such thoughts in his mind, his lips muttered scurrilous and archaic insults endlessly.

Not all the friends had left yet and Hu Niu, out of regard for everyone's face, thought she'd better put a stop to her father's boorishness; but she saw that they were all concentrating on their game and apparently had not noticed the old man's grumbling, so it wouldn't do any good for her to open her mouth and make the situation obvious. Let him grumble. If they all went on pretending not to hear him, it would pass.

How was she to know his grousing and grumbling would work around to her? Well! She wasn't about to take that! She had to spend days running around madly because he was throwing a birthday party and now look, she wasn't getting anything out of it! She couldn't allow that! It didn't matter if he was sixty-nine or seventy-nine, he'd better straighten up! She turned on him.

"You were the one who wanted to spend your money on a party. So what have I done?"

Meeting rebellion, the old man's spirit was suddenly stirred into action. "What have you done? Well, I'll tell you right out! You think my eyes haven't noticed what's been going on?"

"So what have you noticed? Here I've been wearing myself out all day long and now you take your anger out on me at the end of it. Now just you wait a minute. Say it. What have you noticed?" Miss Liu's fatigue dropped away and her words were remarkably apt.

"You needn't watch out for my business, you and your greedy looks! Noticed? I've noticed everything! Humph!"

"Just what are my eyes greedy for?" She tossed her head. "What is it that you have noticed?"

"Isn't that it?" Old Liu pointed to Hsiang Tzu, who was bent over sweeping the ground inside the mat shed.

"Him?" Hu Niu's heart jumped. She had never expected the old man's eyes to be that sharp. "Faugh! What about him?"

"There's no point in beating around the bush!" The old man stood up. "If you want him it'll be without me. If you want me it'll be without him. I'm telling you flat and that's that. I am your Papa! I ought to be the one who rules!"

Hu Niu had never expected the affair to break into the open so soon. Her scheme hadn't even been carried to the halfway point and the old man was already onto it! Now what? Her face turned red, a dark red which the combination of a face powder that made her look half-dead and the greenish glare of the lamps turned into a repellent mishmash of a color very much like overdone pork liver. She was quite tired and now, stirred up and enraged by his remarks, she was in a quandary and couldn't think. She couldn't just retreat into a hole. She had to find a way out immediately, despite her confusion. She'd never given in to weakness in front of anyone before so even a faulty plan was better than no plan at all. All right, she'd get to the point quickly and let everything depend on one blow of the hammer!

"It would be best to speak clearly right now. We'll just assume that you have added the bill up right and now what are you going to do about it? I really want to know. But you are the one who started looking for trouble so don't try to claim that I want to anger you."

It seemed to the mahjong players that they were overhearing an argument between father and daughter but they couldn't bring themselves to divert their attention from the game. All chattered loudly and slapped their tiles down with a clatter to block out the sound of the two voices.

Hsiang Tzu heard all of it and went on sweeping with his head down as usual. He had reached bottom. Or, to put it another way, up theirs!

"You are obviously trying to infuriate me!" The old man's staring eyes got very round. "You think you can make me die of rage so you can buy yourself a man? Don't bother to figure that way. I'm good for quite a few years yet."

"Don't try to change the subject. What are you going to do?" Hu Niu's heart was thumping but her lips were very stiff.

"What am I going to do? Didn't I tell you? You can have him but not me or have me but not him. I'm not going to make things easier for any stinking rickshaw puller!"

Hsiang Tzu threw down the broom and straightened up. He looked directly at old Liu and asked, "Who are you talking about?"

Liu began to laugh wildly. "So you want to make a revolution, do you? You punk! I'm talking about you, who else? Bugger right off! I thought you weren't so bad. I give you face and you think you're on top of the world but boy, you've never even heard of what I can do! Bugger off! Never let me set eyes on you again. Sniffing around for a fucking good deal here, were you? Ha!"

The old man's voice got louder and several rickshaw pullers peeked in at the excitement. As far as the mahjong players were concerned, Mr. Liu was having another one of his arguments with a rickshaw man and, as before, they weren't interested in taking a look.

Hsiang Tzu hadn't any skill at back talk; there was a lot he thought of saying but not one sentence reached his tongue. He stood there silently, swallowing his spit.

"Bugger off! And make it snappy! Came here trying to pull a fast one, did you? When I go out looking for trouble I can do it without you. Humph!"

The old man was simply shouting at Hsiang Tzu for the sake of shouting. He certainly didn't hate him as fiercely as he hated his daughter. In fact, even when enraged he knew that Hsiang Tzu was an honest man.

"All right. I'll go." There was nothing else Hsiang Tzu could say and it was best to get out of there quickly anyway. When it came to an argument with them, he could never win, no matter what the fight was about.

The rickshaw pullers had come in to watch the fracas; they all remembered the scene that morning and were delighted to find Liu chewing Hsiang Tzu out. But when they heard him drive Hsiang Tzu away, they switched over to his side. Hsiang Tzu had worn himself out for Liu and now ingratitude was his reward. The old man turned his face away and would not acknowledge him. They were upset on Hsiang Tzu's account. Several hurried over and asked, "Hsiang Tzu, what happened?"

Hsiang Tzu shook his head.

"Hsiang Tzu! Wait!" Apparently a light had flashed on in Hu Niu's mind and she could see clearly. Her plan was no good now. Speed was better than haste and so she had to grab Hsiang Tzu fast; she must not break the egg now that the chicken had flown! "The business between us is like one cord binding two crickets; neither can get away! Wait. Wait until I make everything absolutely clear." She turned around and confronted the old man. "To be blunt about it, I'm already pregnant. It's Hsiang Tzu's! If he leaves, I go with him. Are you giving me to him or driving us out together? Let's hear what you have to say!"

Hu Niu never thought she would have to play her master stroke so soon. The situation had developed too quickly. Old Liu had simply no idea that things had gone that far. But now the breaking point had been reached, and it was impossible for him to give in, particularly in front of everybody.

"If you really are so brazen as to say such things out loud, then this old face of mine must blush for you!" He slapped his cheeks. "Phooey! How shameless!"

The mahjong players stopped their game. They realized that something had gone amiss but they were in a fog. Since they knew nothing, they said nothing. Some stood up and others stared blankly at their tiles.

Hu Niu, on the other hand, was delighted now that everything was out in the open. "Me shameless? Don't make me tell the world about you! Is there any kind of shit you haven't hauled? This is the first time I've ever put a foot wrong and it's all your fault besides. A grown man should marry and a grown woman should be married. You are sixty-nine and have lived for nothing. Though talk like this is not proper in front of all these people," she pointed all around, "it's best for us to get things straight and out in the open. All you have to do is take this mat shed, put on another party, and that does the job!"

"Me?" Old Liu's face turned red, then white. He put on all the braggadocio of his youth. "I'd burn the place down before I'd let you use it!"

"Swell!" Hu Niu's lips quivered and her voice was excruciatingly hard on the ears. "I'll make up my bedroll and go. How much money will you give me?"

"The money is mine. If I want to give it to anyone, that's who'll get it!" The old man felt very bad when he heard her say she would leave but he hardened his heart because he had to fight things out.

"Your money? After I've helped you all these years? Without me, if you'd just think about it a minute, it would be a miracle if all your money hadn't gone to prostitutes. So let's be fair about it!" Then her eyes sought out Hsiang Tzu again. "So say something, you!"

Hsiang Tzu stood bolt upright; there was nothing he could say.

CHAPTER FIFTEEN

WHEN IT CAME to fighting, Hsiang Tzu would never strike an old man nor would he hit a woman—there was no place here for him to use his strength. Even if he really was a rascal, thinking was the most he could do, or else just get out of there, which he wouldn't have minded if the matter involved only Hu Niu herself. What with the scene in front of him with her at odds with her father and claiming she was ready to leave with him—well, no one knew what was going on inside her but on the outside she was sacrificing herself on his account—there was nothing he could do here in front of everyone except pluck up a little heroic spirit. While there was nothing he could say, and all he could do was stand there and wait until "the water retreats and the stone emerges," at least he could do that much. That would be like a real man.

Father and daughter Liu could only stare at each other. All had been said. Hsiang Tzu was mute. The rickshaw pullers, never mind which side they were on, seemed to find it difficult to put a word in. The mahjong players just had to say something: the silence was already unbearable. But all they could do was cajole the opponents in meaningless words, admonishing the adversaries that there was no need to get heated, take it easy, there was nothing intolerable about the problem. They couldn't say more; nor could they decide anything. When they saw that neither side was willing to give way, it became a case of "it's hard for an honest official to make a judgment in family affairs and he'll get out of it when he can." They'd better slip away now when they had a chance.

Miss Liu grabbed Feng before anyone had time to slip away. "Mr. Feng, isn't there some room in your shop? Let Hsiang Tzu stay there for a few days. Our marriage will be arranged quickly. I won't let him

take up your space for long. Hsiang Tzu, you go with Mr. Feng. See
you tomorrow and we'll talk about our marriage then. And let me tell
you, when I go out these gates it will be in a bridal chair or not at all!
Mr. Feng, I'm handing him over to you. I will collect him from you
tomorrow."

Mr. Feng took a deep breath; he didn't want to take on this duty.
Hsiang Tzu was desperate to get out of there and said, "I won't run
away."

Miss Liu stared at the old man and then went to her room, heaving
great sobs. She locked the door on the inside.

Mr. Feng urged Mr. Liu to go to his room too. But the old man had
recovered his urbane manner and invited them all to stay and have a
few more drinks. "Gentlemen, please don't worry. After all, she's she
and I'm me and we won't argue any more. She'll mind her own business, only as far as I am concerned I never had a slave like her. I've
been a man of the world all my life and I let her do away with my
reputation! Twenty years back I would have sliced up the two of them
alive! Today, I'll just let her go. But if she plans to get anything out of
me, that's just too bad! I wouldn't give her one red cent! Never! Then
we'll see how she makes out. Let her try it. She'll find out whether
Papa or that bumpkin is best in the end. Don't go, have another
drink!"

Everyone made polite talk but they were all anxious to get out of
there.

Hsiang Tzu went to the coal shop.

The whole problem was taken care of very quickly. Hu Niu rented
two small south-facing rooms in a large mixed courtyard. She then
found a paperhanger to paper all the walls white from top to bottom.
She asked Mr. Feng to write some auspicious characters, health,
wealth, long life, and the like, and pasted them on the wall in one
room. When the rooms were ready she hired a bridal sedan chair and
sixteen musicians. She did not want a gold lantern or any of the other
paraphernalia usually carried in bridal processions. When everything
was ordered she got out the red satin wedding dress she had made
herself. She had made it well in advance in order to avoid the taboo
on doing needlework before the fifth day of the new year. The auspicious day for the wedding was the sixth. It was a lucky day and so
there was no need to observe any of the other traditional taboos con-
cerning marriage. She arranged the whole affair by herself and told

Hsiang Tzu to get himself new clothes from head to foot. "There is only one day like this in your whole life!"

Hsiang Tzu had only five dollars!

Hu Niu glared at him. "What? What about the thirty-one dollars I gave back to you?"

There was no way he could avoid telling the truth and so he told her all about the Ts'ao affair. She blinked as if she half believed and half doubted him. "All right. I haven't the time to argue with you. We'll just act according to our consciences. I'll give you fifteen dollars but you'd better watch out if you're not dressed from head to foot like a bridegroom when the day comes."

Hu Niu sat in her bridal chair on the sixth of the month without having said another word to her father, without a brother's escort, and without the best wishes of friends and relations. All she had was the great racket of drums and gongs resounding in the post-New Year streets. The sedan chair moved sedately past the Hsi An Gate and the west double *p'ai lou* arousing a little envy and a little emotional excitement in the wearers of new clothes, the shopclerks in particular.

Hsiang Tzu wore the new clothes he'd bought in the market district. He was red in the face and had a velvet skullcap costing thirty cents on his head. He seemed to have forgotten who he was as he stared doltishly at everything and listened silently to everything without recognizing that he was a part of it. He had been shifted from a coal dealer's shop to a bridal chamber just papered snow white all over and he didn't know what it was all about. His past was just like being in a coal mine where there was one pile of stuff after another and all of it black. Now he'd got into a bridal chamber, somehow or other, and its whiteness dazzled the eye. There were blood-red auspicious characters pasted up here and there too. He felt mocked and uselessly, vaguely, depressed.

Hu Niu's own table, chairs, and bed were in one room. The stove and kitchen table were actually new. A multicolored feather duster stood in one corner. He recognized the table and chairs but felt at odds with the stove, kitchen table, and feather duster. Old and new objects together in the same place made him remember the past and feel anxious about the future. He had let someone else arrange everything while he, himself, was just like some strange object, old and yet also new, which had been placed on exhibition. He did not recognize himself. It didn't occur to him to cry or to laugh as his big frame moved around in this small room. He was like a rabbit in a small cage, eyes redly staring, looking at the outside and knowing how useless it was to have legs that could run like the wind when he couldn't run away!

Hu Niu wore a red dress, her face was covered with powder and paint, and her eyes were fixed on him. He dared not look her in the eye. She, too, was an old and yet new strange something or other. A girl and also a woman, like a female and also like a male. Like a human being and also like some kind of terrible beast! This beast wore a red dress, had got hold of him, and was preparing to finish him off bit by bit. Anybody could finish him off and this beast was especially dangerous for it wanted to keep every single bit of him for itself. Glare at him, smile at him, hug him tightly too, and suck away all the strength he had in him. There was no way out.

He took off the velvet skullcap and stared at the red button on its top until he got spots in front of his eyes. He looked around; the walls were covered with red spots flying in circles, leaping and jumping, and in the middle of them was a huge red grinning Hu Niu!

On their wedding night Hsiang Tzu finally caught on. Hu Niu wasn't pregnant at all. She explained how she had fooled him just as if she were a magician telling all. "If I hadn't deceived you this once, how would you ever have given in? I put a pillow under my waist band! Ha, ha!" She laughed until the tears came. "You dope! There's no point talking about it and I'm not ashamed to face you anyway. What are you and what am I? I quarreled with Papa outright to come here with you and you still don't thank Heaven and Earth?"

Hsiang Tzu went out very early the next morning. Most of the shops were open but some houses still had closed gates. Above the front doors the paper bearing auspicious mottoes was still red but the gold paper ingots hanging there had been shredded by the wind. The street was very quiet. There were quite a few rickshaws out and their pullers were rather more energetic than usual. Most of them had new shoes and squares of red paper pasted on the backs of their rickshaws for good luck. Hsiang Tzu envied these rickshaw pullers a lot and was aware that while they really had a New Yearish look to them, he had been curled up in gloom inside a bottle gourd for many days. They were contented and minding their own business while he had no occupation and wandered idly in the streets. He wasn't happy doing nothing but if he had any intention of thinking about plans for tomor ow, he'd have to go talk them over with Hu Niu, his wife! He was, in act, begging for food from the hand of his wife and what a wife! His great height was all in vain, his great strength was all in vain, both were good for nothing. First off, he had to serve his wife, that red-dressed, tiger-toothed thing, a thing that sucked away a man's virility. Already he was no man, only a hunk of meat. He had lost his selfhood and could only struggle in the grip of her teeth like a little mouse in the jaws of a cat. He didn't want to talk to her about anything. He had to get away. He'd leave as soon as he thought of a plan. There was nothing he had to apologize to anyone for because she was a female monster who had bamboozled him with a pillow! He felt irritated. Not only did he long to rip off all his new clothes, he also wanted to plunge into clear water and cleanse his body from the inside out. He felt like he was smeared all over with some unclean and sickening substance which was vexing him to distraction. He didn't care if he never set eyes on her again!

Where should he go? He had no place in mind. Ordinarily he pulled a rickshaw and his legs took their orders from the mouths of others. Now his legs were independent and his mind was at sea. He went due south from the west double *p'ai lou* and through the Hsuan Wu Gate. The avenue was so straight his mind couldn't wander. He continued southward after going through the gate and saw a bathhouse. He decided to take a bath.

He gazed at himself after undressing and felt mortified. The hot water scalded him into numbness once he got into the pool and he shut his eyes. He had gone limp, as if his body were expelling all the filth accumulated inside it. He scarcely dared scrub himself. His mind was blank and sweat began to pour off his head. Finally, when his breathing became short and gaspy, he crawled out slowly. He was red all over, like a newborn baby. It seemed to him he couldn't just walk around naked. Even with a towel around his middle he was still conscious of his own ugliness. Even though the sweat was running off him in little plops onto the floor, he still felt unclean. It was as if the filth in his mind could never be washed away. He would always be a woman-izer in the eyes of old Liu and all who knew him! He hurriedly put on his clothes and ran out before he had stopped sweating. He was afraid of letting anyone see his naked body! When the cold wind blew on him outside the bathhouse he realized how limp he was.

The streets were quite a bit busier now. The brilliant blue sky lent a little gaiety to people's faces. Hsiang Tzu's mind was still in the grip of indecision and he couldn't think of a good place to go. He went south, then east, then south again. Finally he hurried to the T'ien Ch'iao district.

After the New Year holiday all the shop apprentices would have eaten their breakfast by nine o'clock and come here. Every kind of street stall, every sort of acrobat's platform, had been set up and arranged early in the day. These places were already surrounded by groups of people by the time Hsiang Tzu got there and the drums and gongs were sounding. He hadn't the heart to look at the shows for he was already unable to smile. Ordinarily, the sights here, the mimics, the trained bears, the magicians and fortune-tellers, the folksingers, the storytellers, and the martial dancers, could give him a little real pleasure and make him open his mouth and laugh. T'ien Ch'iao accounted for half the reasons why he couldn't bear to leave Peking. He would recall many comical and delightful incidents every time he saw the booths and awnings of T'ien Ch'iao and the groups of people there. Now he was reluctant to push forward; the laughing voices there would have to do without his contribution. He avoided the crowds and went toward a quieter place and felt even more reluctant to leave! No, he couldn't leave this delightful, exciting place. He couldn't leave T'ien Ch'iao. He couldn't leave Peking. Go away? There was no road he could take! He still had to go back and talk things over with her. With her! He couldn't go anywhere and couldn't loaf. He'd better back up a bit and think, just the way everyone else has to back up a bit and think when they're in a mess and don't know what to do about it. He'd suffered every wrong there was so why did he have to stand all alone on this spot called "honest fellow"? There was no way he could straighten out everything that had gone wrong in the past so he might as well head right on down the road he was on.

He stood still listening to the babble of voices and the sounds of the drums and gongs. As he watched the people coming and going and the carts and horses, suddenly he remembered those two little rooms. He seemed to hear none of the sounds and see none of the sights; only those two small, white, warm, red-character-decorated rooms stood square and orderly before him. Even though only one night had passed there, those two rooms were extraordinarily familiar and friendly, and it did indeed seem as though women in red dresses could not be discarded at pleasure.

Standing in T'ien Ch'iao he was nobody and had nothing. In those two small rooms he had everything. Go back; there can only be a way if you go back. All of tomorrow is in those small rooms. It did no good to feel ashamed, afraid of things and unable to bear them. If you want to go on living, you've got to find the place where there's a way to do it.

He went straight back. It was around eleven o'clock when he went in the door. Hu Niu had just finished making a lunch of steamed buns, simmered cabbage and meatballs, a plate of cold pork jelly, and a plate of pickled turnips. All were laid out nicely on the table except the cabbage, which was still cooking and giving off the most delightful aroma.

She had put away her red dress and put on her everyday cotton jacket and pants, but a red flower made of velvet with a small gold paper ingot stuck in it was fastened in her hair. Hsiang Tzu looked her over; she didn't resemble a bride. Every move she made was like that of a woman who had been married for a long time. She was quick, experienced, and had an air of self-confidence, too. While she didn't resemble a bride, still, in the end, it made him feel that a little something new had arrived. She cooked and she set the house to rights. The slight fragrance and the warmth in the room were things he had never experienced before. Never mind what she was like. He realized that he had his own home and a home always has its lovable points. But he didn't know how to act.

"Where did you go, eh?" She dished the cabbage as she spoke.

"Out to take a bath." He took off his long coat.

"Ah! From now on, when you go out, say something! None of this casual hand-flipping and taking off!"

He said nothing.

"Can't you even grunt? If you can't, I'll teach you."

He grunted. What else could he do? He knew he'd married a mother demon but this demon could cook, keep house, curse him but help him too. Yet whatever she did for him still wouldn't taste good. He bit into a steamed bun. The food was much tastier and hotter than what he usually ate, but eating it was no pleasure. He didn't feel any of his usual delight in wolfish swallowing and tigerish gulping when chewing it, and he didn't sweat while he ate.

When he'd finished, he lay down on the heated brick k'ang and stared at the ceiling.

"Hey! Help me do the dishes! I'm no one's scullery maid!" She shouted at him from the other room.

He stood up very lazily and reluctantly, stared at her, and went to help. Ordinarily he was a diligent worker but now he turned his mouth down angrily and came to work. He had often helped her at the rickshaw agency but now she was more and more repulsive the more he looked at her. He had never hated anyone as intensely as he hated her and he couldn't tell why. He was angry but he couldn't let it out and it curled up in his mind. He couldn't cut this knot in two with one stroke so it was pointless to argue with her. He came to the conclusion as he turned around and around in this little room that his life was one big grievance.

When the dishes were done she looked all around and sighed. She smiled tightly. "Well, what now?"

"Huh?" Hsiang Tzu was squatting next to the stove, warming his hands. His hands weren't really cold but he didn't know what to do with them so he thought he might as well warm them. These two little rooms certainly were like a home but he felt awkward and ill at ease in them.

"How about taking me out? We could go to the White Cloud Monastery. No, it's too late. Then why not go out for a walk and look around?" She was determined to enjoy all the pleasures of the newly-wed to the limit. While her wedding had not been quite the thing, still it had come out all right, unconventional though it was. Being with a husband a lot and enjoying things happily for several days was just grand. She had never lacked food or clothes or spending money at home, but there was no man who understood her. Now she intended to make up for this deficiency. She wanted to promenade, to show herself in the streets, in the temples and shops; she wanted to go out with Hsiang Tzu.

Hsiang Tzu didn't want to go out. In the first place, he felt that to go wandering all over the place with a woman in tow was a disgraceful business. In the second place, he believed that a wife who'd got herself married the way she had was best kept hidden at home. This was not a respectable marriage at all and the less she was waved in front of people the better. And furthermore, if they went out how could they possibly avoid meeting someone they knew? Was there a single rickshaw puller in the whole western half of the city who didn't now about Hu Niu and Hsiang Tzu? He couldn't go out and start them all sniggering behind his back.

"Let's talk about it, all right?" He was still squatting.

"What's there to talk about?" she put in, standing next to the stove.

He drew back his hands and put them on his knees. He stared silently at the tiny flames for a long time and then said, "I can't loaf like this!"

"What a hard life!" She laughed once. "For one day you don't pull a rickshaw and you get itchy all over, right? Look at the old man. He played around all his life and still opened a rickshaw agency when he got old. He never pulled a rickshaw. He never sold his strength. He depended on his brains to eat. Now here's something you ought to study a little. What have you got when you get old if you pull a rickshaw all your life? Let's have fun for a few days and then talk about it. Business isn't good only during these next few days so what's your rush? I had no intention of arguing with you for a day or two so don't you get me angry on purpose either!"

"Let's talk it over first." Hsiang Tzu decided not to give in. He couldn't up and leave so he had to think of some way to get work but he had to take a firm stand first. He couldn't be swaying back and forth as if he were on a rope swing.

"Very well. Let's hear it!" She moved a stool over and sat down next to the stove.

"How much money do you have?" he asked.

"Well, well. I knew you'd ask that question. You haven't married a wife, you've married the money, haven't you?"

Hsiang Tzu felt like he'd had the wind knocked out of him and swallowed his rage several times in succession. Old Liu and the rickshaw pullers at the agency all thought he was after money and so he'd hooked Hu Niu. Now she said the same thing herself! His own rickshaw and his own money had been taken for no reason at all and now he was to be oppressed by his wife's few dollars! He'd eaten her food and it had bumped against his backbone all the way down. He hated not being able to grab her by the neck and squeeze! Squeeze! Squeeze until the whites of her eyes showed! He'd choke everyone to death and then cut his own throat. They weren't human beings so they ought to die. He wasn't a man and he ought to die, too. No one need think about living!

He stood up with the intention of going out for another walk. He shouldn't have come back when he did.

She noticed that his expression was antagonistic and so she softened a little. "Very well, I'll tell you. I had five hundred dollars in cash altogether. Taking the sedan chair, three payments in advance on the rent, wallpapering, clothes, the other things I had to buy, and the money I gave you and adding it all up, it came to a little less than one hundred dollars so I've got about four hundred left. I'm telling you so you don't have to worry. Let's enjoy it, since it can give us a little pleasure. As for you, you pull a rickshaw and stink of sweat all year long. Why not look smart and enjoy yourself for a few days? And I've been an old maid all these years so I ought to have a few days of pleasure too. We can still go to the old man for more when it's nearly gone. As far as I am concerned, if I hadn't had that fight with him, I certainly would never have had to get out. Now my anger is all gone. He is still my father no matter what. All he has is one daughter like me and you are a person he really likes too, so we'll be submissive and make up to him for our mistakes. Probably there's nothing that can't be patched up. It's all really made to order! He has the money. We will get it legally in the proper line of inheritance with nothing the least bit irregular. That's much better than if you went and played beast of burden for someone. You go there first two days from now. He may not want to see you. If he won't see you the first time, go a second time. Give him all the face in the world and he can't help but change his views. Afterwards I'll go and say something nice to him and hope for the best. Very likely we'll be able to move right back in. I guarantee you that after we've moved in we'll hold ourselves erect with our chests out and no one will dare give us any sidelong glances. But if we keep on putting up with things in this place indefinitely we'll always be a pair of fugitives. Right?"

None of this had ever occurred to Hsiang Tzu. Ever since Hu Niu had come the Ts'ao house looking for him he had simply assumed that once he'd married her, he'd use her money to buy a rickshaw and pull it himself. It wasn't very manly to use your wife's money but the relationship between them was the kind you can't talk about even though you have a mouth, so there was nothing to be done about it. It never occurred to him that Hu Niu would have a plan like that in mind. Putting on a show of penitence was a plan, all right, but he was not that sort of man. Thinking over his situation from beginning to end, he finally seemed to understand a little. He had had money himself and had let others trick him out of it. So then he'd had a grievance and no one to accuse. Now you can accept money when someone gives it to you but there's absolutely no way you can regard yourself as a man afterward. Your courage and your strength don't matter and you have to go and be someone's slave. You have to be your wife's toy and your father-in-law's lackey. It was as if a man were, in fact, nothing at all, only a bird which goes out by itself to find food and falls into a net. It eats someone else's grain and then behaves itself inside a cage and sings for others and is sold when they feel like it!

He was unwilling to go see old Liu. He had a flesh to flesh relationship with Hu Niu but there was no relationship at all with old Liu. He'd already gotten the worst of it with her and he wasn't about to go beg from her father! "I don't want to loaf!" One sentence was all he said to avoid wasting words in argument.

"Doomed to toil!" she said, scathingly. "If you don't like loafing go be a street vendor!"

"I don't know how! I wouldn't make any money! I know how to pull a rickshaw. I love pulling a rickshaw!" The veins on his head stood out.

"Let me tell you a thing or two. I simply will not let you pull a rickshaw. I simply will not let you get all stunk up with sweat and get onto my k'ang stinking like an outhouse! You have your plans and I have mine. We'll just see who can drive who to the limit. You got a wife but I was the one who spent the money. You didn't put in a penny of your own. Think it over. Between the two of us, who should listen to who?"

Hsiang Tzu was speechless again.

CHAPTER SIXTEEN

THEY LOAFED until the end of the three-week holiday season and Hsiang Tzu was fed up.

Hu Niu was very happy. She steamed sweet dumplings and made Chinese ravioli. She visited Temples during the day and strolled around looking at all the different lanterns hung in the streets in the evening. She wouldn't let him propose anything but she never stinted his mouth, producing new things for him to eat like magic.

There were about eight families in this mixed courtyard and most of them lived in one room. This one room might have as many as eight persons living in it, both young and old. Some of the men pulled rickshaws, some were street vendors, some were policemen, and some were servants. Everyone had a job to do and no one was idle. Even the small children would take baskets and go off early in the morning to get congee at the soup kitchens and go collect bits of coal in the afternoon. Only the very youngest children would stay behind in the courtyard to play or maybe to fight with their bare behinds bright red from the cold.

Ashes, dirty water, and sweepings all landed in the courtyard and no one bothered to sweep it out. The middle of the courtyard was covered with ice. The children used it as a skating rink when they came back from their coal collecting and slid around noisily.

Worst off were the old people and the women. The old people lacked clothing and food and had to lie on the ice-cold k'ang, waiting until the young ones brought a little money home so they could eat a bowl of congee. Perhaps the young workers managed to sell their strength to earn money but they might also come back empty-handed. They had to find some way to relieve their rage when they came back so they'd look for something to argue about. The old people with their

mpty stomachs had to make their tears serve as water and swallowed
hem down.

The women took care of the old people, tended to the young, and
ad to mollify the men as well. They still had to do their usual work
ven when pregnant and had only bran cakes and sweet potato congee
o eat. Not only did they have to do their usual work, they also had to
get the congee and try to do some sewing on the side. Fortunately,
oth young and old lay down when they had eaten and then the wom-
n could sit close to a small kerosene lamp, washing, cooking, sewing,
nd mending. The rooms were so small and the walls so dilapidated
hat the cold wind could blast right through the openings between the
ricks on one side. Straight across the room it would blow and out the
ther side, taking whatever warmth there was inside along. All that
overed their bodies was some ragged cloth. They might have a bowl-
ul or half a bowlful of congee in their bellies and maybe there was a
ix or seven month old fetus there too. They had to work and also see
o it that the young and old were fed first. They were always ill and
heir hair fell out before they were thirty but they could not rest an
our or even a minute as they progressed from sickness to death.
When they died their families had to go to someone charitable and ask
or the money for a coffin.

The girls of sixteen or seventeen had no trousers. All they could do
vas sit inside wrapped up in some tattered thing in a room that was a
atural prison, helping their mothers get the work done as quickly as
ossible. They had to wait till the courtyard was empty to go to the
rivy and then run like a thief. On a winter's day they never saw the
un or the blue sky at all. Those who grew up ugly would in the future
nherit all that was their mother's. Those who looked like something,
nd even they knew it, would be sold into concubinage by their par-
nts sooner or later to "enjoy happiness"!

It was in just such a mixed courtyard as this one that Hu Niu felt
nost content. She was the only one who had food and clothing, who
lidn't have to worry, and who could wander around amusing herself.
he was arrogant. She was well aware of her elegance and ignored
hat horde of poor people in her goings out and comings in. Besides,
he was afraid they might sully or provoke her.

The street vendors, who sold mostly the cheapest stuff like the meat
craped off bones, frozen cabbage, soybean milk, and horse and don-
ey meat, all came here looking for customers. But after Hu Niu

moved in those who sold sheep's head meat, smoked fish, hard biscuit, and brine-cured fried bean curd also shouted a few times in the doorway. She would get a bowl, put on a haughty expression, and take these dainties back to her room. The little children would all stick their iron-wire-thin fingers into their mouths and watch her, as if she were some sort of princess or other. She was enjoying herself and could not, would not, and didn't want to, notice the misfortunes of others.

Hsiang Tzu was contemptuous of her behavior. He was a child of misfortune and knew what deep poverty was. He didn't want to eat all those goodies and begrudged the money. What made him even more frustrated was something he'd finally got straight in his head. She wouldn't let him pull a rickshaw and she fed him well every day, just the way you fatten up a cow and then squeeze the milk out of her! He had turned into her plaything completely! He'd seen it all before in the streets; a thin old bitch in heat would always choose the strongest and fattest dog. He was not only disgusted with this sort of life when he thought about such incidents. He also worried about his health. He knew how a man who sold his strength for a living ought to guard his body: his physique was everything. If he went on living like this he'd soon be nothing but a dried up skeleton. He'd still be just as tall but there'd be nothing left inside him at all. He began to shudder. He figured he'd better start pulling a rickshaw right away if he wanted to save his life. He'd go out and run and then come back and fall into bed and sleep, blind to everything around him. And then, if he didn't eat her good food, he certainly wouldn't have to serve her pleasure either. He decided that was definitely the way to do it; he just couldn't give in to her again. If she was willing to put up the money for a rickshaw, fine. If she wasn't, he could go rent one. He thought it all out and then went and rented a rickshaw without saying a word about it.

He started in on the seventeenth by renting a rickshaw for the whole day from dawn to dusk. After he'd made two fairly long trips he became aware of aches and pains he'd never experienced before. He had cramps in his calves and aches in the groin. He knew where the source of his trouble lay, but in order to console himself, he told himself it was probably because he hadn't pulled a rickshaw for more than twenty days and his legs were out of practice. He'd make a few more trips and get his legs stretched out and that would be the end of the trouble.

So he took another fare. This time he was part of a group of four rickshaws which made the trip together. They picked up their shafts and let a tall fellow about forty years old go in the lead. The tall fellow laughed. As a matter of fact, he knew he didn't have what it takes anymore, unlike the other three, but he tried hard. He knew quite well that he couldn't outrun the three behind him but he refused to act his age. When they had run about half a mile, words of praise came from behind. "Hey, do you want to run a race? You're not far from it!"

He puffed in response, "How can I go slow when I'm running with you guys?" He certainly did not run slowly and even Hsiang Tzu had to use most of his power to keep up with him. His style of running wasn't much to look at. He was such a tall fellow and ran without bending at the waist. His back seemed to be one plank of wood and so his entire torso had to lean forward. When the torso goes in front the hands go behind. It didn't look much like running but more like pulling something while boring your way ahead. His hips were forced to swing because his torso was such a dead board. His feet almost grabbed at the ground as he twisted himself forward with increasing urgency. The twisting from side to side really wasn't slow but you knew right away that he was putting a lot of effort into it when you watched him. He used his whole body to make the turn when they came to corners. They were all sweating for him whereas he appeared to be concerned solely with getting himself forward and paid no attention to how the rickshaw was managing or not managing to get along.

When they arrived the sweat dripped and splashed from the tip of his nose and his earlobes. He put the rickshaw down and stood up quickly with his lips stretched open. His hand shook so much when he took the money that it looked like it couldn't hang onto anything.

They regarded themselves as comrades now that they had made a trip as a group and parked their rickshaws together. Hsiang Tzu and the others wiped off their sweat and talked and laughed like old friends. The tall fellow kept on sweating for some time. He coughed and coughed, spat out a lot of white stuff, and then, when he seemed to have revived a little, began to talk to them.

"I'm done for. This heart, back, and legs of mine don't have any zip to them at all. I can't get my legs going no matter how straight my back is. I get anxious and upset and there's nothing I can do about it."

"Well, you didn't do too badly just now. You think that was a slow trip?" A short fellow of around twenty joined in. "Don't feel bad. The three of us are stout fellows all right but don't we all sweat too?"

The tall one got a little satisfaction out of that and again, in what seemed to be mortification, he sighed.

Another one said, "Now about your way of running. Isn't it a fact that it holds you back? Do you agree? Age does make a difference. I'm serious."

The tall one smiled slightly and shook his head. "Well, it isn't all a matter of age, brothers! I'll tell you one thing you can be sure of. Guy in our line must not get married and that's the truth!" He lowered his voice a bit when he noticed that they were all listening. "Get married and there's no rest for you night or day. You're just played out! Take a look at me. There isn't a trace of vitality left anywhere so I'd really better not run hard. I end up coughing when I grit my teeth and do it and I feel just awful. There's no point talking about it. Guys in our line of work must be bachelors all their lives, damn it! Even those fucking sparrows can pair up but not us! And besides, after you get married there's one brat a year and now I have five of them! And all of them with their mouths open, waiting to eat. Rental fees are high, food is expensive, work is hard. Is there anything you can do? It's not as good as never marrying and rushing off to a cheap whorehouse when you can't stand it any longer. And if you get the clap, well that's life! When a single man dies, he's dead and that's that. But get yourself this joy of a family and what with all those mouths, the old ones and the young ones, you still can't close your eyes when you die. What do you say, am I right or not?" he asked Hsiang Tzu.

Hsiang Tzu nodded.

At this moment a customer came along. The short fellow made the deal first. Then he stepped aside and said to the tall man, "Elder brother, you go! That joy of a family has five kids in it!"

The tall man smiled. "Good enough. I'll make another trip. But according to the rules things shouldn't be done this way. All right, I can take a few more pancakes along when I go home. See you soon brother!"

Watching until the tall fellow was far away, the short one said to himself, "You have to get through a whole fucking lifetime and never even have a wife to pat! And in those fucking big houses one man has four or five women to himself!"

"So never mind other people," said yet another. "You see, when it comes to an occupation like this one, you really have to be careful. That tall guy spoke the truth and no mistake. Take what you just said. What do you get married for? Can you arrange your wife like a jewel and just look at her? Of course not! All right then, that's where you get into trouble. You eat only bran cakes every day and your vitality is worn down on two sides and even the guy who really has the balls for it will end up crawling!"

Hsiang Tzu picked up his rickshaw when he heard that and said casually, "I'm heading south. There's no business here."

"See you!" said the other two together.

Hsiang Tzu seemed not to have heard. He picked up his feet as he went along; his groin was a little painful still! At first he thought he'd return the rickshaw and not work any longer but he simply didn't have the courage to go home. That was no proper wife at home, she was a bloodsucking monster!

The day dragged on. He made a few more trips and still it was only five o'clock. He turned in the rickshaw and wasted some time in a teahouse. He felt hungry after drinking two pots of tea so he decided to eat and then go home. He ate a dozen meat-filled pancakes and a bowl of red bean and rice congee and, belching, went slowly homeward. He knew quite well there was a thunderhead waiting for him at home but he was calm. He had made his decision. He would not argue with her or yell at her. He'd just put down his head and go to sleep. Tomorrow he'd go out and pull a rickshaw again and she could do what she liked!

Hu Niu was sitting in the outer room when he went in. On the verge of tears, she looked at him. Hsiang Tzu had intended to be nice to her and try a little sweet talk but he wasn't accustomed to that sort of thing and went into the inner room with his head down instead. She made not a sound. The silence in the two small rooms was like that in an ancient cave deep in the hills. The coughs, talk, and crying children of the neighbors could all be heard distinctly and yet seemed very remote. It was just like listening to distant sounds when in the mountains.

Neither of them was willing to speak first. They lay on the k'ang with their mouths closed like two big eternally mute turtles. Waking up somewhat later, Hu Niu spoke, her tone half angry and half amused. "So what did you do when you went out? You were gone all day."

"Went to pull a rickshaw." He spoke as if he were partly asleep and partly awake. His throat felt as if it had a lump in it.

"Oh! So if you don't get all stunk up with sweat you get the itch, do you? You low-life! I cook for you and you don't come home to eat. Is wandering all over the map so delightful? If you dare go out tomorrow I'll just hang myself to show you a thing or two. What I say I'll do, I'll do!"

"I can't loaf!"

"You can't go and look for the old man?"

"I won't do it."

"You really are too much!"

Hsiang Tzu was furious. He had to keep from saying what was in his heart and yet he couldn't put up with any more from her. "I'm going to pull a rickshaw and I'll buy my own rickshaw. If anyone tries to stop me I'll just leave and never come back!"

"Ummm." She made the sound through her nose; it was long, drawn out, and changed its pitch. She used this sound to show her pride and her contempt for Hsiang Tzu but in her heart she turned a corner. She knew Hsiang Tzu was, while very peaceable, a stubborn man. The words of a stubborn man are not spoken in jest. It hadn't been all that easy to catch him and she couldn't let him get away just like that. He was an ideal man; well behaved, diligent and frugal, and strong. It wouldn't be easy for someone like her to get hold of another such treasure. Being flexible, that was capability, so she tried a little flattery.

"I know you're ambitious but you ought to realize that I really love you, too. If you refuse to go see the old man that's how it will be. I'll go see him. I am still his daughter, no matter what, so it doesn't matter if I lose a little face."

"Even if he wants us back I'll still go pull a rickshaw!" Hsiang Tzu wanted to make the situation perfectly clear.

Hu Niu said nothing for some time. She had never expected him to be that clever. His words were simple but he was obviously implying that he wouldn't fall into her snares again. He certainly was not a stupid donkey. For this reason she became even more intrigued with him but thought she'd better use a little caution right now when settling this big fellow, or maybe this big thing, who was quite capable of lashing out with his hind feet when upset. She'd better not curb him too sharply. After all, finding a guy this big hadn't been easy. She must let loose and then tighten up and so ensure he would never leap off the palm of her hand.

"Very well. You love pulling a rickshaw and there's nothing I can do about that. But you must take an oath that you won't go to work for a family and you'll come home every day. You see, I'll get upset if I don't see you every day! Promise me you'll come home early every day."

Hsiang Tzu remembered the story that tall fellow had told that afternoon! He stared at the darkness and saw a crowd of rickshaw pullers, street vendors, and laborers all dragging along with their backs bent. His future would be like that too. But it would do him no good to annoy her again. He figured that as long as he could pull a rickshaw he'd have won for once.

"I'll always be for hire by the day." He made the promise.

She wasn't really eager to go looking for old Liu, even though she had said she would. Of course, the two of them had got into arguments almost every day but the present situation was not the same. It wasn't the sort of problem that could be solved by "saying a few words now and a few words then and soon the clouds and mist will scatter." She was no longer regarded as a member of the Liu clan. Married women are always more or less remote from their parents, so she dared not march in as if she had the right, the way you would enter a law court. Perhaps the old man might actually turn his face away and not recognize her. Then she could only make a big fuss. But there wouldn't be a single thing she could do about it if he refused to let go of his money even if it killed him. And if someone acted as mediator all he could do when they came to an impasse would be to advise her to go away because she had her own home now.

Hsiang Tzu pulled a rickshaw as usual and she paced the floor by herself. She intended to put on her nice clothes and go see Papa again and again. She'd decide to do it and find that her hands were reluctant to move. She was in a quandary. She just had to go back for the sake of her own comfort and happiness, but she thought not going back was justifiable for the sake of her prestige. If the old man melted a little, all she had to do was bring Hsiang Tzu back to the agency. Naturally, she could find something else for him to do. He didn't have to pull a rickshaw. And besides, they could get a firm grip on Papa's business.

Suddenly she realized something. What if the old man was stubborn to the end? She'd lose face. No, she'd not only lose face, she'd also have to admit that she was the wife of a rickshaw man! Phooey! There wouldn't be any difference between her and the other women in this place. Suddenly her mind was full of deep blackness. She almost regretted marrying Hsiang Tzu. It didn't matter how ambitious he was. If Papa didn't nod his head, he'd be a rickshaw man all his life. When she thought of that she almost considered returning home alone and just severing relations with Hsiang Tzu with one stroke. She couldn't lose everything on his account. She went on to the thought that the happy life she had with Hsiang Tzu could not in fact be described in words. She sat up at the head of the k'ang and in a vague sort of way pursued the joy that came after marriage in her thoughts. This joy wasn't here and it wasn't there. It was only a kind of fascination that one couldn't talk about. Her entire body was like a big red flower blossoming warmly, fragrantly, beneath the rays of the sun.

No. She could not leave him. Let him go pull a rickshaw. Let him even go out begging. She'd still stay with him forever. Take a look at the other women in this place; if they could stand it, so could she. That's that. She would not even consider going back to the house of Liu.

Hsiang Tzu had been unwilling to set foot in Hsi An Gate street ever since leaving the agency. For the last two days he'd been heading for the east side as soon as he went out the door with his rickshaw in order to avoid meeting anyone from the Jen Ho agency at any of the west side stops. Running into one of the Jen Ho men would be very embarrassing. But today he deliberately went past the place after turning in his rickshaw for no other reason than wanting to take a look. Hu Niu's words were still on his mind. It was as if he had to test whether he had the courage to go back to the agency or not, just in case Hu Niu and the old man did make up. But he'd better find out whether he had the nerve to walk down this street or not before he went back to the agency.

He pulled his hat down and started sneaking up on the agency when still quite far away. His one fear was that he might be seen by someone he knew. He could see the light over the gate from far off but he didn't know why he felt so very ill at ease. He recalled what it was like the first time he went there, remembered Hu Niu's later enticements, and recalled the events on the evening of the birthday party. All of these memories were extraordinarily vivid and floated before his eyes like paintings.

Among these paintings were still others, all of them quite clear, which were squeezed in here and there: the Western Hills, camels, the Ts'ao house and the detective, all bright, all frightful, and coming one right after another. These pictures were very distinct, yet his mind, on the other hand, was a little confused. It was almost as if he were actually seeing these paintings and forgetting that he was in them, too. He began to get all mixed up when he thought about his relationship with them. Suddenly they whirled around from top to bottom and left to right, all in a muddle of bits and pieces. He could not figure out why he should have been put through all those trials and suffered all those wrongs. The length of time he had spent in these episodes seemed quite long and quite short too. He was baffled by trying to decide how old he was. He knew only that, compared to the first time he had come to the Jen Ho agency, he was much, much, older. Back then his heart had been full of hope; now his guts were full of worry. He didn't understand what they were all about but those pictures certainly were not deceiving him.

And there was the Jen Ho agency right in front of him. He stood across the street staring blankly at the excessively bright electric light. He looked and looked and suddenly his heart jumped. The first word had changed its shape! He couldn't read but he did remember what that first character had looked like and the one there now was a very strange one indeed. He couldn't think of any reason for it. He looked again at the east room and the west room, those two rooms he would never be able to forget. There was no light on in either of them. He got impatient just standing there so he ducked his head and went home.

He tried to figure it all out on the way. Surely the Jen Ho agency hadn't gone out of business? He'd better find out about it by asking around, but it wouldn't do any good to tell the old lady about it right off.

Hu Niu was just sitting there chewing melon seeds to relieve her boredom when he got home.

"So. Late again!" There wasn't the trace of a friendly expression on her face. "I'm telling you I won't put up with this! You go out and stay out all day and I'm stuck here. What with this place so full of tramps,

I'm afraid of losing things. There isn't a single place to go for a bit of talk all day long and that will not do. I'm not made of wood. So you'd better think of something because this arrangement simply isn't good enough!"

Hsiang Tzu said nothing.

"Speak up. What do you want to infuriate people for? Do you have a mouth or not? Do you?" The more she talked the faster and shriller it was, and like the barrage from a piece of artillery.

Hsiang Tzu still had nothing to say.

"Let's do it this way." She was really furious but also seemed a little baffled by his manner. Although she was neither laughing nor crying, her face revealed the fretfulness she could do nothing to relieve. "We'll buy two rickshaws and rent them out so you can stay home and eat up the profits. Will that do? Well, will it?"

"Two rickshaws will bring in thirty cents a day and that's not enough to eat off of. We'll rent one and I'll pull one myself. That way we'll make enough." Hsiang Tzu spoke very slowly but very naturally. When he heard "buy a rickshaw" he forgot about everything else.

"But wouldn't that amount to the same thing? You still wouldn't be home!"

"Doing it that way will work out all right." Hsiang Tzu's thoughts all seemed to turn around the problems of rickshaws. "We rent one out and get a full day's fee. I pull the other one for half a day and rent it out the other half. If I pull in the daytime, I'll go out very early and come home around three. If I work the late shift, I'll go out right at three and come back during the night. That'll be swell!"

She nodded. "Let me think it over. If there's no better solution we'll just do it that way."

Hsiang Tzu was delighted. He figured he'd be pulling his own rickshaw again if this plan was really carried out. Even though his wife had bought it for him he could still save up slowly and buy another one himself. And at that point he realized that she had some good points too, so he smiled at her. It was a naive self-revelatory smile, as if he had canceled all previous woes with one stroke and, by smiling, had exchanged them for a whole new world. It was just as simple and quick as changing your clothes.

CHAPTER SEVENTEEN

GRADUALLY Hsiang Tzu found out what had happened to the Jen Ho agency. Old Liu had sold some of his rickshaws and turned the rest over to a famous west-side rickshaw owner. Hsiang Tzu could guess what it meant. Old Liu's age had caught up with him and he had no daughter to help him. He couldn't keep the business going alone so he simply gave up, took the money, and went off to enjoy it. Where had he gone? Hsiang Tzu never found out.

When faced with this news he couldn't say whether he should be happy about it or not. From the point of view of his own inclinations and stubborn intentions, Hu Niu's plans could be regarded as completely useless now that Liu had decided to reject his daughter. He could now go out and work to earn his own rice properly and not be dependent on anyone else. From the point of view of the estate of old Liu, it was indeed a little sad. Who knew how Liu would waste the money? And he and Hu Niu wouldn't benefit by a penny.

But that's what it had all come to and he wasn't interested in worrying about it, much less being excited about it. This is how he thought: his strength belonged to him no matter what. He was willing to sell it to earn money, so eating would never become a problem. Simply, and without putting any emotion into it at all, he told Hu Niu the news.

But she got upset. She saw her future all too clearly as soon as she heard the story. She was done for! Everything was done for! All she would do for the rest of her life was be a rickshaw man's wife. She was stuck in this place for the rest of her life!

It had occurred to her that her father might marry again but she certainly had never imagined he would wave his hands and leave just like that. If the old man really had married again she could have gone and fought for the inheritance or maybe have formed an alliance with her stepmother and gained some advantage for herself. She had lots of plans but for them to work the old man had to keep the agency open. She'd never dreamed he would be so stubborn and nasty as to convert the whole works into cash and sneak away! When she had that big fight with him she had thought it was merely another method to get her way and of course they'd make up soon. She knew the agency couldn't manage without her but who could have guessed that the old man would toss it away?

There was already some indication of spring; the buds on the ends of the branches were showing a touch of red. But spring in this big mixed courtyard did not arrive on the tips of branches. There wasn't a single flowering tree there. Instead, the spring wind blew little pock marks in the ice in the center of the courtyard first and then blew a fetid stench off the trash heap. It made a tiny whirlwind that piled chicken feathers, garlic skins, and torn paper up in a corner.

Each of the four seasons had its problems for the people living there. The old people dared to bask in the sun and girls rubbed a little of the soot off their noses and now some of the pink and yellow of their skin showed. Mothers could let their raggedy children out to play in the yard without being embarrassed. The little children could drag around bits of paper like kites running about as they pleased and their grubby hands didn't get so cold the skin split here and there.

But the soup kitchen put out its cook fires, the relief agencies stopped giving away rice, and benevolent people stopped giving away money. It was as if they had turned all the poor over to the spring wind and sunlight! It was precisely at the time when the spring wheat was green as young grass and the stored grain ran low that the price of grain followed the rules and went up. The days lengthened and the old people couldn't go to bed early all the time and use their dreams to trick their hungry stomachs. Spring arrived among mankind and in this large mixed courtyard it only increased the distress. Old lice, the worst kind of all, sometimes hopped out of the cotton wadding in the old people's or the children's clothes and gained the experience of a little sunshine!

Hu Niu looked at the melting ice in the middle of the yard and at all those tattered, torn, and inadequate clothes; smelled the varied and slightly warm aromas; heard the old people's sad sighs and the children crying and half her heart grew cold.

Everyone hid inside in the winter and the garbage was all frozen in

the ice. Now people came out and objects revealed their actual shapes.
Even the rubble wall dribbled dirt down, as if preparing to collapse
on the first rainy day. When the "greenery" all over this courtyard
opened its repulsive blossoms the place was much uglier and disgusting than in wintertime by far. Phooey! And this was the time she
realized she would have to stay in this place forever. There would
come a time when all her money was gone and Hsiang Tzu was only a
rickshaw man!

She told Hsiang Tzu to watch the house and went to Nan Yuan to
see her aunt and get some news of the old man.

Auntie said yes, indeed, he had come to her house once. Probably it
was around the twelfth of the first lunar month. He came to wish her a
happy New Year and also to tell her he planned to go to Shanghai or
Tientsin to amuse himself. He said he'd worked all his life and never
left the capital and that wasn't very heroic, was it? So he thought he'd
just go somewhere else and learn something new while he still had
some breath left in him. Also, he hadn't the face to hang around the
city any more because his own daughter had disgraced him.

That was all her report amounted to and her conclusion was even
briefer. Maybe the old man really has gone away and maybe he only
said he was going away and has actually gone and hidden out somewhere. Who knows!

When Hu Niu got home she beat her head on the k'ang and wept furiously. She cried for a long time without a single feigned sob and
made her eyelids all puffy. When her sobbing was over she wiped her
eyes and said to Hsiang Tzu, "All right, you tyrant! Everything will
be done to please you. I bet on the wrong number. If you marry a
rooster you obey the rooster and that's that. I'll give you one hundred
dollars and you go buy a rickshaw."

There was a secret thought behind this move of hers. She had originally intended to buy two rickshaws, one for Hsiang Tzu to pull and
one to rent out, but now she changed her mind. She'd buy only one
and have him pull it. The rest of the money would stay right in her
hands. With the money in her hands the power was also hers and she
wasn't about to let go of it. After all, suppose that Hsiang Tzu
changed his mind about her after he got the money for the rickshaw?
She'd better not be unprepared! Furthermore, having old Liu go off
like that had made her feel that nothing could be relied on. After all,
no one can know for sure what will happen tomorrow and when you

have something to enjoy it's much better to enjoy it while you have it. She had cash in hand and if there was something she liked to eat, well, she'd just buy it, for she had always been accustomed to eating snacks. Living with Hsiang Tzu, that first-class rickshaw man, and having her own money to fill in for her spending money, she would just enjoy whatever she fancied. The day would come when the money was all gone but no one can go on living forever! She had already wronged herself by marrying a rickshaw puller even though she couldn't have done anything else. She could not go to him with her eyes down and her palm up wanting money every day because she hadn't a penny in her own pocket. Her decision made her feel a little better. She knew quite well that the future was impossible but at least she would not have to bow her head immediately.

It was like strolling east when the sun is setting; the distant places are already dark but there is still a little light just ahead of you so you take advantage of it to go on a little farther.

Hsiang Tzu did not argue with her. Buying a rickshaw was just fine by him. As long as it was his own rickshaw he could earn sixty or seventy cents every day no matter what, and that was enough to get along on. Not only did he not argue, he even felt rather pleased. There was no question that he'd put up with all those hardships in the past because he had to buy a rickshaw of his own. Now he could buy another one so what more was there to say? Naturally, you can't save any money when you pull one rickshaw to feed two people and it would be dangerous if he hadn't the money to buy a new one when this one got old. But, after all, buying a rickshaw wasn't all that easy to do and he ought to be satisfied that he could buy one now. Why should he have to worry about things so far away?

A certain Ch'iang, who lived there too, wanted to sell his rickshaw. He had sold his daughter, nineteen-year-old Hsiao Fu Tzu, to a soldier last summer for two hundred dollars. Ch'iang had the air of prosperity for a while after she left. He redeemed everthing he had pawned and bought some new clothes besides. The whole family was very well dressed indeed.

Ch'iang's wife was the ugliest woman in the place. Her forehead bulged, she had heavy jowls, no hair on her head, teeth that stuck out, and a face all covered with spots. It made you sick to your stomach to look at her. She wept for her daughter and wore her new blue dress while she sobbed.

Ch'iang had always been ill-tempered, and he drank a lot after selling his daughter. After several drinks his eyes would fill with tears and he would delight in finding fault with everyone. Although Mrs. Ch'iang wore new clothes and had enough to eat, her joy did not balance her sorrow for now the number of times she was beaten was doubled.

Ch'iang was past forty and figured he could not pull a rickshaw anymore. So he bought a basket rig to work as a street vendor selling a complete line of goods such as fruits, melons, peanuts, and cigarettes. But after doing this for two months he made a rough accounting and found he had not only come out short but was losing a great deal! He was accustomed to pulling a rickshaw and couldn't cope with the technique of selling things. Rickshaw pulling was a matter of picking up business when you met it. It's done once you get the job and if you don't get it, never mind. It takes great skill in bargaining to be a street vendor and he didn't know how to do it. Rickshaw pullers know all about getting things on credit; therefore he would have felt ashamed if he hadn't allowed his friends to have credit. But once credit is given, it isn't always easy to take it back. And so he had no good paying customers at all. Everyone he did business with wanted credit and then wouldn't pay up. There was no way he could avoid losing money. When he lost money he got frustrated and when he got frustrated he drank even more. He constantly got into arguments with policemen and took out his rage on his wife and children. Offending the police and beating his wife was all due to drink. He was extremely sorry and hurt when he sobered up. When he thought about it again, he realized it was his own daughter who had been sold for that small amount of money and he knew it was not manly of him to simply lose it all in trade and then beat people up when he got drunk. At such a time he would sleep in a sort of stupor all day and hand his troubles over to his dreams.

He decided to quit being a street vendor and go back to pulling a rickshaw. He couldn't fritter all that money away to no purpose. He bought a rickshaw. He was utterly unreasonable when he was drunk, but there was nothing he enjoyed more than putting on a handsome appearance when he was sober. He was very fussy about every particular because of his love for an imposing appearance; everything has its standards, after all. He felt that he was a topnotch rickshaw man so, when he had purchased his new rickshaw and was properly dressed, he had to drink good tea and carry handsome passengers. He would stand resplendently with his new rickshaw and his white outfit at a rickshaw stand, chatting with everybody. Trying to get a passenger was always beneath him. Sometimes he would brush off the rickshaw with his new blue cloth duster. Sometimes he would stamp his new white-soled shoes. Sometimes he would stare at the tip of his nose as he stood beside his rickshaw grinning and waiting for someone to come by and praise it. Of course, that would provide a topic for conversation and they would chatter endlessly. He could waste several whole days this way. And when he finally did get a proper fare his legs were no match for his rickshaw and his clothes; he couldn't run! And this made him miserable all over again. When he was miserable he thought of his daughter and then all he could do was drink. In this way, all his money was squandered and all he had left was the rickshaw.

Sometime in early November he had got really drunk. When he came in the two boys, one thirteen, one eleven, promptly decided to slip out. This enraged him and he gave them each a kick. Mrs. Ch'iang said something or other. He threw her down and trampled her stomach. She lay on the floor without making a sound for a long time. The two boys got frantic. One grabbed a coal shovel, the other brandished a rolling pin, and they went after their father at the risk of their lives. They all fell in a tumbling heap. Arms and legs were everywhere. Mrs. Ch'iang was stepped on many times. The neighbors came in and, with great difficulty, got Mrs. Ch'iang up onto the k'ang. The two boys hugged their mother and began to wail. Mrs. Ch'iang came to but never set foot on the ground again. She stopped breathing about a month later. She was wearing the blue dress she made after her daughter was sold.

Her family was upset; nothing would do but an accusation laid against Ch'iang before the magistrate. Old friends mediated the dispute as persuasively as they could and her family retreated a step. Ch'iang had to promise to give her a proper funeral and pay her family fifteen dollars, so he pawned his rickshaw for sixty. When New Year rolled around he thought about getting rid of it for he had no hope of ever redeeming it himself. When he was drunk he thought about selling one son but, indeed, no one wanted him. He also hunted up Hsiao Fu Tzu's husband, who absolutely refused to admit that any such man was his father-in-law. Naturally, there was nothing more to say.

Hsiang Tzu knew all about the history of this rickshaw and he didn't really want it. There were plenty of other rickshaws so why buy this particular one? This ill-omened rickshaw, this rickshaw got in trade for a daughter and sold because of the murder of a wife? Hu Niu didn't see it that way. She figured that getting it for eighty dollars was a bargain! The rickshaw had been used for only six months and even the color of the tires hadn't changed much. Besides, it had been made by a famous west side shop. Don't you have to pay fifty or sixty dollars when you buy one only about seventy percent new? She couldn't let such a bargain go. She also knew that money was tight everywhere right after New Year so Ch'iang couldn't sell it for more. And besides, he wanted spending money in a hurry. She went to look at it herself, settled on a price with Ch'iang, and paid him.

All Hsiang Tzu could do was wait and say nothing. It wouldn't do for him to say anything because the money was not his. He looked the rickshaw over carefully after it was purchased; it certainly was strong and well made but he always felt a little uneasy about it. What made him most unhappy was that the black lacquered body had its brass fittings covered with white enamel. When Ch'iang was making arrangements to buy it he thought the contrast of black and white would be pretty snappy but it had the air of a funeral about it to Hsiang Tzu. It looked like it was in mourning. He longed to change the cover at least. Maybe a yellow or silver one might be enough to add a little color. But he did not discuss this point with Hu Niu to avoid getting her stirred up again.

Everyone paid close attention to this rickshaw when he took it out and some people called it "little widow." Hsiang Tzu wasn't happy about that at all. He kept trying different ways of not thinking about it but the rickshaw was with him all day long. He was always apprehensive, as if he didn't know when trouble would turn up. Sometimes he would suddenly think about Ch'iang and all his hard luck. It was as if he was pulling a coffin, not a rickshaw. Now and then he saw ghosts riding in it, or thought he did.

But certainly nothing had gone wrong since he had started to pull this rickshaw, even though his heart pounded and was jumpy.

The days were getting warmer and warmer. He took off his padded clothes. He really didn't need clothes with linings either and could get by with only a thin shirt and pants. Peking doesn't have much of a spring. The length of the days was almost more than one could stand and everyone felt sleepy and tired. Hsiang Tzu went out early and by the time four o'clock rolled around he knew he'd already sold quite enough of his strength; but the sun was still quite high and while he didn't want to work anymore, he didn't want to quit either. Unable to make up his mind, he would yawn long and lazily.

If these long days made him feel tired and dejected, Hu Niu, sitting at home was even lonelier. In winter she could keep warm next to the stove and listen to the wind outside. Glum though she might feel, she still had one slight consolation: it's just as well she didn't have to go out. Now the stove had been shifted outside under the eaves and she had absolutely nothing to do inside. Besides, the courtyard was foul and stinking and there wasn't a single blade of grass in it. And she couldn't feel at ease about her neighbors when she did go out, so she'd hurry out and come right back every time she went shopping and didn't take the time to stroll around for a while. She was just like a bee trapped in a room, vainly looking at the sun outside and unable to fly out.

She had nothing to say to the other women there. Kids and housework were all they talked about and she was accustomed to ruder topics. She didn't like to join in, or listen to, what they had to say. Their grievances stemmed from their miserable lives and any little thing could bring on tears. Her grievances stemmed from dissatisfaction with her life. She had no tears to let fall so she wondered who she could swear at to relieve some of her gloom instead. She and they could not understand each other for this reason and it was far better to let everybody take care of their own affairs. There was no need for conversation.

When the middle of May came she had a companion; Ch'iang's daughter, Hsiao Fu Tzu, came home. Her "husband" was an army officer. He always set up a kind of basic household everywhere he was stationed. He'd spend one or two hundred dollars on a young unmarried girl, buy a plank bed and some chairs, and then he could enjoy his time there. When his unit was ordered elsewhere, he'd just let the whole arrangement drop and leave girl and planks behind. Spending one or two hundred for a stay of a year and a half was no loss for him at all. If he hired a servant to do the mending and washing of clothes, the cooking, and other such trifles, what with feeding her plus her salary, wouldn't he have to spend at least eight or ten dollars a month? By marrying a girl he got both a servant and someone to sleep with; and what's more, she was guaranteed clean and disease free. If he liked her, he'd have a dress made up for her out of imported cotton print cloth for a dollar or so. If he didn't like her, he'd make her squat in the room naked and there wasn't a thing she could do about it. He didn't regret in the least the chairs and planks when the time came for him to move, because he owed the last two months' rent and would just leave the girl to find a way to pay it. Selling the planks and everything else probably still wouldn't be enough to pay the bill in full.

Hsiao Fu Tzu sold the bed planks, paid the rent, and came home wearing an imported cotton print dress and a pair of silver earrings.

Ch'iang had almost twenty dollars left after selling the rickshaw and paying the pawnshop back with interest. Sometimes he felt that having a wife die on him when he was middle-aged was terribly sad and, since nobody felt sorry for him, he'd console himself by going out to drink and eat good food. It seemed at such times that he hated money and he spent it recklessly. Sometimes he thought he'd really better exert himself and get his boys grown up for then there'd be some hope for the future And when he thought that way about his sons, he'd let out a whoop and buy a big pile of food for them to eat. His eyes would fill with tears while he watched them gobble and wolf down the food and he'd say to himself, "Motherless children! Ill-fated children! Papa goes on struggling, struggling for the children. I don't feel put upon. It doesn't mean a thing whether I eat my fill or not. I must let the children eat all they want first! Eat up! It'll be enough for me if you don't forget me when you are grown up!" At such times he spent quite a lot and gradually the money was all used up.

When he was broke, it was time for him to drink and lose his temper all over again, and he paid no attention to what the boys ate for several days.

The boys were helpless. All they could do was try to think of a way to get some money themselves so they could buy something to eat. They could go lend a hand at weddings and funerals as paid marchers in the processions. They could follow the trashmen and collect little bits of copper and wastepaper. Sometimes they could afford fried pancakes. Sometimes all they could get was bran and sweet potatoes which they ate skin and all. Sometimes they had only a penny between them and then all they could buy was peanuts or dried beans. They didn't stop your hunger but at least you could chew on them a while.

They saw someone who cared when Hsiao Fu Tzu came back; each of them hugged one of her legs. There was nothing to be said so they wept; Mama was no more so Sister was Mama!

Ch'iang didn't react when she came back. All her return did was add one more mouth to feed, but when he saw how happy the boys were, he couldn't help agreeing that the household ought to have a female in it to cook for them and wash the clothes. There wasn't any point to saying something to her; he'd just have to work it out somehow.

Hsiao Fu Tzu had developed into a fairly pretty girl. She had been very thin but she'd put on a lot of weight while living with the officer and had grown a little taller. Although her round face with long and well-matched eyes and eyebrows were not features that were particularly striking, on the other hand, she wasn't hard on the eyes at all. Her upper lip was too short and, when she was either angry or smiling, drew back a little to reveal very white and even teeth.

The officer had been especially fond of those teeth of hers. Her face took on a simpleminded, thoughtless appearance when she showed them and at the same time it seemed to have some attractiveness to it. This expression was just like that of all other poor but pretty girls in its resemblance to a flower which, as long as it had the slightest fragrance or color, would be picked by someone and carried off to the market to be sold.

Hu Niu had always ignored the other residents but now she took Hsiao Fu Tzu as her friend. In the first place Hsiao Fu Tzu looked like something. Second, she had a long imported cotton print dress. Third, Hu Niu assumed that since Hsiao Fu Tzu had been married to an army officer, she must have seen the world. Hu Niu, therefore, was willing to be friends with her.

Women do not make friends easily but friendships form very quickly when they want to. In a few days the two of them were close friends. Hu Niu loved snacks and she'd always call Hsiao Fu Tzu to come over to chat and eat every time she got things like melon seeds. During this gay chatter Hsiao Fu Tzu would show her teeth in her foolish way and tell Hu Niu about all sorts of things Hu Niu had never heard of. She had certainly never "enjoyed happiness" with that officer, but he had taken her to a restaurant or a play when he felt sociable so she had plenty of things to talk about and it made Hu Niu envious.

She had also had quite a number of experiences that should not be mentioned. They had all been horrible to her, but to Hu Niu they were something to be relished. Hu Niu would beg her to tell. She was too embarrassed to talk but also too embarrassed to refuse her hostess. She had looked through *The Spring Palace*, a graphically illustrated "how to do it" book for newlyweds. Hu Niu had never seen it. After hearing about matters of this sort once, Hu Niu wanted to hear about them all over again. She regarded Hsiao Fu Tzu as a person who was most adorable and most enviable and also well worth being jealous of. When she'd heard all there was to tell she took another look at herself, her looks, her age, and her husband, and felt that her life was one enormous grievance. She'd never experienced a springtime in her youth and there was absolutely no hope for one in the future. And right now that Hsiang Tzu was a lump of stuff sort of like an inert glazed brick! The more discontented she was with Hsiang Tzu, the more she loved Hsiao Fu Tzu. Even though Hsiao Fu Tzu was poor and pitiable, in Hu Niu's eyes she was a person who had enjoyed happiness, a person who had really lived. Even if she were to up and die there'd be no injustice in it. In her view Hsiao Fu Tzu was an adequate example of what a woman ought to receive and enjoy.

Hu Niu seemed not to have noticed Hsiao Fu Tzu's suffering. Hsiao Fu Tzu had come home with nothing and now had to take care of her two brothers somehow or other, never mind her shiftless father. But how could she earn the money to feed them?

Ch'iang was drunk and had an idea. "If you really love your brothers, you certainly have a way to get the money to feed them. You all wait for me to feed you, and I have to go out and work all day as somebody's draft animal, but I must eat my fill first. How can I work on an empty stomach? Let me slip and break my neck and how funny do you think that will be, eh? Here you are just sitting around and sitting around and you've got it ready-made the whole time. If you don't sell it, what else are you waiting for?"

Looking from her drunk-as-a-cat father to her two starved-as-mice brothers, Hsiao Fu Tzu could only weep. But tears couldn't move her father and tears couldn't fill up her brothers; she must produce something more substantial. She had to sell her own body in order to feed her brothers. Hugging her younger brother, her tears fell onto his head. He said, "Sister, I'm hungry!" Sister! Sister is a hunk of meat and must be given to brother to eat!

Hu Niu did not offer comfort to Hsiao Fu Tzu. On the contrary, she wanted to aid and abet her, and willingly spent a little money to get Hsiao Fu Tzu all dressed up properly. She could pay Hu Niu back when she earned some money. Hu Niu was willing to lend her a room because her own place was too dirty. Hu Niu's rooms were more or less presentable and besides, there were two rooms, so everybody had some space to turn around in. Hsiang Tzu did not come home during the day, so Hu Niu could take delight in helping her friend and see quite a lot, and learn quite a bit more, about all those things she'd missed out on and had hardly imagined and never done.

Hu Niu made one condition: she must be given twenty cents every time Hsiao Fu Tzu used the room. Friends are friends but business is business and she had to keep the room neat and tidy because of Hsiao Fu Tzu's business. She not only had to work hard at it, she also had to spend more money. How else could she get brooms, dustpans, and the like? Certainly twenty cents could not be regarded as too much. It was because they were friends that she was able to do her such a favor.

Hsiao Fu Tzu showed her teeth. Her tears fell into her stomach.

Hsiang Tzu didn't know anything about any of it and he didn't get a good night's sleep either. Hu Niu had helped Hsiao Fu Tzu to succeed and now she wanted to use Hsiang Tzu's body to find her lost springtime.

CHAPTER EIGHTEEN

THERE WAS SIMPLY no human sound at all in the mixed courtyard when June came. The children went out very early clutching their broken baskets to collect whatever they could. By nine that poisonous flower of a sun was already drying and splitting the skin on their skinny backs and they were forced to come home with what they had gathered and eat whatever the big people gave them. The somewhat older children, if they could scrape up the least amount of capital, would buy some bits of natural ice from an icehouse and, combining it with some they had scrounged, would go out and sell it all quickly.

If they hadn't got together this mite of capital, then they'd all go to the moat outside the city wall and take baths, stealing coal at the railway station outside of town without any extra trouble on the way. Or they'd go catch some dragonflies and cicadas to sell to the children of rich families.

The younger children didn't dare go so far. They all went to places nearby where there were trees and collected locust tree insects, digging their larvae out for fun.

After all the children had gone out, and all the men were gone too, the women would sit in their rooms with their backs bare but none of them dared go outside. Not because of the way they looked, but because the ground in the courtyard was already hot enough to burn their feet.

Finally, when the sun was fast setting, the men and children came back in a continual stream. By this time there was shade from the wall and a little cool breeze in the courtyard. The hot air stored up in the rooms all day made them like the inside of a steamer basket. Everybody sat in the courtyard waiting for the women to get the cooking done. The courtyard was quite crowded then; it was just like a marketplace but one without merchandise. They had all been through one day's worth of heat and they were red-eyed and ill-tempered. Their bellies were empty again and their faces even more anxious and pale. Let one word be spoken out of line and some of them wanted to beat the children, others wanted to beat their wives, and if they couldn't be beaten, at least they could be cursed at furiously. This sort of ruckus continued until everyone had eaten.

After eating, some of the children just lay down on the ground and went to sleep while others went out to the street to chase and frolic around. The adults all felt more cheerful after they had eaten their fill and those who enjoyed talking gathered in several groups to discuss the misfortunes of the day.

But those who had not yet eaten had no place to pawn anything or sell anything, assuming that they had anything to pawn or sell, because the pawnshops were already closed. The men paid no attention to how hot the room was. They dropped their heads down onto the k'ang and made not a sound or, perhaps, cursed loudly. The women held back their tears and tried to smooth things over. Then they went out and, after who knows how many rebuffs, finally managed to borrow twenty cents or so. Clutching this precious money, they went to buy cornmeal to make some mush for the family.

Hu Niu and Hsiang Tzu were not part of this pattern of living. Hu Niu was pregnant and this time it was true. Hsiang Tzu would go out bright and early but she always waited until eight or nine and then got up. It is a traditional and erroneous belief that it won't do to exercise when pregnant and Hu Niu really took it to heart. Besides, she wanted to take advantage of her condition to show off. Everyone else had to get up and get moving early. She was the only one who could calmly enjoy lying in bed as long as she liked. When evening came, she'd take a small stool to a place outside the front gate where there was a little cool breeze and sit there. She went in after almost everyone else in the place had gone to bed. She couldn't be bothered to gossip with them.

Hsiao Fu Tzu got up late too, but she had another reason. She feared the sidelong glances the men gave her, so she waited until they'd all gone to work and then, and only then, did she dare go outside her door. During the day, if she didn't visit Hu Niu, she'd go out walking because her advertisement was simply herself. In the evening, to avoid attracting the attention of the men who lived there, she would go out into the streets for another turn and sneak back when she figured they had all gone to bed.

Hsiang Tzu and Ch'iang were the exceptions among the men. Hsiang Tzu disliked entering this courtyard and feared going into his rooms even more. The endless griping of all the other men made him frantic and he longed to have a quiet place to sit by himself. At home, he felt more and more that Hu Niu was like a mother tiger. On top of that, the rooms were so hot and disagreeable that, with the tiger added in, it was as if he couldn't breathe when he got inside. Formerly, he'd come home early to avoid having her yell at him and scold him. Recently, with Hsiao Fu Tzu for company, she hadn't been keeping tabs on him so much, so he'd been coming home a little later.

Ch'iang hadn't been coming home much recently at all. He knew what his daughter was doing and he didn't have the nerve to come in the gate. But there was nothing he could do to keep her from doing it. He knew he didn't have the strength to take care of his children. It was better for him not to come back and pretend that out of sight is out of mind.

Sometimes he hated her. If Hsiao Fu Tzu had been a boy, he could guarantee that nothing this disgraceful would have been necessary. But this having a daughter! Why did it have to happen to him? Sometimes he pitied her. Here was his own daughter selling herself to feed her two little brothers! He could hate her or feel sorry for her but nothing else. When he was drinking and broke he didn't hate or pity her; he came back wanting money from her. At a time like that, he thought of her as something that could earn money. After all, he was the Papa and to demand money from her was a simply a matter of "calling things by their right names" and carrying out the correct relationship between father and child.

Sometimes he also thought about appearances. Didn't everybody hold Hsiao Fu Tzu in contempt? Her father couldn't forgive her either. He'd force her to give him the money and curse her, too, as if he were cursing her for everyone to hear. He'd show them that he, Ch'iang, hadn't done anything wrong. It was Hsiao Fu Tzu who was born not caring about her reputation!

He'd rail at her and Hsiao Fu Tzu wouldn't even let out a deep breath. Hu Niu, on the other hand, would alternately swear and urge him to leave. Of course he'd take some money with him. It was only enough to keep him drunk because if he sobered up and looked at the money he'd just jump in the river or hang himself.

The heat on the fifteenth of June was enough to drive people mad. The sun had just risen and the ground was already afire. Puffs of gray dust, like clouds and yet not clouds, like mist and yet not mist, floated low in the air making people exasperated. There was no breeze at all. Hsiang Tzu looked at the grayish-reddish sky and decided not to start work until late afternoon. He'd wait until after four o'clock to go out and keep going until dawn if he didn't make much. No matter what the night was like, it would be easier to put up with than the daytime.

Hu Niu nagged at him to get out of there. She was afraid it would hinder business if he were there because Hsiao Fu Tzu would probably bring home a "guest".

"You think it's better here? By afternoon even the walls are scorching!"

He said nothing, drank some cold water, and went out.

The willows along the street looked sick. Their leaves were all curled up and covered with dust; their branches, barely moving, drooped in utter dejection. There was not a spot of dampness anywhere in the main street. It was so dry it shimmered whitely. Then the dust from the dirt streets flew up and joined the dust in the sky to make a poisonous layer of gray dust that burned people's faces. It was dry everywhere, hand-scorching everywhere, depressing everywhere. The whole city was like a fired-up brick kiln which made breathing difficult.

Dogs crawled along with their red tongues dragging. The nostrils of horses and donkeys flared out. The street vendors didn't dare yell and the asphalt pavements began to melt. It was so bad it seemed the sun would even melt the brass shop signs. The streets were very quiet, except for a monotonous banging and clanging from the metalworking shops which annoyed people.

Rickshaw pullers were well aware that they wouldn't eat if they didn't get a move on, but they, too, were reluctant to look for business. Some parked their rickshaws in a shady place, put the top up, and took a nap in the rickshaw. Some burrowed into teashops and drank tea. Others didn't take their rickshaws out at all; they just went out and looked around to see if there was any possibility of working. Those who were out working lost face quite willingly, even if they were the most prepossessing of fellows. They didn't dare run and just shuffled along with their heads down. Every well became their lucky star. It didn't matter how far they'd gone—when they saw a well they hurried over to it. They'd just take a long drink at the trough along with the horses and donkeys if there wasn't any freshly drawn water. And there were those who, coming down with cholera or befuddled by sunstroke, just went on and on until they collapsed and never stood up again.

Even Hsiang Tzu was a little scared! He realized, after pulling an empty rickshaw for a while, that he was surrounded by burning hot air and even the backs of his hands were sweating. But he still intended to take a fare if he got one in the hope that running might make a little breeze.

He did get a passenger, started off, and then realized that the temperature had reached a point that would not allow anyone to work. He'd run a little and then couldn't breathe. His lips were burning and seeing water made him want to drink it, although he wasn't really thirsty. That poisonous flower of a sun would split the skin on his hands and back if he didn't run. He got to his destination one way or another with his clothes glued to his body. He took his palm leaf fan and fanned himself. It was no use. The breeze was hot. He had already lost count of how many times he had had a drink of cold water and still he made for a teahouse. He felt somewhat better when he'd downed two pots of hot tea. The sweat came out of his body as soon as the tea went into his mouth. It was just as if the inside of his body was open at both ends and couldn't hold a drop of water. He didn't dare move.

He sat for a long time feeling very queasy. Since he didn't want to risk going out again and had nothing else to do, he began to think that the weather was determined to make things difficult for him. No, he would not give in to weakness. This wasn't his first day pulling a rickshaw and this wasn't his first nasty encounter with summer. He couldn't just fritter away an entire day this way.

He thought he'd go out but his legs were reluctant to move and his body was unusually weak. It was as if he'd spent too long in a hot bath and still didn't feel any better for it, even though he had sweat a lot. He sat a while longer and then couldn't put up with it any more. Sitting here made him sweat too, so why not go out briskly and try anyway?

He realized his mistake as soon as he got outside. The layer of gray air had already scattered and the sky wasn't so depressing, but the sun was much worse than before. No one dared lift his head to look at it. All anyone knew was that the glare dazzled the eyes everywhere. The glare was all over. There was a whiteness shot through with red in the sky, on the rooftops, on the walls, and on the ground. The sun was a huge burning glass; it was as if every sunbeam had come through it and was heating things to their flash point. In this white glare every color stabbed the eyes and every smell had mixed in with it a fetid stench boiled out of the ground. There seemed to be no one in the streets, which had suddenly become a lot wider and without a breath of cool air. Their glitter made people afraid.

Hsiang Tzu didn't know what to do. He plodded on very slowly, pulling the rickshaw with his head down. He hadn't anywhere to go. He was confused. Covered with sticky sweat, he was giving off a sour smell. After walking a while his shoes and socks and feet were all stuck together, just as if he'd stepped in soppy mud. It was extremely uncomfortable.

He hadn't any intention of drinking more water but he went over to take a drink automatically whenever he saw a well. Not, however, to relieve his thirst. Apparently, it was to enjoy the bit of coolness when the well water went down his throat and into his stomach and produced a moment of sudden chill, gooseflesh, and a cold shiver. It was very pleasant. When he finished he'd hiccup repeatedly. The water wanted out!

He walked a while and sat a while. He was much too listless to look for business and still didn't feel hungry when noon came. He considered going to get something to eat as usual but felt nauseated when he saw the food. His stomach was full of almost every kind of water and sometimes made a little sloshing noise like the sound inside the belly of a donkey or horse which has just been watered.

When comparing the seasons, Hsiang Tzu had always believed that winter was more horrible than summer. It had never occurred to him that summer could be so unbearable. He'd been through more than one summer in this city all right, but couldn't recall ever being so hot. Was the weather hotter now than it used to be or was his body failing him? When he thought of that he was suddenly not so muddled and his heart seemed to have grown cold. His body, yes, his own body, wasn't making it! It frightened him, but there was nothing he could do to change things. There was no way he could drive Hu Niu away. He would turn into another Ch'iang or a man like that tall fellow he'd met or Hsiao Ma's grandfather. Hsiang Tzu was done for!

He got another fare shortly past noon. This was the hottest part of the day, and the hottest day of the year as well, but he decided to make the trip at a run. He didn't care how hot it was in the sun. If he managed it, and nothing happened to him, well then, that would prove there was nothing wrong with him. If he couldn't do it, what was there left to say? He might just as well trip and break his neck on the fiery ground!

He had gone only a little way when he became aware of a cool breeze just like cold winter air coming into a hot room through a slit in the door. He didn't dare believe it so he looked at the willows along the road for confirmation. Yes indeed, they were all moving slightly.

Suddenly a great many people were out in the street. Those in the shops fought to get out and then held rush leaf fans over their heads while they looked around. "There's a cool breeze! A cool breeze is coming!" Almost all of them wanted to shout and jump for joy. The willows suddenly seemed to have been transformed into angels bringing heavenly tidings. "The willow branches are waving! Lord of Heaven grant us a cool breeze!"

It was still hot but hearts were much calmer. A cool wind, even a little one, gives people lots of hope.

This cool wind passed by and the sunlight was not as strong; it was bright and then somewhat dimmer, as if a veil of flying dust floated in front of it. The wind suddenly rose and those willows, motionless most of the day, acted as if they'd had some pleasant news. Swaying and swinging, their branches looked like they'd grown another length. A gust of wind passed by and the sky darkened. All the gray dust flew high up into the sky and then settled back down and inky clouds were visible on the northern horizon.

There was no more sweat on Hsiang Tzu's body. He looked northward once, stopped the rickshaw, and put up the rain cover. He knew that summer rain comes when it says it's coming and doesn't waste time. He'd just got the cover on when there was another gust of wind. The black clouds were rolling onward and had already covered up half the sky. The hot air on the ground combined with the cold air above and the noisome dry dust. The air seemed cooler but it still was hot. The southern half of the sky was clear and sunny. The black clouds in the northern half were like ink.

Everybody was alarmed and frantic as if some great disaster loomed. Rickshaw pullers hurriedly put up rain covers, shopkeepers scurried to take down their signs, street vendors scrambled around stowing away their goods and mats, and pedestrians rushed by.

There was another blast of wind; when it had passed by the shop signs, the mats, and the pedestrians all seemed to have been rolled up and carried off by the gust. All that was left was the willow branches following the wind in a mad dance.

The clouds had not yet covered the entire sky but it was already dark on the ground; the too hot, too bright, too clear noontime had abruptly been transformed into something that resembled a dark night. The wind brought the rain as it dashed wildly from east and west as if searching for something on the ground. Far off on the northern horizon there was a red flash as if the clouds had been split open and their blood gushed out. The wind diminished but it made a loud whistling noise that made people shiver. A blast of this kind passed by and nobody seemed to know what to do next. Even the willows were waiting for something apprehensively.

There was yet another flash, white and clear and right overhead. The fast-falling raindrops came with it and forced the dust to leap upward, giving the ground a rainish look of its own. Many huge raindrops pelted Hsiang Tzu on the back and he shivered twice.

The rain paused. Now the black clouds covered the entire sky. Still another blast of wind came, much stronger than the ones before, and the willow branches stretched out horizontally, the dust flew in all directions, and the rain fell in sheets. Wind, earth, and rain were all mixed up together; that gray, cold, roaring wind wrapped everything up inside itself and you couldn't tell what was a tree, what was ground, or what was cloud. It was a chaos of noise and confusion. The wind passed by leaving behind only the driving rain to tear the sky, rend the earth, and fall everywhere. You couldn't see rain. There was only a sheet of water, a blast of wetness, and then innumerable arrowheads that spurted up from the ground and hundreds of torrents that fell from the roofs. In a few minutes the earth was indistinguishable from the sky as the rivers in the air flowed down and the rivers on the ground flowed across them to make a grayish dark turbid yellow, sometimes white, world of water.

Hsiang Tzu's clothes had been soaked beforehand. There wasn't a dry spot on him and his hair was wet under his straw hat. The water on the ground covered his feet. It was already hard to walk. The rain above pelted his head and back, swept across his face, and wrapped around his loins. He couldn't lift his head, couldn't open his eyes, couldn't breathe, and couldn't move forward. He was forced to stand in the middle of all that water without knowing where the road was or what front, back, left, and right were. All he was conscious of was the water that chilled him to the bone and sloshed over him. He was aware of nothing except a great vague hotness in his heart and the sound of rain in his ears. He wanted to put the rickshaw down but didn't know where to put it. He thought about running but the water held his feet. He could only keep moving, pulling the rickshaw with his head down one step at a time and more dead than alive. The passenger seemed to have died right there in the rickshaw. He let the rickshaw man risk his life in the rain without saying a word.

The rain let up some. Hsiang Tzu straightened up slightly and puffed once. "Sir, let's take shelter somewhere and then go on!"

"Make it snappy! What do you think you're doing just leaving me somewhere!" He stamped his feet and yelled.

For a moment Hsiang Tzu actually thought about leaving the rickshaw and going to find some place out of the rain. But when he looked at how dripping wet he was, he knew he'd only get the shivers if he stopped. He ground his teeth and, paying no attention to whether the water was deep or shallow, began to run. He hadn't been running long when another flash came close behind another darkening of the sky and rain blurred his vision again.

When they finally arrived his passenger didn't give him a penny extra. Hsiang Tzu said nothing. He didn't care if he lived or not.

The heavy rain stopped and then resumed but fell much lighter than before. Hsiang Tzu ran straight home. He hugged the stove to get warm and shivered like the leaves on a tree in the wind and rain. Hu Niu steeped him a bowl of ginger and sugar water and he drank it all down in one draught like an idiot. When he finished he burrowed under his quilt and knew nothing more. His condition was like being asleep and yet not really sleeping. In his ears was the swishing sound of rain.

The black clouds began to look tired a little after four o'clock. Softly and weakly, they let loose paler flashes of lightning. In a while the clouds in the west broke up. The tops of the black clouds were edged with gold and a little whiteness came rushing underneath them. The lightning all went south dragging the not so terribly loud thunderclaps along with it. After another interval, rays of sunlight came out through the spaces between the clouds in the west making gold and green reflections on the water-covered leaves. In the east hung a pair of rainbows, their legs in the dark clouds, the tops of their bows in the blue sky. Soon the rainbows faded and there were no more black clouds in the sky.

The blue sky, as well as everything else that had been newly washed, looked like part of a charming world just risen from darkness. Even the "pond" in the mixed courtyard had a few dragonflies hovering over it.

But, except for the barefooted children who chased those dragonflies, no one in the place cared about taking pleasure in the clear sky that follows the rain.

A piece fell out of a corner in the rear wall in Hsiao Fu Tzu's room and she and her brothers hurriedly tore the matting off the k'ang and blocked up the hole. The courtyard wall had collapsed in several places but no one had time to do anything about it because they were all too busy taking care of their own rooms. Some had front steps that were too low and let the water in. They all had to race around with old bowls and dustpans bailing out the water. Some were on the roof looking for ways to patch it. Some had roofs that leaked like sprinkling cans and got everything inside soaking wet. They were busy moving things outside next to the cook stove to dry or hanging them on windowsills in the sun. They had huddled in their rooms while the rain was falling; rooms that might, when the moment came, collapse and bury them alive. They left their fate to Heaven. After the rain they tried to figure out how to repair their losses.

Although a heavy rain might lower the price of a pound of rice by half a cent, still, their losses were so great that such a trifling drop in price could not make them up. They paid their rent but no one ever came to repair the place unless the dilapidation was so bad that no one could possibly live there. In that case, two masons would come along and fix up the wall haphazardly with mortar and broken bricks, preparing it for its next collapse. If the rent wasn't paid the whole family would be thrown out and have its goods confiscated. The walls were cracking, the roof might fall in and kill someone, and no one cared. A place like this was all their tiny income could afford. It was tumbledown, dangerous, and they deserved it!

The greatest loss of all resulted from the sickness brought on by the rainwater. All of them, young and old, were out in the streets looking for a deal all day and the furious rain of summer could pelt down on their heads at any time. They all sold their strength to make a living and were always covered with sweat. The fierce rain of the north was very hard and very cold. Sometimes there were hailstones as big as walnuts in it. If it did nothing else, the ice cold raindrops striking at their open pores made them lie on the k'ang with a fever for a day or two.

The children got sick and there was no money for medicine. A spell of rain urged the corn and the *kaoliang* upward in the fields but it also sprinkled death onto many of the poor children in the city.

The adults got sick and that was even worse. Poets chant about the lotus "pearls" and double rainbows that come after rain but poor people suffer from hunger when the wage earners are sick. A spell of rain might well create a few more singsong girls and sneak thieves and put a few more people in jail. When adults get sick it's much better for boys and girls to become thieves and singsong girls than to starve! "The rain falls on the rich and on the poor, falls on the just and on the unjust." But the truth is that the rain is not evenhanded at all because it falls on an inequitable world.

Hsiang Tzu was sick and he certainly was not the only sick person in the place.

CHAPTER NINETEEN

Hsiang tzu spent two days and nights in a comatose sleep and Hu Niu was upset. She went to the temple of Kuan Yin and begged the goddess for a prescription. It called for a little incense ash and three herbs. He actually opened his eyes and looked around after she poured it down his throat but went to sleep again in a little while. You couldn't tell what he was saying from the noises his lips made. Then Hu Niu thought of going to a doctor. After he had an injection of camphor and a dose of medicine he opened his eyes again. He woke up and asked "Is it still raining?"

When the next dose was nicely heated he wouldn't take it. He refused to drink that bowl of bitter stuff because he was so stingy and, even more, hated himself for being so inferior as to be unexpectedly laid low by a rainstorm. He decided to put on his clothes and get up right away to prove he didn't need any medicine. But when he sat up his head seemed to have a bulge as big as a boulder on it, his neck was weak, and he had spots in front of his eyes. He fell back again. There was no need to say anything; he took up the bowl of medicine and drank it.

He was in bed for ten days, becoming more and more anxious the longer he lay there. Sometimes he huddled on the pillow and wept soundlessly. He knew he couldn't go out and work so all their expenses had to be met by Hu Niu. The two of them would spend all of her money and then they would have to rely entirely on his rickshaw. He couldn't make enough to satisfy Hu Niu what with her love for spending and eating; and besides, she was pregnant.

The longer he lay there the more he indulged in fantasies and exaggerations. The more he thought, the more upset his melancholy made him, and getting well was all the harder. As soon as he cared about living again he asked Hu Niu, "The rickshaw?"

"Don't worry. It's rented out to Ting."

"Ah." But he did worry about his rickshaw. He was afraid that it would be wrecked by Ting or some other man. But he couldn't get up so of course it had to be rented out. Could it be left unused? He added finances up in his head. If he pulled it, he'd always average about fifty or sixty cents a day. That was just enough to pay for the rent, coal, rice, firewood, kerosene, tea, and water for two people, not counting new clothes. He had to economize everywhere he could; he couldn't be as unconcerned about money as Hu Niu was. Now all they took in each day was the fifteen cents rental fee. They had to make up the remaining forty or fifty cents, not counting the money for medicine. If he didn't get well, what then? Don't blame Ch'iang for drinking. Don't blame those suffering friends for doing what they liked so recklessly. This rickshaw pulling was a dead end street! No matter how hard you work or how ambitious you are, you must not start a family, you must not get sick, and you must not make a single mistake. Humph! He remembered the first rickshaw he had and that bit of money he'd scraped together himself. Had he ever annoyed or provoked anyone? It wasn't because he'd got sick or had started a family that both rickshaw and money had been taken from him so cruelly and unreasonably! Being good wouldn't work and being bad wouldn't work either. There was only death ahead on this road and no telling when the time would come because he wouldn't know a thing about it. When he thought of that his melancholy changed to despair. Ugh. Screw it! If you can't get up, then just lie there. That's all it will amount to in the end anyway! His mind a blank, he lay there peacefully.

But he couldn't stand it before long and wanted to get up right away because he still had to go on struggling. The road was deathbound but a man's heart is alive and until he entered his coffin he would always go on hoping. But he couldn't stand up. He could only mutter to Hu Niu in a hopeless, pitiful manner, trying to say to her, "I said that rickshaw was unlucky, and really unlucky!"

"Get yourself well! Always talking about that rickshaw! You're rickshaw crazy."

He didn't say any more. Right; he was rickshaw crazy. He had believed a rickshaw was everything ever since he had started to pull one but as a matter of fact. . . .

He got up when he felt a little better and looked in a mirror. He didn't recognize the man he saw. There were whiskers and angles all over his face, his temples and cheeks had fallen in, he had eyes sunk in two deep pits, and there were many lines across his scar.

The room was extraordinarily hot and depressing but he didn't dare go out into the courtyard. His legs seemed to have no bones in them they were so weak. Furthermore, others would see him. It wasn't only the people in this place. Everyone at every rickshaw stand in the whole city knew that Hsiang Tzu was a first-class topnotch fellow. How could he be a sickly ghost like this? He did not want to go out. It was so boring in his room it drove him wild. He hated not being able to regain his health with one mouthful of medicine and go pull his rickshaw. But sickness ruins a man and it comes and goes as it pleases.

After resting for another month he just went out and worked. He didn't care whether he was completely well or not. He pulled his hat down low so no one would recognize him and he could run slowly. Hsiang Tzu was the same as speed so how could he slog along openly and make people despise him?

Actually, he was not in good shape. On top of that, he was greedy for all the fares he could get to make up the deficit that piled up during his illness, so in a few days he had a relapse and this time dysentery was added. He slapped his face in a rage at himself but it was no use. The skin on his belly seemed to be meeting his backbone when he bent over on the privy and still the flow went on. After a lot of trouble the dysentery finally stopped, but his legs were so weak that just squatting and standing up took all his strength. What was the use of saying he thought he'd go out and work? He had to rest for another month! He knew Hu Niu's money would probably be used up soon.

On the fifteenth of September he decided to take the rickshaw out again. And if he got sick this time he vowed he'd jump in the river!

Hsiao Fu Tzu often came to see him when he was ill the first time. Hsiang Tzu never got the last word with Hu Niu and felt so glum, too, that sometimes he'd say a few words to Hsiao Fu Tzu. This infuriated Hu Niu. Hsiao Fu Tzu was a good friend when Hsiang Tzu wasn't at home. But when he was home, Hsiao Fu Tzu was, to Hu Niu's way of thinking, a manchaser who didn't care what other people thought at all. She pressured Hsiao Fu Tzu into returning the money she owed her. "From now on I won't let you come in here!"

Hsiao Fu Tzu had lost her place to entertain customers and her own place was so ramshackle and tumbledown with the mat from the k'ang blocking up the hole in the back wall that all she could do was go off and register at a "transport company," that is, a placement agency for singsong girls.

Transport companies, however, certainly did not want a piece of goods like her. They sponsored female students and "cultured girls of good family." It took a lot of money to get a girl outfitted for high-class jobs and they didn't want a common person like her.

She considered going to a low-class brothel because she had no cash to set herself up in business. What else could she do but mortgage herself to a low-class brothel? But if she took that course of action she'd lose absolutely all her freedom and who would take care of her brothers? Dying must be the easiest, simplest thing there is because living was hell already.

She wasn't afraid of dying but didn't think about death either. She wanted to do something braver and finer than dying. She wanted to see both her brothers capable of earning their own living. Then, when she died, it would be with an easy heart. She would die sooner or later but not unless killing one would save two!

No matter what she thought of, there was still only one road for her: sell for less. Of course, anyone willing to come to her room wouldn't want to pay much. Very well, then. It didn't matter who came. Whatever he paid would be fine and she could economize on clothes and cosmetics. Men who came looking for her needn't hope to have her dressed fashionably and they'd only get what they paid for. She was very young and that was something.

Hu Niu found moving about uncomfortable. She was even afraid there might be a mishap when she went out shopping. Hsiang Tzu was out all day long and Hsiao Fu Tzu didn't want to come over either. She was as lonely as a dog tied up in a room. The lonelier she got, the more she hated. She was convinced that Hsiao Fu Tzu had deliberately cut her price in order to anger her. She wasn't about to swallow this humiliation so she sat in her outer room with the door wide open, waiting. When a man came along to Hsiao Fu Tzu's place, she'd stretch out her neck and make scurrilous remarks which embarrassed the men and upset Hsiao Fu Tzu. Hu Niu was delighted when Hsiao Fu Tzu's business fell off.

Hsiao Fu Tzu knew that if things went on like this, eventually everyone in the place would agree with Hu Niu and they'd throw her out. All she could do was be frightened; she couldn't afford to get angry. People who have come to such a pass as hers know that facts have to be placed ahead of anger and tears. She took her little brother along and knelt before Hu Niu. She said nothing but her expression did; if this supplication was not enough, she had no fear of death herself but Hu Niu need not think of living! The most admirable of sacrifices is to bear disgrace. The most admirable way to bear disgrace is to prepare for rebellion.

Hu Niu was thrown for a loss. Nothing she thought of had any appeal and, with such a big belly, she didn't dare get into a fight. Warfare was out of the question so she'd better find a way to get herself down from her pedestal. She claimed she was only teasing. Who could mistake the false for the true? Besides, Hsiao Fu Tzu was taking things too seriously.

Once she had explained it all away, they became good friends again and she supported Hsiao Fu Tzu in her enterprise as before.

Beginning in mid-September, when he took his rickshaw out again, Hsiang Tzu increased his caution in all respects. Two bouts of illness had brought him to realize he certainly was not made of iron. His zeal for earning more money had not been discarded and completely forgotten but repeated assaults had made him fully aware of how puny a man's strength is. A time will come when even the stoutest of fellows can't do anything but grind his teeth and he'll spit blood, too!

His dysentery was over but he still had stomachaches. When he was about to see what his legs could do by speeding up a little, it felt like his stomach had knots tied up inside it. He had to slow down almost to the point of stopping altogether and forced himself to endure the pain with his head down and his stomach pulled way in. He could still manage well enough when working by himself, but when running as part of a group his abrupt halts would make the others wonder if he knew what he was doing and make him very embarrassed. What would happen when he was thirty or forty? A thought like that made him break out in a sweat!

He wished for his health's sake to get private work again. After all it was a job that had its slow times. You had to run fast when you went somewhere but the rest periods were long and it was a much easier job than pulling individual passengers.

But he knew that Hu Niu would never let him do it. You lose your independence when you marry and Hu Niu was a terrible shrew besides. He'd have to put up with it.

The year reached its halfway mark. He got along as best he could during the fall and early winter, afraid of taking on too much work and afraid to risk taking time off. He struggled on with his head down, depressed at heart. He didn't dare be as reckless as before when he ran, and he really didn't much care about anything at all. He still earned a little more than most rickshaw pullers and, unless his stomach really hurt, was never willing to pass up a fare. Pulling a rickshaw is what you ought to do, so you do it. He was still free from the contagion of bad habits. He had never learned how to shake down a passenger for a higher fare, or overturn the rickshaw in the middle of the road, or sit around all day waiting for a profitable deal. And so, while he didn't work harder, he did have a regular income every day. He never cut corners in his methods so he was never in any jeopardy.

His income, however, was still too small. There was never anything left over. Money was taken in with the left hand and given out by the right. He was cleaned out every day. He didn't dare think about saving. He knew how to economize but Hu Niu knew how to spend.

The end of Hu Niu's ninth month was in early March. Her belly began to show in early winter and she loved to stick it out on purpose to get a look at her own importance. What with contemplating her belly, she was simply too lazy to get off the k'ang. The job of making tea and cooking was handed over to Hsiao Fu Tzu. Naturally, Hsiao Fu Tzu had to be allowed to take home any leftover soup and the water from soaking dried meat to give to her brothers. This practice wasted quite a bit.

Hu Niu also had to have snacks in addition to her regular meals. The more obvious her belly became, the more she felt she must eat tasty things; she couldn't stint her mouth. She not only bought anything and everything when she felt like it, she ordered Hsiang Tzu to bring more home every day. Hsiang Tzu would earn a certain amount and that was how much she spent. Her demands rose and fell with his income.

Hsiang Tzu couldn't say anything. Her money had been used when he was sick, and now it had to be paid back, so of course he had to let her spend it. She immediately got sick whenever he tried to keep a little back.

"Being pregnant is simply to suffer a nine month long illness and what would you know about it?" What she said was true.

She had even bigger plans when New Year's came. She herself couldn't leave the nest so she sent Hsiao Fu Tzu out to do the shopping

constantly. She hated herself for not being able to go out and yet wa
so in love with herself that she didn't want to leave. But staying a
home was boring to distraction. Therefore, as she saw it, buying mor
things was a comfort of sorts. She insisted over and over again that th
food she wanted wasn't bought only for her but because she loved
Hsiang Tzu.

"Here you work hard all year and you still won't take a bite? Yo
haven't got all your strength back yet since you were sick. Here it i
New Year's and you still won't eat. Are you waiting until you get s
hungry you look like a dried up bedbug?"

Hsiang Tzu didn't care to argue about it and didn't know how t
object anyway. Yet whenever whatever it was was ready, she was th
one who ate two or three big bowlsful. She ate everything in sight an
never exercised. When bloated from overeating she'd clasp her belly
and actually complain that her swelling was an offense against he
pregnant condition!

She wouldn't let Hsiang Tzu go out at night after New Year's, n
matter what. She wasn't certain when her time would come and sh
was afraid. And now she finally began to think about her real age
While she wouldn't say right out what it actually was, at least she di
stop telling him she was only a little bit older than he was. Hsiang Tz
was very confused when she made remarks like that.

Life is extended only by having children. Hsiang Tzu's heart auto
matically felt a little joyful. Even though there was no need for him t
have a child at all, that most simple and mystical word, father, tha
the future would give to him, could make even an iron-hearted ma
close his eyes and reflect. No matter what else a man might thin
about it, this word was still one to move the heart.

Hsiang Tzu, the clumsy one, had never thought he had anything t
be proud of, but when he thought of this wonderful word, he suddenl
became aware of his own status. When there is nothing, then nothin
matters. But if there were a child, then his life would not be empty. A
the same time, he wanted to do all he could to serve Hu Niu and wai
on her. She was not one person now, and, repulsive though she was, i
this single instance she had all the merit. Only no matter how muc
merit she had there was simply no way he could put up with he
shrewishness. She changed her mind every minute and carried on an
fussed as if she was possessed.

Hsiang Tzu had to go out and work to earn money and had to ge ome rest at night. Even if the money were spent frivolously, he still had to sleep soundly at night so he could go out again and work the next day. She wouldn't let him work at night and wouldn't let him get a good night's sleep either. He was in a daze all day long, hadn't a thought in his head, and didn't know what to do. Sometimes he was happy, sometimes he was anxious, sometimes he was glum. Sometimes he was happy and then ashamed of himself for being happy. Sometimes he was anxious and had to comfort himself because he was anxious. Sometimes he was glum and then had to cheer himself up because he was glum. Emotions revolved in his heart in circles and made this simplest of men so upset he couldn't tell east from west or south from north. One time he actually took a passenger past his destination. He had forgotten where the man wanted to go!

At the end of the three-week New Year holidays Hu Niu sent Hsiang Tzu out to get the midwife because she couldn't stand it any longer. The midwife came, told her the time hadn't come yet, and described some of the signals that would tell her when her time was near. She bore her condition for two more days and then began complaining again. She asked for the midwife to come and still it wasn't time. She wept and wailed and wanted to go die somewhere because she couldn't take any more of this agony.

There was nothing Hsiang Tzu could do for her. But, to prove to her that he was doing what he could, he complied with her demands and did not work.

The ruckus contined until the end of the month when even Hsiang Tzu could tell that her time had really come. She no longer looked like a human being. The midwife came again and gave Hsiang Tzu a dark hint; she feared it would be a difficult birth. Hu Niu's age, combined with a first pregnancy, lack of exercise, and the large size of the baby caused by all the rich food she'd eaten during her pregnancy, led the midwife to conclude that there could be no hope for an easy normal birth. Furthermore, Hu Niu had never been examined by a doctor, the position of the baby had not been corrected, and the midwife did not have the skill to shift it herself. She could, however, say that she was afraid it would be a breech birth!

The birth of children and the death of mothers were topics everyone in this mixed courtyard was accustomed to discussing simultaneously. But Hu Niu was in much more danger than most. Other women continued to work right up until their time came and, since they never had enough to eat, the baby was not very big so it was easy for them to give birth. Their danger lay in their inability to take care of themselves after the baby was born. Hu Niu was in precisely the opposite situation. Her great advantages were, in fact, the cause of her catastrophe.

Hsiang Tzu, Hsiao Fu Tzu, and the midwife kept watch over her for three days and nights. Hu Niu called on every Buddha there was and made all sorts of vows but none of it did any good. At last she lost her voice and could only moan softly. The midwife couldn't do anything; nobody could do anything; but Hu Niu had an idea of her own. She told Hsiang Tzu to go out and get old lady Ch'en, a shaman of the Mystic Toad. Old lady Ch'en wouldn't come unless she got five dollars so Hu Niu took out her last eight dollars.

"Good Hsiang Tzu, hurry! Spending money isn't important! Wait till I'm all right again. I'll be good to you every day. Hurry!"

Old lady Ch'en and her "boy," a big forty-year-old yellow-faced fellow, arrived just before it was time to light the lamps. She was around fifty, wore a blue silk dress, and had a red pomegranate flower and a complete set of gold-plated head ornaments in her hair. Her eyes were wide and staring. When she came in, she washed her hands and then set up incense and stared blankly at the tiny flame.

Suddenly, her whole body swayed and gave a great shudder. Her head drooped down, her eyes shut, and she remained motionless for some time. Even a falling needle could have been heard in the room. Hu Niu ground her teeth and made not a sound. Very slowly, old lady Ch'en raised her head and nodded as she looked towards them all. The "boy" pulled at Hsiang Tzu and told him to hurry up and kowtow.

Hsiang Tzu didn't know if he believed in the gods or not. All he knew was that it wouldn't be a mistake if he kowtowed so, in a daze, he kowtowed he didn't know how many times. He stood up and looked dully at that pair of staring "god" eyes, at the red light from the burning incense, smelled the aroma from its smoke, and hoped vaguely that something good would come of this attempt. His palms were wet and clammy.

The Mystic Toad spoke with vigor and a little stammer.

"Doesn't . . . doesn't . . . matter. Draw a charm for hastening . . . hastening birth!"

The "boy" quickly passed a piece of yellow paper to the shaman, who waved her fingers above the incense, spit on them, and drew on the paper. When the charm was drawn the Mystic Toad stammered out some more words. The general idea was that Hu Niu had owed a debt to this child in a previous life and now must suffer this torment to repay it.

Hsiang Tzu beat his head. He couldn't understand what he heard and was a little frightened by it all.

Old lady Ch'en gave a great long yawn, sat with her eyes shut for a little longer, and then opened them wide, as if awakening from a dream. The "boy" hastened to report the words of the Mystic Toad. She seemed to rejoice! "Today the great god is happy! He enjoys talking!" And then she told Hsiang Tzu how to get Hu Niu to swallow the charm and gave him a pill to be taken along with it.

Old lady Ch'en waited eagerly to see how effective the charm would be so, of course, Hsiang Tzu had to get her something to eat. He gave this task to Hsiao Fu Tzu. She went out and bought some sesame sauce, pancakes, and stewed pork. Old lady Ch'en grumbled because there was nothing to drink.

Hu Niu ate the charm and pill. Old lady Ch'en and the "boy" ate up the food. Hu Niu went right to thrashing and groaning. After half an hour of turmoil her eyes rolled slowly upward.

Old lady Ch'en had still another idea. Without any alarm or haste, she told Hsiang Tzu to kneel and hold a tall incense stick in penance. Hsiang Tzu didn't have much trust left in her but, since he'd already spent five dollars, he might as well try out her methods good-naturedly. He wasn't going to beat her so he'd have to do things her way just in case they worked!

He knelt with his back straight, holding the incense. He didn't know what god was being prayed to, but he thought in his heart he ought to respect it. He watched the dancing of the flame and pretended to see a shape of some kind in the flame itself. He prayed to it. The incense got shorter the longer it burned. A little black line appeared right in the middle of the flame. He let his head droop, his hand felt for the floor, and he felt confusedly drowsy for he'd had no proper sleep for three nights. His neck suddenly relaxed. He gave a start and looked around. The incense had burnt down and there wasn't much left of it. He didn't care whether this was the time for him to stand up or not. He pushed at the floor and stood up very slowly because his legs were slightly numb.

Old lady Ch'en and the "boy" had already sneaked away.

Hsiang Tzu couldn't be bothered to hate her. Worriedly, he hurried to look at Hu Niu and saw that nothing could be done now. Hu Niu was drawing her last breath and couldn't speak anymore. The midwife told him to think of some way to get her to a hospital for she'd done all she could.

It seemed to Hsiang Tzu that his heart had suddenly split; he wept loudly. Hsiao Fu Tzu also let some tears fall, but since she was in the position of a helper, her mind was a little clearer.

"Brother Hsiang, don't cry now! Should I go to the hospital and ask?" Without noticing whether he answered her or not, she rubbed away her tears and ran out.

She was gone for an hour and then came running back, puffing so hard she couldn't speak. Holding onto the table, she panted for a while and then said it cost ten dollars to have a doctor make one visit and that was only to look, not to do anything about the delivery. It was twenty dollars for that. If it was a difficult birth and you had to go to the hospital that took lots more dollars.

"Brother, what do you think we can do?"

There was nothing Hsiang Tzu could do except wait for those fated to die to die!

Stupid barbarism and thoughtless cruelty only contributed to the situation here. There were, in addition to stupid barbarism and thoughtless cruelty, other causes.

At midnight Hu Niu brought forth a dead child and stopped breathing.

CHAPTER TWENTY

Hsiang tzu's rickshaw was sold!

Money was just like running water; his hands couldn't hold onto it. A dead person must be taken away and you even have to pay for a license to carry the coffin out of the city to the graveyard.

Hsiang Tzu watched stupidly while everyone else rushed about. All he did was toss money away. His eyes were terribly red and sticky stuff was piled up in their corners. His ears were deaf and, while he followed everyone else's confused turnings in a dazed and wooden way, he didn't know what he was doing himself.

He finally got things a little clearer in his head on the way out of the city with Hu Niu's coffin, but he still didn't want to think about anything. There was no one in the procession except Hsiang Tzu, Hsiao Fu Tzu, and her two brothers. Each of them carried a bit of paper "money" which they scattered along the way to feed the road-blocking ghosts.

Woodenly, Hsiang Tzu watched the pallbearers bury the coffin. He did not cry. His chest seemed to have a fierce fire burning inside it which had dried up his tears. When he wanted to weep, no tears came. Watching blankly, he almost didn't know what was going on. Only when the head pallbearer came for his money did it occur to him to go back home.

Hsiao Fu Tzu had already cleaned up the room. He fell onto the k'ang when he got back, too tired to move. His eyes were so dry they wouldn't shut and he stared dully at the stains from leaks on the ceiling. He couldn't sleep so he sat up, looked around the room, and didn't dare look again. He didn't know what to do with himself. He went out to buy a pack of cigarettes.

Sitting on the edge of the k'ang, he lit one. He really did not enjoy smoking. Blankly, he watched the blue smoke at the end of the ciga-

rette and suddenly tears dropped one after another, for he was not only thinking of Hu Niu, but of everything else besides. All those years of
hard work since he had come to the city had amounted to nothing. He
didn't even make a noise when he cried!

A rickshaw, a rickshaw, a rickshaw was his rice bowl. Bought, lost;
bought again, sold. Two rises and two falls. It was like the shadow of
a ghost; you can never catch it. He'd suffered all those hardships and
wrongs in vain. Gone, everything was gone, even his old woman was
gone! Hu Niu was a terror but how could he have a family without
her?

He looked at the objects in the room. They were all hers but she was
buried outside the city wall! The more he thought, the more he hated,
but his tears were now shut off by the fire of his rage and he puffed
furiously at the cigarette. The more he hated smoking, the more he
perversely wanted to smoke. When the cigarette was finished he held
his head in his hands while an acrid heat came out of his mouth and
heart. He wanted to shout wildly and blow out all the blood in his
heart and then he'd feel much better.

He didn't know how long he'd been sitting there when Hsiao Fu
Tzu came in. She stood in front of the kitchen table in the outer room
and looked at him silently.

He suddenly lifted his head and when he saw her his tears began to
flow again very fast. Right now he'd cry even if he saw a dog. When
he saw another living thing he wanted to let his whole heartful of
grievances loose. He wanted to talk to her because he thought he'd get
a little sympathy but there was too much to say and his mouth would
not open at all.

"Brother Hsiang!" She came a little closer. "I straightened everything up."

He nodded and didn't thank her. Polite usages are empty and false
in the midst of grief.

"Have you figured out what to do?"

"Huh?" He seemed not to understand but shook his head when he
finally comprehended. He wasn't interested in making plans.

She took two more steps forward and suddenly blushed. She stuck
out a few white teeth but couldn't say anything more. Her life had
forced her to forget shame, but when it came to proper matters, she
was still a woman who had an honest heart. When it comes to shame,
a woman's heart knows how to use the greater part of it with skill.

"I think . . . " was all she said. She had a lot to say in her heart but all the words fled when she blushed and she couldn't remember them.

Actually, people don't say all that many sincere words to each other but the blush on a woman's face is far more expressive than a long speech, and even Hsiang Tzu understood what she meant. She was, in his eyes, a very beautiful girl. Her beauty was in her bones and even if her entire body had sores all over it which rotted the flesh right off, she would be as beautiful as ever in his mind. She was beautiful, young, ambitious, frugal, and diligent. If he thought of remarrying, she was the ideal person. He certainly was not thinking about remarrying right away. He didn't care about anything. But since she was willing and forced by the oppressions in her own life to bring up the subject immediately, it seemed to him there was no way to reject her. She was such a fine person and she'd helped him so much that he could only nod his head. He even thought of hugging her and weeping away all his grief. They would struggle forward together afterwards, with all their strength and will united. In her person he saw all the peace and comfort a man could have and all that he ought to have. He didn't like to talk much but, looking at her, he was quite willing to say what he pleased. His words wouldn't be wasted at all if she were to listen to them. Her every nod and smile was the most satisfying of answers and made him feel he did have a family after all.

Just at this moment her little brother came in. "Sister! Papa is coming!"

She frowned. When she pushed open the door Ch'iang had just come into the courtyard.

"So what are you doing in Hsiang Tzu's rooms?" Ch'iang's eyes were big and round. His legs wobbled and stumbled, and he wavered from side to side. "So you've been selling and that isn't enough for you and now you want to let him play around for free? You shameless thing!"

Hsiang Tzu came out and stood behind her when he heard his name.

"I say, Hsiang Tzu." Ch'iang, in his truculent way, thought that he'd just puff out his chest and put on a bold front, but he couldn't even stand up steadily. "I say, Hsiang Tzu, do you still think you're a man? Who are you taking advantage of now? Think you can use her? What kind of a fool are you?"

Hsiang Tzu didn't want to humiliate the old drunk but the woe piled up inside him made him unable to control his anger. He took a step forward. Two sets of red eyes flashed at each other, as if they were about to clash in the middle of the air and let off sparks. Gently, as if he were picking up a child, Hsiang Tzu put a hand against Ch'iang's shoulder and pushed him away.

The reprimand of conscience had borrowed a little baigan and turned into mad violence. Ch'iang's drunkenness was, in fact, mostly a pretense. He almost sobered up after this shove. He wanted to counterattack but knew he was no match for Hsiang Tzu; yet to leave politely without a murmur was even less appealing. He sat on the ground, unwilling to stand up, but it would be even more inconvenient to go on sitting there indefinitely. His wits were in a jumble and left his mouth free to say what it wished.

"I'm the one to discipline my sons and daughter! What business is it of yours? You push me? You old woman! You'll pay for it all right!"

Hsiang Tzu wasn't interested in replying; he just waited for the counterattack.

Hsiao Fu Tzu held back her tears and didn't know what to do. Trying to tell her father how to behave was useless but to have to watch Hsiang Tzu thrash him was upsetting. She felt in all her pockets and dredged up ten pennies which she handed to her little brother. Ordinarily he would never have gone near his papa but today, after seeing him shoved down on the ground, he was a little braver.

"For you. Go away."

With squinty eyes Ch'iang took the money, stood up, and grumbled, "To hell with all of you, you offspring of a slave! You provoke a respectable gentleman like me and I'll be damned if I don't take a knife to you and slit your throats!" He hurried to the front gate and then yelled, "Hsiang Tzu, I'm not finished with you yet! We'll meet outside!"

Hsiang Tzu and Hsiao Fu Tzu went back inside together after Ch'iang had gone.

"There's nothing I can do," she said to herself. All her sorrows were gathered together in these words, words which also contained an unlimited hope; she'd have a way out if Hsiang Tzu were willing to take her.

Hsiang Tzu had been through this sort of scene before. He could see quite a few dark shadows gathering behind her. He still liked her but he couldn't take on the responsibility of rearing her two brothers and supporting her drunken father! He didn't dare think that with Hu Niu dead he had his freedom. Hu Niu had had her good points, too. At least she had given him a lot of help with money. He didn't think for a moment that Hsiao Fu Tzu would sit on the side eating and doing nothing to help him, but it was unquestionably true that this family of hers couldn't earn its keep.

Poor people must decide whether to love or not to love on the basis of cash. The seeds of love can sprout only in the homes of the rich.

He began to gather his things together.

"Do you want to move out?" Even her lips were white.

"I'm moving out." He hardened his heart.

In a world without justice, poor people must rely on hard hearts to keep their freedom, trifling bit of freedom though it is.

She looked at him and then went out with her head down. She did not hate him, nor was she angry; only without hope.

Hu Niu's hair ornaments and all her best clothes had gone with her in the coffin. Only a few old outfits, some wooden utensils, and some plates and pots and such remained. He took some of the nicer clothes out of the pile and put them to one side. Everything left over, clothes and utensils, was to be sold. He called in a junk man and got ten dollars for the lot. He was anxious to move and anxious to get rid of those things so he had no interest in getting another junk man in and having the offer raised. The junk man gathered the stuff together and left. All that remained in the room was a bedroll and the clothes he'd held back, spread on the matless k'ang.

The room was completely empty and he felt much better. It was as if he'd cast off yards and yards of entangling ropes and could now leave and go fly high and far away. But in a moment he thought about the things again. The table had been taken away but its legs had left their traces behind in the little piles of dust that had gathered around their ends and now outlined four empty squares on the floor. He looked at these marks and thought about the objects, thought about the person, and now all were gone like a dream. Never mind if they were any good or not, or if she were any good or not; without them all, there was no place he could be at rest. He sat on the edge of the k'ang again and pulled out another cigarette.

A worn ten cent note came out along with the cigarette. Then, without really thinking about what he was doing, he got out all the rest of his money. These last few days he hadn't kept track of the money at all. He made a pile; silver, copper, paper, he had all kinds. It wasn't a small pile, but when it was counted, it wasn't more than twenty dollars. Add to it the ten he'd got from the junk man and his entire estate was thirty dollars and change.

He put the money on a k'ang brick and stared at it. He didn't know if it was better to laugh or to cry. There was nothing in the room except himself and this pile of old worn moldy disgusting money. What was it all for?

He gave a long sigh. Listlessly, aimlessly, he put the money inside his shirt. Then he rolled up his bedroll and those few clothes and went to find Hsiao Fu Tzu.

"Here, you keep these outfits to wear. Hold onto my bedroll for me for a while. I'll go look for a good rickshaw agency first and then come back and get it." He dared not look at her and said his piece all in one breath with his head down.

She said nothing, just made two sounds that meant yes.

Hsiang Tzu found an agency and came back to get his bedroll. He noticed that her eyes were swollen with crying. There was nothing he could say, really, but he did his best and came up with two sentences. "Wait, wait until I get settled. I'll come, I'll come for sure!"

She nodded and said nothing.

Hsiang Tzu rested for only a day and then went out to pull a rickshaw as before. He wasn't the firebrand for business he had once been, but he wasn't deliberately lazy either. He just got through each day calmly and without disgust, and in this way a whole month passed. He was serene at heart. His face filled out somewhat but it wasn't as ruddy as it once had been and didn't look entirely healthy, but it didn't show any signs of actual ill health either. His eyes were very bright but without expression. They were always so bright they seemed to be full of energy and yet they never seemed to take notice of anything. His demeanor was very like that of a tree after a tempest which stands quietly in the sun, not daring to move again.

He had never enjoyed talking and now he liked opening his mouth even less. The days were already very warm and the willow trees were covered with soft leaves. Sometimes he'd put his rickshaw down facing the sun and sit with his head lowered talking to himself with his lips moving slightly. Sometimes he'd put his face up towards the sun to receive its rays and take a nap. He simply never talked to anyone unless he had to.

But he'd already got a hankering for cigarettes. He'd sit in the rickshaw and his big hand would immediately grope around under the footrest. He'd exhale slowly after lighting the cigarette and his eyes would follow the smoke rings upwards. He'd stare dully at them and then nod his head as if he'd seen something interesting in them.

His running, when he began working again, was still more skilled than most but he no longer ran as if his life were at stake. He was particularly cautious, almost excessively cautious, when turning corners and going up or down slopes. No matter how much he was teased and provoked by someone who wanted to race with him, he would hold his head down and silently keep on running at a steady pace. He seemed to have seen through this business of rickshaw pulling. He knew it for what it was and never thought about gaining glory from it again.

But he made some friends in the agency. Although he didn't like to talk, a mute gander still enjoys flying with the flock. His solitude would, he feared, be unbearable if he didn't make some friends.

His package of cigarettes was passed around as soon as he took it out. Sometimes they noticed that there was only one left in the pack and were embarrassed to take it. He'd say curtly, "I'll buy more!" When they were gambling he did not, as he used to, shrink off to one side; now he came to watch and sometimes he'd bet, too. It didn't matter to him whether he won or lost. He would gamble just to show them he was very much one of the bunch and agreed that they ought to have a little fun after working frantically for days. They drank and he did too. Not a lot, but he'd put up his own money to buy pickled vegetables and such to go with the drinks and ask everyone to have some.

Things he had previously held in contempt he now thought were rather interesting. The road he had chosen had turned out to go nowhere. Since it was blocked, he was forced to admit that the roads others chose were all right after all. In the past, he had not known how to fulfill his social obligation when one of his friends had a family wedding or a birthday or a funeral. Now he'd put up his forty cent share too, or join in a pool to buy presents. Not only did he now contribute money. He also went in person to congratulate or to mourn, because now he understood that these affairs were not staged to waste money. They were necessary in order to fulfill the obligations involved in human relationships. There was sincere laughter and sincere weeping with people like these. They weren't making a lot of meaningless noise.

But he didn't dare disturb his hoard of money. He got a piece of white cloth and with his own clumsy hands took a needle and sewed the money up inside the cloth and always kept it next to his body. He didn't consider spending it and didn't think about buying another rickshaw. He just kept it with him as a kind of precaution because who knew what sort of catastrophe the future held! Sickness, accident, either could hit him any time, so he'd always have to be prepared. A man is certainly not made of iron; he had come to realize that.

He got another private job around the beginning of autumn. The work this time was much easier than what he'd had to put up with in other households. If it hadn't been that way he simply would not have taken the job. He knew how to choose his work now. If the position was agreeable to him he'd take it. Otherwise pulling fares was not impossible. He wasn't so eager to work at a private job any more. He knew his body was something he had to take care of. When you are a rickshaw puller and risk your neck as he used to, you only do yourself in and never get any good out of it. Experience teaches a man that he ought to be a little wily about everything because life is a one-way trip!

The place he went to work this time was near the Lama temple. His employer, named Hsia, was an educated man of about fifty. His family included a wife and twelve children who lived in his home town. He had recently taken a concubine but didn't dare let his wife find out so he had rented a small house in a quiet district and in this small house near the Lama temple there was only Mr. Hsia and his new concubine, one female servant, and a rickshaw man and he was Hsiang Tzu.

Hsiang Tzu really enjoyed this job. First of all, the house had only six rooms altogether. Mr. Hsia had three of them, one was the kitchen, and the other two were for the servants. The courtyard was very small. Leaning against the base of the south wall was a small jujube-date tree with about ten or so half-ripe jujubes hanging on its branches. When he swept the courtyard it seemed to take only two swipes of the broom to get from one side to the other, which saved a lot of work. There were no flowers or grasses to be watered. He often thought about straightening up that tree but he knew that a jujube tree is very headstrong and recalcitrant. It simply will not accept correction so it wasn't worth trying.

The other work didn't amount to much. Mr. Hsia went off to his office every morning and came back at five. Hsiang Tzu merely had to take him and bring him back. Mr. Hsia did not go out again once he was back home. It was just as if he were avoiding some problem. On the other hand, Mrs. Hsia went out often but always returned around four to let Hsiang Tzu get Mr. Hsia. Hsiang Tzu's daily tasks were pretty much over with when he had brought Mr. Hsia home. What's more, Mrs. Hsia only went to the Tung An market or Sun Yat-sen park and other spots on the same side of town so he had lots of time to sit around when they arrived. This job was a snap for Hsiang Tzu.

Mr. Hsia was very tightfisted; he wouldn't let the tiniest coin slip out of his fingers without cause. His eyes never glanced sideways when coming or going, as if there were no one in the streets and nothing else to look at either. But Madam was a spendthrift; she was always out buying something. If it was something to eat, she'd give it to the servants when she didn't like it. If it was a household item, she'd wait until she was ready to buy a new one but gave the old one to the servants first; then she could go negotiate with Mr. Hsia for the required cash. The course of Mr. Hsia's lifetime seemed to be spent wearing himself out bowing to his superiors and taking whatever energy and money he had and respectfully offering all of it to his concubine. Beyond this he had no other activity or pleasure. His money must be used to enlist the services of his concubine and then it was gone. He couldn't spend it on himself, not to mention giving it to anyone else. It was said that his first wife and his twelve children lived in Paoting in Hopei. Sometimes they wouldn't get a penny from him for four or five months.

Hsiang Tzu despised this Mr. Hsia. His back was hunched over all day and his neck was pulled in. He went out and came in like a sneak thief, eyes watching his toes. He never made a sound, never spent any money, never smiled. He looked like a scrawny monkey even when riding in the rickshaw. But if he should happen to speak a sentence or two, he would say it in a tone that was quite offensive, as if everyone else were a low scoundrel and only he an educated, perfect, Confucian gentleman. Hsiang Tzu did not like that kind of person. But he regarded business as business; as long as the money came in every month

why bother about anything else? Besides, Madam was still very amiable and there was always a little extra of what she ate or used for
him. So he let it go at that and simply regarded this job as one where
he hauled a monkey who was ignorant of human feelings.

Hsiang Tzu, however, still regarded the wife merely as a woman
who could give him a little extra money. He certainly did not like her.
She was prettier than Hsiao Fu Tzu and was soaked in perfume and
scented powder and wrapped in silk and satin; she was certainly not a
person Hsiao Fu Tzu could ever be compared with. But although she
looked very beautiful and was dressed very prettily, still, and he
didn't know quite why, when he looked at her there was always something about her that resembled Hu Niu. But it wasn't her clothes and
it wasn't her looks either. It was something in her manner or in the effect she had on people. Hsiang Tzu couldn't find the right word to
describe it. All he knew was that she and Hu Niu were, to use the only
words he could think of, the same line of goods.

She was very young, at most twenty-two or twenty-three, but her
manner was very worldly and certainly nothing at all like that of a
new bride. Just like Hu Niu, she, too, had never had any of a young
girl's bashfulness and gentleness. She curled her hair, wore high-
heeled shoes, and her clothes were cut so as to make every curve of her
body curvier. And Hsiang Tzu also noticed that although she dressed
in the appropriate style, she still hadn't a married woman's manner.
But she didn't resemble someone who had begun life as a singsong girl
either. Hsiang Tzu couldn't get hold of what sort of thing she was. He
only knew she was a little terrifying, the way Hu Niu had been terrifying, though Hu Niu hadn't been as young and had had none of her
beauty. So Hsiang Tzu feared her even more, as if she had brought
with her all the harmfulness and destructiveness of the female sex
which he had already tasted once before. He dared not look her in the
eye.

He grew even more frightened of her after several weeks. Hsiang
Tzu had never seen Mr. Hsia spend any money when he was being tak-
en around. Once in a while, however, Mr. Hsia went shopping too.
He'd go to a big pharmacy and buy medicine. Hsiang Tzu didn't
know what kind of medicine he was buying, but the two of them
seemed very happy afterwards everytime, and Mr. Can't-even-take-a-
deep-breath-Hsia was remarkably energetic. Well, energetic for a few
days and then he couldn't even take a deep breath again and his stoop

was even more pronounced. It was all very like the live fish you buy in the market. Put it in the cook pot to enjoy the heat for a while and it jumps a bit, then pretty soon it's very well behaved indeed.

Hsiang Tzu knew it was time to go to the pharmacy again when Mr. Hsia sat in the rickshaw like a dead ghost. He didn't like Mr. Hsia but couldn't help feeling sorry for the scrawny old monkey every time there was a trip to the pharmacy. And after Mr. Hsia brought his package of medicine home, Hsiang Tzu would think of Hu Niu and there would be some nagging and undefinable discomfort in his heart. He didn't want to harbor hatred toward any ghost, but, looking at himself and then at Mr. Hsia, there was no way he could not resent and hate her. No matter what anyone said, his body wasn't as strong as it had been; and Hu Niu ought to bear the greater part of the responsibility for it.

He thought of quitting but to quit because of such a side issue did seem ridiculous. He smoked a cigarette and said to himself, "Why bother about other people's business?"

CHAPTER TWENTY-ONE

CHRYSANTHEMUMS had arrived in the markets and Mrs. Hsia and Yang Ma, the woman servant, got into an argument because Yang Ma had broken one of the pots of flowers Mrs. Hsia had bought.

Yang Ma came from a village and really did not believe that flowers were anything important. Since, however, she had broken someone else's property due to her own stupidity and carelessness, it didn't matter that flowers weren't important and she bore the reprimand in silence. But when Mrs. Hsia's scolding went on and on and she lambasted Yang Ma for her crude and bumpkinish manner, Yang Ma couldn't hold her fire any longer and answered back in kind. When country people get angry they don't take out a ruler and measure their words. Yang Ma scraped the bottom and came up with the crudest of barnyard curses. Mrs. Hsia jumped up and down screaming with rage and told Yang Ma to pack up and bugger off.

Hsiang Tzu never tried to make peace. He didn't know the right words and was even less able to mediate in an argument between two women. When he heard Yang Ma tell Mrs. Hsia that she was only a snatch, a stinking cunt that a thousand men had ridden and ten thousand had fingered, he knew Yang Ma's job was gone for sure. At the same time he also realized that if Yang Ma's job was gone, his would have to go too. Mrs. Hsia probably would not want to keep a servant who knew such things about her around.

Yang Ma left and he waited to be fired. He figured that the time for him to pack up his bedroll would come when a new woman servant arrived. But he wasn't depressed about it, for experience now enabled him to take a job coolly and calmly and leave it coolly and calmly. It wasn't worth getting upset about.

But Mrs. Hsia was surprisingly polite to him after Yang Ma left.

Having lost a servant, she had to go to the kitchen herself and cook. She gave him some money and told him to go out and buy vegetables. When he came back she told him how to peel this and wash that. He peeled and washed vegetables; she sliced up meat and boiled rice and searched for something to talk to him about while she cooked.

She was wearing a pink smock, a pair of black trousers, and a pair of heelless white satin slippers embroidered with flowers. Hsiang Tzu kept his head down and fumbled on with his job. He didn't dare glance at her but kept thinking about looking at her again and again. The scent of her perfume flowed into his nostrils strongly and constantly. As a fragrant flower lures bees and butterflies, it seemed to tell him he must look at her.

Hsiang Tzu knew about the cruelty of women and was also aware of their good points. One Hu Niu was quite enough to make a man afraid of women and unable to do without them, too. And wasn't this even more true of Mrs. Hsia who was far beyond comparison with Hu Niu in everything? Hsiang Tzu glanced at her twice involuntarily. Even if she was more dangerous than Hu Niu she still had many more desirable features than Hu Niu by far.

If this situation had taken place two years ago he certainly would not have dared take those two glances. Now he didn't much care. He had already experienced the seductive wiles of a woman and there was nothing he could do to control himself. Furthermore, he had already slipped into the ruts of the ordinary rickshaw man. Whatever they thought was all right he also thought was all right. His efforts and self-restraint had been a waste. Everyone else's actions, therefore, were perfectly reasonable. A rickshaw man was what he had to be regardless of whether he wanted it that way or not. Being different from the group was self-defeating.

Well, then, since taking advantage whenever you could was something all poor people thought was right and proper, why shouldn't he take an advantage when he saw one? He took two glances at this woman. Yes, she was only a woman! He wouldn't refuse if she were willing. He didn't dare believe she could actually be that cheap but just in case. . . .

She didn't make a move so of course he didn't either. He wasn't quite sure what to do if she did show some interest first. Had she shown interest already? If not, why had she got rid of Yang Ma and then not gone out to hire a replacement right away and told him to help make lunch instead? Why put on so much perfume just to go to the kitchen to do the cooking?

Hsiang Tzu didn't dare draw any conclusions or hope for anything but still, in his heart, he faintly wanted something decided, wanted to have a little hope. He seemed to be having an improbable dream and yet wanted to keep on dreaming it. The dynamic power of life was forcing him to admit he would never amount to anything, and yet, in this profitless affair of living was concealed the greatest of joys or, perhaps, the greatest of miseries, but who cared!

A glimmer of desire drummed up a little courage. A little courage aroused a hot strength. A fire sprang up in his heart. There was nothing demeaning here at all. Neither he nor she was base; the fires of desire are equal!

A murmur of alarm awakened reason. A little reason dampened and put out the fire in the heart. He almost decided to run away on the spot. There was only trouble here; taking this path would make him a laughingstock for sure!

Sudden fright followed sudden desire; his heart seemed to have caught malaria. This situation was much more uncomfortable than his encounter with Hu Niu. He didn't know anything about anything then and was like a little bee on its first flight who'd flown down into a spider's web. He knew how to be careful now and also when to be bold. Yet he was in a complete quandary, longing to sink and afraid of falling!

He was not contemptuous of this concubine, this unregistered prostitute, this beautiful one. She was everything and she was nothing. If he had any need to make excuses to himself, he's say it was all Mr. Hsia's fault for being so despicable a scrawny old monkey. Someone like that deserved to be paid back with evil. With a husband like him nothing she did was wrong. With a boss like him nothing he, Hsiang Tzu, did made any difference. His nerve increased.

She, however, wasn't noticing whether he was looking at her or not. She sat by herself at the kitchen table and ate when the food was ready. When she had finished she called to Hsiang Tzu and said, "You eat now and you can clean up when you've finished. Buy the vegetables for dinner when you go out to get the master this afternoon and save having to make an extra trip. Tomorrow is Sunday so he'll be at home. I'll go out and look for a serving woman. Do you have a friend you could recommend? These serving women are really hard to find. All right, eat up now, don't let it get cold."

She spoke easily and naturally. That pink smock suddenly looked very chaste indeed! Hsiang Tzu, on the other hand, felt disappointed and his disappointment led to a feeling of chagrin. He saw quite clearly that he was a man with no goal in life; and not only was he a man without a goal, he was also a scoundrel! He got down two bowls of rice somehow or other. He felt awful. He went to sit in his own room after he'd washed the dishes and chain-smoked he didn't know how many cigarettes.

By the time he went to get Mr. Hsia late that afternoon he didn't know why he hated the scrawny old monkey so much. He even thought about running flat out and then dropping the shafts and letting the old thing go smash and half kill himself. And at that moment he understood something.

At one time he had worked for a wealthy family and the master's third concubine and his eldest son were up to something. The master caught on and the eldest son, somehow or other, came close to poisoning him. He used to think the eldest son was too young and didn't know what he was doing but now he knew why the old master had to die. Yet he didn't want to murder anybody; he just thought that Mr. Hsia was obnoxious and hateful and there was no way to give him what he deserved. He deliberately bobbed the rickshaw up and down and gave the old monkey a shaking up. The old monkey said nothing at all. Hsiang Tzu, on the other hand, felt a little guilty. He had never done such a thing before. Even if there happened to have been a reason for it he still couldn't make excuses for himself. His guilt made him feel indifferent to the whole business. Why should he deliberately go out looking for trouble? He was a rickshaw man and so he'd do his best for everyone and that would be that. What was the use of thinking about anything else?

His mind was tranquil now and he forgot about that inconclusive scene in the kitchen. He thought it was all rather ridiculous when he happened to think about it again.

Mrs. Hsia went out to look for a servant the next day. Pretty soon she came back with one to try out. Hsiang Tzu had given his project up and it left a bad taste in his mouth no matter which way he thought about it.

Mrs. Hsia sent the servant away after lunch on Monday. She was afraid the woman was not very cleanly. Then she told Hsiang Tzu to go out and buy some roasted chestnuts.

He stood outside her door and called to her when he came back with the hot chestnuts.

"Bring them in," she said from inside.

Hsiang Tzu went in. She was just putting powder on her face while seated in front of her mirror. She was still wearing her pink smock but with a pale green underskirt. She watched him enter in the mirror and then turned around very quickly and smiled at him. Hsiang Tzu suddenly saw Hu Niu in that smile. A young and beautiful Hu Niu. He stood there paralyzed. Nerve, hope, fear, caution, all were gone. All that remained was a large, or maybe a small, gust of hot air that surrounded his entire body. If this gust of air pushed him on, he'd go on. If it pushed him back, he'd go back; he couldn't consciously decide one way or the other.

The evening of the next day he took his bedroll and went back to the agency.

He found himself in a predicament that ordinarily he would have feared. It was extremely humiliating. Now he announced it to everyone as if it were a joke. He couldn't piss!

They all told him what medicine to buy or which doctor to go to. No one thought it was shameful and every one of them gave him suggestions sympathetically. And some, with their faces slightly red, would smugly tell him about their own experiences in this line. Quite a few young men had already bought this particular illness. Quite a few middle-aged men had got it for free, and quite a few who'd had private jobs told of experiences that differed in detail but were of the same nature. Then, too, quite a few who'd had private jobs, while they had never had such an experience themselves, recalled a few stories about their masters which were well worth telling.

This illness of Hsiang Tzu's opened all their hearts towards him and they told him their own stories. He forgot about being ashamed but still didn't think of his sickness as something to brag about. He endured it calmly, in a manner not much different from the way he would have put up with a chill or a slight case of sunstroke. He felt a little remorse when he ached and recalled the sweetness when he felt good. And he did not get anxious, no matter what. His experiences had taught him to have little regard for life. What was the point of getting upset?

This bit of medicine, that prescription, took ten dollars away from him and the sickness still hadn't been uprooted. He vaguely thought he was better and stopped taking anything. On dark days, or maybe every two weeks or so, his bones would ache again. He'd take a little medicine for the time being or he'd get through it grimly. He certainly didn't regard his illness as anything that mattered. Life just goes bitterly on to its end. What does a body count for? To make this statement clearer: even a fly in a privy pit has its fun and wasn't that even more true of a living man as big as he was?

He seemed to have become a different man after his illness. He was still as tall but there was none of that upright spirit. His shoulders sagged deliberately and his lips drooped with a cigarette stuck in between them. Sometimes he'd stick a cigarette butt behind his ear, not because that was a convenient place but because he wanted to show how tough he was. He still had no love for talk but when he had to be tough he could, with only a little difficulty, manage a sarcastic retort. And even if what he said wasn't skillfully phrased, at least he said it brusquely. All the same, his fervor slackened and his figure and spirit hung loosely.

But, when compared with most other rickshaw pullers, he still wasn't all that bad. He'd think about his former self when sitting alone. Bettering himself was still in his thoughts and he really did not want to let himself slide. While ambition had no meaning, destroying himself didn't look very smart either. And at such times he would think again about buying a rickshaw. More than ten of his thirty-odd dollars had been spent on account of his illness—spent on an injustice! But he did have about twenty as a foundation. He had, when you came right down to it, a lot more hope than the other guys with their empty guns.

That sort of idea often made him consider throwing away his half-smoked pack of cigarettes and never touching cigarettes or drink again—he'd just grit his teeth and hoard his money. His thoughts would move from hoarding money to buying a rickshaw and from buying a rickshaw to Hsiao Fu Tzu. He realized he owed her an apology. He hadn't seen her since he left the mixed courtyard and not only was he not well fixed but he'd got a rotten disease instead!

But with his friends he'd smoke as before, drink a little when he had the chance, and forget about Hsiao Fu Tzu completely. With his friends he certainly wasn't the one to start anything, but he couldn't help going along when someone else wanted to do something. One day's suffering and its bellyful of grievances could be forgotten for a short time only when he chatted and amused himself with them.

Pursuit of the pleasures before him led to willingness to forget his high-mindedness. He just wanted to be happy for a while and sleep in oblivion for a long time afterwards. Wasn't that what everyone wanted? Life was so boring, so painful, so hopeless! The poisonous boil of life could be numbed for a while only by using tobacco, drink, and women. When you take a poison to cure a poison the day will dawn when the poisonous vapors return to your heart. Didn't everyone know that? But did anyone know any better method to take the place of this one?

The less inclined he was to work hard, the more his self-pity increased. He used to fear nothing. Now he looked for peace and comfort. If there was rain falling or a cutting wind he didn't go out. If he had a few aches and pains, well, he'd just take two or three days off. His self-pity increased his selfishness. He wouldn't lend anyone a single dollar out of his pile. It was reserved solely for his support on windy or rainy days. You can offer people a cigarette or a drink but you don't lend your money.

He was much more spoiled and pitiable than the others. The more he rested the lazier he became, and with nothing to do he became glum and upset. Amusement was frequently necessary or he'd buy himself something good to eat. He always had a ready-made answer whenever it occurred to him that maybe he shouldn't waste his time and money that way. It was a sentence that many experiences had coined for him. "I had lots of ambition at the start and it didn't get me a damn thing." No one could dispute the truth of those words. No one could take them and explain them away. Well, then, who could keep him from heading right on down to the bottom?

Indolence can make a person very ill-tempered. Hsiang Tzu knew how to glare at his passengers now. He wasn't about to be obedient and ingratiating to any passenger or policeman or anyone else again. He had never, when he was working so hard at selling his strength, asked for more than a fair price. Now he knew how valuable his sweat

vas and he'd reduce it by even one drop if he could. He didn't fool
around when someone tried to take advantage of him. He'd just put
he shafts down and refuse to take another step. He didn't care if it
vas a legal stopping place or not.

When a policeman came to intervene he would move his mouth but
not his body. He would drag things out for a while and then wait. And
vhen he saw that he'd have to move along, his mouth certainly did
not take a moment off. He knew how to swear, all right. And if the
policeman refused to put up with being sworn at, well, a fight wasn't
anything either. The important thing was that Hsiang Tzu knew he
vas very strong and hitting a policeman and then sitting in jail wasn't
degrading. He was even more aware of his strength when arguing.
Everything looked glorious to him after he'd socked someone with all
his might and the sun seemed to have become especially bright. Stor-
ng up his strength to get set for a fight was something that had never
occurred to him in the past. Now, surprisingly, it had become a fact
and a fact that made him happy for a while. When he thought of that
t was very funny!

But never mind those bare-handed empty-fisted cops. He wasn't
even afraid of those motor cars that ran around all over the streets. A
car would come at him head on, rolling up the dust on the street, but
Hsiang Tzu wouldn't flinch. It didn't matter how the horn blasted at
him. He didn't care how frenzied his passenger got. There was nothing the driver could do about it either: he would have to slow down.
Hsiang Tzu would turn aside after the car slowed down in order to
avoid eating dust. He would use the same trick if the car was coming
up behind him. He had it all figured out; cars did not dare injure people, no matter what. Well, then, why move over and let them bring
along all that dust? All the cops cared about was keeping the road
open for motor cars. Their sole fear was that the cars wouldn't go fast
enough and wouldn't bring along enough dust. Hsiang Tzu was no
cop. Why should he let the cars race by?

Hsiang Tzu, in the eyes of the police, was a first-class thorn in the
flesh but they didn't dare aggravate him. The shiftlessness of the poor
is the natural result of having their bitter toil amount to nothing.
There was a certain righteousness in a poor man's thorniness.

Nor was he polite to his passengers. When they told him to take
them someplace he'd go there and not one step farther. When they

told him to go to the head of a side street and then, when they got there told him to go down it, he'd do no such thing. The passenger would glare. Hsiang Tzu's eyes would get even bigger. He knew that gentlemen wearing western suits were, for the most part, domineering and stingy. Fine. He was ready for them. Let them change their minds and he'd grab the sleeve of their fifty or sixty dollar suits and give them a grimy handprint at least! They'd have to pay up once they had a handprint bestowed upon them. They realized how strong that big hand was. Its grip made their scrawny arms hurt.

While he did not run slowly, he wasn't about to waste effort by going especially fast. His big feet would drag along if his passenger urged him to hurry. "How much more do I get if I hurry?" He had no manners, for what he sold was blood and sweat. He no longer had hope that their "benevolence" would reward him with extra pay. You pay so much money for so much in goods so you'd better get it all arranged ahead of time and exert yourself if you're paid for it.

He didn't cherish a rickshaw as much as before. His ardor for buying one had already cooled and he was quite careless with rented rickshaws. A rickshaw was only a rickshaw. Pull one and you can figure that making enough to look after yourself and pay the rental fee takes care of everything. You don't have to hand over a rental fee if you don't work, so there's no need to work if you have enough money on hand to eat for a day. That's all the relationship between a man and a rickshaw amounts to.

Naturally he wouldn't damage someone's rickshaw on purpose but he couldn't be bothered to be excessively protective of it either. Sometimes, when he wasn't paying attention, another rickshaw man would run into him and some damage would be done. He certainly did not jump up and down in a frenzy screaming at the man. Very coolly, he'd go back to his agency. If fifty cents was what he ought to pay for the damage, he'd pay twenty and that would be the end of it. If the boss didn't agree, well, all right, the final solution was generally to start a fight. If the boss wanted to fight, Hsiang Tzu would match him!

Experience is the fertilizer of life. When you have certain kinds of experiences you become a certain kind of man. You can't grow peonies in a desert.

Hsiang Tzu was in a rut. He wasn't any better than any other rickshaw man and he wasn't any worse. He realized that he was surprisingly more at ease this way than ever before and others liked him. All crows are black, and he did not long to be the only one with white feathers.

Winter came again. One night's worth of yellow dust-laden wind blowing from the desert could freeze many people to death. Listening to the voice of the wind, Hsiang Tzu put his head under his quilt and hadn't the nerve to get up. But when the wind had finished its wolfish howling and demonic screeching he had to get up anyway. He couldn't decide whether it was better to go out or take the day off. He was in no hurry to take hold of those ice cold shafts and was afraid of this wind that made you sick to your stomach when it moaned.

But the wild wind was afraid of the sunset and was quite still by four o'clock. When the twilight sky was shot through with the pale red of sunset, he stirred himself and took a rickshaw out. He wandered listlessly along, his hands tucked away and his chest against the crossbar joining the two shafts. A cigarette dangled from his lips. It was dark soon and he decided to get two quick fares and quit nice and early. He couldn't be bothered to light the carbide lamp until the police patrol told him five times. Then he lit it.

He finally picked up a fare in front of the Drum Tower and headed for the east side. He just went plodding along at a trot without bothering to take off his padded coat. He knew he didn't look like much but if he didn't he didn't. Whoever paid extra for style? He wasn't pulling a rickshaw, he was muddling through. He didn't want to take off his coat even when sweat broke out on his forehead. Taking it off for form's sake was merely for form's sake. When he entered a side street a dog, which probably didn't like the look of a rickshaw puller in a long coat, tried to bite him. He stopped, grabbed his long-handled duster, and chased the dog for all he was worth so he could beat it. After the dog had gone without a trace he waited a while to see if it dared come back. The dog didn't return and Hsiang Tzu was a little happier. "Fuck you! Think I was afraid of you?"

"Do you think that's the way for a rickshaw man to behave? Hear?" The man in the rickshaw asked ill-temperedly.

Hsiang Tzu's heart jumped. His ears knew that voice. It was very dark in the side street. The rickshaw lamp was bright but all its light went downward so he couldn't see the man in the rickshaw clearly.

The man was wearing a big hat with earflaps and most of his face was covered by a muffler. All that showed was two eyes. Hsiang Tzu was trying to figure out who he was when he spoke again.

"Aren't you Hsiang Tzu?"

Hsiang Tzu had it. It was old Liu! What a bombshell! His whole body was on fire and he didn't know what to do.

"What about my daughter?"

"Dead!" Hsiang Tzu stood there stupidly. He didn't know if it was himself or someone else who said that word.

"What? Dead?"

"Dead."

"Once she fell into your motherfucking hands could she have done otherwise?"

Hsiang Tzu suddenly found himself. "You get out! Get out! You're too old. You couldn't live throught the beating I'd give you. Get out!"

Old Liu's hand shook. Hanging on to the rickshaw, he got down, trembling. "Where is she buried? I'm asking you."

"None of your business!" Hsiang Tzu picked up the rickshaw and went off.

He turned to look back when he'd got quite far away. The old man was still standing there like a big black shadow.

CHAPTER TWENTY-TWO

HSIANG TZU forgot where he was going. With his head thrown back, his hands gripping the shafts tightly, and his eyes flashing, he marched onward with long strides. He paid no attention to his direction or destination; to keep moving was his only concern. His heart was full of joy, and his body light and relaxed, for it seemed to him that all of the hard luck that had landed on him after he'd married Hu Niu had been blown onto old Liu. Forgetting the cold, forgetting his business, he thought only of running on and on. It was as if he were heading for someplace where he would be able to recover his original self: that carefree, pure, ambitious, hardworking Hsiang Tzu. It seemed to him, when he thought about that old man, that black shadow standing in the street, that nothing more needed to be said. A victory over old Liu was a victory over everything. While he hadn't punched the old wretch, and hadn't kicked him either, still the old man had lost his only family. Hsiang Tzu, on the other hand, was carefree and contented. Who says this isn't getting your just deserts? If the old man hasn't died of fury yet, he can't be far from it!

Old Liu had everything. Hsiang Tzu had nothing at all. But Hsiang Tzu could pull his rickshaw happily and the old man couldn't even find his daughter's grave! All right, so you've piled up a heap of silver and have a temper as huge as the sky, but you can't lord it over a poor guy who has to scrape up the money before he can eat and is as poor as a polished egg!

He got even happier the more he thought about it. He actually thought of shouting something out loud and letting everyone in the whole world hear about this victory. Hsiang Tzu is alive again! Hsiang Tzu has won!

The cold night air slashed at his face but he didn't feel it. On the contrary, the cold made him happy. The streetlight glowed coldly but

Hsiang Tzu's heart felt comfortably radiant. The light was every where, illuminating his future. He hadn't smoked for some time and didn't want a smoke now. He wouldn't touch cigarettes or drink from now on. He must start out anew and be hardworking and ambitious as of old. Today he had triumphed over old Liu, triumphed over him forever. Old Liu's curses were just what Hsiang Tzu needed to succeed, to have more hope. He could, with the evil spirits expelled, breathe fresh air from now on.

He took a look at his hands and feet. Wasn't he still very young? He would always be young. Let Hu Niu die, let old Liu die, but Hsiang Tzu would go on living; happily, ambitiously living. Evil people would all come to a bad end. They would all die. The soldiers who stole his rickshaw, Mrs. Yang who would not give her servants any thing to eat, Hu Niu who deceived and oppressed him, old Liu who despised him, detective Sun who swindled him, the old witch Ch'en who humiliated him, Mrs. Hsia who seduced him, they would all die. Only loyal and honest Hsiang Tzu would go on living and live for ever!

"But Hsiang Tzu, you must work hard from now on!" he ordered himself.

"Why wouldn't I work hard? I have the willpower, the strength, the youth!" he answered himself. "I'm content at heart so who can prevent me from having a family and a livelihood? How could anyone have been happy with all the things that happened to me heaped up on top of him? Who wouldn't have slid downhill? That's all in the past now. You'll see a new Hsiang Tzu tomorrow. Much better than before, much, much better!"

His legs began to move more strongly while his lips were muttering as if they were the visible proof of what he was saying. "I'm not talking nonsense. Of course I have what it takes. So what if I've had a little trouble with sickness and had a nasty disease. What difference does that make?" His body would get strong right away now that his heart had changed. Whether he had the mettle or not was no problem!

He had broken out in a sweat and his mouth felt dry. He wanted a drink of water and then realized that he was already at the Hou Gate. He couldn't be bothered to go to a teahouse. He put the rickshaw in the parking place at the gate and called to a small boy who went around with a big pot and a yellow clay bowl selling tea. He drank two bowls of tea that tasted like dishwater. The stuff was extremely ard to get down but he told himself that's what he'd have to drink from now on. He couldn't spend money on good tea and good food any more.

Having made this decision, he cheerfully got himself something cheap to eat to begin his new life of endurance and hard work—he bought ten fried buns that had nothing inside them but cabbage cores. They were not crisp on the outside and were gritty in the teeth. He gulped them all down, regardless of how unappetizing they were, and used the back of his hand to wipe his mouth when he'd finished.

Where should he go?

There were only two people he could rely on. He must, if he intended to work hard and get ahead, find these two: Hsiao Fu Tzu and Mr. Ts'ao. Mr. Ts'ao was a sage and would certainly forgive him, help him, and tell him the right thing to do. He'd do what Mr. Ts'ao advised him and get Hsiao Fu Tzu to help. He'd take care of the support, she'd take care of the house, and they'd succeed. They must succeed. How could there be any doubt about it?

Who would know if Mr. Ts'ao had come back or not? It didn't matter. He'd go to the old place to inquire tomorrow. If he didn't find out anything there, he could go to Mr. Tso's house to ask. Everything would work out well if only he could find Mr. Ts'ao. All right. Keep working until late and go look for Mr. Ts'ao tomorrow and, once he's been found, go look for Hsiao Fu Tzu to tell her the good news! Hsiang Tzu hadn't done very well so far but he definitely was on the comeback trail and now they could go forward together and work as one!

With this plan made, his eyes lit up like a hawk's and flashed as they swept around in all directions. He almost flew over to a passenger when he spotted him and had his coat off before he named the price. His legs weren't what they had once been at all when he began to run, but a kind of heat filled his entire body and he ran as if his life were at stake! Hsiang Tzu was Hsiang Tzu after all. Hsiang Tzu ran for all he was worth and no one could run faster. He'd race past another rickshaw when he saw one as if he had gone mad. His sweat flowed very fast and, when he had completed the trip, he realized that his body had become quite a bit lighter and his legs had their bounce again. He decided to take still another run. He was like a famous racehorse which hasn't run enough and stamps its hooves and paws the ground after standing still awhile. He went on running till one in the morning and, when he went back to the agency and returned the rickshaw, he found he'd made almost a dollar after subtracting the rental fee.

He went to bed and slept until dawn; then he rolled over. When he opened his eyes again the sun had been high for a long time. A good rest following great exertion is the sweetest of pleasures. He got up and stretched; his joints cracked lightly. His stomach was completely empty, and food was all he thought about.

After having something to eat he told the boss with a grin, "I'm taking the day off. I have something to do." He'd got it all figured out; he'd take one day off to get everything arranged nicely and begin his new life tomorrow.

He went to Pei Ch'ang street right away to take a look in case Mr Ts'ao had come back. He prayed in his heart as he walked along, Mr Ts'ao must have come back. Don't let me clutch at air! If this first plan doesn't work out then nothing will ever work out! I have reformed. Can it be that Heaven won't protect me?

He arrived at the Ts'ao's front door and his hand shook when it pressed the doorbell. His heart almost jumped out while he waited for someone to open the door; he simply did not want to think of all that had happened to him in the past as he stood facing this familiar door. All he hoped for was to see a familiar face when the door opened. He waited and began to wonder if anyone was there. Why was it so quiet? The stillness was almost terrifying. Suddenly there was a sound at the door. He almost fell over. It was as if he were a watcher by a coffin at night who suddenly hears a noise inside it. The door opened; in the sound of its opening was a most treasured, a most familiar and lovable "Oh!" Kao Ma!

"Hsiang Tzu? Well, we haven't seen much of you, have we? How did you get so thin?" Kao Ma had put on a little weight.

"Is the Master at home?" Hsiang Tzu didn't take time to say anything else.

"He's home. You're a fine one. The only one you think about is the Master. As if the two of us didn't know each other! You didn't even ask how I am! Well, you've said what you've said and once the carpenter cuts the board it's too late. Come in! How are you doing? All right?" She asked as she turned to go in.

"Humph! Not well at all!" Hsiang Tzu laughed.

"What do you think, Master," Kao Ma called outside the library, "Hsiang Tzu has come!"

Mr. Ts'ao was just shifting some narcissi into the sun. "Come in!"

"Ah, you go on in. We'll have our talk in a little while. I'll go tell Madam. We've been talking about you the whole time. A fool has a fool's luck but you just don't see it." Kao Ma went off chattering.

Hsiang Tzu went into the library. "Sir, I've come!" He knew he ought to ask Mr. Ts'ao how he was but the words didn't come out.

"Ah, Hsiang Tzu." Mr. Ts'ao stood there in the library wearing a short jacket and long gown, a kind smile on his face. "Sit down. Well. . . ." He thought for a moment. "We came back pretty soon. We heard old Ch'eng say you were . . . right, at the Jen Ho agency. Kao Ma went to look for you once but didn't find you. Sit down! How are you? Is everything all right?"

Hsiang Tzu wanted to cry. He didn't know how to tell anyone about his troubles because his tale was written entirely in blood and lodged in the deepest part of his heart. He was silent for some time. He longed to take those words of blood and let them flow out. They were all there in his memory and, when he thought about them, would come flowing back, so he had to get them into the right order and arranged well. He wanted to tell the history of his life. While he did not now know what it all meant, that string of injustices was plain and clear.

Realizing that Hsiang Tzu was pondering something, Mr. Ts'ao sat down quietly and waited for him to speak.

Hsiang Tzu sat silently with his head down for quite a long time. Then he raised his head and looked at Mr. Ts'ao as if to indicate that if he couldn't find anyone willing to listen to him, not saying anything at all would be all right with him.

"Go ahead!" Mr. Ts'ao nodded his head.

Hsiang Tzu began with events in the more distant past, starting with how he had left the country and come to the city. He hadn't intended to mention all that useless stuff but his situation would not be completely explained and he wouldn't feel right if he didn't. His memories were composed of layers of bloody sweat and bitter pain and he couldn't speak of them casually or jokingly. He was unwilling to leave anything out once he began. Each drop of sweat, each drop of blood, came from the core of his being and every detail had a value that made it worth mentioning.

He told how he had worked so hard when he first came to the city and then how he'd switched to rickshaw pulling. How he'd hoarded his money to buy a rickshaw and how he'd lost it . . . and so on, right up to his situation at the present time.

Even he was aware that this was all very strange. How could he talk for so long and so openly and rapidly? Events and all his thoughts came leaping out of his heart one after another. The events themselves seemed to find the right words. One sentence pressed after another. Every sentence was a true one, this one to be cherished, that one to be lamented over. His mind could not keep anything back nor could he stop himself from talking. He seemed determined, without any hesitation or confusion, to get out all that was in his heart in one breath. The more he talked the happier he became. He forgot himself because he was already wrapped up inside the story. He, himself, was in the heart of every sentence, that ambitious, wronged, suffering, and downfallen self. His head was sweaty when he had finished and his heart was empty. It was a comforting emptiness, like the emptiness you feel when breaking out in a cold sweat after you have fainted.

"Do you want me to decide for you now?" asked Mr. Ts'ao.

Hsiang Tzu nodded. He had told his story and seemed reluctant to open his mouth again.

"Can you still pull a rickshaw?"

Hsiang Tzu nodded again. He couldn't do any other kind of work.

"Since you can still pull a rickshaw," Mr. Ts'ao spoke slowly, "you really have only two alternatives. One is to get the money together and buy a rickshaw. The other is to keep on renting one, right? Since you haven't any money saved, you'd have to borrow to buy a rickshaw and pay interest. So isn't it all the same? It's no better than going ahead and renting one. Therefore working privately would be better. The conditions are set and you can count on food and housing. I think you'd do well to come back here. My rickshaw was sold to Mr. Tso so, if you do come, we'll have to rent one. How about it?"

"That's great!" Hsiang Tzu stood up. "Master doesn't remember about that business?"

"What business?"

"That time Master and Madam all fled to the Tso house."

"Oh!" Mr. Ts'ao began to laugh. "It was nothing! I was a little too upset. Madam and I went to stay in Shanghai for a few months but, in fact, it was entirely unnecessary. Mr. Tso put in a good word for me right away. That Yuan Ming fellow has a government job now, too, and we're on pretty good terms. Well, you probably don't know about him. Never mind. I don't remember much about the whole business. Let's talk about what concerns us now. This Hsiao Fu Tzu you just mentioned, what's to be done about her?"

"I don't have any plan."

"Let me work it out for you, then. If you were to marry her and rent a room outside, that wouldn't be very practical. Household expenses take money and you won't be making enough. If the two of you were to work as a couple, how could you expect to be lucky enough to find a place where you'd pull a rickshaw and she would work as a maid? Places like that aren't easy to find, so that certainly wouldn't be a good scheme to try." Mr. Ts'ao shook his head. "You must not be offended by what I'm going to say, but is she actually reliable?"

Hsiang Tzu's face got red and he gulped before answering. "She can't help doing what she does. I'd stick my neck out . . . she's very fine . . . she. . . ." He was upset and the many conflicting emotions that had been frozen together in a lump inside him all wanted to rush out at once.

"Now if we were to think about it that way. . . ." Mr. Ts'ao spoke doubtfully. "Unless I brought both of you here . . . you'd take up one room by yourself. Two of you would also take up one room so then there'd be no problem about where to live. I don't know if she can do laundry and cook or not, but if she can we'll have her help Kao Ma. Madam will be having another baby soon and there'll be more work than Kao Ma can handle by herself. She'll get her food free but I can't pay her anything. What do you think about it?"

"It's great." Hsiang Tzu smiled innocently.

"But I can't make this decision all by myself. I have to talk it over with Madam."

"You won't be making a mistake! If Madam is worried about her, I'll bring her here and let Madam see for herself."

"Fine!" Mr. Ts'ao smiled too. He had never expected Hsiang Tzu to be so perceptive. "This is what we'll do. I'll mention it to Madam first, then you bring her here in a day or two and, if Madam nods her head, we'll figure we've succeeded!"

"Well then, sir, shall I go now?" Hsiang Tzu was in a hurry to find Hsiao Fu Tzu to tell her this good news, news that even his wildest hopes had never dared hope.

It was around eleven o'clock, the most pleasant time of day in winter, when he left the Ts'ao home. It was especially bright and beautiful out today. There wasn't a cloud in the sky and the sun beamed down through the cold dry air giving people a warm and joyful feeling. The cackling of chickens, the barking of dogs, and the calls of the street vendors all carried very far; like the cry of the crane falling down from the sky you could hear those clear sharp voices a whole street away.

The rickshaws all had their tops down and their brasswork shone with a yellow gleam. Camels moved slowly and stolidly along the sides of the streets while automobiles and trolley cars hurried down the middle. Pigeons flew in the sky and pedestrians and horses passed by below. There was excitement and silence everywhere in the old city: an excitement that delighted and a silence that also delighted. There was a layer of sound, there were a million different lives there, all spread out beneath the clear and exhilarating blue sky while trees stood silently everywhere.

Hsiang Tzu's heart wanted to leap out and fly straight up into the sky and swirl there with the pigeons. He had everything: a job, pay, and Hsiao Fu Tzu. Everything had been arranged satisfactorily in a few sentences; it was all beyond belief! Look at that sky! Look at how sparkling and dry it was, just like the straightforward joy of the Northerner. When something nice happens to you even the weather is good. It seemed to him he'd never experienced a winter day as delightful as this one.

To demonstrate his joy in a real way he bought a frozen persimmon. He took one bite and his whole mouth was frozen! A coldness that struck to the roots of his teeth went slowly, coldly, down inside his chest and made him shudder all over. A few more bites finished it, leaving his tongue a little numb and his heart at ease.

He hurried on his way to find Hsiao Fu Tzu. He could see that mixed courtyard in his mind's eye already and the small room and the woman he loved. All that was missing was the pair of wings to fly him there. Everything in the past would be wiped out as soon as he saw her and another world would open up in that same instant. His eagerness at this time, went far beyond what he had felt when he went to see Mr Ts'ao. The relationship between him and Mr. Ts'ao was one of friendship and one of master and servant; each party exchanged good for good. She was not only a friend. She had handed her whole life over to him and now two people, trapped in this hell of life, could wipe away each other's tears, smile, and go forward together hand in hand.

Mr. Ts'ao's words could move him. Hsiao Fu Tzu didn't need to use words to move him. He had spoken the truth to Mr. Ts'ao. Now, to Hsiao Fu Tzu, he must speak of things much closer to his heart. He could say things to her that he couldn't say to anyone else. She was now, simply his life and nothing meant anything at all without her. He couldn't work solely to feed himself. He had to rescue her from that tiny room and then they would live together in a clean, warm, comfortable place. Like a pair of little birds, they would be happy and respectable! She could forget about Ch'iang and forget about her two brothers, too. She had to come and help him. Ch'iang could, in fact, earn his keep himself. Those two little brothers could work together. The two of them could pull one rickshaw or go do something else. But he couldn't do without her. For the sake of his body, his spirit, and his work, there was just no place where he could do without her; and surely she needed a man like him, too.

He became more excited and elated the more he thought about her. There were lots of women in the world and not one of them was as fine as Hsiao Fu Tzu or as well suited to him! He'd been married and he'd been an adulterer. He had already encountered beautiful ones and ugly ones, old ones and young ones, but not one of them could hold him. They were all merely females, not mates. But make no mistake, she was not the pure chaste girl of his dreams; and yet that was precisely the reason why she was even more adorable and could help him even more. A bumpkinish village girl might well be extraordinarily pure but she certainly would not have Hsiao Fu Tzu's ability and tactfulness. Furthermore, what about himself? There were plenty of black spots on his heart! Well, then, she and he were a proper pair all right. No one was high, no one was low. They were like a pair of pitchers that had cracks in them but could still hold water. It was right to put them side by side. Theirs was, no matter how you looked at it, a very fitting union.

He began to think a little more practically once he'd got that all thought out. First off, he'd have to get an advance from Mr. Ts'ao so he could buy her a padded gown and proper shoes before taking her to see Mrs. Ts'ao. Clean from top to toe, dressed in a new gown, with her youth, manner, and appearance to rely on, why, with all those in hand, she'd make Mrs. Ts'ao pleased with her all right. There was no mistake about that!

He was covered with sweat by the time he got there. Seeing that sagging gate again was just like coming back to your old home after being away for years. The sagging open gate, the ruinous wall, and the tufts of grass growing in the gateway were very dear to him all of a sudden. He went right inside and straight to her room. He didn't bother to knock or call out; he just pulled the door open. He pulled the door open and stepped back instinctively.

A middle-aged woman sat on the k'ang. There was no fire in the room so she had surrounded herself with a tattered quilt. He stood in the doorway, stunned. Her voice came out of the room.

"What is it? Come to report a death? Why do you charge into somebody's room without a word? You looking for someone?"

He couldn't think of anything to say. The sweat that had covered him was gone and he gripped the sagging door. He didn't dare give up all hope so he said, "I'm looking for Little Lucky One—Hsiao Fu Tzu!"

"Never heard of her! Next time you go looking for someone, yell before you open the door. What's all this little lucky one big lucky one anyway?"

Stupefied, he sat in the gateway for quite a while, his heart a void. He had forgotten what it was he was doing. Slowly, he began to think again. He thought about how she had walked into his heart and then walked out, coming and going like the paper cutout figure in a magic lantern and good for nothing at all. He seemed to have forgotten the connection between them. Slowly, slowly, her shadow grew smaller and his heart began to beat a little faster. And then he knew he couldn't make it.

When people aren't sure whether a situation will turn out for better or for worse, they always hope for better. Hsiang Tzu thought that maybe she'd only moved and nothing more than that had happened to her. He'd done badly. Why hadn't he gone to see her before? Chagrin leads people to make up for their mistakes. The best thing to do now was go ask around. He went back into the courtyard to find an old neighbor to question. He didn't get definite news. He still didn't lose all hope and started off to look for Ch'iang without bothering to eat. Finding those two brothers would do just as well. The three of them were always around in the streets so it wouldn't be hard to find them.

He asked everyone he saw at the rickshaw stands, in the tea houses, and in the mixed courtyards. He went around all day until his legs were worn out, asking everywhere, but there was no news.

He went back to his agency that night completely worn out but not ready to give up and forget it. Yet a day of disappointment had left him with little hope.

Poor people are the ones who die easily and their deaths are easily forgotten. Was there any doubt that she was already dead? Go back a step and think. Of course she hadn't died! Ch'iang had gone and sold her again. She had been sold and sent to some faraway place. It was a possibility. It was even worse than death!

Cigarettes and drink became his friends again. He couldn't think if he didn't smoke and how could he stop thinking if he didn't get drunk?

CHAPTER TWENTY-THREE

DOWNHEARTED, Hsiang Tzu was wandering aimlessly along the street and met Hsiao Ma's grandfather. The old man was no longer pulling a rickshaw and his clothes were even more tattered and thin than before. He carried a long pole made of willow wood with a big pot hanging from the front end and a broken basket hanging from the back. Some oil cakes, pancakes, and a piece of tile for balance were inside the basket. He still remembered Hsiang Tzu.

He told Hsiang Tzu that Hsiao Ma had been dead for more than six months and he had sold that broken-down rickshaw. Now he sold tea, fruit, and fried cakes at the rickshaw stands every day. The old man was as affable and endearing as ever but his back was very bent, his eyes watered in the wind, and his red eyelids looked like he'd just been crying.

Hsiang Tzu drank one of his bowls of tea and told him about his own troubles in a few sketchy sentences.

"So, you think getting along on your own is best, do you?" The old man gave his judgment of Hsiang Tzu's story. "Who doesn't think that way? But who gets on well? My body and bones were sound and my character good when I started out, and I came straight on down the road to where I am now and ended up like this! Sound body? Even men of iron can't get out of this snare of a world we're in. So you have a good character. What good is that? " 'The good are requited with good, the evil with evil.' " There never was any such thing! When I was young they called me a zealous fellow. I took everyone else's problems for my own and did it do me any good? None at all! I've even saved lives. People who jumped in the river, people who'd hanged themselves, I saved them all. And did I get anything for it? Nothing at all! I'm telling you, I'm not the one who decides what day I'll freeze to death. I figure it's perfectly understandable that any poor

guy who thinks he can succeed by himself will find it harder than going to heaven. How far can one man hop? Have you ever seen a grasshopper? It can go a long way in one hop by itself. Let a small boy grab
it and tie a thread around it and it can't go anywhere. But if it joins up
with a whole lot of other grasshoppers in a horde and they all move
together, whew! One swoop and they've eaten up all the crops and
there's no way you can control them. Now you tell me if that's right or
not! I couldn't even protect one grandson, no matter how good my
character was. He got sick and I had no money for medicine and I
watched him die in my arms. It's useless to talk about it, useless to talk
about anything! Tea here! Who wants a bowl of tea?"

Hsiang Tzu had things straight now. Old Liu, Mrs. Yang, detective
Sun, none of them would come to a bad end because of his curses. He
wouldn't gain any advantage because he was ambitious, either. By
himself, and relying only on himself, he would be just like the grasshopper the old man had described, with his legs tied up by a kid.
What good did it do to have wings!

So he didn't even think about going back to Mr. Ts'ao. He'd have to
want to be a success if he went back there and what was the use of being a success? Just go on blindly. Take a rickshaw out when you don't
have anything to eat and take a day off when you've made enough for
one more day and let tomorrow take care of itself. It was not only one
method, it was the only method. All you are doing when you hoard
your money to buy a rickshaw is set things up for someone else to
come and steal it. Why suffer? Why not just enjoy things when you
have them?

Even if he did find Hsiao Fu Tzu, he'd have to work hard for her
sake if not for his own. But he hadn't found her, so wasn't he in the
same situation as Hsiao Ma's grandfather? Just who was there to work
for?

He regarded the old man as a real friend and had told him about
Hsiao Fu Tzu too.

"Who wants a bowl of tea?" the old man called. Then he told
Hsiang Tzu his thoughts. "It was probably as I'd have guessed. There
were only two routes for her. If Ch'iang didn't sell her to someone for
a concubine then he indentured her to a white house. Ahem. Most likely she's gone to a white house. Why do I say that? She has, as you have
just told me, been married, so it's unlikely that anyone would want
her. People who buy concubines want their goods intact. Well, then,

it's probably eight out of ten chances she's gone to a white house. I'm almost sixty and I've seen a lot. Suppose you go look for a young and strong rickshaw man who hasn't been out in the streets for a couple of days. He's bound to be crawling around a white house if he isn't working privately. And if, all of a sudden, we stop seeing a daughter or a wife of one of us rickshaw men, it's seven or eight chances out of ten she's there too. We sell our sweat and our women sell their bodies. I understand it and I know! You go to those places and take a look. Don't hope that she's really there only. . . . Tea here! Who wants a bowl of hot tea?"

Hsiang Tzu ran straight out of the city through the Hsi Chih Gate.

He was immediately aware of how open the land was when he got out in the countryside. The trees stood scrawnily along the road with not a single bird in their branches. The gray trees, gray earth, and gray houses stood silently in a yellow-gray world. Beyond all this grayness he could see the wild cold Western Hills. North of the railroad tracks was a stretch of woods with a few low buildings close by them. These, he figured, were probably the white houses. He looked towards the woods and saw not a sign of movement.

Farther away to the north he could see as far as the marshy area outside the former Zoological and Botanical Gardens. A few decaying rushes and defeated mulberries were left in the hollows of the ground.

Looking back again he still could see no one outside those low buildings and nothing disturbed the silence. The whole place was very quiet and he doubted whether the buildings were the famous white houses after all. He got his nerve up and went towards them.

All the doors had new glossy yellow grass curtains hung in front of them. He had heard others say they'd found out that, in the summertime, the women here sat outside the huts with no blouses on and called to passersby. The men who patronized them always sang the songs currently fashionable in the city whorehouses to show they were no novices at this game. Why was it so quiet now? Was it possible this place didn't do business in winter?

He was squarely in the middle of these doubts when a curtain in one doorway moved a little and a woman's head poked out. Hsiang Tzu jumped. At first glance that head was extraordinarily like Hu Niu. He said to himself, "I came looking for Hsiao Fu Tzu but if I find Hu Niu that's really seeing ghosts!"

"Come in, you dear dolt!" This head spoke but the sound wasn't like Hu Niu's voice. It was hoarse, just like the old fellows selling herbs at T'ien Ch'iao, hoarse and anxious.

There was nothing in the room except the woman and a small k'ang. There was no mat on the k'ang but there was a fire under it. The stench inside made it hard to breathe. An old quilt was spread on the k'ang. The edge of the quilt and the bricks on the k'ang both glistened greasily.

The woman was about forty. Her hair was messy and she hadn't washed her face yet. She wore a pair of trousers and an unbuttoned black cotton jacket. Hsiang Tzu had to duck to get through the doorway. She grabbed him as soon as he got inside. The little jacket popped open and two enormous pendulous breasts hung out.

Hsiang Tzu had to sit on the edge of the k'ang because he couldn't stand up in there without bending his neck. He was inwardly delighted to have met her. He'd often heard others say there was a "white flour sack" in the white houses and this must be the one. This nickname, White Flour Sack, came from her two big breasts which she could flip up and onto her shoulders. When traveling salesmen came to patronize her they would all ask her to demonstrate this talent of hers on the side. But her fame was not due entirely to this pair of spectacular dugs. She was the only free person in the place. She had come here to make her living of her own free will. She'd been married five times but her husbands had all died off quite soon looking like shriveled-up bedbugs. So she gave up being married and came here to enjoy herself. She had the nerve to talk about what went on because she was free, so anyone who wanted to find out about things had to get hold of her. The other women didn't dare let anything leak out. And so everyone knew about White Flour Sack and there was no end to the people who came here to ask her questions. Naturally, the questioner had to give her a little "tea money" so she was better off than the others by far and had a much easier life. Hsiang Tzu was aware of all this so he handed over her tip first. She caught on right away and didn't expect anything more. Hsiang Tzu asked her straight out if she'd seen Hsiao Fu Tzu or not.

She didn't know her.

Hsiang Tzu described her appearance and manner.

She thought it over.

"Yes, there was someone like that. She wasn't very old and had a few white teeth that stuck out. Right. We called her Tender Little Morsel."

"What hut is she in?" Hsiang Tzu's eyes suddenly flashed balefully.

"Her? She was done for long ago!" White Flour Sack pointed outside. "Hanged herself in the woods."

"What?"

"Everyone liked Tender Little Morsel but there was one thing about her no one could stand. She was too thin. One day around lamplighting time, I still remember it clearly because I was sitting in the doorway with some lady friends. Ah, just at that time of day along came a customer who went to her hut. She didn't like to sit with us in the doorway and she was beaten for that when she first came here. But she got famous later and the boss let her be by herself in her own hut. Fortunately, men looking for her never looked at anyone else. Ah, after about the time it takes to eat a meal her customer left and headed straight into the woods. We didn't notice anything in particular and no one went to her hut to see her. When the madam went to get the money from her she saw a man lying inside with no clothes on at all and sound asleep. Actually he was drunk and that "tender little morsel" had stripped off his clothes, put them on herself, and run away. She really was a smart one. But she couldn't have got away if it hadn't been dark, no matter what. But it was dark so she dressed in his clothes and hoodwinked everybody. The madam sent people in all directions right away. Um, they went into the woods and there she was, hanging. They got her down but she'd already stopped breathing. Still, her tongue wasn't sticking out very far and her face wasn't too hard to look at either. Why, people liked her even when she was dead! There haven't been any incidents in the woods these last few months at all so she doesn't come back to frighten people. Now that's what I call well behaved!"

Hsiang Tzu just staggered out without waiting for her to finish everything she had to say. He came to a cemetery with pine trees planted on all four sides. There were many grave mounds there. The sun was very weak and the pines dismal. He sat on the ground, which was covered with dry grass and pinecones. There was no sound at all except that made by a few magpies perched in the trees dragging out their long doleful cries. He knew that Hsiao Fu Tzu's grave couldn't be here but his tears flowed down one after another anyway. He had nothing anymore. Even Hsiao Fu Tzu had gone into the earth! He had wanted to amount to something and so had she. Now all he had left was a few good for nothing tears and she had become the ghost of a hanged person! To be wrapped in a mat and buried in a potter's field was the final stage for those who'd worked hard all their lives. Just that and nothing more.

He slept for two solid days after returning to his agency. He didn't think about going to the Ts'ao's at all. He didn't even think it necessary to send word. Mr. Ts'ao could not save his life for him after all.

He took a rickshaw out again after his two-day sleep. His mind was a complete blank. He didn't think any more, he didn't hope any more. He went out to suffer solely on account of his belly and once his belly was full he'd just go to sleep. What was the use of thinking any more? What was the use of hoping?

He watched a dog so thin his bones stuck out at angles waiting next to a sweet potato vendor to eat the peelings and sprouts and knew that he and the dog were the same; all one day's labor got you was a bit of peel and sprout to eat. To keep on living was all that mattered; there wasn't any need to think about anything else.

Men have separated themselves from the animals but now drive their own kind back among the beasts. Hsiang Tzu remained in this "cultured" city but he was being transformed into an animal. Not a bit of it was his own fault. He had stopped thinking and, therefore, the human being in him was destroyed. He bore no responsibility for that at all. He'd never hope again. He'd just sink blindly, stupidly, lower and lower, into a bottomless pit. He ate, he drank, he whored, he gambled, he cheated, and all because he had no heart left in him. Others had taken it from him. All that remained was his big frame and now he waited for it to burst open like an abscess. He was getting ready for the potter's field.

Winter passed. The spring sun is the garment nature gives to everyone. He rolled up his padded coat and sold it. He wanted to eat and drink well. There was no need to keep winter clothes and there was even less necessity to be prepared for the next winter. Live happily today and die tomorrow! Who cares about winter! If he was unlucky and still alive when next winter came, he'd worry about it then. When, in the past, he mulled things over, he used to think about all the things that had happened to him. Now he noticed only what was right in front of him. Experience told him that tomorrow was merely the continuation of today and inherited all today's grievances. He sold the padded coat and felt remarkably happy. Getting hold of ready cash to use as you wanted was great. Why did he have to keep that coat around while waiting for winter with its wind that can choke a guy to death?

Eventually he thought of selling not only his clothes, but everything else he had too. Any item he didn't really need promptly left his possession. He enjoyed watching his things turn into money that he spent himself. Money he spent himself wouldn't fall into anyone else's hands and spending it was the best way to guarantee that nothing else would happen to it. He could buy things when he needed them once he'd sold everything. He would simply do without if he didn't have the money to buy them. It didn't matter much if his face went unwashed and his teeth unbrushed. It not only saved money, it saved trouble. Who were appearances meant for, anyway? You may wear ragged clothes but you can still fill your belly full of good wheat pancakes rolled around soy-soaked meat—that was what mattered! With good things in your belly, there'll be a little gloss to you when you die and you won't end up looking like some starved to death rat.

Hsiang Tzu, that very handsome Hsiang Tzu, became a scrawny and filthy low-class rickshaw man. He never washed his face, his body, or his clothes. His head hadn't been shaved in more than a month. He wasn't particular about a rickshaw either; new one or old one, all he wanted was a low rental fee. He'd offer a passenger a low rate as bait to get the fare and then head in the wrong direction halfway along. If the passenger refused to pay more, he'd glare and start an argument. Spending two days in jail for it didn't mean much!

He moved very slowly when he was by himself. He was quite solicitous of his own sweat. If he was feeling good when going as part of a group, he was still willing to run fast, but just to put the others behind him. He could, on these occasions, be a real troublemaker. He knew all about cutting in front of another rickshaw, how to cut wide around corners deliberately, how to pester those behind him, and how to take advantage of those in front of him and force them to pull over to one side when they least expected it.

He used to believe that you held someone's life in your hands when you pulled a rickshaw. If you weren't careful, you might get someone killed in a crash. Now he deliberately looked for trouble. It didn't matter if someone did get smashed up and killed. Everyone was doomed anyway!

He also reverted to his silent ways. He didn't make a sound. He ate, he drank, he made trouble. It is by means of speech that human beings exchange opinions and transmit feelings. Hsiang Tzu had no opinions and and no hopes, so what was the point of talking? He'd keep his mouth shut all day long except when discussing fares. His mouth now seemed to specialize in eating, drinking, and smoking. He didn't even make a noise when he was drunk. He'd go to a secluded spot and weep. Almost every time he got drunk he went to the woods where Hsiao Fu Tzu had hanged herself. When he stopped crying, he just went over to a white house and stayed there. He had no money when he sobered up and he felt ill. He had no regrets at all and if, now and then, he did have regrets, it was to regret that he had been so ambitious, diligent, and trustworthy at the start. Everything he might have regrets about was in the past; there was nothing to be regretted now at all!

If there was any way to gain an advantage he'd take it. He smoked lots of someone else's cigarettes and paid for things with counterfeit coins. When he bought soybean milk to drink, he'd take more pickled vegetables on the side than he was entitled to. He put in less effort when he worked and demanded more money for it. All of these tricks made him feel satisfied. He got the advantage and other people took the loss. This was a kind of repayment.

Slowly, he expanded his methods. He learned how to borrow money from his friends though he never intended to pay it back. If you were to press him for it he might well act like a thug! At first no one had any doubts about him. Everyone knew he was a respectable man concerned for his honor, so he got the loans when he asked for them. He found it to his advantage to use the remnants of his reputation whenever he went to borrow money. But borrowing, to him, was just like finding. The money would land in one hand and be spent on a whim with the other. He'd put on a most pitiable air when anyone wanted to be paid back and beg for an extension of the time. But if this tactic didn't work, he would borrow twenty cents more, pay back fifteen of the earlier debt, and have five cents left for a drink. When he got so deep in debt that no one would lend to him again, he began to wheedle people for money.

He decided to pay "respectful calls" on all the households he'd worked for. It would be fine by him if he saw the master but servants would do. Anyone would do. He planned to unroll a string of lies and trick them out of some money. If he couldn't get any money out of them he'd beg to be rewarded with some old clothes instead. The clothes could be turned into cash in a jiffy and the cash would become cigarettes and baigan right after that.

He sat with his head down contemplating something even more unscrupulous. As part of this great plan for making even more money than he could get by pulling a rickshaw all day and saving his energy too, he had an idea he thought was absolutely perfect. He went so far as to think about finding Kao Ma.

He waited some distance from the doorway for her to go out shopping. When he saw her come out he caught up with her in almost one jump. He called her name in a very mournful voice.

"Huh! Scared me to death! Who's calling me? Hsiang Tzu! Why do you look like that?" Kao Ma's eyes opened wide and round, as if she were looking at some weird creature.

"Who needs to bring that up!" Hsiang Tzu kept his head down.

"Didn't you get everything all arranged with Master? So how come you didn't come back? I even went and asked Old Ch'eng about you but he said he hadn't seen you. So where have you been, anyway? Master and Madam have been really worried."

"I was sick for a long time. I almost died. You ask Master to help me out. I'll come start work when I'm better." He unrolled his prepared speech and spoke it simply and heartrendingly.

"Master isn't home now. You go in and see Madam, all right?"

"Oh, that's no good! Not with me in this condition! You go do the talking."

So Kao Ma went in and came back with two dollars for him. "From Madam, with orders to take medicine right away!"

"Oh, I will. Thank Madam for me!" He took the money and began to plan where to spend it. Kao Ma had just turned away as he ran off towards T'ien Ch'iao. He had enough to roister for a whole day.

After slowly making his tour of all the households in turn, he went back for a second round but his technique wasn't as productive the second time. He saw that this path wouldn't take him much farther. He'd better think of some other, easier way to earn money than rickshaw pulling. His hope, in the past, had lain solely in pulling a rickshaw. Now he detested pulling a rickshaw. Of course he couldn't cut his connections with rickshaw pulling all at once, but he certainly was not going to fumble with rickshaw shafts as long as he could find some other way of getting hold of three meals a day.

His body might be lazy but his ears were sharp and he'd be right there at the head of the line when he got wind of a job. He knew what to do at a political rally or private celebration or funeral, and at all those events where people paid for help in the processions. Thirty cents, even twenty cents, was fine. He enjoyed going around carrying a banner all day, following the wanderings of the processions or the crowd. He was convinced that anything, no matter what, was better than pulling a rickshaw. He wouldn't get much but he wasn't selling any of his strength either. He'd hold his little banner up and keep his head down. He'd have a cigarette stuck between his lips and go along apparently, but not really, smiling, and without saying a word. He'd open his mouth wide when the time came to cheer but there'd be no sound at all. He was very concerned about his voice. He'd sold his strength in the past and never got anything good out of it so he never considered using it now. If, during a political demonstration, he saw danger looming, he'd be the first to run away and he ran very fast besides. His life might well be ruined by his own hands but he wasn't about to sacrifice anything for anybody. He who works for himself knows how to destroy himself. These are the two starting points of Individualism.

CHAPTER TWENTY-FOUR

THE TIME to take incense to the temple on Miao Feng Mountain had come again and it was very hot. Sellers of paper fans seemed to have emerged from somewhere all at once with boxes hanging from their arms and strings of jingling bells to attract attention hanging from the boxes.

Many things were for sale in the streets; green apricots were heaped in piles while cherries gleamed redly and brightened your eyes. Swarms of bees swooped over bowls of roses or dates and the agar agar jellies on porcelain plates had a milky glow. Peddlers of cookies and jellies had their wares arranged with remarkable neatness and spices of every kind and color were also set out on display.

People had changed into brighter and more colorful unpadded garments and the streets were suddenly filled with their colors, as if many rainbows had come down into them. The street cleaners worked faster, going down the road sprinkling water without a pause, but the light dust soon flew around as before and vexed people. There were longish twigs of willow in the slightly dusty air and lightly and delightfully swooping swallows as well which made people feel cheery in spite of themselves.

It was the sort of weather that really made you wonder what to do with yourself and everyone yawned great lazy yawns while feeling tired and happy too.

Processions of various kinds set out for the mountains continuously. Lines of people beating on drums and gongs, or carrying baskets on shoulder poles, or waving apricot yellow flags went by one on the heels of another, lending an unusual kind of bustle to the entire city, lending an elusive and yet familiar thrill to the people and lingering sounds and fine dust to the air. Those in the processions and those who watched them all felt a kind of excitement, devoutness, and exuberance.

The hurly-burly of this chaotic world comes from superstition; the only solace the stupid have is self-deception. These colors, these voices, the clouds filling the sky, and the dust in the streets made people energetic and gave them something to do. The mountain goers climbed mountains, the temple goers went to temples, the flower gazers looked at flowers. Those who couldn't do any of these things could still watch the processions from the sidelines and repeat the name of Buddha.

It was so hot it seemed to have roused the old capital from its spring dream. You could find amusements everywhere but everyone wondered what to do. Urged on by the heat, the flowers, grasses, fruit trees, and the joy among the people, all burgeoned together. The newly furbished green willows along the South Lake enticed harmonica-playing youngsters; boys and girls tied their boats up in the shade of the willows or floated among the lotuses. Their mouths sang love songs and they kissed each other with their eyes.

The camellias and peonies in the park sent invitations to poets and elegant gentlemen who now paced back and forth while waving their expensively decorated paper fans. They would sit in front of the red walls or under the pine trees when tired and drink several cups of clear tea, enough to draw out their idle melancholy. They'd steal a glance at the young ladies of wealthy families and at the famous "flowers" of the south and north who strolled by.

Even places which had heretofore been quiet had visitors sent to them by the warm wind and bright sun, just as the butterflies were sent. The peonies of the Ch'ung Hsiao temple, the green rushes at the T'ao Jan pavilion, the mulberry trees and rice paddies at the site of the Zoological and Botanical Gardens, all attracted the sounds of people and the shadows of their parasols. The Altar of Heaven, the Temple of Confucius, and the Lama temple had just a little bustle in the midst of their usual solemnity as well.

Students and those who like short tips went to the Western Hills, the hot springs, and the Summer Palace. They went to sightsee, to run around, to gather things, and to scribble words all over the rocks in the mountains.

Poor people also had somewhere to go: the Hu Kuo temple, the Lu Fu temple, the White Pagoda, and the Temple of Earth. All the flower markets were busier. Fresh cut flowers of every sort were arranged colorfully along the streets and a penny or so could take some beauty back home.

On the mats of the soybean milk vendors fresh pickled vegetables were arranged to look like big flowers topped with fried hot peppers. Eggs were really cheap and the soft yellow egg dumplings for sale made people's mouths water.

T'ien Ch'iao was even more fired up than usual. New mats had been hung for tea sheds, one right next to another. There were clean white tablecloths and entrancing singing girls who waved to the ancient pines above the wall at the Temple of Heaven. The sounds of drums and gongs dragged on for eight or nine hours and the brisk heat of the day made them sound especially light and sharp in a way that struck and disturbed people's hearts.

Dressing up was simple for the girls. One calico frock was all they needed to go out prettily dressed and it revealed every curve of their bodies as well.

Those who liked peace and quiet also had a place to go. You could drop a fishing line at the Chi Shui reservoir, outside the Wan Shou temple, at the kiln pits east of town, or on the marble bridge west of town. The little fishes would bump into the rushes now and then, making them move slightly. When you finished your fishing, the pigshead meat, stewed bean curd, and salted beans you ate with your baigan could make you both satiated and drunk. And afterwards, following the willow-edged bank and carrying fishing pole and little fish, you entered the city at a leisurely pace while treading on the beams of the setting sun.

There was fun, color, excitement, and noise everywhere. The first heat wave of summer was like an incantation that made every place in the city fascinating. The city paid no attention to death, paid no attention to disaster, and paid no attention to poverty. It simply put forth its powers when the time came and hypnotized a million people, and they, as if in a dream, chanted poems in praise of its beauty. It was filthy, beautiful, decadent, bustling, chaotic, idle, lovable; it was the great Peking of early summer.

It was precisely at this time of year that people hoped for news to relieve their boredom, news they could read two or three times without finding it tiresome, news interesting enough to get them to read the entire newpaper and then go themselves to see what it was all about. The days are so long and boring, you know!

This kind of news came! The trolley cars had just left their barns when the newsboys were heading out in all directions yelling at everyone in their high-pitched voices. "News of the execution of Yuan Ming! To be taken through the streets at nine o'clock!"

One penny after another was collected by their little black hands. Every page in the trolley cars, in the shops, and in the hands of pedestrians spoke of Yuan Ming. There was Yuan Ming's photograph, his history, the transcript of his interrogation; all was explained in the captions for the photographs and in large and small type. Yuan Ming was all over every page. Yuan Ming was on the trolley cars, in the eyes of the pedestrians, in the mouths of the talkers. There seemed to be no one in the entire city except Yuan Ming. Yuan Ming would be paraded through the streets today. He would be shot today! This was valuable news, ideal news. Not only was he in everyone's mouth. Wait a while and he would be in everyone's eyes too!

Women hurried to get dressed up. Old people had already left early, worried only that their legs would be too slow and they'd fall behind and be late. Even the schoolboys thought they'd play hooky for part of the day and go learn something.

By eight thirty the streets were already full of exuberant, thrill-seeking, pushing, clamoring people waiting to see this living news. Rickshaw men forgot to look for business. Weights and measurements were got all wrong in the shops. The street vendors were reluctant to shout. Everyone was waiting for the tumbrel and Yuan Ming.

History has its Yellow Turbans, T'ai P'ing rebels, and Chang Hsien-chung; all were killers and all loved to watch killing. Execution by firing squad seems too simple. People love to listen to tales of execution by slicing, beheading, flaying, and burying alive. Hearing these tales is like eating ice cream; delightful and a trifle chilling. But this time, in addition to the execution, they were to be given a procession, and they wanted to offer heartfelt thanks to whoever had made the decision. Letting them see the half-dead prisoner tied up in the cart was a thrill to their eyes. They were not executioners themselves but that didn't matter a great deal. There wasn't much in the minds of these people. They couldn't distinguish between right and wrong at all clearly. They kept a deathlike grip on formalities and polite usages and wished to be known as civilized people. Their pleasure in watching one of their own kind cut to ribbons was just as direct and cruelly barbaric as that of a small boy murdering a puppy. If one morning they had the power in their hands, any man among them could do as

Chang Hsien-chung did in 1630: have the inhabitants of a city butchered and then order the women's breasts and feet to be cut off and piled into two heaps. That's what they'd enjoy doing. They haven't got this terrible power but that doesn't prevent them from staring at butchered pigs, slaughtered sheep, and executed men to satisfy a little of their craving. And if they can't find sights like those to look at, they can still scream at children, threatening them with a "thousand-cut death" or a "ten-thousand-cut death" and releasing some of the evil in their hearts.

There was a brilliant blue sky and a great red sun high in the east. The willows along the road waved gently in several gusts of light east wind and along the east side of the road there was a great dark shadow. The roadside was crammed with people: old and young, male and female, ugly and handsome, fat and thin. Some were dressed beautifully in the latest fashion; some wore only short jackets and pants. All were talking and laughing expectantly, constantly craning their necks to look to the north or south. When one person stretched his head to look, everyone else did the same and their hearts all leapt happily together. And so the more they peered, the more they shoved forward until the horde reached the edge of the street and made a wall of flesh with an uneven top of erratically shifting heads.

Policemen came along in squads to keep order. They blocked off, they shouted, and sometimes they grabbed a grubby urchin and boxed his ears, which made everyone laugh delightedly. The people waited and waited. Their legs were already sore from standing but they were unwilling to leave without seeing something. The ones in front wouldn't move and the new arrivals in back kept shoving forward and met resistance. The contenders didn't use their hands or feet; they relied on verbal warfare and railed and cursed at each other while others cheered. The children got impatient and were cuffed by the adults. Pickpockets plied their trade and their victims shouted and cursed. The clamoring, quarreling, and shouting merged into one sound. No one was willing to budge. The more their numbers increased the less willing anyone was to move as they demonstrated as one man how much they looked forward to seeing the prisoner.

Far off a squad of police was coming and everyone was silent all of a sudden. Someone shouted "They're coming!" The voices of the people close behind rose in a babble and the whole horde pressed forward like a mechanical man, one inch, another inch, they're coming!

They're coming! Their eyes all flashed and their mouths all said something or other, making a layer of voices. The whole street smelled of sweat. The citizens of a courteous nation dearly love watching an execution.

Yuan Ming was a shrimp. As he sat with his hands tied behind him in the cart he resembled an apprehensive monkey. He hung his head and a white placard over two feet high was stuck onto his back.

The shouts of the people were like waves on the ocean; those in front rushed back to meet those behind. Everybody turned their mouths down and complained to each other. They were all disappointed. He was only a little monkey like that after all! And he was so floppy and blah! He didn't look up, his face was deathly pale, and he wasn't even making a sound! It occurred to some of them to taunt him. "Brothers, give him a cheer!" And right away shouts of "Bravo!" came from here and there as if they were cheering a female impersonator in a Peking opera. They shouted contemptuously, malevolently, and nastily, but Yuan Ming still said nothing and didn't even look up.

Some of the onlookers were actually annoyed. They really looked down on a weak prisoner like him. They crowded up to the edge of the road to shout their contempt and spit at him a few times. Yuan Ming was still motionless and without any reaction at all. People became less interested the longer they watched, and yet they were still reluctant to leave because of the chance that, like an operatic hero, he might just up and shout "After twenty years I'll come back as a hero!" Or want a couple of drinks and some barbecued meat to go with them like a proper bold and fearless criminal. No one wanted to move because they all wanted to see what he was really like. The cart passed by so they had to follow it. He still hadn't made any move but who knows? Maybe he'll stop holding back when they get to the single *p'ai lou* and he'll bellow a hero's song from an opera to show his defiance. Follow them!

Some people had run directly to T'ien Ch'iao. Yuan Ming hadn't done anything along the way to make people respect him and feel satisfied, but they'd see him eat bullets even so and wouldn't have wasted the trip after all.

Hsiang Tzu, during these exciting moments, was all alone, walking slowly and dejectedly along the inside of the wall near the Te Sheng Gate. He looked around in all directions when he reached the Chi

Shui reservoir. There was no one about so, slowly and gingerly, he went towards the edge of the embankment. He found an old tree at the water's edge, leaned against the trunk, and stood there awhile. Hearing no human sound in any direction, he sat down gently. A slight motion in the rushes or perhaps the cry of a bird made him jump up abruptly, sweat beading his forehead. He listened and looked but there was really nothing to disturb the silence anywhere so he sat down slowly once more. He finally became accustomed to the slight motions in the rushes and the birdcalls after several more such incidents and wasn't alarmed any more.

He stared dully into a ditch running into the reservoir. A few little fish with eyes as bright as pearls were suddenly clustering and scattering just as suddenly, coming here and going there. Sometimes there was a bit of duckweed on their heads and sometimes they blew out little bubbles. A few tadpoles swam along the side of the ditch. Their hind legs had already grown and they wagged their big black heads with their bodies straight out behind them. The water suddenly began to flow faster and carried the fish and tadpoles along with it. Their tails curved as they went by with the current. The water brought another little school of fish with it which struggled to stop. A water lizard came racing by. Gradually the inflow of water diminished; the fishes made their school again and opened their mouths wide to nip at floating green leaves and bits of grass.

The somewhat larger fish lurked in the deep spots. If by chance their backs showed above the water, they would turn quickly and dive, leaving little whirlpools and a few ripples behind on the surface. Kingfishers swooped across the surface of the water like arrows. Little fish and big fish were no more to be seen and nothing was left but the duckweed.

Hsiang Tzu watched all of this blankly; he seemed to see and yet appeared not to see. He picked up a stone without thinking and tossed it into the water scattering a few water flowers and alarming quite a lot of duckweed. He startled himself and, frightened, almost stood up again.

He sat for a long time and then his big black hand groped stealthily in his waistband. He nodded. His hand stopped, paused, and then clutched a bundle of bank notes. He counted them and hid them away again very carefully.

His mind was alive solely because of that money and thoughts of how to spend it all, how to keep others from finding out about it, how to simply enjoy it and still be safe. He wasn't thinking of himself any more for he had become a dependent of that money and had to follow its instructions in all things.

The manner of this money's coming had already determined its departure. Money like this could not be spent conspicuously. Money like this, and those who took it, did not dare look upon the sun. The people had all seen Yuan Ming in the tumbrel but Hsiang Tzu was concealed in a quiet place near the wall, planning how to get to an even quieter and darker place. He didn't dare appear in the streets or the market-places because he had informed on Yuan Ming. And so he sat alone, facing the quietly flowing water close to the base of the city wall, where there were no traces of others, not even daring to lift his head as if some ghostly shade were pursuing him constantly.

Yuan Ming, who had fallen in the midst of the bloodstains at T'ien Ch'iao, lived on in Hsiang Tzu's mind, lived on in those bank notes in his waistband. Hsiang Tzu certainly had no regrets but he was afraid —afraid of that ghost which was close on his heels wherever he went.

After becoming a bureaucrat Yuan Ming had rather enjoyed some of the practices he had previously denounced. Money can entice a man into vile company and cause him to set his loftiest ideals aside and march willingly to hell. Yuan Ming wore expensive and well-tailored western suits; he went whoring, gambling, and even went so far as to smoke opium. He told his conscience, when it showed itself, that it wasn't his fault. This utterly evil society had ensnared him! He admitted that his way of life was not entirely respectable but he laid the blame for it on the enormity of society's powers of seduction; there was no way he could resist them. He went into debt because he didn't make enough to cover his expenditures and that led him to reflect on those old radical ideas he'd had. Not because he wanted to do good by putting them into practice. Oh no, his notion was to use them to his advantage by exchanging them for money. Taking ideas and converting them into cash was on a par with his vain attempt to use friendship with his teacher to get a passing grade.

The ideas of an indolent person cannot stand on the same footing as character. Sooner or later, every one of those ideas that can be exchanged for cash will be handed over for sale. So he took in a little on the sly by working for left-wing causes in secret. He was eager to publicize revolutionary organizations so he could not be too selective.

He was willing to let anyone who turned up be his comrade. People who get paid for working on the sly, however, must get results, regardless of the methods they use to get them. Reports are what organizations want. Yuan Ming couldn't just take their money and do nothing. So he had a hand in organizing the rickshaw pullers. Hsiang Tzu was already an old hand at flag-waving and shouting in demonstrations and Yuan Ming knew Hsiang Tzu for that reason.

Yuan Ming sold his ideas for money. Hsiang Tzu accepted ideas for money. Yuan Ming knew that when the moment of need came he could sacrifice Hsiang Tzu to save his own skin. Hsiang Tzu had certainly never figured things that way, but when the time came he simply did the same thing: he informed on Yuan Ming.

Those who do their work solely for the sake of money fear being confronted with too much money; their loyalty does not take precedence over cash. Yuan Ming believed in his own ideas and used the virtue of his radicalism to excuse all his evil deeds.

Hsiang Tzu listened to what Yuan Ming said and thought it sounded reasonable, but he also saw how many pleasures Yuan Ming enjoyed and envied him. "If I had lots more money I could be happy for quite a while too! Just like that Yuan fellow!"

Money diminished Yuan Ming's character and money dazzled Hsiang Tzu's eyes. He informed on Yuan Ming for sixty dollars. What Yuan Ming had wanted was the strength of the mob but what Hsiang Tzu wanted was even more of life's pleasures, pleasures just like Yuan Ming's. Yuan Ming's blood was sprinkled on Hsiang Tzu's payoff. Hsiang Tzu stuffed the bank notes in his waistband.

Hsiang Tzu sat until the sun had settled in the west and gold and red rays glimmered on the rushes and willow trees. Then he stood up and went westwards along the base of the wall. He was already habituated to getting money by fraud but this was the very first time he had informed on a man and doomed him. And, even worse, he still took what Yuan Ming had had to say as entirely reasonable!

The open spaces along the base of the wall and its height made him more and more fearful the longer he walked. He happened to catch sight of several crows on a garbage dump and all he could think of was going wide around them because he was afraid of startling them and making them croak a few unlucky caws at him. He quickened his pace when he reached the base of the west wall and, like a dog that has stolen something to eat, he slinked out through the Hsi Chih Gate.

The ideal place for him that night was somewhere where there was someone to keep him company, get him stone drunk, and make him unafraid. The white houses were that sort of place.

When autumn came Hsiang Tzu's chronic illness would not allow him to pull a rickshaw, but his credit was utterly lost and he couldn't have rented one anyway. He was a patron of the lowest dives and could stretch out at night when he had a few pennies. In the daytime he worked at jobs that could provide only a bowl of congee or so. He couldn't beg in the streets because no one would show benevolence toward a man his size. He couldn't make some colored spots on his body and beg outside a temple because he had never "received the doctrine" so he didn't know how to fix himself up to make people feel sorry for his "misfortune." Nor had he the skill to be a thief. Besides, thieves had cliques and organizations. He was the only one who could earn his food. There was no one else to rely on. He exerted himself for his own sake and would accomplish his own death. He waited to take that last breath of all for he was merely a still-breathing wraith and Individualism was his soul. This soul would follow his body and rot in the mud with it.

After Peking was honored as a former capital, the things it was known for, its handicrafts, food, dialect, and police, had gradually spread outwards in all directions. That westernized Ch'ingtao had Peking-style "rinsed lamb" too. You could hear the gloomy calls of street vendors selling noodles late at night in bustling Tientsin. Shanghai, Hankow, and Nanking all had policemen and official messengers who spoke in Peking dialect and ate sesame seed pancakes. Jasmine tea traveled from south to north, passed through a double smoking, and went south again. Even the pallbearers sometimes took the train to Tientsin or Nanking to carry the coffins of high officials.

But Peking itself was slowly losing its original distinctions. You could buy flower cakes in the snack shops well after the Mid-Autumn Festival. Sellers of the sweet dumplings reserved for the last night of the New Year holidays might be found in the markets in autumn. It even occurred to shops three or four hundred years old to celebrate an anniversary by spreading handbills around advertising a sale. Economic oppression drives out idiosyncracies; respectability isn't fit to eat.

Weddings and funerals, however, still kept up most of the ceremonies and practices of old. It was as if they were still worth paying attention to and families needed to put on a good show. But, even so, you could not get hold of the required paraphernalia, the noisemakers, sedan chairs, and coffins, in just any market in the city. The paper figures, scrolls, and such carried by mourners, the banners carried by members of a bridal procession, and its twenty-four musical instruments still showed off the official style and reminded people of the extravagant displays and attitudes of peaceful times before revolutions.

Hsiang Tzu's livelihood now depended primarily on these vestigial ceremonies and customs. He'd hold a flag or an umbrella when someone got married. He'd hold up a funeral scroll when someone was buried. He didn't rejoice, he didn't wail, he was there solely for the sake of ten or so pennies. With a poorly fitting black hat on his head and dressed in the outfit provided by the rental agency for such occasions, he could conceal his ragged clothes and be a little handsome for a short time. If he ran into an affair put on by a great family, all hired hands were given a head shave and new shoes, so he had an opportunity to get himself cleaned up. Venereal disease made it hard for him to walk fast. The best he could do was dawdle along by the side of the road with a banner or two funeral scrolls.

But he wasn't regarded as a good hand even at this sort of thing. His golden age had already passed him by. He had never founded a family or got a livelihood out of pulling a rickshaw. And so, everything had followed his hopes and turned into "that old stuff." That big frame of his now struggled to hold up a flag or a pair of narrow funeral scrolls. He refused to touch any of the heavier items such as red umbrellas, grave tablets, and the like. He could still argue with old men, children, and even women. He wasn't about to let anyone take advantage of him.

Carrying his trifling object, he'd hang his head, stick a cigarette butt found on the street in his mouth, and drag along, slowly and listlessly. He might well keep on walking when everyone else had stopped. He might well stand around when everyone else had started off again. He didn't seem to hear the clang of the signal gong. He was even more eternally oblivious to whether he was the same distance from those ahead of him as he was from those behind, or whether he was in line with those to his left and right and at an equal distance from them. He went at his own pace with his head down as if in a dream and even more, as if pondering some lofty principle.

The man in red beating the going and the man with the silk flag urged the procession forward and used all the village slang they knew to swear at him.

"You boy! I'm talking to you, Camel! Look sharp, you mother-fucker!"

He still seemed not to have heard. The gong beater came over and clouted him. He rolled his eyes and looked around in a daze. He paid no attention to what the gong men said. He concentrated on searching the ground to see if there were any cigarette butts worth picking up.

Handsome, ambitious, dreamer of fine dreams, selfish, individualistic, sturdy, great Hsiang Tzu. No one knows how many funerals he marched in, and no one knows when or where he was able to get himself buried, that degenerate, selfish, unlucky offspring of society's diseased womb, a ghost caught in Individualism's blind alley.

⚜ Production Notes

This book was designed by Roger J. Eggers and typeset on the Unified Composing System by the design and production staff of The University Press of Hawaii.

The text typeface is California and the display typefaces are California and Friz Quadrata Bold.

Offset presswork and binding were done by Halliday Lithograph. Text paper is Glatfelter P & S Offset, basis 55.

2252